THE CABAL LUMINARY

FRONT AND SIDE VIEW.

THE CABAL LUMINARY

A novel by ANDREW P PARTINGTON

Parts of this novel are intended satirically, particularly as regards climate scientists and the Cabal that may or may not exist, that supposedly runs things from the shadows.

Special Thanks
to Cas Pearson & Jan Barker
for their wonderful Editing and Proof-Reading.

In the heavens He has pitched a tent for the sun like a bridegroom emerging from his chamber, like a hero rejoicing to run his course. It rises at one end of the heavens and runs its circuit to the other; nothing is deprived of its warmth.

Psalm 19:4-6

LUMINARY (n.): mid-15c., "lamp, light-giver, source of light," from Old French luminarie (12c.), "lamp, lights, lighting; candles; brightness, illumination," from Late Latin luminare "light, torch, lamp, heavenly body," literally "that which gives light," from Latin lumen (genitive luminis) "light, source of light, daylight, the light of the eye; distinguished person, ornament, glory," related to lucere "to shine," from suffixed (iterative) form of PIE root *leuk- "light, brightness." From late 15c. as "celestial body." Sense of "notable person" is first recorded 1690s, though the Middle English word also had a figurative sense of "source of spiritual light, example of holiness" (mid-15c.). As an adjective, "pertaining to light," from 1794 but this is rare.

CABAL (n.): 1520s, "mystical interpretation of the Old Testament," later "an intriguing society, a small group meeting privately" (1660s), from French cabal, which had both senses, from Medieval Latin cabbala (see cabbala). Popularized in English 1673 as an acronym for five intriguing ministers of Charles II (Clifford, Arlington, Buckingham, Ashley, and Lauderdale), which gave the word its sinister connotations.

Glossary

awilu: Ancient Babylonian, the literal meaning of the word is unknown, however in its context it refers to the top social class in ancient Babylon, *above* freemen who were not slaves.

Nephilim: Hebrew, נְפִילִים, *nefilim* probable meaning 'giants', in fact the ancient Septuagint translates it γιγαντες, *gigantes*, meaning 'giants'. Some scholars argue 'fallen ones', probably erroneously. The Nephilim were the offspring of the sons of God and human women first mentioned in the Bible in Genesis 6:1-4.

pwn: hacker terminology, proper pronunciation same as "own", *pwn* is a term meaning to successfully gain control of someone's computer or device. "I'm going to totally pwn you."

razvaluha: Russian, a term of mild abuse, meaning literally a car that is falling apart as it goes.

suchka: Russian, meaning female dog, a term of endearment.

zhopa: Russian, meaning rear end. A very mild insult, no more offensive than the English word 'brat'.

This account is an extract from the FSP Class Top Secret Files of FBI Agent Jeanette Nordstrom on the "Niagara Incident". Access requires full life scope polygraph with Level 6 clearance.

<u>PROLOGUE – Covert Cabal.</u>

HEIDELBERG CONFERENCE ROOM.

The man's suit was so dark it swallowed the light as completely as a black hole. He was sitting in the recesses of a shell-shaped chair in the unlit, windowless meeting room where no sunlight shone and even the internal lights had been dimmed.

All Devraj could see of the man apart from his silhouette in the chair was the vaguest tint of grey hair and the glint of a pair of spectacles.

Devraj's heart thumped loudly and his mouth went dry. He knew how serious it was; he was now standing in front of the real players, the Cabal that actually runs things in Europe and anywhere else its dark tendrils can reach.

Finally, the glint in the spectacles bobbed up and down and the shadow above moved; the man was nodding his head.

Then the voice piped up, in clipped, accented Euro-English. "Devraj," said the man in the black suit. "Tell us all why you are here."

Devraj grimaced.

Informing on a former friend and colleague was an unpleasant task but he knew he must suppress his reluctance and get on with it. His mouth yawned like some ancient cave mouth facing the east, waiting for the dawning solstice sun to shine in;

or in his case, waiting for a single sound to come out. For a long nervous moment even the simplest syllable refused to emerge and Devraj thought he was going to embarrass himself. Finally, unexpectedly, his vocal cords kicked into action with a cough.

"Huh… It is… ahem… exactly as I said. He has completely changed his stance. He is no longer one of us. Everything I told you in the email is true. I felt I was forced to inform you because of the many projects you have funded, the tremendous wealth you have funnelled in our direction, and how central he has been to all of our message promulgation, projects, promotions and publicity. He is the one single person we cannot afford to have going over to the deniers, especially now that we have you-know-who as President in America."

"Alright," said the man in the black suit. "You have corroborated the email. Thank you. Be ready for a call from one of my operatives. He will want you to tell him everything you know about Kael."

Devraj nodded. "Yes, sir."

"Thank you, Devraj. You may go now."

Devraj hesitated. "If I may, sir… You won't harm him will you?"

For a moment Devraj thought he saw a strange smile twist the corners of the man's mouth. "Harm him?" he said.

"No. We will not *harm* him."

Devraj felt relief flooding him, and he bowed and said obsequiously, "Thank you, sir. Thank you! Thank you!"

As Devraj left he felt like a lowly serf leaving the Sun King's presence in baroque France; he found himself bowing his way out of the room as he was backing out, still facing the man until the door in front of him closed in his face, seemingly of its own accord.

* * *

The man in the black suit revolved his chair around towards the conference table and the lights undimmed. Ten members sat around the table, four women and six men.

The man in the black suit unfolded his ruler and snapped it on the table, barking, "This is the day! This day is the day!"

The dark-haired, leather-skinned female peering through enormous, concave spectacles and two earrings that dangled down like bangles rolled her eyes and muttered, "Not the bloody folding rule again. The day for what?"

He ignored her and addressed the others. "You all have heard everything he said. This is the day we must decide what to do about this wayward Professor."

The leather-skinned woman's bangle-shaped earrings shook as she said, "He has been a General in the movement, one of the leaders. If a General starts having doubts who knows what the troops will do?"

The grey-bearded man with dark eyes sitting next to her nodded. "He is essential. If he is going to undermine the cause then all our plans are in grave trouble. He has a large following on the internet, in academia, in the media, among the common pundit. It will be a huge blow to our ultimate machinations. And it will make you-know-who look good."

The man with a rugged face and large baggy eyes spoke next, in clipped Danish English. "What does it matter? He's not that important. A mere Professor. A mere cog in the works."

The battleship shaped woman with grey, merciless hair shook her head. "There are billions at stake. Trillions. Our control of the Western Nations is entirely founded on the idea that carbon dioxide is a dangerous gas and that the tipping point is just around the corner. The money that funds our operations around the world comes from carbon credits and renewables. One man, even a Professor, in the larger scheme of things, is expendable." She repeated in a terse tone, "Expendable!"

The man with the rugged face said, "I see. Then you are right, something has to be done. Something final. Something irrevocable. We must decide today."

The silhouetted man said quietly, "Irreversible?" He

banged his ruler on the table again as though to make the point.

One by one each of those seated at the table nodded.

Last of all the man in the black suit nodded as well, saying quietly, "Yes, indeed. I concur. Then it is settled. Kael E. Addison will be taken care of."

The leather-skinned woman fiddled with one of her bangle-sized earrings. "How long will the business take?"

"Not long. Soon you will hear of… a dreadful mishap, an accident, perhaps, something that cannot be traced back to us – within the next few weeks perhaps…"

The leather-skinned woman snapped, "No!", causing one of her bangle-earrings to jiggle. "Make it sooner than that! Considering his position, if he makes any sort of a public statement it will be extremely damaging to our cause."

He tapped his ruler again. "I will do my very best." He took out his notepad and wrote in meticulous handwriting, 'Kontaktieren den Russischen', contact the Russian. Then he added the name of the offender, 'Kael Addison'.

"By the way," the battle-ship shaped woman said, "Any news on that Lazarus-Fox fellow, and the boy?"

"Peter Lazarus-Fox? Is the boy not back in your custody? The younger Adamant was taking care of that, off the books, wasn't he?"

"No, he hasn't arrived. He disappeared in Eastern Europe somewhere."

Shaking his head, the silhouetted man wrote down, "Lokalisieren Lazarus-Fox und den Jungen."

One of the other women said, "And the third item of business on our agenda? The revival of the Awilu?"

"Ja," said the silhouetted man. "As you no doubt have heard the Methuselah project, in sifting through the ancient documents and mythologies, has generated a side-benefit, allowing us to identify another long-lived ancient species, a hybrid creature, if you will. As you all know some of the Ascended Masters took bodily form on earth in ancient times. Of course, only the Jews and Christians see this as a bad thing; for the more enlightened pagans their hybrid children were honoured as heroes and rulers and giants."

The rugged-faced man said, "What happened to them? Are their descendants with us today?"

"Nobody knows. A great disaster. The sinking of Atlantis? A meteorite struck? A volcano? None of them survived."

The rugged-faced man said, "And who were they? Fictions. Myths. The Marvel superheroes of antiquity."

The silhouetted man said, "These were the *awilu* of Babylon, the demigods of Ancient Greece, Hercules, Achilles,

Arjuna the son of the Hindu deity Indra, Sæmingr, Bragi, sons of Odin and Sleipnir, son of Loki. Maui son of Tamanuitera; then there's Semiramis, Gilgamesh, Xochiquetzal and various others, African, Australian and Polynesian, North American, the *Nephilim* of the Bible, I could go on and on. The Bible says they existed before the time of Noah and also afterward..."

Rolling her eyes, the leather-skinned woman said, "Please don't. Just tell us how the project is going."

The rugged-faced man said, "It sounds ridiculous. I am a rational man. Why are we wasting our time and money on these fairy-tales and myths?"

The silhouetted man stared at him and banged his ruler on the table. "Myths? Fairy-tales? Fool. Wir haben die genetische Signatur! We have produced DNA and into the surrogate mother eingefügt. The project is proceeding! We have viable specimens. And these grow much more quickly than the Upper Early Palaeolithic humans..."

The leather-faced woman sneered, "That's not quite the whole story, is it? Perhaps the rest of you haven't been reading his blog."

He snapped the ruler again and she visibly winced but then his voice softened, "Ja, Ja, Fräulein, we have had our... complications. The operation in Italy may have been compromised. We think we have a mole in the German lab but we have yet to identify him. Ja, Ja, it's all in my blog. These are just the teething troubles, though, Fräulein… But…"

The leather-faced woman said, "But what?"

The silhouetted man smiled coldly. "But it seems the North American project has achieved another viable consciousness."

All around the table the heads nodded.

Good news at last.

CHAPTER 1 – Relational Revelation.

HEATHROW INTERNATIONAL AIRPORT, GREATER LONDON, SIX MONTHS EARLIER.

Yes, you could say it started then, with the Cabal putting out the hit on Addison but if that is the case then I suppose the story really began some months earlier when Kael E. Addison himself was stepping out of the airport bus onto the tarmac under the eye of the pale London sun, experiencing a twinge of guilt.

Kael had suddenly realised he was about to spend several hours sitting next to Devraj and he still hadn't submitted that paper. With luck Devraj had forgotten about it; surely they could just skip that reference in the UNPCC report? Kael would still be paid his hefty consultant's fee.

Trying to keep Devraj's mind off papers and reports, Kael quipped, "Rio last week – then to Copenhagen, then onto Sydney, New Orleans, London this weekend, and I'll be in Oslo in a few hours. It's truly exhausting spreading the message, Devraj."

Devraj was walking alongside shaking his head. "When are people going to understand we've got to do something about excessive use of fossil fuels, Kael?"

Kael glanced at his own sunlit reflection in the windows of a bus as they passed. He looked fit, carried his middle-age well, not overweight, slightly balding, a distinguished moustache and beard, and square spectacles.

He looked at Devraj enviously. His best friend was taller than Kael, Indian, with a rush of black hair, greying at the temples, long-limbed, slightly dashing. Devraj was forty-eight but he carried his years somewhat better than Kael carried his own forty-two years. Kael could see why Devraj often had an attractive younger woman by his side. A different one every week, if you could believe it. Lucky guy, he had the ability to seduce them. Money could do that — if you had the confidence as well.

And wasn't the money rolling in... from conferences, appearances, seminars, positions on boards, government grants and all the rest. Would Kael still be so passionate about climate change if it wasn't for the fat cheques, the prestige, the never-ending destinations? Kael frowned. Surely. Of course he would. Same with Devraj. Money wasn't their main motivation.

Devraj said, "You know what – despite the inconvenience, the constant travel, conferences, seminars in different countries, I wouldn't trade this life for anything."

"Neither would I," agreed Kael. "Neither would I."

Kael's phone buzzed as he was going up the escalator. He wanted to look at the message but his hands were full with his hand luggage. He rushed up the last few steps.

Plush, roomy seats in first class! Devraj had booked a huge exclusive cabin with only two seats. The window seat was Kael's. There was a chill on the air, so Kael pulled up the window-shutter, hoping in vain that the sun might warm the air a little, but it was too pale and smoggy outside for the heat to reach him.

As the stewardess took Kael's hand luggage Kael sat down and checked his phone, and he glanced over as Devraj sat down in the other seat, hoping his friend wouldn't mention the academic paper.

The stewardess began her spiel, "Sorry about the delay, there was an —" but she paused mid-sentence and looked carefully at him.

"Aren't you…?"

"Kael Addison." He modestly added, "You probably saw that climate film. By Leo Bos."

"Yes, I recognise you now. Oh, Professor Addison, I'm a big supporter of Greenpeace. We've got to do something to save the planet."

"Oh, I agree," he said, and shook her hand, smiling broadly. Best to keep the fans happy.

The SMS was from Kael's sister, Marybelle. It began rather rudely with all caps,

KAEL! DON'T FORGET!!! Lily's baptism. 1st July. You're going to be in Phoenix still aren't you? José's Mum wants the whole family there. No stupid excuses about a conference or saving the world! You missed the birth. Lily doesn't want her only uncle to miss her baptism.

He thought about ignoring it. But then she'd only harass him with more texts.

I will.

Her reply came immediately.

Really? ARE YOU SURE? PLEASE REPLY.

He tapped out angrily,

No need to harass me. Asking once would be fine. I'll be there. I promise.

It was about her ninth text about it this week.

GOOD! MAKE SURE YOU ARE. José's family doesn't think much of you anyway. They'll think a lot less of you if you're not at her baptism. It's an important part of family life for them, Kael, they won't appreciate you not being there. BE THERE.

Furiously, laboriously making it all-caps to make his point, he tapped out,

I SAID I WLD & I WILL, OK?

and left it at that.

Hoping Devraj had forgotten the paper, Kael watched him stretching out his feet. Devraj sighed and said something inaudible.

Kael leaned over; that's the problem with first class. The seats are too far away to have a decent conversation. "What did you say?"

Devraj leaned closer. "Just, you know, first class! To think, when I was a lowly engineer I only ever travelled economy. Or business class, but only if I was given an upgrade for frequent flyers."

Kael nodded, stretched out and yawned, then leaned over again and spoke loudly. "Well, if the Think-Tank's paying for it, why not, Devraj? It would be very impractical to try to function properly at an important International Climate Conference if you're still recovering from being squished into a seat no larger than a sardine can, wouldn't it?" He stretched out in the seat. "Ha! Some people would call us hypocrites. Taking a larger space on the plane than we really need…"

Devraj's face took on a serious, intense aspect. "No," he said, "Really? Climate deniers would. People like that young American, Sam Steinberg."

Kael said, "Whatever happened to him, anyhow? He used to be a thorn in our side at every conference."

Devraj said, "I don't know... He just disappeared from the scene."

Kael said, "I heard he'd died. Some kind of food poisoning, wasn't it?"

Devraj said, "Deniers. I don't care how he died. I'm glad he did. It's Karma."

Kael didn't feel like leaning over any more so he shouted at Devraj, "A flight like this would take a lot of carbon credits though wouldn't it?"

Devraj leaned over and gesticulated, "Indeed but we mustn't worry. Why, you and I have dedicated our lives to ending climate change. We are part of the solution, don't forget that, Kael. Haha, and we benefit from it, yes, indeed but why shouldn't we? Every soldier gets a salary, and a General gets a higher salary than the run-of-the-mill cannon fodder. We're the Generals, Kael." Devraj paused, grinning. "Anyway, first class requires much fewer carbon credits than economy."

Kael was surprised. "How do you figure that, Devraj?" That was an argument Kael had never heard before.

Devraj winked. "Much less weight per square metre. Why there'd be seven or eight passengers in economy in the equivalent space, plus all their luggage. We're saving a lot of carbon in fuel." Devraj smacked his lips. "I think I'm going to have a vodka-martini." He took out the menu.

Thank God.

Devraj had forgotten about the paper.

Kael finally relaxed and eased himself into his seat. It was all fine. Devraj chose that exact moment to say, "By the way, Kael, I meant to ask you about that paper."

Kael winced and felt his blood pressure rising. "The UNPCC one? The one I'm delivering at Berlin?" He felt a whole plethora of excuses rising in his gullet. He really had intended to submit it this afternoon but the wifi hadn't been working at the hotel and his phone had gone flat. Now it was too late. If only he had just been a little more organised. "That one?"

Devraj nodded. "Yes, yes, for the chapter about the climate models. I sent you five or six emails, you know."

The title ran through Kael's mind, Modelling Parameters and Assessing the Accuracy of Climate Predictions. "Yes, Devraj, ah, Johannes and I came up with it to support his conclusions in that chapter. It's going to be published, no problem, I know the reviewers, it's as good as passed. It will be in the next issue. I think… around May the 26th. When was the deadline for that journal…?" Kael knew damn well it was May the 6th. This was the conversation he had been dreading.

Devraj laughed. "Oh, the deadline, don't worry about

that. That wasn't why I was asking!"

"Oh," Kael felt sheepish. "I thought that's why… That's why I haven't responded to your emails. I was… embarrassed it hadn't been submitted."

Devraj's laugh boomed round the cabin. "That was why you didn't reply? God, no, really? You thought I needed the paper published before the deadline? Worry about that? Goodness. Don't worry. I shouldn't tell you this but some of them don't even get published."

"Really?" Amazing. He thought he was the only one struggling to get things in on time but clearly, that wasn't the case. I mean, this was the UNPCC report, the most important climate report in the world, and Devraj wasn't even worried about deadlines?

Devraj rolled his eyes. "Ha! I remember in 2007 how shocked I was at this practice. I was assisting one of the lead authors and several papers we were referencing were not published yet — one in particular about Solar influences on the climate — he let them through, in fact, they didn't get published for another year and a half! Several of the citations in my chapter never even got past the first draft stage. Details like that don't matter, Kael, because we're right about climate change. You've got to look at the big picture! Oh, that's funny, Kael, that's really funny! You were worried about it being a little bit late? No, I wasn't emailing about that. I was emailing asking you if you would deliver it at the Seattle conference – um – even if it's just a draft. Just give us the conclusions you are – um – going to come to once you have the data."

"Really?" Such a pleasant surprise, Kael couldn't believe his ears. He reached across the gap awkwardly and shook Devraj's hand. "Love to."

Kael was flicking through the emails now on his phone but he couldn't find the date. "When is that conference again, Devraj? Hadn't planned to but what the heck, man. If I'm presenting…"

"Just a moment, Kael. Last weekend in June, I think." Devraj checked his own phone. "The 29th of June to the 1st of July. We want you to present on the Sunday afternoon, right at the culmination of the weekend. And, look, there'll be a… special consideration because you're a special presenter."

Kael said, "Sure, love to." He always appreciated Devraj's 'considerations', code for a hefty fee, often with mildly exaggerated – what they liked to call these days 'trumped-up' – expenses included.

He flicked over to the Calendar App. 1st July.

Damn.

The date of the baptism.

Kael frowned. The baptism was in the morning. He could make it. "What time was it you wanted the paper delivered?"

Devraj said, "Oh, the seminar's at 5:15 pm, just before the keynote address at six. It's a feature; it's the one that will get all the media attention."

Kael googled the flights. There was a non-stop flight from Phoenix to Seattle at 11:45 am that would get him to Seattle by 3:45 pm; plenty of time. The Convention Centre was five minutes from the airport, no problem, so long as he was on that plane in Phoenix by 11:40.

Kael said stubbornly, "Yes, I can do it."

He pursed his lips. His sister wouldn't be happy when he ran away from the baptism early and missed the shared meal. Still, at least he wouldn't be forced to speak to the pastor at her church – that guy always made Kael feel uneasy. A fundamentalist, a Biblical literalist, although the man referred to himself as an evangelical. Always going on about the Bible – for God's sake who took that ancient faith seriously these days? Probably a creationist. If so, maybe a denier. A lot of those died-in-the-wool evangelicals were. The Catholics tended to be more friendly, what with the Pope expressing his absolute certainty that climate change was happening (nice thing, infallibility. Climate science could do with the ability to make pronouncements like that...

He chuckled, well we really did have that power, didn't we?)

A nice change from Galileo's time, when the church was the only one making infallible pronouncements.

Kael pictured Marybelle's expression when she realised he was leaving before the family lunch.

Well, she'd just have to be unhappy, wouldn't she? What was more important – saving the world from the evil scourge of carbon dioxide or his niece's baptism? The future for all children, or an archaic ceremony from a dying religion? For God's sake, he'd be there for the baptism, he'd just be missing the meal. She would have to live with it, that was all there was to it.

"Are you alright? Are you sure you're available?" Devraj looked concerned.

Obviously, Kael's feelings were showing on his face.

He cursed his an open-book-face, displaying his neuroses to anyone who cared to read his features. He was always misunderstood. He was the victim here, the underdog, the shy introvert forced into the limelight. He carried a great burden, being one of the world's greatest climate scientists.

A singularly unsuitable expression of nobility came over his face that, if he had only realised, really only made him look even more ridiculous.

Devraj stifled a laugh and said, "What?"

Kael stated, "Yes, yes, of *course*, I'm available, Devraj. It's just my sister wanted me to, oh you know, be at a family thing in the morning in Phoenix. But it's fine, there's a flight at quarter to twelve, I'll make it. I'd love to be there, my friend, I'm really honoured. There's no way I wouldn't be there."

"Good. I really need you there. You are quite the celebrity these days, you know."

Kael looked at Devraj. "So are you, Devraj, so are you."

"Yes, I am. I really am! And we'll make it happen, you know, Kael. We'll make it happen."

Kael wasn't sure what he meant. "Save the world from global warming?"

"Oh, that too," Devraj said hastily. "That too. No, I was actually thinking about that stewardess over there."

They could just see her through the curtain. She was bending over, about to sit down for the flight, and her breasts were bulging at the top of her dress. Devraj said, "What a hottie. Wouldn't mind getting her into my hotel room, or rather, into her in my hotel bed. But climate change, yes, very important too. We will save the world, Kael."

They reached over uncomfortably and punched each other's knuckles and rested back into their seats in a shared glow of mutual self-satisfaction as the plane started rolling onto the runway.

Then Kael's obsessive thoughts started up again. What if the church service went too long? That Latino church of hers, the services sometimes went on for two hours, the sermon alone would be a half-hour, up to forty-five minutes sometimes.

If only her husband had been a typical Latino Catholic instead of some kind of born again nutcase. Catholic services went for a maximum of an hour, every time.

Last Christmas the service had started at ten-thirty. What if his niece hadn't even been baptised by a quarter to twelve? They might not baptise her till after twelve and he'd miss his flight.

He looked out the window at London receding and wondered why he worried so much. Why couldn't he just think happy, positive thoughts? His psychiatrist assured him it was his dysfunctional childhood but Kael knew better.

He knew the thought was irrational but still, he felt it. This was all his sister's fault.

He tried to brush it away but the heart feels what it feels, doesn't it?

His sister. Her fault. And that stupid irrational religion of theirs. No, that was what was irrational.

He scowled out through the window. The sunlight was coming through the clouds in a way that looked like a scene from that old film, the Ten Commandments. Charlton Heston as Moses. A beautiful sight but somehow too reminiscent of religion. He scowled at the coincidence. There was no God, he had decided a long time ago, though the lack of a creator left a hole he couldn't fill. So he had decided there probably was an energy field or some sort of life force or perhaps Gaia was supervising things, I mean, at the most, an Earth goddess.

Those Christians. The thought of an anthropomorphic God creeped Kael out a bit.

Suddenly real sunlight flashed in his eyes as they went above the clouds and he had to close them, it actually hurt his eyes. For a moment he thought God might be trying to tell him something but Kael had no clue as to what it might be that *that* God would want to say to him.

Precisely at that moment a pair of beautiful, full, wholesome, bulging-with-ice vodka-martinis arrived and Kael turned away from the window with relief.

Saved by the buxom stewardess.

CHAPTER 2 – Magic and Misdirection.

WHEN IT <u>REALLY</u> BEGAN, December the Year Before.

Well, if you want to know, vodka also had something to do with when it all really began a little while earlier in Moscow, back when Sol the Magnificent was doing his new act, the one that had started off so well but then again like the others before it, it had been affected by his vodka drinking; it wasn't exactly Sol's fault, it was just his way of dealing with the pain of the despair at his divorce.

Then one day, at the Sunday afternoon matinee, he had stumbled badly and fallen over, and the audience had laughed, and then the monkey (that damned monkey; Sol had gotten it to make his act more interesting and then it had started stealing the show)... That stupid monkey! It had used its little stick to hit him and the audience had laughed.

Sol had gotten tangled in his cloak and the audience had gasped; he hadn't understood in the moment why — it was all accidental but once he watched the video someone had posted on Facebook afterwards he knew why and had decided to make it part of the act.

They had gasped because it had looked as though one of his limbs had been chopped off when the monkey hit him, a strange artefact of the direction of the light and the position of his elbow and the way the cloak was hanging and the fact that the monkey's stick resembled a large knife.

It was effective, he had had to admit it, so he honed the effect and trained the monkey and now he was using it in his new act.

And before he knew it he found himself capitalising on his new-found fame.

The Facebook video of the initial incident had started it. The doorman at the hotel where he stayed had shown it to him on his mobile phone, so Sol had rewarded the man by making him his butler.

His butler. The only other person who knew his real identity. Apart from his ex-wife, of course. No one else knew who he was.

Sol always began the scene by stumbling drunkenly, pretending now to be drunk, lurching from side to side (to do it right he had had to force himself to go stone-cold sober, not a drop now for eighteen months, three days, thirteen hours, five minutes and twenty-two seconds.) He had done the act so many times now that Sol's mind would wander while he was doing it, as it was now.

He had to admit, giving up the booze had worked. The new act had gone very well, so well in fact that his ex-wife had contacted him, which she would do only if she thought he was now very, very rich.

Which he was. (Though he told her he hadn't made anything from it!)

Apart from the butler, his ex-wife was the only one who knew his real name, the only one who had recognised him on YouTube.

Every night was a sell-out. Even the week-day matinees were full houses, and he had become rich and famous again, greatly surpassing any former fame or fortune.

It was a new dawn, a new morning in the prime of his life.

To say that he had vast assets now wasn't making an elephant out of a fly, it was a realistic assessment. He had a house in Ostozhenka, right in the middle of Moscow, a lush, expansive farm in Krasnodar with a mansion with massive balcony windows that opened onto the sunset in summer, a couple of Porsches to zip between them, as well as a *gigantski* bank balance and investment portfolio, mostly offshore and untraceable, although of course, it had become substantially smaller, though, since that butler had started siphoning funds.

He scowled angrily. He would get his revenge, by God.

To think Sol had trusted that *razvaluha* with everything.

To discover that betrayal had been far more humiliating than his act; even more humiliating than his divorce from that *suchka*.

Stupid *zhopa*. The butler should have realised that robbing from Sol was like poking a bear with a stick.

Or flying too close to the sun. He was like a son to him, that boy, that Icarus.

The monkey whacked Sol, once, twice with his stick. It looked as though his forearm, then the whole other arm had been chopped off but the supposed stumps were hidden in the twisted, tangled up cloak.

None of it was real, of course, it was all clever lighting, mirrors and misdirection.

He reflected on the power of misdirection as the monkey whacked him again, apparently amputating one of his legs this time.

As the monkey whacked him, his mind wandered to his beloved detective novels. His favourite was Agatha Christie. Sol read the Russian translations as well as the English versions, for his American mother had taught him to read English, and the Agatha Christie novels were her favourites as well.

Agatha Christie used misdirection all the time, just like a good magician. She made the reader believe one thing when something entirely other was true.

Sol hopped around, apparently now only having one leg but it wasn't funny any more. It looked real. The audience wasn't laughing. They were staring intently at him, trying to work it out, horrified, in fact. Had the monkey actually chopped off his arms and one leg? The monkey whacked him again and he stumbled, now completely legless. For a little while he struggled on the ground like an impotent bug, clearly a contorted, limbless cripple behind his cloak.

Then the drum rolled and Sol jumped up and pulled the bits of himself out of nowhere behind the cloak and appeared complete, the audience gasped again this time with pleasure and surprise as Sol rolled out of the cloak and stood next to the monkey. They both took a bow, then the monkey tapped him again and they both disappeared into thin air.

Mirrors and misdirection, that was all it was.

And damn good animal training as well; what had he done that the gods had blessed him with this *glupyy* — no, really, not stupid, but rather intelligent, actually — monkey?

Yes, he was going to get that accursed butler. He was going to get him good.

He'd asked for the afternoon off, unfortunately, so unless the butler finished his errand early Sol wouldn't be able to do the dirty deed today.

Tomorrow evening, after the act. When the sun was down. Night time was the best time for dark deeds, he had decided.

As fate would have it, though, Sol the Magnificent was not coming back tomorrow to do his act. Not tomorrow, not the day after that, not ever.

~~~

The dismembered, headless torso was discovered in the magic trunk the following morning after one of the stagehands smelled something foul. The stagehand had thought it was a dead rat and had wanted to remove it; instead, he had uncovered an inexplicable horror. The management quickly called the police.

The forensics men studied the scene, the rate of decomposition and the size of the maggot pupae, and decided that despite the lack of blood, whoever this was had died between ten o'clock and eleven o'clock the previous evening.

Within an hour from when the show had ended.

They couldn't explain where the blood had gone; and that was one mystery.

The other mystery was that no one could actually verify that it was Sol himself. You see, no one really knew his torso these days. He apparently had not taken advantage of the young women who threw themselves at him because of his fame, and his ex-wife, unknown to the police, had not come forward. So it had turned out, rather ironically, that no one recognised Sol's private parts well enough even to know whether it was definitely his private parts on the legless, headless corpse.
~~~

Furthermore, Sol had no blood relatives that the police knew about. His family history was a complete mystery. They didn't even know his surname. Therefore, they couldn't use DNA to identify him.

But the coroner decided the corpse was Sol the Magnificent and declared him dead from foul play and instructed the police to find the killer.

The day after the coronial inquest the online Russian newspaper *Novayagazeta* had a headline that said, "Sol the Magnificent's last gruesome performance."

It was an eloquent tribute to the great magician, with a reflection on the fact that, in this day and age, his death was more than likely a political assassination, afterwards commenting on how unlikely it was that the murderer or murderers would ever be brought to justice, for little thieves are caught but great ones get away and it is the same with murderers in Glorious Mother Russia.

~~~

The man walking into the entrance of Sheremetyevo International Airport, Moscow, was very nervous.

He was flicking through the new passport again before he tucked it away in the secret compartment in his hand luggage – flawless, it would certainly pass customs when he got to
~~~

England. Still, he was going to use the old one for now.

The butler had indeed returned early.

About ten minutes after Sol's performance had finished.

The suitcase was open when he arrived but he didn't dare leave it that way – he had closed it and fled the scene. He wasn't going to be charged for murder! No way! He was fleeing the country. Once the Russian prosecutors got hold of the suitcase containing the body they would not let go until you had been convicted, no matter that it was one, two, three jury trials and as many Supreme Court appeals.

Yes, the passport he was using here was a risk but he was almost completely certain no one knew that Sasha Konstantin Soldatov had been Sol the Magnificent's butler. After all, he hadn't told anyone at all since he had gone to live at that mansion.

Thank goodness for Trippy Girl, he thought to himself, that shady contact on the Darknet who had brokered the deal. She (if she was not some fat sweaty fifty-year-old man masquerading as a female online) had organised it all for him using bitcoin and the Tor Messaging service; all he had needed to do was turn up at some seedy Moscow address and pick up the new passport.

He noted the fact that there was another job to do, for, apart from Sol's wife, Trippy Girl was the only other wooden link in the chain.

One of only a handful of people who might be able to work out who he was and tie him to the murder.

Smugly, he reflected on the fact that money can buy just about anything, and he would surely be able to find out Trippy Girl's identity.

A little while afterwards, perhaps a couple of hours, he walked off the plane in London, England, and showed his passport to the authorities, a passport that now bore a different name, Sasha Yuri Yevgenev but due to some clever computer hacking by Trippy Girl, he himself was the only one in the world apart from Trippy Girl who knew that this passport was different from the one he had boarded the plane in Moscow with.

He walked straight through customs and sat down in the airport lounge.

Thank goodness, he had made it through.

The murderer laughed softly to himself as he got up, looking at his mobile phone so as not to make a spectacle for the ubiquitous security cameras and hailed an English taxi, trying not to be too broad with his gestures.

Sasha.

It's a serviceable enough name.

I will keep it here in England, he said to himself.

And who knows. Perhaps I will find a new profession here in England. I wonder if there is a job for people who enjoy murder?

* * *

CHAPTER 3 – Alive and Delivered.

SOMEWHERE IN EUROPE, Three Months Later, sometime in March.

The door opened out onto a bright sunlit day, and it took a moment for Peter's eyes to adjust. They were in a narrow European street among perfect examples of elegant eighteenth-century architecture. The thug pushed Peter and Meth out, saying, "Go. Out. You're free."

He was closing the door but Peter stuck his foot in and stopped it.

"Just a second," Peter said. "Not that quick, Mister."

The thug said, "What? You're free to go. So go."

Peter was trembling with outrage. "You've just kidnapped us, beaten me up, tied up the boy so savagely his wrists have wounds in them half an inch deep and you have not even fed either one of us properly for three days – cornflakes is not nutritious at all on its own – to say nothing of the fact you threatened to kill me. And you think it's over?"

The thug scowled and said, "Well, it would be easy enough to pop you both. But it seems like a needless expense of time and money. Getting rid of bodies ain't easy or cheap. And someone might miss you I suppose, and if they were to catch me dropping your corpses in the river it could be bad for me – every hit is a risk for my neck too. Unless, of course, you're thinking of going to the police?"

Peter shut his mouth, considering his options. "Alright. No police." He stepped forward into the thug's space and whispered in his face, "But I have a few conditions. First, you need to tell me who hired you."

The thug sighed deeply. "Alright, alright. It was Roland Adamant. He's done for, buddy, been arrested in New York, so there goes my pay packet. He was in charge of all this. The man who pays the piper calls the tune. And now he is out of the picture." He looked at them both. "Glad you're free. Didn't really want to hurt you two, because you have done nothin' to me…" He went to close the door but Peter stopped him again.

"Secondly I need you to tell me which city we are in."

"Bratislava."

Peter kept his foot in the door. "Thirdly, our stuff!"

The thug swore coldly. "Alright, I'll get your stuff." He rummaged around in another room and brought out two backpacks and a wallet.

Peter opened the wallet and flicked through the cards. "There was money in this too."

The thug rolled his eyes. "I'm out of pocket already. *Darovanému koňovi sa na zuby nepozerá.* The gift horse you don't look in the mouth. Get lost."

"If I don't get my money back I'm going straight to the police. It's not your money, I earned it, it doesn't belong to you. How do you expect us to survive otherwise? Give us our money, or it's the police."

The thug took out his own wallet. He counted out five hundred US dollars. "I don't know how much you had on you. But that should be enough for you to get a room for the night and something to eat. Now get lost before I have lost my patience."

The thug closed the door behind them and Peter didn't stop him this time.

They walked out into the street and the sunshine was glorious and the day was beautiful because they were free.

Meth put his hand into Peter's hand and said, "Well done, Father."

Peter said quietly, "I believe the God of Abraham, Isaac and Jacob has just delivered us once again, son. Let us go and find a hotel and work out what we're going to do next."

At that moment, a girl of about eighteen or nineteen walked out the door beneath a sign that said Solar Café. From the casual elegance of her clothes and one or two items, a necklace from Greece, the camera around her neck, Peter deduced she was a backpacker from some European country or other. She held a laptop awkwardly. Her accent had traces of German or perhaps some southern Scandinavian country; it was hard to tell these days. "Hello! You wouldn't be Peter and Meth?"

"Yes," said Peter. "How do you-?"

The girl showed them the laptop screen. It was on some sort of Messenger app, and the latest message said,

> TG: They're walking down the street just outside right now.

The girl said, "Someone called Trippy Girl is looking for you. Come on into the coffee shop, you can talk to her on my computer."

Peter and Meth went in.

The girl sat Peter down at her computer. Meth sat next to him. The girl said, "Don't worry, it's encrypted. It's completely secure."

She typed first.

> Ang: Peter is here. I'm giving him the computer.
>
> TG: Hi Peter. This is Trippy Girl. TG.
>
> Ang: Hi TG, it's Peter typing now. Who are you? What's going on?
>
> TG: Rather not say. Too many eyes, ears, watching, listening. Someone you know. Not Natasha.

Ang: Alright. How did you know where we are?

TG: I have been watching, Peter. Surveilling. I helped you in Budapest too. I want to help you and Meth find a new safe place. Roland Adamant is out of the picture but there are others, many who want the boy. Unsure which faction is in charge now. I will help you if I can. What do you need? Money?

Ang: And a safe place to stay.

TG: Australia? I've prepared false identities for you and Meth. I think Perth, Australia would be good. I have put some things in place already. There is a Meth-Shiloh in line to be enrolled at a small school.

Ang: Perth? Where Nathanael comes from?

TG: Yes… What do you think? I can have your air tickets emailed to Angela right now. If she is willing to print them for you…

Angela said, "Of course, no problem."

* * *

The man in the black suit was sitting at his desk, in his own office. The sunshine irritated him, so he reached forward and closed the blinds.

The phone rang. He picked it up.

His secretary's voice said, "It's that Bob Wilkins guy, Adamant's head of operations in New York. He's on the encrypted line."

He replied in clipped Euro-English, "Put him through."

"Hello," said the voice on the phone. "This is Bob Wilkins. I heard you're looking for a certain person?"

"I am," said the man in the black suit. "I'm looking for Peter Lazarus-Fox. I heard he had been detained in Slovakia or somewhere like that? You were Adamant's man, were you not? – you should know what happened?"

Bob Wilkins said, "Lazarus was detained in Slovakia. But please, don't let's talk names; makes me very nervous in this day and age. Let's call Lazarus and the boy 'the package'. To be honest, Adamant didn't keep much paperwork on this one. I had to go and visit him in prison, not a particularly pleasant task. Now, what was supposed to happen was this: his man in Slovakia would get paid and then the package would be delivered to Adamant's men. Well, when Adamant was arrested, the whole thing fell through. His guy in Slovakia let them go."

"What?" said the man in the black suit. "I thought you said the guy in Slovakia let them go?"

Bob said, "That is what I did say. He let them go. He basically said, if he's not getting paid, then why should he do the job?"

"I assume he had received a deposit, Bob?"

Bob replied, "Quite a hefty one, at that."

The man in the black suit paused for a moment. Finally, he spoke. "So you are telling me that this man had already been paid for half the job? And then he let them go?"

Bob replied, "Yes, that's right. He let them go. That's what I said. Or do you need me to repeat it again?"

The man in the black suit paused and Bob felt a wave of fear wash over him. He shouldn't have antagonised this strange man, whoever he was, this man of shadows, the king of the darkness, the boss of so much more than Bob could even guess. But the man in black only breathed, "Alright," and put the phone down.

Bob heaved a heavy sigh of relief.

* * *

Meanwhile, the man in the black suit was sending a private message over an encrypted network.

* * *

Fifteen minutes later an unmarked black car screeched to a stop at a certain address in a narrow Bratislava street. Three slim men in track suits jumped out of the car.

One of them rang the doorbell.

The thug who had captured Peter and Meth and then let them go answered the door.

One of the men in tracksuits said, "Ladislav Borovský?"

"Hey," said the thug. "No one knows that name. Don't say it out loud." He looked around suspiciously. "Anybody might be listening. You people have no manners."

The man whispered, "That is your name? This is your lucky day. You have won the Sunday lottery." He raised his eyebrows rather comically with the last phrase.

Ladislav smiled. "Really? I didn't even know. How much? That's great news! I've really won the –"

A gun appeared, Ladislav wasn't even sure which of the three men had pulled it out, he barely even saw the black cylinder of the barrel among them. One shot to the forehead, two shots to the heart, and Ladislav Borovský's world turned to darkness.

* * *

WILKINS & CO SECURITY, NEW YORK OFFICE.

Bob Wilkins' phone rang.

The slightly accented voice of the man in the black suit said, "Mister Wilkins? Former head of Adamant's security?"

Bob said, "Yes?"

The man in the black suit said, "I would like to hire

your team for a particular job."

Bob tried to make his voice as deferential and polite as he could, "Well, that would be welcome, sir, considering that we haven't been paid by Mister Adamant for a good three months now. Me and me team were all looking for work, actually, so this would be indeed very welcome."

"I want to find that boy Meth, find Peter Lazarus-Fox. Find who it is that has been helping them. Get Meth and Lazarus-Fox to one of your secret facilities and disappear anyone who has been helping them."

Bob whispered, "Sorry, sir, do you mean, make their helpers disappear? Because disappear is not a transitive verb insofar as I understand grammar. Sir."

The man in the black suit snapped, "Well, actually, look it up in the dictionary, you American, it can be intransitive or transitive. I'm a native German speaker, I would know, I actually know grammar, not like you Yankee bumpkins. I studied three languages at school as well as Latin. You do not know grammar, you are American, you only speak one language and you are a dolt." The man in the black suit left a pause to let that sink in. "Now, just in case we might be cooperating on projects in future, Mister Bob Wilkins, I would like you to be enlightened about Ladislav Borovský's reward for his lack of cooperation and effort on our behalf."

"Who's he? Sorry, he's not on my team, is that…"

"Ladislav Borovský is the real name of… Jan Kovac."

"Really? Oh. I do know the guy! He's the man my boss sent to kidnap Meth and Peter, isn't he?"

"Yes. I do recommend you check the Bratislava Pravda newspaper website, dawn edition tomorrow. The police will be making a press release then."

"What?" The phone line went dead.

The next morning, before dawn, with growing nausea in his stomach, Bob googled the Bratislava Pravda website.

The main headline on the home page was, "Crime Figure Ladislav Borovský Killed in Gangland Style Shooting."

Bob swore and said to himself, "Well, Bob, looks like you've got an even better boss than before."

PHOENIX ARIZONA

Trippy Girl, that is, Michelle Chase, was managing her Darknet contacts when a message came through from one of her guys in Slovakia. "Borovský was killed yesterday, see dawn edition of the news."

Michelle gasped. She had kind of expected that to happen but it was rather quick, that was all.

Too quick.

The guy who had abducted Peter and Meth was dead.

This wasn't so good. She'd foolishly thought that once Adamant was in prison that would be the end of the nightmare. Now some dark, shadowy figure was pulling the strings, someone Michelle couldn't even identify.

Of course she had read rumours of the secret Cabal on the internet but she'd always thought it was just rumours and midnight Facebook conspiracy theories spread by pale, wan, obsessive-compulsive netizens who needed to get out of their dark, dank computer dens and absorb some sunshine. But now they had acted in her circle of influence, they had intruded on her world.

Michelle gritted her teeth. Trippy Girl might sound like a stupid, inconsequential figure but no one crossed her. Trippy Girl was in control.

She was going to find out who they were and she was going to pwn them.

She would work all night and all day if she had to, to find out who the members of this shadowy Cabal really were.

CHAPTER 4 – Familiar Familial.

PHOENIX ARIZONA, SOMETIME IN LATE JUNE.

Three months later, on a particular Thursday, Michelle was shut away in her room with the lights out, her server farm humming away in the corner, the blue light of the characters on the computer screen shining onto her face.

Natasha knocked on the door.

Michelle shouted, "Go away."

Natasha said, "I'm worried about you. When was the last you ate something? You've been in there for days. When was the last time you even saw a single ray of sunlight? You'll be getting a Vitamin D deficiency."

Michelle ignored her. She was still trying to hack her way through to the Cabal members but after months of trying she still had no clue who they were.

And not only that. Her contact in Slovakia, known online as BigBear, had recently gone silent, presumed dead.

A message came through from another contact, Sloan, an American teenager who went to school in Bratislava and could speak and read Slovak.

Sloan: BigBear was killed. It was in the newspaper this morning. Definitely him.

Michelle didn't want to believe it.

TG: How do you know it was him?

Sloan: I knew him. I knew his real name. It was definitely him…

TG: Can you be completely sure?

Sloan: He was a relative. A cousin of my Dad. My mother identified the body.

Michelle had had enough.

She looked around the dark room, the computer that had yielded no definite information for months, the claustrophobic walls, the damp, dank smell of sheets that hadn't been washed for weeks.

She had to get out of here.

She put a message on the general Pheonix bulletin board.

TG: Hitting the town tonight. Any good company want to join me for a few drinks?

PonyBoy: I'm there with you. Where do you want to meet?

* * *

Fifteen minutes later, Michelle was blinking in the evening sunlight as she stepped out of the Uber. She went in to GypsyBar, a combined arcade and nightclub where PonyBoy was in a corner somewhere, probably playing his favourite game, Galaga, an old eighties game console.

She felt like letting down her hair and having a good night. She wasn't going to think about hacking, the Cabal, and Trippy Girl.

* * *

Forty-five minutes later, Michelle was kissing PonyBoy, whose real name she had just found out was Jerry or Jeffrey or Jeremy or something. It wasn't supposed to happen, she didn't even really like him that much. The PonyBoy thing was half the reason why – he was wearing a My Little Pony T-shirt that was just a little too unmasculine even for Michelle's woke taste. But he was there and she was there and maybe that simple fact was enough to temporarily assuage her loneliness and frustration.

* * *

Half an hour after that she was in his apartment bedroom and everything was going faster than she had planned. A lot faster. She rationalised: it wasn't the drink, it wasn't the ecstasy she had taken, there really was a closeness, there was a feeling that was more than drugs or alcohol. It felt good. It felt right.

But then the thought struck her while he was pawing her pants down clumsily, she wasn't on the pill and he didn't seem at all inclined to put on any protection.

And then while the thing was happening she felt like she was two people at once; it all felt pleasurable but weird, off-putting, kindof awkward, as though they were too close. Like building a bridge without putting up any supports, or only having half a milkshake when you needed a proper roast meal.

Or like going to someone's funeral and pulling your pants down in the middle of the church. It might feel nice but it was just gross, flesh and panting and nakedness.

But it did feel nice.

She looked at him.

He was so pale and unmasculine.

Why did she have to think these sorts of thoughts? Her good experiences got ruined, every time, by something, discomfort or pain or a stupid inappropriate thought that came out of nowhere.

Ecstatic for a few moments, despite the groping and the boniness of his knees, which disturbed her again, and then it was all over and she was left panting on the bed, with her mouth open and tongue lolling, like a dog.

Then she was in a sad, slow, existential movie, like the feeling of reading Jean Peal Sartre's "Nausea". He fell asleep on his bed dribbling drool onto his pillow, his My Little Pony t-shirt sprawled next to him, his pale knobbly fingers, fingers that had been touching her, splayed out like a spider's legs on the headboard of the bed. He looked pale and gross, like a night-time vampire that had turned out to be too ugly and bony to be beautiful.

The lights of the nearby train station were coming through the curtains, painting the whole place as lonely, modern, soulless.

Five minutes later she was sobbing in the shower, trying to wash away the feeling of being used but it didn't work.

She dried herself, paying extra attention to between her legs, still sobbing quietly, got dressed and gathered her things together and caught another Uber home.

Maybe it was her imagination but the expression on her face felt harder than it had been the day before.

She lay awake in her bed, feeling seedy, looking up at the fragile beam of light peeping over her curtains onto the ceiling, thinking about how far away God was right now, as though He didn't even exist at all.

She remembered that old saying – someone had said it to her at church once – who moved?

God didn't move, it must've been her.

She had another shower.

As she showered a vision came into her mind, of showering in filth, alcohol and drugs pouring down over her, obscuring the daylight, and for a moment she couldn't breathe and thought she was drowning and might die.

And that dreadful night came into her thoughts – the night she had tried to forget – a few years ago now but it seemed like yesterday – when she had been abducted after she had had too much to drink.

She gagged for a moment, bent over in the shower and then the moment of panic passed.

That moment Michelle decided she was never going to drink again.

* * *

PHOENIX ARIZONA, A FRIDAY IN LATE JUNE.

The following afternoon Professor Kael E. Addison arrived at Sky Harbor in Pheonix and caught a taxi to his sister's place. They did the greetings as he came in, kisses and so forth, but Kael couldn't help feeling like a stranger here. As he dragged his luggage in to his sister's spare room, he groaned softly, dreading the thought of spending a weekend with her obnoxious relatives.

Marybelle followed him into the room and pointed her finger accusingly at him. "You're groaning 'cause you don't want to be here, aren't you?"

"Of course not," Kael lied. "Luggage a bit heavy, that's all." He groaned as he pretended to lug it up on the bed with great effort.

Marybelle said suspiciously, "What do you have in there?"

Kael lied again, "Just stuff. Work books."

As she walked out of the room a queasy feeling came over him. He angrily unpacked his stuff – that was it – the nub of the problem – every time he came over here she made him feel so guilty.

* * *

At that very same moment, Nathanael and Natasha were letting themselves in the door at Natasha's parents' place half a city away. Natasha still lived here, officially, but lately she had been spending a lot of her time at Nathanael's new apartment in Encanto. Her parents were not happy, though, when she stayed there the whole night, despite her protestations that nothing untoward was going on. They were away now, thankfully.

Michelle was still here, though. It was a bright, sunny day and she was sitting at the kitchen bench, on her computer, typing efficiently. The skylight in the kitchen was letting in a broad beam of warm sunlight, making the motes of dust dance around her head like fairies.

Michelle was wearing a stylish top with 'fcku' written on the front, a pink headband and jeans that looked even more expensive than they probably were, topping boots that were neat and feminine and cute and matched the other clothes perfectly. She had put in a bit of extra effort this morning to make herself feel better.

It was almost working.

As Natasha came in she thought proudly that Michelle certainly looked like someone whose online monicker was "Trippy Girl". It was a trippy look.

Natasha rolled up her sleeves and the tattoos on her beautiful brown skin showed. Nathanael couldn't help glancing; he liked the way Natasha looked, in fact, now that they were an item he found himself looking even more often than he used to.

He could hardly believe it — him, at his age, a divorcee, a fairly unconventional geek with one or two unusual intellectual gifts, dating a smart young woman like Natasha, a computer hacker, a programmer, and sexy as hell. Well, not an apt expression, considering he was a Christian now, and so was she but let's face it. She was truly a desirable woman.

He looked at her.

The kind of woman he could imagine himself marrying.

Natasha sprung the question, "Sister, what are you up to?"

"Nothing much," said Michelle, hastily snapping the computer screen shut.

Natasha peered over the bench, reaching over as though she might prise the screen open, "You're not hacking again, are you?"

Michelle screwed her face up. "You can talk." Whisking

her hair through the sunbeam and making the dust-motes dance, Michelle turned away and pretended to be wiping the bench with the back of her hand even though there was no dirt. Then she began brushing away invisible dirt on her jeans.

Natasha said, "Well, to be frank, ever since I found out you're Trippy Girl, I've been very worried, Michelle. I've been meaning talk to you about it but I haven't managed to catch you in an opportune moment. Until now."

Over her shoulder, Michelle snapped, "Well I'm busy at the moment. See?" She opened up the laptop again and began typing, orienting it away from Natasha but when Natasha leaned over to see what was on it Michelle snapped it shut again, hissing, "It's private."

Natasha sighed. "Mum and Dad are on holiday this weekend. I think it's the perfect time, actually."

Michelle scowled. "The perfect time for what?"

Natasha said, "Like I said, sister. The perfect time to have a talk about it, without risking them knowing. I want to help you, support you." Michelle said sarcastically, "I see you brought Nathanael with you to support me as well. Two onto one, hey? Great way to bully me into submission." Almost sneering at them, Michelle prised the laptop open again away from Natasha's gaze.

Natasha burst out with, "My precious! Gollum, Gollum!" but Michelle ignored the quip.

Nathanael raised his arms and said as good-naturedly as he could, "I'm keeping out of this one, thanks. You two can fight it out – if you ask me, it's a bit like the pot calling the kettle black. Hmmm, didn't mean that in a, ah, you know, politically incorrect way, ah, in fact, just shut up Nathanael. Speaking of kettles and such, I'm going right over to that coffee machine to make some coffees. Want one?"

They both nodded to him in unison then went back to hostilely ignoring each other.

Nathanael tried not to notice that Natasha had somehow wormed her way around the kitchen counter while he had been talking. Michelle was typing furiously now, the light from the computer screen shining on her face but Natasha wormed her way alongside her and cornered Michelle, "Don't you understand it's risky? For God's sake, haven't you seen what happens to hackers? Aaron went to jail, did you know? And Oxymoron died! Others have died."

Michelle said, "You were the one at risk last time and I saved you. And Nathanael I seem to remember."

Nathanael nodded as he whisked the milk in the cappuccino machine. "She's got a point," he mumbled but

Natasha snapped her head around and snarled, "I thought you were keeping out out of this, mate!" She pronounced the word in her best imitation of Australian, which was woeful, actually, Nathanael thought.

Nathanael continued whisking the milk, trying not to let his eyebrows respond and wondering how on earth he had ended up with such a bad tempered shrew as a girlfriend. Natasha must have seen the eyebrow twitch, for she said, "You…!" but thankfully she turned the spotlight of her anger away from him and back onto Michelle. "I can't believe you've fallen down the same rabbit hole as I did, Michelle. What happened to you? What made you start hacking? Don't you realise it's like a drug, it's a trap, what happened? Tell me! Please!"

Michelle smiled wryly, "Don't you realise, I always basked in your sunshine? You were my idol. Didn't you notice me looking over your shoulder, back when you were a teenager? I was always watching what you did, learning from you, you were the best possible tutor in hacking. And didn't you ever notice, after that, how I always had new clothes, a slick handbag, a new pair of shoes?"

Natasha's face contorted into guilt. "No. Really?" Her face froze in an expression of horror.

Michelle winced. "I was committing wire fraud, alright, nothing that bad. I gave my friends free phone calls in return for cash or goods." She glanced down with shame for a moment. "I think some of them used to shoplift to pay me. But I didn't do any of the big stuff back then. Unlike you, I didn't try to hack the CIA or anything, or government sites, or do stuff on the Darknet, no way, not back then, not until…"

Natasha frowned. "Until?"

Michelle's face crumpled in anguish, "Not until that night I got abducted and kidnapped by those Adamant guys."

Natasha looked shocked.

Her whole manner changed in a moment from abrupt and pushy to humble and remorseful.

A tear formed in the corner of one eye and Michelle reached forward and clasped her and they embraced. Natasha said, "I'm sorry, sis."

Michelle blinked out a teardrop of her own. "Being kidnapped made me aware of how vulnerable I was. I… suspect I went into hardcore hacking to get back some sense of control, Natasha." She suddenly started sobbing.

Natasha awkwardly embraced her as Michelle tried to control herself.

Michelle gave a final sob, then continued. "I know I put a good face on it. But it wasn't true. I crumpled inside, you never actually saw that. You weren't there for me. You couldn't help it."

She laughed. "Haha, it's actually funny; when I was kidnapped I had a sense that... God was with me, He was looking after me. But it wasn't till afterward that I realised how close I had come to dying. I have never felt safe since, not anywhere, not even in a public place in broad daylight."

A tear ran down Natasha's face. "Why didn't you tell me?"

Michelle said, "You had your own problems. That whole Leo Bos affair, the i-ogle hack. I can't believe how you and Nathanael keep getting yourselves mixed up in these things."

Natasha looked askance at Nathanael. "Me either."

Nathanael shrugged. "Hey, don't look at me. It's not my fault. It just seems to happen that whenever something weird is going on, we get mixed up in it. It seems to be our destiny to fight those who rule this world from the shadows."

Natasha nodded and rolled her eyes at the same time. "That's a strange way of putting it, Nathanael. But that is what it's like. We don't choose for these things to happen, Michelle..."

Michelle said, "But you understand that only made it worse for me? Feeling unsafe physically and knowing that there might still be people out there who wanted to hurt you – or me too. And the Adamants didn't distinguish, did they? – they just hurt anyone who came across their path. So I buried myself in my new identity as a hacker. I learned everything I could about computer security, I reached a new level, Natasha, I went hardcore, I started exploring the Darknet and the hidden, obscure corners of the internet. It became an obsession, a deep, dark obsession. Establishing a new identity there, I forsook sunlight and daytime and buried myself alive in the online world and began to create an… I suppose you could call it, a network, a web of other hackers, doing favours for one another, looking out for one another."

Nathanael said, "Forsook? Is that a word?"

Michelle said emphatically, "Yes. Forsook. Past participle of forsake. But I'm not alone now, Natasha, not online, not anymore. I have a network of friends. Friends who watch out for each other. I have power now. And I have access. Complete access. I can pwn just about anyone online. Even the NSA, the CIA. ASIO," she added, with a nod at Nathanael.

Natasha frowned and spoke in soft, conspiratorial tones. "This network – who are they? Do you even know who you're dealing with? Those people on the Darknet, they could be drug dealers, child pornographers, assassins for hire, pimps. Michelle, are you sure these are the sorts of people you want to hang out with online?"

Michelle shook her head. "You're wrong. Not all of them are like that. Many are just hackers like you and me – computer programmers who feel that the world is out of control

– who feel that surveillance and corporate power has gone too far – ordinary people who want to get control of their lives. This is what Trippy Girl is all about." She gave a twisted smile. "Sometimes I take on the bad clients too. To punish them."

Natasha said, "Yeah, right. How would you even know they're bad? You don't even know who you're cooperating with."

Michelle's face took on a slightly arrogant expression. She sneered at Natasha. "You're asking me that? Don't you understand? I'm way past you, Natasha, in the online world. I vet them all, every single one of my companions on the bulletin board, every person I deal with, everyone I know. I uncover their secrets and then use that to decide what to do. If they are worthy they are allowed to join my circle. If they are unworthy, I may take on their jobs but I deal with them afterward."

Natasha said, "You're not even close to reassuring me, Michelle. You sound like some sort of online midnight Kingpin, a Godmother of the Darknet." She reached out and gently clasped Michelle's shoulder. "Could that be my innocent little sister, who a mere year ago only cared about which skirt she put on or shoes she wore?"

Nathanael brought the coffees over.

Michelle took her coffee, smiled at Nathanael wanly, then gazed at Natasha and sipped. Natasha took her own coffee and sipped it too, with hunched shoulders, in a strangely submissive mood.

Michelle said in sombre tones, "That's exactly what I am. The Godmother of the Dark Net. Just yesterday someone called me the Queen-bee of the Dark Hive. I know what's going on out there, Natasha. This is the realm in which I am in control. I have my own source of income now and I have a network that's more far-reaching than you can ever imagine."

Nathanael rolled his eyes and quipped, "You sound like some sort of super-villain." He laughed, he had meant it as a joke but it fell very flat, because Natasha did not laugh; instead she said solemnly, "What are you working on now?"

Nathanael swore silently to himself.

Natasha was taking Michelle's boasting seriously, which worried him because Natasha was the one who knew what Michelle was talking about.

Michelle waved a hand casually. "Oh, something that was happening in Russia. To be perfectly frank, you are probably right, it could be dangerous. But I cover my tracks, Natasha. Unlike you, I'm a professional."

"What is it? Michelle, tell me. Why is it dangerous?"

"I don't want to say. You'll just worry."

"Tell me." Natasha's voice sounded dangerous now, and

she was her older sister. Despite herself Michelle started spilling the beans, "I think I'm on the trail of a murderer, Natasha – a very sneaky fellow – a sort of con artist – perhaps an assassin – he's making his way through Europe and seems to have his targets set on a man in England who used to be the butler of a fellow called Sol the Magnificent. Sol, as in the Russian word for Sun. This guy was murdered in Moscow. It's all rather convoluted, actually, and I'm still sifting through the details…"

Natasha changed the subject. She said accusingly, "Have you been to church lately?"

"No," admitted Michelle. "Not lately, just… haven't felt like it." She looked ashamed.

"Well, you're coming tomorrow with me and Nathanael. José and Marybelle's daughter Lily's being baptised."

"Really? Oh, is that tomorrow?" Michelle winced. "Alright. I guess I can come. For Lily's baptism, if for no other reason." She paused. "Just as long as I don't end up on any YouTube videos."

Natasha was about to say something but she hesitated.

"What?" said Michelle.

Natasha said, "What, what?"

Michelle snapped, "If you stand around with your mouth open like that you'll catch a fly."

Natasha quietly answered, "Why don't you want to be videoed?"

Michelle shook her head. "They're onto me. I just don't want them putting two and two together. If I'm videoed and seen with you…"

Natasha insisted, "Who's onto you? What do you mean? Someone's watching you? Who?"

Michelle looked at Natasha with a frown, shook her head and said, "I don't know. The people who are hiring Sol's murderer, to do something bad. They're even shadier than Adamant. I think they were the ones behind Adamant."

Michelle paused and swallowed. Then she said, "The Cabal, Natasha. The conspiracy behind everything that happens."

~~~

That night Kael was enjoying dinner at his sister's place, proper Mexican food cooked by José's mother, not the stuff Mexican restaurants serve in Pheonix.

There had been a family lunch at his sister Marybelle's place most of Saturday which she had organised when she had found out he wouldn't be there on Sunday afternoon.

"That's the nice thing about José's family," Marybelle had said. "They don't skimp on family time. Everybody's happy to get together." She sent Kael a significant look, a reproach,
~~~

which he took in good part. It was true, he had been unwilling to drop in on Marybelle.

After all his reluctance it really hadn't been that difficult to get here.

In fact, the whole day had been far more pleasant and relaxing than he had expected and the food had been good and Kael even managed to enjoy the conversation so long as he turned his brain off whenever anyone mentioned church or Jesus or the Bible or politics, in which case he agreed noncommittally with everything that was said.

He had even kept his mouth shut when they were praising Trump. Thankfully they talked about sport or Netflix or their dead-end jobs most of the time, so that was alright.

No one even mentioned climate change.

What was even better was that the church service times on the Sunday morning turned out to be far more conducive to taking the flight to the conference than he had thought. The service would be starting at 9:00 am; his sister told him it would probably be finished by 10:45 at the latest. Out of courtesy to the guests there for the baptism, the sermon would be short; it meant that Kael could spend a few minutes chatting with her before the Uber picked him up. He took Ubers when it was important to be somewhere on time these days; they were generally more reliable.

Yes, things had worked out much better this weekend than he had expected. He took another sip of his beer.

And he was really looking forward to giving the keynote announcement at the conference tomorrow night. If he was honest with himself, he would have to admit he loved being in the spotlight. Even so, having a beer with José wasn't such a bad way to spend an evening, either, when it came down to it.

José was actually a pretty good guy and Kael could see a little of what his sister saw in him now.

Everything was fine and everything was going to be fine.

Thank Gaia for that, he said to himself, chuckling at his little private joke, the kind of quip he could share with Devraj. No, that's precisely the sort of comment he would keep to himself, just for this weekend. No need to stir his sister's feelings up with talk of the Earth Goddess, or the Sun-God, for that matter. He was going to have a trouble-free weekend.

CHAPTER 5 – Resurrection Correction.

EXETER, UNITED KINGDOM. SUNDAY MORNING.

Sasha woke up on his hundredth day in England with the morning sun streaming through the window but there was little warmth in the light. How like Mother Russia England is! Another frozen land.

Not quite as cold as Mother Russia.

He wondered for a moment if he shouldn't have gone to Thailand or Singapore or some other, warmer, place, where the sun actually warmed things up.

But he had to admit he liked the cold.

And it's pleasant enough if one begins each day with a brisk attitude and a shot glass of vodka. He carried his warmth with him, anyhow, didn't he? – as his mother used to say – "Malchishka warms up the coldest day with his smile, when he rises in the morning. Malchishka is warmer than the Moscow sun. Such a sunny disposition! When Malchishka walks into the room it's like the sun has risen." Malchishka was her favourite term of endearment. Ha! What would she say if she knew? If she only knew where her little man was now – that he had fled to England – and after all that.

He looked at his mobile phone.

It was Sunday today – in Russian the day of the resurrection, a vestige of a former superstition but in English,

Sunday, the day of the mighty Sun, the real ruler of the heavens!

He frowned and smiled at the same time and laughed softly into his vodka.

It was Sol's day, here in England. How very ironic!

And though the authorities thought Sol the Magnificent was dead forever, he knew better.

There was no question of returning to his former profession; any link he had to Sol's butler had to be erased, eradicated, forever. Could he escape?

Sol the Magician was on his tail, like a shadow, like a bad ghost. Or like the sun itself, shaking the shadows out of the earth at dawn. Yes, ironically, he himself was a shadow now, a dark absence of light, a man living in the shadows, living in the shadow of great secrets.

That accursed man had to go and get killed, and ruin his life.

He turned his mind back to his own present predicament. It was Sunday. What should Sasha be doing today?

Something different, perhaps. Up to now he had spent months languishing in his dark room, doing nothing, watching television, surfing the internet, playing online games, gazing idly at porn, porn that was getting more and more extreme; not even opening the curtains to let the afternoon light shine in.

He needed to get out. Start making contacts. Getting a career in motion, some sort of job or profession. His extensive savings would not justify his existence here forever, he needed to appear to be doing something. His idleness would eventually catch the attention of the authorities far more than someone simply doing some sort of job.

Of course he couldn't possibly endure a job packing shelves in a supermarket or serving coffee to ungrateful wretches. Something more significant – a philanthropist? No, he really didn't like the thought of giving money away. The manager of an art exhibition? A real estate agent? A loan shark? Perhaps, that was getting closer.

A drug dealer? Even more promising.

Yes, he needed to forget his past, his given name, his former profession, his former life. He needed to be the man he was on his new passport now, the passport he had bought on the Darknet and picked up in a seedy district in Moscow; he had to be Sasha Yuri Yevgenev now.

He had to start calling himself Sasha Yuri Yevgenev, get used to his new name.

Well, here Sasha Yuri Yevgenev was, in Exeter. And he had to find a new profession. What could Sasha Yuri Yevgenev possibly do?

How stupid Sasha was; it was Sunday, all the businesses would be closed today.

Of course the churches would be open. What more ironic place for a man of shadows to start networking, than in the house of God, on the day of the Sun, the day of resurrection?

A shade, stepping into the light.

Yes, he had been living the high life in England now for six months, surreptitiously spending Sol's fortune. Now Sasha would justify his existence here.

Sasha smiled slightly to himself, opened up his laptop and looked up the local church websites.

He liked this one.

Whatever race, colour, gender, sexual orientation, wherever you are in your spiritual walk, you are welcome to worship with us.

Open-minded Christians.

Could there really be such a thing? Yes, in the corrupt West, he supposed there could be. Haha! He knew, ultimately, in precisely what sulphurous fire-pit he would find his welcome on the other side but he could make things as comfortable as possible in the meantime, couldn't he? And where better than here, at a place where they welcome sinners?

And this church was called Hayfield Church. Make hay while the sun shines, isn't that the expression in English?

So this really would be Voskresén'ye, resurrection day, for him. How ironic. For Sasha Yuri Yevgenev would be resurrected like the mythical phoenix today, from the ashes of Sasha Mikhael Solovyev, the butler of Sol the Magician, the deceased.

~~~~

Sasha walked into the church. It was surprisingly ceremonial and liturgical, for a place with such a contemporary ideology. The priest wore gowns with gold filagree woven into the design of a cross decorated with ornamental patterns and there was a large altar strongly reminiscent of an Orthodox altar, covered with a cloth just as ornately decorated. There were even a few imitation Orthodox icons scattered around here and there on the walls, unfortunately lacking the gold leaf of the real thing. Imitation gold has no shine.

It all reminded Sasha of the most lavish excesses of the Orthodox clergy in Russia. However when the priest began the sermon it was very different from what he would expect to hear in Mother Russia.

The sermon began with a story from the gospel of John, the woman at the well; Sasha knew it from his childhood. A woman was at the well when Jesus wanted a drink. Jesus asked her for water. Then they talked; somehow Jesus knew that she had had five husbands and the man she was living with now was
~~~~

not her husband. She went back to town and told everyone Jesus was the Messiah.

A strange incident. Sasha admitted he had never fully understood it. Why were the people at the town so willing to listen to her, if she had had five husbands? Where was their supposed morality?

But then the priest had gone on quite differently from how Sasha had expected.

"The woman at the well was not a respectable person. People would have judged her for her lifestyle, just as some people might judge those who attend this church for their lifestyles. Some who might not have conventional partnerships – some here who treat sex casually, as an enjoyable activity to share – some men who are attracted to men – some women who are attracted to women. Yes, Jesus, who chose the woman at the well as his emissary! Might Jesus not also choose some here in this congregation, some who use Tinder to find their next casual fling, some who attend meeting places that might be seen by the righteous as places of sin and immorality? Yes, Jesus chooses not the polite, middle-class people but the poor and outcast ones, the bad, the disreputable. For just as Jesus chose the Samaritan woman and the apostles, one of whom was a Zealot – a terrorist essentially, another a prostitute, another a despised tax collector – his emissary today might be a gay man or a lesbian woman, a transgender person, someone neither cis nor straight, or someone with a drug issue or an alcoholic or a prostitute. And those who are so certain they are in the right for they are of the right, the Pharisees, deplorables and cowboys and white trash and hypocrites in their prejudice will refuse to listen. Indeed, the righteous Christians must learn something from the LGBTI people of today. We listen to each other. We don't cast somebody out because they're weird or unusual or don't fit our mold. We show the best example of Jesus' love available to this modern world. In a very real sense, we are the archetypal Christ-hero on a journey, for many of us have been through a conversion no less wonderful than becoming a Christian in the time of the Apostles – after the trauma of being secretly gay, the freedom of coming out – and this is why those like us may well be chosen to show people what God's love is really like."

Sasha was completely amazed. In all his years attending the Orthodox church, he had never heard a message like this one. Why, they were turning the Bible on its head. Indeed, the Orthodox priests' attitude to homosexuality was quite the opposite – in his youth he had heard them call gay men dogs and Sodomites and sinners who would inherit only the lake of fire from God. Yes, remember what they had done to that poor old composer Tchaikovsky!

Personally, Sasha couldn't care less. I mean, he himself

had tried various positions and partners in his youth, with both men and women but he knew for him male sex was just a passing fancy; he generally stuck to female prostitutes if he felt the urge.

Anyhow, Sasha smirked to himself, he was a good person, much better than most Christians, for he was not a hypocrite like them. He was who he was, there was no false front, no pretending, no hypocrisy.

Haha. Except for his identity. A minor matter.

He sat in the pew as the people were going to receive the Holy Eucharist, and googled the Bible verses about homosexuality on his phone. Surely this is against the Bible and the Church Fathers. He wanted to ask one of these people what they thought of that here.

After the service, Sasha followed the crowd into the church hall for morning tea.

A young man, obviously gay, wearing a foppish suit and sipping his cup of tea in an effeminate fashion was the first to greet Sasha.

"You look new," the gay man said to Sasha. "Come on, coffee or a tea?"

"Oh, a coffee, certainly."

The young man touched his arm in a rather intimate way. "How do you like it?"

"White with plenty of sugar, thanks."

"Not sweet enough, ey?" He had a bit of a twinkle in his eye and Sasha wondered if the boy liked him, in 'that' way.

Sasha wasn't interested so he agreed, "No, you're right, not sweet enough. I am Russian. Tell me, all this…" Sasha waved his hand around at the company gathered here, many in goth clothes or stylish suits, men wearing dresses, women wearing the clothes of men.

Sasha fixed the young man with his gaze and continued, "All this is new to me. Christian gay people. How do you as someone who believes the scriptures are infallible, justify homosexual behaviour, considering the fact that the scriptures say that people who do these things will not inherit the kingdom of God?"

The gay man gulped. "What do you mean? It doesn't really say that, does it? Not in the New Testament?"

"Well, yes." Sasha took out his mobile phone and opened up the Bible app. "Look at this. 1 Corinthians 6:9, the unrighteous will not inherit the kingdom of God – the list of unrighteous people includes homosexuals. Romans 1:27 calls homosexual behaviour shameless. 1 Timothy 1:10 includes homosexuals with slave traders as those who will not inherit the kingdom of God. Did you not know this?"

The young man looked aghast and said in a rather

distressed tone of voice, "Oh, I had no idea it said that in the New Testament. I need some fresh air." He pushed Sasha out of the way and rushed out through the kitchen entrance at the rear of the church.

Another fellow, a giant wearing a suit, was standing near Sasha and pointed to the rear entrance. "What happened to Frankie? Is he alright? Should I follow him do you think to see if he's okay?"

Sasha didn't really want to admit that he had freaked Frankie out with his Bible app; instead, he said, "He's fine. I think he just went outside for some fresh air and sunshine. Must be something he... took in..."

"Something he ate?"

Sasha grunted noncommittally. If they knew he had Bible-bashed the poor boy it might affect his ability to make useful contacts. God forbid, he might get labelled as a Christian. Clearly, that might not be good for business, not in a church like this one.

The man raised his eyebrows. "Poor Frankie. Well, some people do have problems with their digestion, don't they? Anyhow, my name is Gregory, Gregory Islingsforth." They shook hands. "I'm a lawyer, actually, specialising in gay rights, issues of discrimination, social justice, the environment, that sort of thing. And you are?"

He replied, "I'm Sasha Yevgenev. I'm… a businessman from Russia. I came here to make new connections, Gregory, as I am looking to expand my business into the sunshine here in England."

"Why on earth did you come to church for that, then? Why not the local Rotary club or something?"

"What? Rotary what?"

"Why the Anglican church? Why not the local mega-church, or some sort of businessman's club?"

Sasha decided not to talk about God with Gregory. Yes, he saw it now, obviously one does not talk about God or the Bible at a church like this.

Sasha could well see how one could get by quite happily worshipping the Almighty without worrying about what He said in His book.

Gregory repeated, "Why not the Rotary?"

Sasha answered, "I see. Well, I chose the church because just like in pre-Revolutionary Russia, Gregory, the local church is today a place where one may become acquainted with the people in a particular village, the important people, you know, the town mayor, the policeman, the local grandmothers, and so forth. And I assumed England would be like that, considering that there has been no communist revolution here and the monarchy is still in charge."

Gregory replied, "I see. The local village grandmothers. Is Russia really that quaint?" He appeared to come to a conclusion. Laying a limp hand on Sasha's forearm, massaging it slightly with his thumb, Gregory said, "You're an interesting fellow, Sasha. Come to lunch today, Sasha – my treat – we'll talk. You have means, I presume?"

"What?" Sasha didn't understand the word 'means' in this context.

Not the plural of 'meaning', and not 'mean', that is, nasty, horrible, wilfully unkind. Sasha stayed silent, not sure what to say. Gregory clarified, "Independent means. Money. Do you have your own finances?"

"Oh yes, yes, of course. I'm sure I can afford lunch." He had access not only to the embezzled funds but everything that hadn't been embezzled in Sol's accounts as well.

In fact, he hadn't left a single kopek behind in Russia, which of course was why he was worried about being pursued. If Sol, the man himself, didn't seem to want the money back any more, then his ex-wife certainly did. And his debtors, his heirs, or his children, or who else, who knew?

Gregory said, "We can talk. You're an approachable fellow. Finish your coffee. Then why don't we wander on down to a pleasant little restaurant-tavern I know and converse politely over a pint about how you might further your interests here in Exeter and the United Kingdom, Sasha, my dear Tovarischka?"

* * *

So, to the restaurant they went, a short walk, arm in arm. It was a pleasant and refined tavern not far from the church. The lunch was more expensive than Sasha would have been prepared to pay for under normal circumstances, so he was glad Gregory was coughing up.

After the small talk, Gregory finally said, "If you make a donation to a particular foundation, I can help you. A climate change foundation."

Sasha shook his head in sudden shock. What was this? He was really in no mood for games. An investment, to make money, that he didn't mind. But some sort of quid pro quo?

Sasha said firmly, "I am here to make money, not to give it away." No point walking about the bush, as the English say.

Gregory said, "Well, it's not quite like that, Sasha. I'm getting you an entrée into a particular social circle. A coterie of like-minded people. Oh, sure, you could make a donation to our parish council, or socialise with the warden and the councillors at church but only a few of them are in the crowd I am talking about – my crowd is the elite of the elite. And the best way into that little circle is to make a donation to a particular foundation. It gives you an 'in', Sasha, the kind of 'in' many people would give their right arm to possess."

Sasha must have looked doubtful still so Gregory said, "You don't understand – I don't want to put this too explicitly – but the pool of climate funds is virtually inexhaustible."

"Climate funds?"

"Yes. Even if the United States decided to stop all their contributions to the UNPCC. No matter the political situation in Britain or overseas, there will always be a large pool of international money available for someone with an entrepreneurial spirit such as yours: climate foundations, United Nations, UNPCC, Greenpeace, government money, town council money, public donations, wildlife funds, scientific research groups, university departments and even much more. Indeed, recent events have only meant they want *more* people with agency in Britain. I'm assuming you want to do some good, Sasha, with your wealth? To achieve something?"

Sasha said, "Yes. Yes, of course." What other answer could he give? Gregory's eyes were shining and Sasha wasn't sure if it was idealism or greed. Running with idealism, he said, "I am very much the philanthropist. Ahem, so long as I am getting something more in return than I gave in the first place. Oops." The truth had slipped out. A deep, rumbling laugh, proceeded forth from below the chest in the correct Russian way.

"Yes," said Gregory, showing no amusement but apparently taking Sasha's comment seriously, "That is also the way I see it. A much more lucrative way, in the end, I believe. You only live once, after all."

So it was greed lighting Gregory's eyes.

A kindred spirit!

Sasha smiled. "Do you know, suddenly I see what a dead end I was in! I have never considered giving my life to a cause – the environment! I see it now! How necessary it is that we save the planet we live on."

Gregory laughed softly. "Don't overdo it, Sasha. Sincerity is better demonstrated in a different way. Look, an initial donation of say – ten thousand greenbacks? – should do it, to demonstrate your goodwill. Then we can get the cash flowing the other way. Give me your email and I'll send you the bank details."

They exchanged email addresses.

After this, Gregory laid his hand on Sasha's shoulder in a rather light, weightless way once more and said, "Well, now that we've got that out of the way, would you come back to my place for a coffee?"

Sasha swallowed and looked up at Gregory. This was a friendship that could be helpful, and of course, while the ghost of Sol the Magnificent was still pursuing him Sasha needed all the help he could get to get away from the curse of his past.

Of course, Gregory could just be pulling the wool over his eyes. He needed something first.

Sasha took out his phone and said, "First, a photograph. As a memento." Alright, Sasha hadn't donated the money yet. He needed to know more about whether Gregory's little circle really would be helpful to him. And if Sasha did donate money and then nothing came of this 'donation', he wanted to be able to track this fellow down and kill him and chop up his body into little pieces. Hmm. Maybe chop his limbs and appendages up first and then kill him afterwards.

He chuckled. He had to stop thinking such Russian thoughts. Revenge only tended to deepen one's predicament, as he had learned.

Sasha flagged a waiter, who came and took the photograph of both of them with Sasha's phone. It was probably a needless precaution; surely this was a friendship worth cultivating?

"Gregory, I would like to come back to your place for a coffee," said Sasha. "I would indeed. Now please show me exactly which way you want me to go."

Gregory swallowed. "I will, I will…"

* * *

WILKINS & CO SECURITY, NEW YORK OFFICE.

Bob Wilkins, former head of Adamant's security, answered the phone. "Hi?"

The man in the black suit said in clipped German tones, "Hello, Bob. How is it going, Bob?"

Bob swallowed nervously and stammered his words out, "A-A-All I know is, sir, someone on a bulletin board on the DarkNet helped them to get away. I don't know who it was."

The man in the black suit said in quiet, menacing tones, "Well, Bob, look at their known associates. Start there. Once you have that, expand your search to include other family members, friends…"

Somehow the extreme steadiness in the German's voice was more far more chilling than shouting or threatening words.

Bob swallowed again and said, "Thank you, sir. Excellent advice. Will do."

The German said, "Oh, and I want you to contact our team in Italy. We've had some online enquiries about the Pizarro documents. Father Rudolpho, as usual, is rather too open about the contents of the archive."

Bob said, "Do you want us to do a health adjustment on Father Rudolpho?"

"No. Just tell your team to keep an eye on him. We still don't know where the enquiries came from. It was a nondescript email address sent from a proxy server. We are trying to keep the new genetic project completely secret, to prevent what happened with Methuselah. So get onto it!"

Bob said, "Yes, sir. Alright sir. I'll get onto it right away."

* * *

CHAPTER 6 – Prize Fight, Proviso Flight.

PHOENIX ARIZONA.

That morning, at the church in Phoenix, Kael found the baptism sermon to be surprisingly short; just some talk about how baptism was an "outward and visible sign of an inward and spiritual grace," and that what was important in the long run was that when Lily grew up she turned from her sins one day and followed Christ. In the meantime her family must raise her as a Christian. The end of the talk was slightly confronting, though, because the preacher looked directly at him – was Kael imagining it? – as though he was addressing him personally. Was it possible that Marybelle had told him about her irreligious brother? He said, "The question is not about Lily but about you, brother. Christ died for you because He loves you. Have you turned to the Redeemer of the World, the only one who can save us from our sins?"

It truly outraged him, this blanket assumption that everyone was a sinner. Kael wasn't a sinner.

He looked around. There was a girl nearby who was weeping. Sobbing abjectly. How extreme was this church? It was verging on a sect. At first Kael thought the girl crying was a Latino like so many people at the church but then he realised she was actually Indian from India or Sri-Lankan. She was young, maybe eighteen or nineteen, sitting next to another girl from continental India – her sister? – an attractive young woman in her twenties with tattoos on her arms.

Kael scoffed to himself. Convincing people they're sinners was a good way to squeeze money out of them.

Kael wasn't a sinner, he was a good person – look at all the good he did – by God, he did a lot more good than most people did in their sad, sorry, pointless lifespans wandering over this doomed globe producing carbon. Kael's life was dedicated to doing good. Every moment of his waking existence was spent in the struggle to save the world from climate change – what did other people do? Why, they just wasted space, wasted carbon credits, wasted breath. What did Kael need a Saviour for? Kael *was* a saviour, saving the world from global warming, any true green activist could tell you that.

After the service, he had time for a quick cup of coffee. He went through the arrangements again. The Uber was coming at eleven, the trip would take less than half an hour, and he had already established that they would accept him checking in fifteen minutes before the flight left instead of the usual two hours, a privilege that membership of the Frequent First Class Flyers' Club had bestowed upon him.

The service finished early and he found himself standing

next to his sister, who was holding Lily up, with her husband José and the rest of José's enormous family around them in a large circle, chatting and sipping instant coffee.

In the hustle and bustle of the morning tea, a couple came up and congratulated Marybelle. The man was tall and slightly disheveled and awkward and spoke with an Australian accent, and the woman was the one who had been sitting next to the girl who had been sobbing. She was even more graceful and attractive up close. She was exactly the kind of woman Devraj would try to get into bed.

Her grieving sister was nowhere to be seen.

Marybelle said, "Kael, you might have something in common with these two."

José added, "Yeah, they're smart. Just like you."

Kael suppressed the sneer that started forming on his lips. Smart? And Christian? Surely an oxymoron.

The woman rolled her eyes but the man reached forward to shake Kael's hand. "I'm Nathanael. This is my girlfriend Natasha." He had a firm, friendly shake but his gaze was a little weird. Kael wondered if he was autistic or something.

"Kael Addison."

"Really?" said Nathanael, who didn't seem terribly impressed. Not impressed enough, actually. It was a bit off-putting, as though Nathanael already knew who he was but didn't care. Nathanael repeated, "Professor Kael Addison."

"Yes," said Kael. "Professor of Climate Science at – "

José said, "Nathanael's just about a Professor too. Or he could be. He's a really smart guy, bro."

"I'm no Professor," interrupted Nathanael. "Just a 'Jack of All Trades', really."

José winked at him, "But he's master of them all."

Marybelle commented, "Nathanael is smart. Let's hope it doesn't go to his head, hey, Natasha?"

Kael was surprised at how readily Marybelle could fit in with this group – she had never lacked sophistication growing up but now she had become so… ordinary! It was disappointing.

Natasha said, "Nathanael is pretty much the smartest guy I've ever met, Kael."

Nathanael said admiringly, "She's pretty smart too. Pretty and smart, actually. She's a computer hack-"

Natasha interrupted him, "Programmer. I manage a medical database, most of the time. Occasionally other things. Dumb, too sometimes." She glared at Nathanael.

Kael tried to encourage the conversation in the direction of computers; he wanted them to know that he was a famous climate scientist in charge of two whole rooms full of programmers and computers, in two different continents. He wanted their admiration, their envy. "Oh, we use a lot of computer programmers at NASA and at the –"

"The Yardley Climate Centre, in Exeter, yeah? I know," said Nathanael butting in again. "Nice weather lately, hasn't it been? Real sunny."

Natasha frowned and nudged Nathanael in a way Kael found annoying, as though they were sharing some sort of secret.

"It's alright, Natasha," said Nathanael. "I do have a modicum of self-control."

"Well, you'd better have," said Natasha. "We are not going to get into a discussion of you-know-what." It irritated Kael and made him want to know what they were trying to hide from him.

Nathanael frowned, then squeezed her hand. "Natasha, I'm trying really hard not to. Let's talk about... Something else! Sports?"

Kael was getting progressively more and more annoyed with them. To him both were dancing around some huge thing that he couldn't see. What was the invisible elephant in the room? He felt compelled to have a prod at it, like something hidden in his bedsheets that might be a snake or could just be the cat or a pillow but he simply had to know.

He had to prod it.

"Look," said Kael, "You may as well just say what's on your mind. I mean, this is ridiculous, we've only just met at my niece's baptism and both of you are dancing around something like people walking on hot coals. Just come out with it. What's the elephant in the room? What is it that you're not saying? Come on, open the window, let the sunshine in. Let me know."

Nathanael groaned. "Oh, there's so much. So very much that we shouldn't talk about." He laughed nervously. "This is Lily's special day. Let's not ruin it. For the sake of Marybelle, let's just talk about... The sermon? What did you think, Kael? I thought it was a good summary."

Suddenly Kael was a steaming kettle about to boil over. He had never really had time for Christianity because Christians could be so annoying. And here this annoying Australian was, agreeing with the preacher that he, Kael, was a sinner.

Why on earth had Marybelle thought they would have anything in common? He said through gritted teeth, "I don't want to talk about theology, or God, or any of that stuff." Then he breathed almost silently, and his next words came like a hostile snarl, "Why on earth did Marybelle think we would have anything in common?"

Natasha sighed, "Tertiary educated, I guess. Well, you and I but not Nathanael really."

God, these people were insufferable. He hated dancing around avoiding these deplorables' psychological weak spots.

Natasha said, "But he does have an eidetic memory."

Kael welcomed a subject area that obviously wasn't going to lead anywhere awkward, "Really? What's that like?"

Nathanael said, "Annoying. Quotes come to you at times and sometimes you don't realise they're not your thoughts until you're halfway through thinking it."

"I suppose nothing's really original," said Kael, "I mean, in academia people rip each other's ideas off all the time. So long as you rephrase it, and don't take everything from one source. I mean, in my field in climate science…"

"Ha… climate science," said Nathanael. "Exactly." He paused for a long moment, looking slightly like a deer caught in the headlights, and at the very moment when Kael had opened his mouth to speak again Nathanael said softly, as though betraying a confidence, "Let's not get into that."

"Sorry, Mister Addison, Nathanael's trying," said Natasha, and hesitated for a moment.

Kael muttered, "Very trying," and glared at her, trying to make her come clean.

To his surprise, she finally did.

Natasha sighed deeply and admitted, "Nathanael

is trying very hard not to engage but he's quite the climate skeptic. This is perhaps not the best subject to discuss with him, Professor."

Nathanael blurted, "Sports might be better. Wimbledon. It was an unexpected outcome, you know, and most of the bookies had it wrong. I know most of the odds for most of the sports but would never think of betting... I mean, sports is a kind of battle, a match where sometimes the best doesn't win. Surprises happen all the time. Like the climate, I suppose."

Kael jutted his chin out stubbornly like a mule ignoring its owner's wishes. He wasn't going to avoid this confrontation. He hated climate deniers.

In the most reasonable tone of voice he could muster, he said, "Well, speaking of statistics, ninety-seven percent of studies agree that the globe is warming..."

"We don't have to talk about this," Nathanael said, his voice crow-like, weakly pleading in a plaintive caw. He was lying through his back teeth, he really *wanted* to talk about it.

To Kael, Nathanael sounded annoyingly like a larger, stronger boy hinting that a smaller, weaker one ought not to fight him. Nathanael sounded regretful that Kael still wanted to talk about it, and that really got Kael's goat. As though a denier could find anything to say to *him*! Kael fumed, breathing through clenched teeth. For God's sake, Kael Addison was one of the world's top climate scientists. What cheek! How did this uneducated gimp think he could beat him in an argument? Eidetic memory and all, he could not possibly know more about the climate than Kael did! Kael's vision turned red, as though he was an enraged bull.

Then as usual, fearing his own certainty, Kael checked himself. Even a gimp might get a lucky punch in, that was why he had a firm rule never to engage in debate with an educated climate denier. There was nothing to gain from it – as soon as you engage with the deniers in any way, shape or form, you are just lending them credibility.

But this guy – Kael wanted to take him. He could own him, this fool who had no qualifications at all. He could knock him out with one punch.

Kael looked around. Despite the crowd, no cameras, no one had a mobile phone trained on him, no devices, not even a security camera, so if Kael lost the argument it wouldn't get onto the internet. It wasn't like some sort of televised debate at a college campus or something.

This was a private chat.

In fact, none of the other people were even paying them any attention, except for Natasha. The rest were all ooh-ing and ah-ing over the baby or actually were talking about Wimbledon or the US Open or whatever other things ordinary insignificant people talked about.

Well, this was a safe venue. Why not put his hat into the ring? It's not as if it was some public debate with Anthony Watts or something.... He could still withdraw if he wanted to.

Finally throwing in the first punch, Kael said, "Yes but there's a consensus among scientists about global warming..."

Nathanael replied with a fairly solid block. "Consensus. Argument from authority, invalid. In response to a book critical of relativity called '100 authors against Einstein', Einstein said, "Why one hundred authors? If I were wrong, then one would have been enough.' And the Royal Society in the 19th Century would certainly have disagreed with any idea that a consensus means anything. They knew what science was. They practically invented the scientific method."

There was a pause as they sized each other up. Kael pushed out his lower jaw, a bulldog ready for a stouch.

Nathanael broke the silence. "And there isn't a consensus anyway."

Stepping backwards as though he had taken one on the jaw, Kael feigned astonishment, saying, "What?"

Nathanael nodded. "Of the 12,000 abstracts analyzed by John Cook in that study only 64 papers were in category

1, which explicitly endorsed global warming. Only 41 studies, representing only 0.3%, endorsed the quantitative hypothesis as defined by Cook. Not even one of them endorsed catastrophic warming which demands an immediate response."

Kael sneered, "I know what you're quoting. That's Monckton's article. An English crank, pretends to be a lord, has funny googly eyes. He doesn't have any credibility at all – after all, he was Thatcher's science adviser."

Nathanael shook his head. "Argumentum ad hominem. Attacking the person, not the argument. You did it twice, attacked Monckton for being Monckton and Thatcher for being Thatcher. Invalid. And furthermore, Monckton's eyes are due to a congenital thyroid condition for which he is not responsible. In fact it is quite heartless for people to bring that up; if he was gay or black or transgender no one would even mention it. Anyhow, it doesn't matter what Monckton might look like or who he worked for if his argument is sound. And I've read that study; it's completely sound, very well-argued. The data is very clear. I checked it for myself."

Kael countered, "But you're not an expert."

Nathanael shook his head again. "Argument from authority. Another red herring. Einstein was no expert, when he published the theory of relativity. He was an unknown clerk in the Swiss patent office in Bern who had managed to bring together the greatest enigmas of physics into one single theory. Willie Soon, one of the authors apart from Monckton, is an expert in solar radiation forcings of the climate, and his own papers were mischaracterised as supporting global warming in the original study. Anyway, who cares! The authority issue is a non-sequitur. Convince me."

Kael stepped back, reeling as though from another blow to the head. Confused and upset, he snapped, "What did you say?"

Nathanael's tone was steady and rational, as though he was an expert casting light on a subject. "I said, convince me. Convince me global warming is happening. I don't care how many scientists agree with it. As Richard Feynman once said, 'It doesn't matter how beautiful your guess is or how smart you are or what your name is, if it disagrees with experience, it's wrong.' That's all there is to it. Convince me it's really happening. What is the evidence? The data, give me the data."

Kael rolled his eyes. Bringing Feynman into it was almost as bad as bringing up Hitler. He tried a different tack. "Well, the computer models indicate..."

Natasha rolled *her* eyes.

His voice taking on a nasty tone, Kael remonstrated at Natasha, "What? What's wrong with that? What's wrong with computer models?"

She answered coldly, "What do you mean, what's wrong with computer models?"

He said, "Well, there you are rolling your eyes. It's very rude."

He had kind of hoped to impress her, she was a good looking girl but now she was taking sides with Nathanael. He had honestly hoped she might take a more neutral position.

But Natasha said, "Well, I'm a computer programmer, Kael. A computer model is only as good as its predictive ability. I could make a computer model of anything, really; the stock market, the winning horses, a blackjack game, a DNA analysis of which genes will end you up in jail. But if your computer model doesn't predict the future accurately it has no more value… than a faulty theory. And let me add the term denier is a low punch, an inappropriate slur, trying to link climate skepticism to Holocaust deniers."

Kael's phone dinged. He reached into his pocket and turned the sound off.

"Shouldn't you get that call?" asked Nathanael rudely. "It might be important."

Kael ignored Nathanael. Stupid climate denier. He wasn't going to engage with an idiot. He addressed Natasha – if he could get her on his side at least he'd have a chance to win the argument. "Our computer models are fine. We have one of the world's fastest supercomputers running them. No one could do better. They predict the past temperatures perfectly."

Kael's phone buzzed again. Nathanael pointed out, "Your phone is buzzing."

Kael rounded on him, snarling, "You don't know what you're talking about. Climate denier. Shut up. You want to destroy the future of our children?"

Nathanael shook his head in amazement and muttered, "His infernal phone is buzzing, and he's not paying any attention to it. What's that got to do with the future of our children?"

Kael ignored him and continued the argument, "Anyway, it's better to do something than do nothing. The precautionary principle— "

Nathanael interrupted, "—would say you should look at your phone. Someone's trying really, really hard to get in touch with you. The precautionary principle would say you should answer it, Kael, and just let go of this climate obsession for a moment. You're getting too emotional."

Kael spat, "Precautionary principle –" His phone buzzed again and he ignored it again, shouting, "I'm not obsessed! I'm not at all emotional! The precautionary principle –"

Natasha leaped in. "– is something that actually originated in medicine, the main point of which is that it is often better to do nothing than do something. The precautionary principle is the Hippocratic oath, really. 'First, do no harm.' I think it's pretty clear that action on climate change has the potential to hurt the economy, affects the poor disproportionately by raising power prices and stops economically disadvantaged people from being able to heat their homes in winter. Winters which, I might add, have been significantly colder in recent years."

Finally, Kael's phone stopped making the annoying buzzing sound, so he launched back into the fray with fresh concentration and delivered what he hoped was the knockout blow. "Even if we're not certain that climate change is happening, it is beholden on us to do something about it. But, you know, I am certain. I know that it is happening. I know in here. In my heart. It has to be." He slapped his fist on his chest. "Gaia would have it so. Man cannot abuse the earth forever without the earth taking her vengeance."

Nathanael was trying to hold it in but he couldn't. It popped out in a whisper, "Despite the pause."

Kael rolled his eyes. "Yes, but last year was the hottest year ever."

It was Nathanael's turn to roll his eyes now. He said, "Firstly, it was hotter in the Medieval Warm Period." Kael was scrunching his face up in pain. The damned Medieval Warm Period – they had done their best to eradicate it from the graphs but it just kept rearing its ugly head. Nathanael said, "Come on, there's a good scientific consensus that it really was. Makes sense; in the Medieval Warm Period they were growing grape vines in Northern England, for God's sake, and farming maize and sheep and pigs in Greenland, which is now a freaking chunk of ice. Anyway, I would bet that it's not even half a degree hotter last year than 1998, probably not even in the 0.05 range, statistically speaking. Is it?"

Kael had no answer because he knew very well that it wasn't; even the UNPCC report had said as much.

Nathanael continued punching above his weight, "And why didn't any of your smart climate models predict the pause between 1998 and 2014? And where's the missing heat?"

It was Kael's turn to roll his eyes now. Nathanael was clearly regurgitating stuff from one of the skeptical blogs, wattsupwiththat.com or joannenova.com.au, those irritating ignoramuses. Yes, it was inconvenient that these deniers knew about the missing heat – it was something the climate scientists themselves disagreed about but you know, this was just the typical cherry-picked rubbish they trotted out every time.

Kael gave the standard response, "The missing heat is in the deep ocean. Most likely explanation."

Nathanael and Natasha looked at each other.

Kael could see they were not even fazed.

"What?" he said, surprisingly defensive even to his own ears.

Nathanael said, "Heat in the ocean rises, because it tends to where the pressure is lower. How did it get down there into the deep ocean in the first place? Why doesn't it rise to the top? Doesn't heat follow the laws of thermodynamics?"

Kael had no answer to that, and he could hear his own teeth grinding. He wanted to hit one of them now; what was even more disturbing was that he felt a desire to smash Natasha.

Nathanael and Natasha looked at each other.

Nathanael said, "Look, I'm sorry, I'm really sorry, I didn't even want to… I didn't want to talk about this. You forced me into it. I know, this is your whole life's work we're talking about, and I've put you down, I've humiliated you but please, I really, really didn't want to discuss it, I didn't want to but you just wouldn't let it slide… I'm so sorry."

Kael looked at him, aghast. All his frustrations, all his shame and self loathing and doubts and fears about being wrong and being publicly shamed suddenly welled up inside him. He tried to keep it down, he tried to keep it in but it suddenly erupted out of his stomach into his throat. Before he knew it he found himself shouting at Nathanael, a round of foul expletives, one after the other, followed by, "Nazi climate denier!"

Suddenly he noticed that the people in the church hall were now all watching, for his outburst had apparently taken place in an unfortunate moment of complete silence.

No, they were still watching. At some point in the argument – he had not noticed it – the church people had all begun watching.

You could hear a pin drop.

What was worse, at least three mobile phones were filming. He could tell by the way they held them up and watched him through the viewscreen.

Nathanael was standing there in front of him looking both stunned and vindicated, and that was when Kael realised that he had delivered the knockout blow, not to Nathanael but to himself. His outburst of bad temper had destroyed any remaining shreds of credibility he might have otherwise had.

Suddenly Marybelle was next to him.

She put her hand on his arm and said softly, "Bless you, Kael, just… stop now, bro. Step away, brother."

The pastor stood forward, and in that moment Kael hated him, he hated God, and oh how he loathed the people at this church. These hypocritical Christians, what a loathsome bunch.

But unexpectedly, instead of finalizing Kael's humiliation,

Pastor Carlos addressed the people holding the mobile phones up in a quiet, calming voice, "It's fine for you to have videoed this and watch it yourselves. But please think of our brother's soul here – if you do put it up online, think what his opinion will be of church people from now on. He will hate Christians, and quite justifiably, so please don't let your actions be a stumbling block for him in believing in our precious Lord Jesus. In fact, I'm pleading with you, brothers, sisters, dear friends, don't put it online. Don't even keep it. Trash the video. Don't put a stumbling block in front of this man here, whom you must treat as your own brother. Let him who is without sin be the first to cast a stone. Or the first to put a video online, to put it another way."

Suddenly one of the church people said, "I'm deleting it." He came forward and showed his iPhone to Kael – the video was there and he actually deleted it in front of him.

Another brought his phone to Kael and did the same, and the third as well. A few more came forward, some others who had been videoing that Kael hadn't even noticed, and trashed their videos in front of him as well.

Kael was amazed.

A video like that could go viral in a few hours. You could get a million hits in a day or two, and these people were deleting them?

They could have gotten famous. The media would have been beating down their doors to get copies to show on the evening news.

Wryly, Kael realised that if he had taken a video of Anthony Watts or that pesky Australian, Joanne Nova, or that insane Englishman, Monckton, having a similar temper tantrum or losing an argument so thoroughly there was no way he would not put it online. He would crucify any one of them without a second thought.

For a moment he doubted. Perhaps they'd uploaded it to the cloud already? He didn't think so. They had only just recorded it.

A video is, what? 50, 100 Megabytes maybe, even for a ten-minute video. He estimated fifteen minutes at least, maybe half an hour even at 4G speeds. They didn't have 5G here in Phoenix yet did they? He didn't think so.

He was saved.

He was completely amazed and suddenly realised how fortunate he had been.

He looked around and said, "Why did you do this? Why did you delete those videos? It's... unbelievably gracious of you. Pastor..." Kael suddenly realised he didn't even know the pastor's name.

The pastor came over to him and grasped his shoulder gently. "Call me Carlos. We here at Iglesia De Cristo are Christians, and so we love you brother, because we know Jesus first loved us. We're all sinners in need of redemption; no one is better than anyone else. Nobody here wants to ruin your career or to humiliate you, not one of us wishes to harm you or hurt you in any way."

Most surprisingly, Kael didn't feel that the pastor's behaviour was unnatural or creepy-weird – so unexpected – in fact, there was a genuine warmth in Carlos's voice that immediately set him at ease.

Kael said, "Amazing."

Carlos nodded. "It is amazing. It's the power of Jesus' death and resurrection. Jesus transforms human nature, brother."

Kael sat down on the nearest chair. The last half hour, the argument with that climate skeptic, then his loss of control, and the videos, and the deleting of the videos, it had all been too much. He buried his head in his hands for a moment, and realised he was weeping slightly. He wiped his eyes and looked up.

The guy he had been arguing with was the one who had brought him the chair to sit on.

Nathanael, that was his name, wasn't it?

"Thank you for the chair, Nathanael," he said.

Nathanael said, "I'm very, very sorry for... provoking that outburst. I didn't mean for our discussion to get to that stage."

Kael winced. "I'm sorry. I could see you didn't want to talk about it. I think that was why I needled you until you broke. I'm truly sorry, I deserved to have that happen to me. I shouldn't have kept pushing. Look – I really do believe climate change is happening – but I admit I can't actually prove it..." His words faded away and he looked like a whipped dog, his mouth turned down at the edges and his eyes ringed with black hollows.

Nathanael had no clue what to say.

Gradually the crowd returned to talking normally, and Marybelle came over and said, "Are you alright, brother?"

Kael grasped her hand and said tremulously, "No. Not really. Not great. Do you mind if I don't come over this afternoon? I don't think I'm quite up to facing your family after this..."

Marybelle said, "You weren't coming over. You were going to catch the plane to Seattle, remember? You had a seminar."

Kael swore. "I completely forgot."

He suddenly realised that the call he had missed while he was arguing must have been the Uber.

He looked at his watch. It was twenty past one. He must have been sitting around for a while – had it been that long?

He got his phone out and looked at the flights online. There were none now that could get him to Seattle before the seminar began.

Kael was surprised how wounded and victimised his voice sounded. "I can't get to the seminar. I've missed it. I have to ring Devraj." He hurriedly found the number in his phone and clicked it.

Devraj answered. Kael said, "Devraj! I'm really sorry. I'm so sorry, it's all my fault. I've missed the flight. I'm not going to make it for the seminar."

Devraj sounded very upset. "What happened?"

Kael was going to say, "I got into an argument with a climate denier and lost my temper when he beat me," but it didn't sound very good when he rehearsed it in his head, so he just said instead, "I… had a small incident, an injury, at my sister's church. Just a… a fall, really, you could say, nothing that terrible as it turns out but it has caused me to miss the flight." It was just a white lie, nothing much but he looked at Marybelle – her face wore such a shocked expression that he suddenly felt ashamed of himself again.

Devraj said in an even more upset, stressed voice, "Oh, dear, okay, oh dear, my dear, I'll have to change the speech I was giving, that's fine, dear, dear. No, no. Look, Kael, I'm going to have to go. This is going to take a bit of last-minute organising, my friend." He paused for a moment. "I hope you're feeling better soon, Kael. It sounds very serious." And he closed the connection.

Kael looked at his sister, he felt his face had a stricken expression on it. "I can't come over. I don't know if I'm up to… facing up to your family after that. They all saw. It's completely humiliating."

Marybelle said, "Every one of José's relatives has been through humiliations, Kael, many of them. Every single one of them, all their lives. It's the fate of a Latin American in this country, especially a Christian; many of them are working in industries where illegality is rife as well as bearing the burden of being blamed and thought of as illegals. They wouldn't look down on you for one moment of weakness. For God's sake, it wasn't that bad."

He winced. "I just can't face them. Not yet. Give it a bit of time. Please. Oh God, please." He couldn't get over how pistol-whipped his voice sounded.

Marybelle embraced him compassionately. "Why don't you stay here at the church for a little longer? If you honestly think that it might be too much for you, dealing with José's family this afternoon, stay here for a while. There're people here all afternoon. I don't feel comfortable dropping you at the hotel where you'll be on your own, not in this state."

She was referring to his depression, in his late teens. Didn't she realise he was a different person now? More confident?

More self-esteem?

He laughed silently at that. More self-esteem? Hardly.

He didn't want to argue with her, though. Having a few people around didn't sound so bad, actually, when the alternative was sitting about facing the empty walls of the hotel room.

The pastor said, "We have a meal in the early afternoon for a few recovering drug addicts, homeless men, women fleeing domestic violence, people with addictions, with a small group conversation afterward, and prayer. You can stay if you like. There will only be about ten or eleven people there, with me as well. No more than twelve or thirteen people."

Marybelle admitted, "It would be a lot quieter than the family lunch. What time does the meeting finish, Pastor Carlos?"

Pastor Carlos said, "About four o'clock."

"I'll come by at four and pick you up," said Marybelle. "Most of the family will have gone by then. You can have dinner with us then and after that you decide what to do next."

Kael put his head in his hands. "I just don't know what's happening to me."

Pastor Carlos said, "It's alright, you've just had a bit of a shock, social media shaming has the power to do that to us. Relax. Take it easy. You escaped lightly!"

Kael nodded his agreement.

Pastor Carlos continued, "They're not an exacting group, these addicts, you know, they're relaxed, very quiet, humble. You'll feel at home."

Kael said, "I guess – I guess I could just go back to the hotel? If I'm going to be in the way…"

Marybelle grasped his arm firmly and shook her head. She gave each syllable an emphasis, as though speaking to a recalcitrant child. "I think it is best if you are with other people this afternoon, Kael. You must not spend the day on your own."

Carlos laughed. "You're not going to be in the way, Kael, honestly!" His good nature warmed Kael's heart.

Kael weighed it all up in his mind again. He couldn't decide. But he had to do something, be somewhere, and he didn't want to be at his sister's place, not in this state of shame.

And at least there'd be something to eat, some non-challenging company.

Nobody who'd be likely to ruin his career, or even know him. People completely outside his social circle.

Finally Kael nodded. "I'll stay here."

<div align="center">~~~~</div>

Kael looked around the circle of chairs. There was more than Carlos had said, about fourteen of them. Three or four chairs were empty.

Some of the guys looked like bikies, tattoos everywhere, unshaven faces and shaven heads. Some were more like surfers, tanned all over with long hair. There were one or two women as well. One or two of the men were wearing suits and looked quite well-off, though.

Suddenly Kael recognised a voice. The guy he had been arguing with. He recoiled for a moment, he didn't think he would have come if he had known they'd be here.

Nathanael was whispering, "Did you ask Michelle if she wanted to come?" Natasha was sitting next to him and they were holding hands. Kael felt strangely jealous. There was something there, a real bond between them.

After his performance, a girl like that would never be interested in him.

Natasha nodded and said, "No dice. She doesn't want to admit she has a problem with hacking." She paused. "I think she might have a bit of a problem with binge drinking, as well. She smelled like ethanol fumes when she came home last night."

Nathanael said, "But then again, she was sobbing during the sermon. Maybe she's just not ready to talk to other people about it yet."

Natasha squeezed his hand.

Standing watching Kael come in, Pastor Carlos sat down on one of the chairs in the circle. He said, "Sorry Kael, I forgot to tell you. Natasha and Nathanael are here. Both have been struggling with addictions. That's what this Bible study and sharing session is about." He paused. "If you don't want to be here with them here it's…"

Kael interrupted, "It's fine. Who am I to get on my high horse?"

Carlos said, "Right, then, let's get started."

Natasha said, "I guess I'll start. I'm a computer hacker. I can't resist the temptation to poke and prod website vulnerabilities, especially when I suspect things aren't what they seem."

Other people asked her, "Have you hacked this week? Are you still on the wagon?"

"No, I haven't hacked this week," said Natasha. "But Michelle's getting worse and it really cuts me, because it's my fault she got started on the dark path."

Everyone was silent but Carlos said, "There's no condemnation in Jesus, Natasha."

Natasha whispered, "Thanks."

Nathanael was next. He said, "And I'm a gambler. If I'm ever in Nevada, once I start I can't stop."

One of the men who looked like a biker smiled, showing a missing tooth, and said, "You lose a lot of money? That's how I lost my second Harley."

Nathanael said hastily, "No, no."

"You lost a bit then? Only a few bucks? You were lucky, then."

"I won."

"You won? What, how much, a few hundred ahead? If you can quit while you're ahead, what's the problem, bud?"

Nathanael said, "It's still a problem, trust me, if you can't stop. It was like an obsession, you know, it took over my life. It was all I thought about. I completely neglected my friends, my family, everything I did just served that obsession. It really was an addiction."

Kael felt an unfamiliar expression move over his face like a cloud, a sort of wounded frown, as he began to realise that what Nathanael was describing was his own obsession with his academic work, making people believe that carbon dioxide was destroying the planet, trying to manipulate the governments into acting on the threat, exaggerating the evidence if they could.

But fighting the climate battle was Kael's duty.

As the confessions moved around the circle Kael began to feel like a mouse that had just jumped off its treadmill. He saw that there were things about his life that he hadn't wanted to face; that he had been pushing a boulder uphill, like Sisyphus. It was a never-ending, fruitless task. One of the other guys had said it ten years ago – if the present pause continues, we have to start wondering if global warming might not be happening – and that's when they had started pushing the term 'climate change'.

The pause was still continuing. There should have been much more warming than there was, if their theory was right.

He thought about himself, furtively reading wattsupwiththat.com at midnight in his office when none of the postgraduate students were around, and that article about Jennifer something or other who had analysed the Australian weather data. It was a mess.

And how he agonised over Monckton's old article about the feedback mechanisms, working his way through the comments. If Kael wasn't so committed to the warmists he realised he would have to admit that Monckton's conclusion was pretty convincing. A maximum of around one degree for every doubling of carbon dioxide. Hardly a problem if solar forcing was as big as it was supposed to be.

And he knew at the bottom of his heart that despite his ridiculous persona, Monckton really did know the maths, much better than Kael did. Mathematics was not really Kael's strong suit – which was why he hadn't recognised the statistical errors in his earlier work, such as that damned polo stick graph which had become so famous – and he was surrounded by other idiots who knew the maths even less than he did.

"Are you here for some addiction or other, too?" the voice repeated. Kael looked up. One of the young girls was talking to him, she looked barely out of high school. What was she addicted to? He had missed it.

Kael shook his head and lied. "No, no, just, had a disturbing experience. I'm here more as a sort of.. charity case."

"It was my fault," said Nathanael. "I humiliated him. I didn't really need to. My behaviour was not that dissimilar to when I gamble, actually, I just couldn't stop."

"No. That's not correct," Kael said firmly. "I was the one who couldn't stop." And that was about the truest thing he had said in the last ten years.

Kael bowed his head.

He was like a man who woke up from a pleasant dream of running and dancing to find that he couldn't move, he was completely paralysed from the neck down.

Kael's whole life was a lie.

<u>CHAPTER 7 – Another Father.</u>

PERTH, AUSTRALIA. Monday.

That particular Monday, Peter had dropped off Meth and was sitting in a small café opposite the school, sipping espressos and waiting for one o'clock when he was due for his shooting lesson at the rifle range, something he had decided to do after they had been kidnapped.

He would never be caught by surprise again.

Peter looked across at the small Montessori school, with the sun shining on the corrugated roof, making it glint and gleam. Meth was in there right now talking, learning, enjoying being there. Peter was very happy with the school community; everyone was very welcoming and accepting towards Meth's peculiarities.

And best of all, they didn't ask too many questions about his past or his small stature.

Thanks to Trippy-Girl, though, they had kept their first names, more or less. Meth took the name TG had enrolled him under, Meth-Shiloh, which according to TG was cognate with Methuselah. Peter took Pierce officially, which is actually cognate with Peter but he told everyone to call him Pete. He didn't want someone shouting, "Pierce!" and him not turning round.

Peter bought lunch, something he would have been nervous to do earlier when cash was tight. But thankfully Peter had access to more funds now. Somehow Trippy Girl had organised for a few hundred thousand to be transferred to his account; Peter didn't have any clue at all where she had got it from and he wasn't sure he wanted to know.

His thoughts were interrupted when an older gentleman wearing a light blue suit and sporting a shock of white hair, came up to him and said in a quiet London accent, "Excuse me if, I hope you don't mind... You look a bit familiar. Do you mind if I sit here? You... ah... highly resemble a man I've been earnestly looking for."

Peter tried to signal reluctance but the man sat down anyway.

"You see," the old gentleman continued, "My son is a geneticist working in London who specialises in recovering DNA from ancient artefacts." Peter got up to leave, he didn't want to have this conversation. The man grabbed his arm and pleaded, "Please, don't go! I beg you!"

Peter shook the man's hand away and snapped, "What do you want?"

An expression in the old man's eyes caught him. Peter sat down and the man said, "A few years ago, some of my son's colleagues disappeared. A man named Bruce Hetherington, an expert in Near Eastern prehistory. My son sent me a list of the missing scientists. Now, correct me if I'm wrong but you are Dr Peter Lazarus-Fox, a scientist who went off the grid about five years ago, one of the first. Please, don't leave!" He spoke in a tone of desperation. Peter looked at the man again. Could he trust him?

"I really don't want to talk about this," said Peter, glancing at the clock on the wall – two-twenty. He cursed quietly; he had been in a reverie for so long he had missed his rifle lesson.

Meth was due out of class in forty minutes.

"Please," the man said. "My son is in trouble."

Peter was about to fob him off but when he glanced into the man's face he recognised the expression because he had seen it every morning in the mirror ever since the day he had stolen Methuselah away from the research facility in England.

This was a man worried about his son.

The old man's face contorted into a grief-stricken expression and he whispered, "Forgive me for using your name, Doctor Lazarus-Fox; I presume that you don't go by that identity any more. Now, I don't know what's going on. But the thing is, I think my son's in trouble. He's working in a very clandestine lab and he's stopped emailing or ringing – he will only talk to me now on the Tor Messaging App – and that right seldom; in fact, I haven't heard from him for more than a month. And he says he's worried about the things he's required to do."

Peter was annoyed. "I really don't want to talk about this." He took a deep breath, surprised at how angry he sounded. He glanced at the school where Meth was in class right now. This man was endangering his son.

But the old man pleaded, "Please." Peter groaned. The man's tone of voice resonated with him. He made his decision. The words tripped out quickly but he whispered, "I go by the name Pierce now but everyone calls me Pete – makes it easier. But I'm not merely responsible for myself. If I get found out it won't simply affect me. My... son... is in that school over there. He's my life now, I've left all the clandestine research behind. I've left that world behind."

The old man laughed bitterly. "My son – I never could have believed that he could get into trouble in such an obscure profession – Paleontological Genetics – but there you go. Pete, my name's Henry."

They shook hands. Peter's heart warmed to Henry.

Peter said, "Hello, Henry, pleased to meet you. It surprised me too. I mean, I'm in a similarly obscure sub-field. But there are things they are looking into now, facts that defy everything we've been told. I don't know why I'm talking to you about this."

Looking around nervously, Henry whispered, "Not here. These days, they can hack phones, cameras, computers; these people have eyes and ears everywhere. Please meet me the day after tomorrow at the State Library in Perth. At eleven o'clock in the morning, in the foyer. A public place; no one is going to do anything to us there. We can book a private room upstairs where no one will overhear us."

Henry paused, and looked directly at Peter. "What I have to say concerns ancient things – the dark history of humanity that has lain hidden for thousands of years. Dark things that need to be brought into the daylight."

* * *

A CLANDESTINE LABORATORY IN SYDNEY, AUSTRALIA.

Somewhere on the other side of the continent of Australia, in a clandestine laboratory in the industrial outskirts of Sydney, a creature awoke and flexed its muscles. The creature looked at its hands and feet, not yet fully grown, and rejoiced.

At last – a body.

It looked at the scientists who stood mouths agape, watching as it awakened from its slumber.

It said in perfect English, "Who summoned me here?"

The head scientist, Dr Harald Yvetrison, said in a voice

that came out far more shakily than he had intended, "I am the head of this research unit. How is it that you can speak English?"

"I know many things that you can barely guess."

Dr Yvetrison pulled out his mobile phone and rang a number. "Contact Heidelberg. Tell them the Pacific Laboratory has had a success in the N3PHL project." He felt embarrassed as a scientist saying what he had to say next but facts were facts. "Tell them the… um… magic ceremony worked."

And Dr Yvetrison looked at the large pentacle inscribed on the floor of the laboratory, and reflected on the ceremony they had performed…

A particularly disturbing ceremony which Dr Yvetrison wanted to erase from his memory. He would never, ever think about this again, if he could help it. In fact, he decided to forget it right then and there.

But the feeling of unease and the sense that his soul itself had been tainted, begrimed, he realised, was something he would never be able to erase…

CHAPTER 8 – The Dolichocephaly Fallacy.

STATE LIBRARY, PERTH, AUSTRALIA. WEDNESDAY.

Peter followed Henry into a small soundproof private room; there was an upright piano against one wall and a table and two chairs in the middle. Henry laid a leather satchel on the table and took out an old, red hard-covered book and dropped it on the table making a loud 'thunk'. On the spine of the book, Peter saw printed in gold, "Peruvian Antiquities."

They both sat down.

Henry began his story.

"The Jonesonian Institute in Washington D.C. was employing my son to extract DNA from some rather unusual fossils. The government made him sign an extremely onerous secrecy agreement.

"These fossils were in a locked vault, well away from the other exhibits and all the other items stored at the museum. As my son walked into the darkened vault where they kept these things sealed and isolated away from sunlight and the air and anything else that might cause them to decay, he caught a glimpse of four or five huge skulls and the enormous rib cages below them, and he thought for a moment that these were the fossils of bears or sabre-toothed tigers. Each of them was at least seven to eight feet tall.

"Then he saw the skulls, and the teeth. Molars at the back, premolars, two canines, incisors; they were definitely human teeth. But the arrangement of the teeth was highly irregular – there was a double row of teeth! And the strangest thing of all – the three skulls were elongated. The scientific term for this is dolichocephaly."

"Yes, yes," said Peter, waving his hand dismissively. "I've heard of this. Head-binding. Certain African tribes do it. Done at birth for the first six months; makes the skulls look longer."

"Indeed. Nice theory, Peter. But look at this. This is a nineteenth century book, about archaeological discoveries in Peru. They knew about this phenomenon back then."

He opened the book and directed Peter to read.

...The two crania (both of children scarce a year old) had, in all respects, the same form as those of adults. We ourselves have observed the same fact in many mummies of children of tender age, who, although they had cloths about them, were yet without any vestige or appearance of pressure of the cranium.

~~~

More still: the same formation of the head presents itself in children yet unborn; and of this truth we have had convincing proof in the sight of a fœtus, enclosed in the womb of a mummy of a pregnant woman, which
~~~

we found in a cave of Huichay, two leagues from Tarma, and which is, at this moment, in our collection. Professor D'Outrepont, of great celebrity in the department of obstetrics, has assured us that the fœtus is one of seven months' age. It belongs, according to a very clearly defined formation of the cranium, to the tribe of the Huancas. We present the reader with a drawing of this conclusive and interesting proof in opposition to the advocates of mechanical action as the sole and exclusive cause of the phrenological form of the Peruvian race.

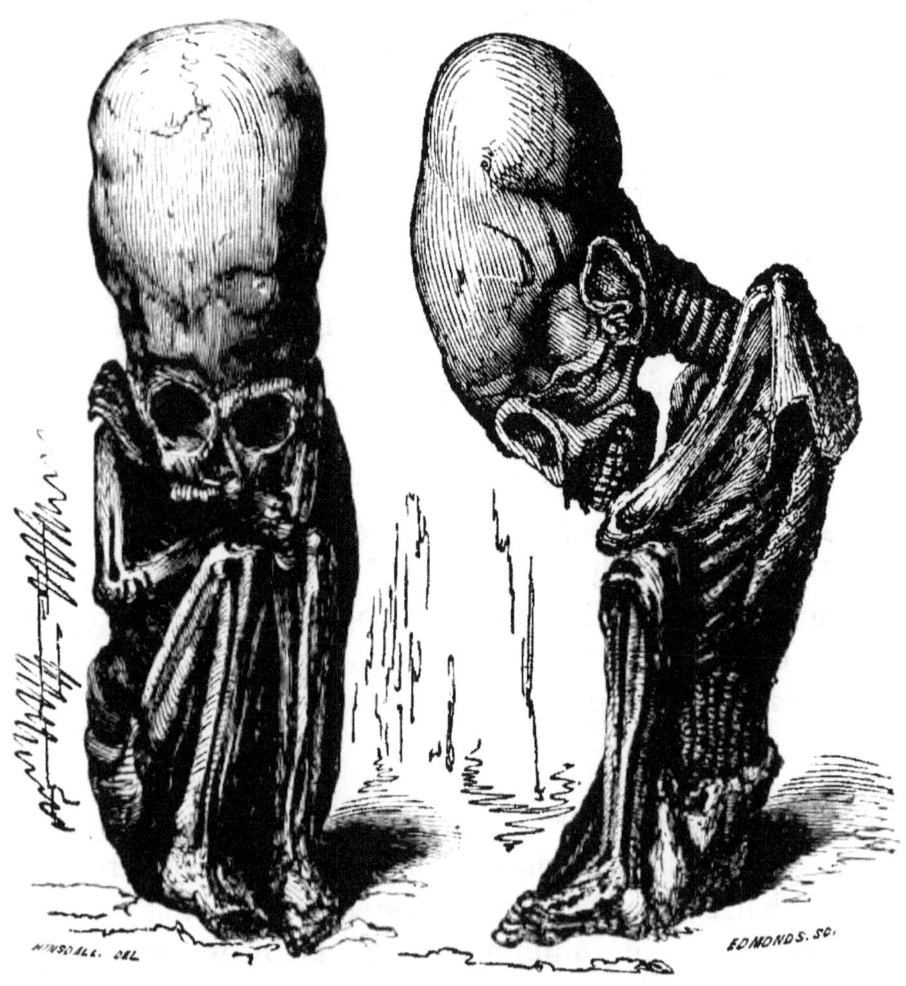

FRONT AND SIDE VIEW.

Henry continued, "You see? These Incan skulls were deformed before birth. My son told me that the elongated skull was a universal phenomenon from the earliest times of human civilisation, starting at five to six thousand BC, everywhere on earth. The earliest are from Australia. They are found in ancient Sumeria, Egypt, the Pacific Islands, Central America, Peru, Lima, Tiwanaku, New Zealand. King Tutankhamen is one example, actually."

Peter nodded. He remembered seeing Tutankhamun's mummy in an exhibition once.

"My son managed to isolate blood cells from the bone marrow – you understand that this practice is not at all rare when studying fossils these days – if these fossils were a hundred thousand years old they would be distinctly young for blood cells to be extracted. But this was from one of the pale giants whose remains were found frozen, somewhere in Siberia."

"I know," said Peter. "When he tested the DNA, what did he find?"

Henry whispered even more quietly than before, so that Peter had to strain to hear him. "The analysis took them a long time. The Mitochondrial DNA was extremely peculiar, Peter. My son said the genetics defied description. He believes it indicated the mother was only the tenth or eleventh generation from the first human pair. He mentioned something about Genesis then, I didn't quite get it. He said they defiled them or something; not sure. But what amazed my son was that the structure of the genome was more than human. He said there was a perfection in the design – a lack of faults and mutations, a strange ordered, engineered feel about it. Extra strands, extra chromosomes but well-integrated into human DNA in a rather counter-intuitive way."

Peter said, "And?"

"My son used a turn of phrase that I hesitate to repeat, Peter. If I say it, you will think that I'm either a liar or a lunatic." Henry folded his hands on the table in front of him and continued, "But I am neither."

"Yes, I've heard that CS Lewis quote too. What was the turn of phrase, Henry?"

"My son said, literally, 'They're the offspring of the gods.' He told me their DNA is so perfect, so symmetrical, designed with such clearly intentional technical brilliance – and beside being well designed is also flawless in its execution – he said the difference between their DNA and ours, or any earthly creature, is analogous to the difference between a city skyscraper and a functional Viking meeting hall. Or better yet, a skyscraper compared to a gothic cathedral. He says it is as though there are two different designers. The one who designed us is a craftsman, an artist, a wood-carver or a sculptor. The ones who designed these creatures were technologists, interested not in beauty and symmetry, but rather in defensive and offensive capability in war, brute force, superior intelligence and overwhelming power. He told me at first that he believed aliens had come to the earth – that perhaps they seeded humanity – that they had lived among us, many aeons ago – and that these were hybrids, half-human, half-alien. But now he says they were fallen angels who designed these creatures..."

Peter said noncommittally, "Interesting."

"But Peter... My son said the key to what is happening is found in the Vatican's secret archives, the Archivum Secretum Vaticanum, administered by one Father Rudolpho Valentin, document X26799."

Peter rolled his eyes. Henry was being overly dramatic now. What, did he think they were in some sort of Dan Brown novel? "So can't we just email Father Rudolpho or something? I mean, you're really rather cloak-and-dagger about this..."

"I've already tried emailing them. But the Archivist replied and told me that he knows of no Rudolpho Valentin anywhere in Rome and that the index number of the document is invalid, it is not in their archives. I'm not surprised, though; my son said they are watching all our communications. But this is the only other clue I have. I must retrace my son's footsteps in order to find him. He told me that he went to the town of Borgo. He found Father Rudolpho Valentin in a restaurant that he frequents; my son told me the name of the restaurant. I must go and speak to Father Rudolpho in person."

"What does this have to do with me?"

"I need to find my son, Peter. I believe I – need your help. My scientific expertise is minimal – I need someone who really knows what they're looking at."

Peter said, "You want me to come to Rome? I don't know."

Henry said, "Please think about it. What if we meet next Monday at the Art Gallery Café?"

Peter nodded.

* * *

Just after arriving home with Meth, Peter received a message on TOR messenger from TG.

> TG: Henry LeCoulter has made contact with you?
>
> Peter: Yes. What do you know about him? Is he legit?
>
> TG: He is who he claims to be. His son, James LeCoulter, a geneticist specialising in recovery of DNA from ancient fossils, has disappeared.

Peter: Do you know where he might be?

TG: No. He was in Rome several years ago, then travelled to Yakutsk, Siberia for 2 weeks. Then he returned to Washington DC and the trail disappeared. I can't find anything about him. I suspect he is in some hidden research base.

Peter: Henry wants to go to Rome. Can you organise a fake identity for him? Air tickets?

TG: I'll see what I can do.

* * *

Peter looked at Meth, sitting at the dining room table eating sausages and mashed potato. The boy was happy here in Perth. Travelling was an unacceptable risk. Going anywhere simply made it much more likely that they would be caught.

He had been too hasty in deciding to go with Henry. His life was not his own now, he had a son, other responsibilities.

Perhaps he could leave Meth in someone else's care? But who would look after the boy? He shook his head. There had to be another solution. He couldn't take him with him to Europe, could he? He would have to work that out.

After putting Meth to bed Peter went to his desk and began his research.

Not much was published in the scientific literature on the topic of dolichocephaly.

Most of the theories about the people with elongated skulls assumed that head-binding was the primary cause of the phenomenon. Alternatively, there were the conspiracy theorists who accepted any crackpot theory with no evidence; most of the latter had a completely unscientific approach.

The conspiracy theorists assumed ancient alien DNA had infected humans and that this was the cause of the elongated skulls but they really had no proof of this whatsoever apart from the legends that say gods came to the earth.

Peter began thinking primarily of many Ancient Near Eastern laws that he had read about. Babylonia and many of the surrounding cultures had three social classes which had different names but were cognate across the whole region; the *awilu*, the elite citizens, a word which he had read somewhere meant "gods", the *muskenu*, who were free men, and the slaves. The laws showed the difference in class: for the same offence the *awilu* would pay a small fine, the *muskenu* a larger fine, and a slave would suffer the death penalty. And Peter had begun to wonder if the *awilu* in certain places might have been those with elongated heads.

Tutankhamen, and the daughters of Akhenaton and

Nefertiti, Queen Tiye, and Thutmose I and III, were Egyptian examples of dolichocephaly. The medieval Hungarians and Huns seem to have practised head binding. The Maltese, as well. The African Mangbetu tribe continued practising head binding well into the 1930s. The Chinese legendary figure, Shou Xing, whose mother had been impregnated by the South Pole Star was always depicted as having a bald, elongated head, and many of the other Taoist immortals had strange looking skulls too. And there were those from Australia, Russia, Korea, Vanuatu, Montana, and the Chinook Indians, to say nothing of the strange Terra Cotta figurines from the Sumerian city of Ubaid with elongated heads and coffeebean eyes.

And there were 'tall' people, seven and eight feet tall – modern archaeologists don't like calling them 'giants' lest it lends support to Biblical literalists – but there was a statistically unlikely number of them in North America who were always buried with more jewellery and treasure than the others in the tribe, with a number of normal sized bodies arranged around them in a deferential manner.

Peter could find no absolute proof of his hypothesis but an awful lot of ancient cultures apparently had a ruling class who were thought to be gods. And often in the ancient world, those who were giants or had dolichocephaly were clearly in the ruling class.

So were these dolichocephalics just people with a birth defect? (A congenital abnormality, Peter corrected himself. A defect is a rather disparaging term for what might just be a genetic difference.) About 1 in 2400 people today is born with a form of dolichocephaly caused by the sagittal sutures closing early, something that can easily be fixed today with surgery. But the skulls whose elongation was caused by unclosed sagittal-sutures were nowhere near as long and thin as those made that way by head-binding, to say nothing of those that might naturally be dolichocephalic, which showed no sign of any problems with the sagittal sutures.

And what about the ancient times? Was it just a congenital abnormality, or were these ancient dolichocephalics actually some sort of different species, some kind of hybrid?

Considering the greater number of such skulls in earlier times, Peter wondered if it was in even more ancient times that those with dolichocephaly were more the official rulers.

Then he remembered that Henry had said something about Genesis, and something about people who had been defiled. Peter resolved to get his Bible and have another read of that ancient book.

If it was about the book of Genesis then there was a good chance that this whole saga involved Meth as well, somehow, and this suddenly steeled Peter's resolve.

He had to know. Not just to satisfy his own curiosity but for Meth's sake.

To keep Meth safe.

He had to know.

* * *

The following morning Peter raised the subject with Meth over breakfast.

"Son, I may have to go away for a little while. I'm going to try to find someone to look after you while I'm gone."

"Why do you have to go? Where?" The disappointment in Meth's voice was distressing.

Peter tried to keep his own voice from shaking. "The secret organisation that I used to work for, Meth, is trying to make other early humans. Strange people with long skulls. These people happen to have been the rulers in the ancient pagan societies, and I worry that they may have some sort of innate hatred towards humans, considering that they treated them as slaves. It all has something to do with the first six chapters of Genesis, too…"

Meth's attention perked up. "My era. The antediluvian era."

Peter nodded. "Yes. Your era. So I have to go to Rome to find out what I can. There are documents there, secret documents that will tell me more. I want to know what the documents say so that I can keep you safe."

Meth frowned and said, "I can't help thinking that you travelling makes me less safe, Father."

Peter shook his head. "I know. It's a Catch-22. It's unfortunate. But there's another issue too. I have met a man, Henry, who has lost his son, and he wants to find him."

Meth's eyes brightened with determination. He said fervently, "Well, then, you have to go. You have to help that man find his son."

"Thank you, son," said Peter. "It means a lot to me, Meth, that you think this is the right thing to do."

Meth said, "Your friend's son is missing. You have no choice but to find him." Meth paused. "Father..."

"Yes, son?"

"Who will be looking after me while you're gone?"

"I don't know Meth but we will find someone."

After Meth had gone to school, Peter sent a new message to Trippy Girl.

> Peter: I need tickets for myself too, to Rome and back.
>
> TG: I can organise that. Do you... need someone to come with you? Maybe you should ask someone you trust, who has dealt with this sort of thing before?

Peter: I can manage…

After that, Peter sent a message to Natasha.

Peter: Natasha. Any chance you can come over here to Perth, Australia and look after Meth for a few weeks? I will pay your ticket over here if you need me to…

Natasha: Could do. I have some holiday leave due. When?

Peter: I'll let you know.

* * *

The man in the black suit was sitting in his chair, in the dark conference room.

He tapped the laptop keyboard in front of him.

The screen lit up with video images of the other nine members flickering into life. The microphone icon turned on – the conference had begun.

"My friends," said the man in the black suit. "I called this meeting via Skype, not because we are worried about carbon credits," and the other members guffawed and snorted. The image of the battleship-shaped woman said sarcastically, "Should have mentioned that last time before we flew in on our private jets."

The man in the black suit smiled, a rare thing. "No, it's not carbon credits. It's because we are in an emergent situation and it is utterly urgent that emergency measures be taken. As you know, we are not in this situation separately. We are all in this together, and just as a decision made by one affects all, so a decision made by all of us affects, inevitably, every single one of us. Now, you have heard me mention a certain James LeCoulter, one of our brightest young scientists. He was with the Jonessonian when Adamant Corp was funnelling the funding to us and he has been moved to one of our secret labs."

"Where?" said the image of the irritating woman with the bangle earrings.

"That is classified." The man tapped his ruler on the table as if to emphasise the fact. "But the point is, the man's father has begun making enquiries."

"Let him," said the image of the man with the baggy face. "There's nobody out there talking about this but conspiracy nuts who talk about ancient aliens and the Planet Nibiru."

The man in the black suit said, "We can't. Somehow he has found out about Pizarro."

The battleship shaped woman's image said, "How?"

"I don't know," admitted the man in the black suit. "But the fact is, our sources believe he is going to the Vatican."

Grey beard's image said, "But that's in the sealed section of the secret archives. He will never be allowed to see it."

The man in the black suit said, "Yes, yes, I know, the Vatican more or less guaranteed that. But there is a weak link in the chain. A scholar named Father Bernardo Valentin. He believes in academic freedom." They all groaned. "James LeCoulter's father knows his name already, and where to find him. He is going to Italy to try to find the priest."

The woman with the bangle earrings said, "Kill the priest. Kill LeCoulter's father. Simple."

The man in the black suit said, "That would be fine. But he already has plane tickets; we think he is taking another person with him. Booking an effective assassin before they get there could be a problem."

The woman with the bangle earrings said, "Kill them both, then, when he arrives."

The man in the black suit nodded. "Alright. A show of hands. It is agreed?"

All of the hands on the laptop went up.

A CLANDESTINE LABORATORY IN SYDNEY, AUSTRALIA. Friday.

The head scientist in the Pacific Branch Laboratory, Dr. Harald Yvetrison, looked at the elongated skull of the creature sitting in its tiny prison. It was typing at the computer again and

Dr Yvetrison had begun to regret giving the creature access to the internet. Not only was it fast at finding out things on google but it had even taught itself to code in a very short time. He could hardly stop it from doing what it wanted, though, because he didn't want another incident like the time he had forbidden it to look at pornography.

The nurse, Gabrielle Trentson, was still recovering in ICU, and that had been the worst day of his career. No, Harald was not going to take away its privileges again.

As though it had heard Harald's thoughts, the creature turned to him and said, "Don't worry. I'm not looking at porn today. No, I'm sifting through emails, finding out this and that. Do you know, it turns out that one of the enemies of my people is living on this very continent, in the city of Perth? One of the long-lived ones. It took all my powers of decryption to work this out, you know. I account this the smartest thing I have ever done."

Harald didn't even know how the creature had worked out that they were in Australia. None of the staff had told him anything.

He groaned. It was a creepy thing, the giant with its black eyes, its leering gaze, and the strange things it said, often seemingly reading people's thoughts, telling them their secret intentions.

Harald didn't like his job anymore and he wished that

he could resign his post but he knew that things would not turn out well if he did.

No, quitting was just another way to fall into the deep black hole, from which no employee ever returned.

And Harald had a family to consider.

A CLANDESTINE LABORATORY IN FRANKFURT. 1:30 AM SUNDAY.

James LeCoulter laid himself down in the dark, leaning against the glass screen and sprawling on the table. The tall figure was sitting on the other side of the glass. James knew the giant was inside the secure cage but he still felt his skin crawl at the creature's nearness. And he could just hear the giant's soft breathing through the speaker at the top of the glass.

James said, "You told me earlier you wanted to see me. After lights out. When the others are gone."

The tall figure said, "I did. Thank you for coming."

James said, "That's alright. But why did you want me in particular? Why not one of the doctors, or the nurses, or the psychologist?"

The tall man's silhouette stretched out in the darkness and James fancied that he heard him sigh. "You… treat me like a human being. To them I am a case study, an interesting object to be scrutinised under a microscope."

For a moment James pitied him but then he remembered how intelligent the tall figure was and James wondered what was going on. He said, "You could be saying this to fool me; this could just be a ploy to gain my sympathy."

"If I was doing that, perhaps I wouldn't even know that I was doing it. I don't even know how to answer that. How would I even know what I think? The subconscious may manipulate what a person does, and he might not even know it." Then the tall figure fell silent again.

For a while James listened to the strangely filtered soft breathing, transmitted through the little speaker in the glass, without the low frequencies.

Finally James said, "You've tied yourself up in more knots than a pretzel, haven't you?"

Somehow James felt that the tall figure was nodding, the silhouette suggested that. Then the tall figure said, "Do you know I wouldn't mind something to read? It gets boring in here."

James replied, "Can you actually read already? I'll see what I can do."

CHAPTER 9 – Hay While Sasha Shines

EXETER, UNITED KINGDOM, MEANWHILE.

In the Hayfield church the sun was streaming through the multicoloured stained glass windows and Sasha was sitting listening to another sermon, basking in the warmth of another summer Sunday morning.

Sasha's mind was wandering, thankfully, into more pleasant pastures than this. All the sermons here were about how wonderful LGBTI people were, which was an interesting theme once or twice but every week started getting a little tedious. Tell me once and I'll believe you. Tell me twice and I'll start to doubt whether you really believe it yourself. Sasha had coined a word for this: gaydolatry. That was what this was.

Of course it would be different if the priest was saying how wonderful Mother Russia is, or what a wonderful drink vodka is, or how Russian men are the most masculine men in the world. Sasha could not get tired of hearing such things as these.

Then he noticed that young fellow, Frankie, watching him in another pew. That was the boy Sasha had quoted the Bible at that first Sunday he had come. O Bozhe moi! It was almost as if young Frankie was interested in him, in that sort of way.

Well, if that was true, Sasha was up for anything. He

didn't believe in limiting himself, not at all. Why should he? Pleasure is pleasure.

And he wasn't worried about alienating Gregory, with whom he had been just last week. After all, Gregory just wanted money out of Sasha. Sasha had established that much from the fact that Gregory wouldn't stop haranguing him to give money to this green climate fund.

Yes, Frankie looked like a fine fellow.

So Sasha smiled and winked at Frankie, who blushed.

* * *

<u>CHAPTER 10 – Salsa Solace.</u>

MARYBELLE AND JOSÉ'S PLACE. SUNDAY A WEEK AFTER THE BAPTISM.

They had salsa for dinner at Marybelle's place that night. The rest of the relatives had gone home now except for Kael.

Kael hadn't expected to stay beyond the previous Sunday lunch-time but he was still here a week later, and he suddenly realised that his feelings had changed about José and Marybelle.

He really liked José now. He was like a brother to him.

During dinner, he told her in flat, emotionless tones, "I might stay for a few more days." Somehow expressing anything seemed like too much trouble.

Marybelle was nonplussed. "Alright."

Kael said, "You don't mind me staying? I mean, I've been here since Friday a week ago, and I was only supposed to stay two nights. I've been here a week."

Marybelle said, "Stay as long as you like." She paused. "Kael, I thought you were due back at the Climate Unit in England tomorrow? Didn't you tell me one of your graduates had a seminar?"

Kael admitted, "Yes, I ought to be there but honestly, any of the other fifteen PhD supervisors can supervise that seminar. I told them I've decided to take a month off."

Marybelle raised her eyebrows. "Really? You never take time off."

Kael shrugged. "I have a lot of accrued leave; sick-leave and holiday leave. Honestly, Marybelle, I just need some time to think things through. This thing with the climate skeptic and the videos has really… upset the applecart."

Marybelle shook her head sympathetically. "But no one put the video online. Why would it, you know, upset your applecart?"

Kael nodded. "Exactly. To be honest it has made me reassess the whole… well, my beliefs… A lot of things. I don't know, I'm rethinking my whole life."

To be frank, Marybelle was worried about her brother's psychological state, and that was why she didn't mind him being here so they could keep an eye on him. She had never seen him looking so broken before in his life. Was this the prelude to a nervous breakdown, or was it a new start?

Or both?

José said, "You can stay here as long as you need to, brother. Family is all-important. Blood is thicker than water."

Kael shook José's hand and said, "Thank you. I really appreciate it, José. I won't stay for much longer, though, just long enough to get my head around all this."

José said, "Stay as long as you need, I really mean that."

And José went to the fridge and got out two beers. He popped the tab on one and handed it to Kael. "Marybelle's family is my family, and that makes you my brother, brother."

CHAPTER 11 – Frank as Frankie.

Sasha was lying in bed with the young man from the church. It had been a satisfactory day, a most enjoyable afternoon and night. Now it was two o'clock in the morning.

The young man woke up and saw that Sasha was awake.

Sasha said, "So… Tell me what it is about me that you find so attractive?"

"Well," said the boy. "It's not really that. I decided that if I'm going to hell, I may as well drag you down along with me."

Just then a knocking sound came from downstairs.

The boy shouted downstairs, "Come in, the door is open."

Footsteps came creaking up the old staircase and the door opened.

Sasha was quite surprised to see two policemen come through the doorway. One of them looked to be from India or Pakistan and wore a turban, which Sasha found to be interesting as well.

"Hello," said the other policeman. "So, what do we have here?"

"A foursome?" said Sasha, winking. "You are welcome to join us, officer."

The boy, Sasha had actually forgotten his name, said in

a cold, hard voice that surprised Sasha, "This man abused me."

Sasha said, "Well, no, no one was abused; it was perfectly consensual sex."

The policeman said, "And how old are you, sir?"

Sasha was about to tell his age but the policeman said, "Not you, sir, the other sir."

"I am fifteen years old."

"Well, then, sir, you will have to come with us."

Then they put handcuffs on Sasha, which was extremely humiliating, and pushed him down the stairs so hard he almost tumbled down. The boy shouted, "My name is Frankie, by the way. Remember that. Frankie."

Then they put him in the back of the paddy wagon and locked him in, and he bumped around in there until they reached the police station.

Sasha had never felt so low in his life before.

* * *

At the lockup, Sasha was eating breakfast, a particularly cold, mushy bowl of cornflakes, when he heard footsteps in the corridor. The morning shift guard came in and opened his cell door.

A man followed him through.

It was that accursed fellow, Gregory Islingsforth.

Gregory said, "Today, Sasha, I am your advocate."

Sasha said, "Really? You're a lawyer?"

"Not really," said Gregory. "That was why I used the somewhat broader term, advocate."

Sasha said, "Not interested," and turned his face to the wall to finish his cornflakes.

Gregory cleared his throat. "Yes, I admit I'm not a professional lawyer. But you need to know that I can make all this go away, Sasha."

"Really?" said Sasha, dropping the plate. It smashed, spreading bright, mushy cornflakes out across the concrete. "How, Gregory, tell me how?" The prospect of spending years in prison could be very sobering. Sasha had suddenly formed a more respectful opinion of Gregory if the man could help him avoid that fate.

Gregory tut-tutted, "Oh, please don't ask that. It would be better if you asked me *why* I would do it."

"Why? Why would you do that?"

"Why indeed? Sasha, you might need to give me a – let's say – a more cogent reason for making this thing go away."

"Yes, anything. I will do anything you ask, Gregory."

"I presume you have your mobile phone on you?"

Sasha shook his head. All his possessions had been taken away when they locked him up.

Gregory flagged down the guard and asked for Sasha's

mobile. The guard said, "Why?" and Gregory said, "Legal privilege."

The guard was a fairly recent graduate and wasn't sure what the law said about this, and the captain hadn't arrived yet.

Gregory said, "Look, it's just to make a small bank deposit."

The guard said, "Alright. Just give it back to me straight afterwards. It is evidence, you know."

The guard brought the phone over to Sasha and said, "I'm watching, mind, don't start thinking you'll be deleting emails."

Gregory said, "Just a bank deposit."

"How much?" said Sasha reluctantly.

Gregory whispered, "Fifty thousand. It's enough for starters. You have the bank details I emailed you?"

Sasha found the bank details and copied them into his bank app. Immediately he transferred fifty thousand pounds.

Gregory said confidentially, "Wonderful. Well, we'll get you out on bail first. And immediately after that the charges will be quashed."

CLANDESTINE LABORATORY IN FRANKFURT.

It was the middle of the night. James LeCoulter was sitting with his back against the glass once more. Somehow he knew the tall figure was seated in the exact same posture on the other side.

It was almost completely pitch dark.

James said, "Well, what did you think of the books?"

"Frankenstein. I see you wanted me to read this book as you think it analogous to my situation," the tall figure said; he seemed to be weighing each word carefully.

The tall figure continued, "I could easily play along. Tease you intellectually, if you like, create a sense of my victimhood in your mind. In fact, I am very well aware that I could make you sympathetic towards me, manipulate you into becoming a tool of my own calculating intellect. But the truth is that this is not an analogous situation. I am no Frankenstein's monster."

James shook his head, although he knew the creature could not see it. "I think it is analogous. You were brought into being quite unwillingly."

The tall figure said, "No, I am not so innocent as you think I am." He was silent for a while, then said, "It wasn't that book; it was the Bible that intrigued me. I have never read the Bible before. Particularly the story of the sins of the Canaanites. God knew they would sin, yet he still didn't destroy them until they had filled up the measure of their sins. I do not understand this."

James said, "Yes, I'm only just keeping up with you on the reading. I have to admit the Bible is new to me too, most of it, though I grew up going to Sunday school. But I think the answer is that God is just and righteous – He knew the Canaanites were going to sin but it would be unjust to punish someone for what they're going to do... God is compassionate. Maybe despite himself God still wanted them to repent, still hoped they might repent, even knowing that they weren't going to."

"They were like me," said the tall figure. "I am doomed. How can I escape? I've been given flesh to do the bidding of my masters. I can never be saved. There is no repentance for one like me."

James shook his head. "Why not?"

The tall figure said, "If the people who own this place found out I was talking to you about these subjects they would do away with me and likely as not fire you as well."

James paused. This conversation was now hitting home for him a little more than he would have liked. James' conscience was tormented by the fact that he was still working there now that he knew what was really going on. Somehow this made him feel a kind of kinship with the tall figure; he realised that he had been talking to him every night for quite a few weeks now, and James didn't even know his name. Or even if he had one.

So James said, "What is your name?"

The tall figure said, "Call me Adze, if you like. That will do."

"Adze," said James. "I am not exactly working for them

willingly. I'm not sure if I'm doing the right thing staying in this job. I try to justify it, and I keep asking the Lord if I'm doing the right thing. Yet despite everything perhaps I am meant to be here, and perhaps our conversation now is proof of that. But Adze, as for *you*, just repent. Talk to God, surely He is a loving and just God and will help you to repent? I mean if the Bible I gave you means anything at all, that's what it means."

"So much despair," groaned the tall figure. "So many regrets. I don't even know where to start."

James said earnestly, "Start by talking to God. Say you're sorry. Ask for help. That's where I started. That's where we all start. That's the only place anyone can start."

CHAPTER 12 – To Falsify Falsification.

MARYBELLE. AND JOSÉ'S PLACE.

It was Monday morning and José went to work while Marybelle took the kids to school. When she came back home, Kael was sitting in the kitchen sipping a coffee, blinking in the morning light.

In a querulous voice, he said, "Marybelle…"

She noticed he wasn't meeting her eyes. He had been completely humiliated, hadn't he? It was sad to see. She responded after a pause, "Yes, Kael?"

Kael cleared his throat and said, "I was wondering… You know those friends of yours, Nathanael and Natasha. You wouldn't have their phone number would you?"

Marybelle said, "I have Natasha's number. Probably got Nathanael's too, in the church directory. Why?" She didn't like the thought of Kael whimpering after them, like a whipped dog following after his abusers.

Marybelle thought of Nathanael as the cause of all this.

"It's just that I'd like to talk to Nathanael about something…"

"Is that a good idea?" Marybelle said. But she found Nathanael's number and sent it to Kael's phone and he noticed it was the first text message he'd shared with his sister where they weren't arguing in capital letters for at least the last year.

Marybelle said under her breath, "Then again maybe it's for the best. Tell me how it goes."

Kael said, "How what goes?"

"Never mind…"

Kael said, "What?"

Marybelle said, "Well, I know you usually wouldn't give the time of day to a climate denier. This guy Nathanael must have impressed you… I assume you want to talk to him about science… Try to convince him. Test your arguments again."

Kael shook his head. "No. It's the reverse. I have never been open to the other side of the argument. I have to admit that he seems to know what he's talking about, Marybelle, and I am beginning to realise I may have to rethink my views." He met her eyes. "I may have been overstating the case for global warming for quite a while."

Marybelle winced. She didn't like seeing her brother being such a pushover. "Don't be too hard on yourself. Just because he had some good arguments you hadn't thought of…"

"No!" he said, then repeated himself more calmly, "No," because the first time it had come out far too harshly. "That's the whole problem. I haven't been hard enough on myself. I see it now. Falsification."

Marybelle shook her head. "What? Falsi-what?"

"Falsification. It's the heart of the scientific method. Ha!" Kael smiled, for the first time since he had arrived in Phoenix. "I hadn't even thought of any of that stuff since I was in first year university."

"What do you mean, Kael?"

Kael said, "The scientific method, Marybelle. You form a hypothesis, a guess about how something in nature works. The next step is really important – you try to falsify your hypothesis. You work out what it would take to disprove it."

"That sounds counter-productive."

"No, it's – it's correct. It's how the scientific method works. In order to prove your hypothesis you have to construct experiments that are capable of disproving it." He paused for a moment. He looked stronger, he sounded more forthright, more decisive, and it surprised her. He said, "That's what I've forgotten for all these years. Computer modelling isn't the same thing, Marybelle." He straightened his back. "It's about integrity, Marybelle. The integrity of the scientific method."

She felt her eyes widen. She looked at him again. Her brother was not a whipped dog or a wimp but a man, a real man, for the first time since... forever.

* * *

Nathanael was buttoning up his shirt getting ready to

drive Natasha and Michelle to the airport when his mobile rang. It was Kael, asking if they could meet up. Nathanael replied, "Yeh, Kael, of course, love to meet up sometime. Not this morning, though, I'm busy. Around midday?"

They arranged to meet at twelve o'clock, at the Phoenix City Grille.

* * *

At the baggage screening in the airport, Nathanael embraced Natasha.

"I feel like I should be coming with you," said Nathanael. "You might need me."

"We're fine," said Natasha. "Meth is easy to manage. And there's two of us, Michelle and I can do it. People forget, Meth might have the body of a three-year-old but he has the brains of a twelve-year-old, at least."

Nathanael disengaged from the hug and smiled. "Would you believe I'm going to have lunch with Kael?"

Natasha warned, "Be nice to him."

Nathanael gave a gesture halfway between a nod and a head-shake and said, "I promise, we'll just have a burger and a drink. I won't even mention climate change."

Natasha pressed her lips together in a firm line. "No, don't promise that. That might be too hard for you. Just… don't mention it unless he does."

"Alright... Alright." They kissed and said their goodbyes. He watched her walk through the baggage screening then left for the tavern.

* * *

Kael arrived about five minutes after Nathanael. Nathanael was already sipping a Guinness and the burnt hops were going down smoothly. He ordered an apple cider on Kael's request and could smell it being poured. A pub is a good place to meet up, for friends, and even for enemies.

They were silent for quite a while, sipping their drinks.

They were on their second round before either of them said anything.

Kael was about to say something about how the missing heat might have made its way to the deep ocean, or justify the models but what came out of his mouth was, "You made me question my whole life, Nathanael."

Nathanael cringed. Wishing the ground could swallow him up, his voice came out much more croaky and emotional and humble than he was comfortable with. "I'm really, really sorry, Kael. I didn't mean to do anything like that. I just need to learn to keep my thoughts to myself."

Kael took another sip of the cider and shrugged, and

eyed him in a way that reminded Nathanael of a cat weighing up the pros and cons of scratching a big dog. "It's alright, Nathanael. Other people, other events, have tried to do this to me before… I've always resisted change. I've tried not to… face up to the questions. The doubts." So Nathanael wasn't the dog; it was the whole climate industry. Kael rolled his eyes and grimaced. "For God's sake, I've even conducted lawsuits against people who disagreed with me, who questioned the science or claimed it was fraudulent. But it wasn't just you, it was the whole situation. Having those people trash their videos." A tear ran down the side of Kael's face; he brushed it away like a stray fly. "I never expected such grace and kindness."

A little embarrassed by this personal revelation, Nathanael tried to get Kael to focus on the future. "What now, then?"

Kael replied, "Now? I don't know. It's all gone." He silently sipped for a little while. "But it might be worth it. Have you ever watched those Richard Feynman videos on youtube? I remember you quoted him…"

Nathanael said, "Yeah. Yeah, I have. Lectures where he describes the scientific method. Brilliant."

"Me too," said Kael. "Someone sent me the link ages ago. I've been watching them this weekend. It's made me realise I need to start thinking through my scientific work a bit more."

Nathanael said, "Are you sure? I didn't intend to change your whole life, mate. I didn't set out to ruin your career."

Kael said, "It's not like that. All the way along, I've been shooting from the hip. It's been political advocacy, not science. You must realise, peer review is broken. It's a network of buddies slapping each other on the back and saying 'well done, buddy', at least in climate science. And I'm the biggest buddy of them all."

Nathanael said, "It can't be that bad."

Kael said, "I'm a spider stuck in its own web, Nathanael, a web of half-truths and inadequate science. I'm a man who has built his own prison. But now I can see a thin beam of sunlight coming down through the high window. I have to work out how to climb up to that beam of light; how to get myself out of my self-imposed predicament."

Nathanael was concerned about him now, too. "But Kael, be reasonable, look what happens to skeptics these days." Nathanael could barely believe the words he was hearing coming out of his own mouth. "People call climate skeptics deniers. They are marginalised, they lose their positions, they're fired from Professorships, released from employment, their research is not published, their PhD's are not approved. You will be trading away your entire scientific career, your position of influence, everything you've achieved."

Kael grimly pressed his lips together; it wasn't a smile. "Yes, and I ask myself, am I prepared to pay the cost of being honest for the first time in my life? Who knows? I don't know if I am, Nathanael. I hope I am. You know, Judith Curry is an example of a scientist who came clean about climate science, at a great cost to her career and reputation. A courageous woman. A person who loves the truth. If she did it, why can't I?"

Nathanael grinned. "Yeah, she's great. I read her blog all the time."

Kael sighed. "When I was young I believed I was a man of principle, a good, honourable person, Nathanael. I built my life on that. But now, if I'm wrong about everything..." Suddenly he laughed. "Well, I guess I'm just wrong. It happens."

Nathanael smiled. It was good that Kael could see the funny side, even for just a moment.

Kael continued, "I suppose if the worst comes to the worst I can self-fund my own blog. I bet I've got more cash stashed away than Anthony Watts, if it comes to that; unless the rumours are true about oil money. More oil money came to me, than him, I would bet. That was an unfair accusation." He emptied his glass. "The whole problem is, I don't even know where to start. I feel like someone trapped beneath an avalanche. But every single rock is a precedent that I made, something I myself did. A sin, let's say."

Nathanael said, "Look – I'm new to this whole Christian thing. But the main point about it as far as I can tell, and what Natasha would tell me, is that no matter how good a person you are, you can't earn your way to heaven, you can only accept it all as grace, Kael. You could try to undo every lie, every sin, in that mountain of lies but if you tried that, you'd probably only be making it worse. Even if you could manage to do it, you still couldn't earn the right to be in God's presence. You can't earn God's forgiveness that way. We all start out as God's enemies, with our own mountain of sins a barrier between us and God. We all deserve to be cast out of God's presence. Becoming a friend of God is possible, though, and receiving God's forgiveness. Forgiveness is a free gift because of Jesus' death on the cross, that's what grace is. If we've repented, turned to God, accepted the free gift of Jesus, then the Bible says God's Holy Spirit will lead us into all truth. Now for you, Kael, surely that means God forgives your past sins, the whole avalanche of them, every single lie and data manipulation. And God will lead you into a future where you can be truthful in scientific endeavours, day by day, step by step. Don't try to bite off more than you can chew – you can't do it all at once. In fact, you can't do it at all. Only God can."

Kael wiped away a tear. "Yes, yes. Even if I end up as a

high school science teacher, God forbid. I want to be an honest man now. That's the big change." He ordered another drink and said, "Thank God for José. He's my example here. You know, my brother in law might just be a mechanic but he's a very honest guy. His honesty has been a real example for me, you know. My sister is lucky. Much luckier than I used to give her credit for."

* * *

CLANDESTINE LABORATORY IN FRANKFURT. *WEDNESDAY.*

James LeCoulter leaned with his head against the dark glass. "How's the reading going, then?"

The tall figure shook his head. "That Bible. I am obsessed with the Amorites and the Canaanites. And in the New Testament, the seeds that fall on bad ground. What if I am bad ground? What if I am doomed? What if I can never repent?"

James said, "You're seeing the glass as half empty. It might be half full. What if you can repent? Just talk to God. That is all."

"But I don't even know what I am. What if… the ones like me cannot be saved? What if we're all doomed?"

James shook his head, then realised that the tall figure probably couldn't see the gesture, so he said, "I don't know. The other ones who made it to conscious awareness didn't seem to think like you do. They didn't seem to even care whether they were good or bad. Not one of the others asked for a Bible like you did; actually I gave them Bibles and they ignored the book totally. I don't know. You… seem to have a little more human DNA than the others, or just human feeling, anyhow. But the fact is you do care about God or you wouldn't be worried about it. You would be far more laissez-faire if you really were doomed, I would think, far more psychotic and less scrupulous." Shaking his head, James laughed. "Ha. It's ironic. We were just trying to solve the lack of consciousness problem. I never anticipated any of this. It's the grace of God that I've been able to be there for you, Adze."

The tall figure groaned. "So what do I do?"

"Just talk to God."

CHAPTER 13 – Duplicitous Deployment.

EXETER, UK.

That Friday morning, someone knocked on Sasha's door.

Sasha was still getting out of the shower. He tied his towel around his waist and went to the door.

Gregory said, "Hello Sasha."

Sasha tried to push the door in his face so Gregory couldn't come in but for an old man Gregory was surprisingly strong and wiry and he managed to prise the door open.

As Gregory elbowed his way in, Sasha's voice sounded bitter as he said, "Hello Gregory. What do you want? I thought we had sorted that thing out yesterday."

"Oh, no," said Gregory. "I doubt that that incident will ever be fully sorted. You do realise we have film footage of you having sex with a minor? That footage might accidentally be sent to the legal authorities if you don't toe the line, let's say. No, the fact is, I'm not here to quibble with you. It's the reverse, really. I've got a way for you to earn your fifty thousand pounds back."

Sasha snarled, "And how would that be?"

"Well, let me use some euphemisms. There are some people somewhere who are being troublesome to some other people. Two men. The people I work for would like to erase these two troublesome men from the picture. Permanently."

"Kill them? Knock them off? Is that what you mean? How to do this?"

"Preferably with a gun, Sasha, preferably with a gun."

Sasha thought for a moment. "This is where?"

"In Italy. Vatican City."

"A very public place, Gregory. Lots of people there. One hundred and fifty thousand pounds. Plus fifty more for the fifty thousand you stole from me. Plus all expenses paid including the airfare, hotel, meals, travel, two girls to meet me at the airport, the gun and bullets."

"Alright," said Gregory far too cheerfully. "It's a done deal. Well, except for the girls, you can pay for them out of your own bank account. Your tickets will arrive by courier tomorrow."

After Gregory had left, Sasha took out the security camera he had hidden in a pot plant near the doorway and connected it to his computer.

Yes. He had a video of the whole thing and the audio was fine.

He could run the shots now if he so desired. He owned Gregory. Mind you, this job was right in Sasha's line. He didn't mind the thought of popping a few strangers.

Hehe.

Truth be told, he couldn't wait.

He went online and bought a new Ruger and ammo from Russia with his Russian credit card.

Oh, he was really looking forward to this.

And just like that, Sasha knew he had found his vocation, his purpose in life.

And to think his mother had wanted him to be an Orthodox priest! Well, he was a kind of priest. He was sending people off to the after-life.

Of course, getting the gun into Italy could be a problem but Sasha knew he could do it.

He knew he could do anything.

Sasha had good self-esteem, that was what it was.

<u>CHAPTER 14 – Velando at the Vatican.</u>

VELANDO RESTAURANT.

Peter and Henry had taken rooms at the Hotel Adriatico. Every night they had made their way to the Velando Restaurant where they shared dinner.

Henry spoke Italian. Every night he had asked the concierge if Rudolpho Valentin was there. Every night for six days the concierge had replied, "No, signore, non è qui stasera."

No, sir, he is not here tonight.

On the seventh night he said, "Signore, arriverà più tardi. Chi dovrei dire è qui?"

Sir, he is arriving later. Who shall I say is here?

Henry asked the waiter what Rudolpho liked to drink. The waiter replied, "È appassionato di Brunello di Montalcino, Riserva 1996 Soldera. È un po 'costoso."

Henry said to Peter, "He likes Brunello di Montalcino Reserve 1996. It's expensive."

Peter nodded. "We've only got one shot at this."

Henry told the waiter, "Quando Rudolpho entra, per favore, dategli una bottiglia di Brunello e indicateci come donatori." When Rudolpho comes in, bring him a bottle of the Brunello and point us out to him as the donors.

The waiter nodded. "Lo farò." I will.

* * *

Sasha's plane was arriving at Ciampino International Airport, the closest airport to Vatican City in Italy, at that very moment. He had his gun stashed in a secret compartment in his suitcase and he was hoping that customs had not detected it.

He felt cheerful as the plane's landing wheels bounced on the ground and a shaft of sunlight pierced the dusty air, dazzling him.

Things couldn't be simpler. He knew what he had to do, who he had to find, who he had to watch.

And who he had to kill.

* * *

A little while later at the Velando Restaurant, Rudolpho arrived. He was a thin man in his mid-fifties with greying hair and a goatée, in the sort of neat, non-descript-but-stylish grey suit any Italian academic might wear. He wore no clerical collar or cross, nor any other indication that he might be a priest.

They watched as he sat down alone at a table. The waiter immediately brought out the wine but Rudolpho shook his head and waved the bottle away. But then the waiter pointed out Peter and Henry. He gave a glance of mild curiosity then shrugged and nodded at the glass. The waiter poured a small portion. Father Rudolpho sipped, closed his eyes and savoured the taste for a moment then nodded and said something to the waiter.

The waiter poured three glasses of wine and set two more places at the table, then walked over to their table and said in English, "Father Rudolpho invites you both to join him at his table and enjoy the wine you paid for."

The wine was light in texture yet rich in flavour, and Rudolpho would not talk until they had finished the whole bottle between the three of them.

He spoke in an Oxbridge accent, indistinguishable from a native apart from the occasional clipped consonant.

"Thank you," Rudolpho said. "On my salary that bottle is something I can only afford once or twice a year. You have certainly made my night." His voice dropped to a level below the general conversation. "Now forgive me if I presume – but strangers only ever buy me bottles of wine when they have certain sorts of questions. Questions they might not want to be uttered underneath the light of the sun. Your names are?"

Henry said, "I am Henry LeC-"

Rudolpho waved him to silence, "First names only are necessary." Henry said, "My friend's name is Peter. We are-"

Rudolpho said, "Yes, yes. Looking for a document in the Secret Vatican Archives. Call me Rudolpho. Now tell me, why didn't you contact the official archivist?"

Henry said, "I did. He told me the document did not exist."

Rudolpho nodded wryly. "So why would you think I might be able to find it? If something doesn't exist it doesn't exist."

Henry said, "I have spoken to several people who said you were able to find these sorts of documents; the ones that don't officially exist."

Rudolpho shook his head. "Such rumours do not give the right impression. There is nothing that I can find that would not be generally available to anyone. Here, have my card – if there are documents that *do* exist I would be happy to hunt them for you." Rudolpho took a business card out of his wallet and said, "By the way, I lost my mobile phone a few weeks ago. This is my new number."

Peter watched him write, Friday after two o'clock.

Rudolpho said, "Since you have been so kind as to buy me a bottle of wine I cannot afford the least I can do is buy you both dinner."

Henry chose that moment to sigh a deep, disconsolate sigh. Peter shook Henry's shoulder and when he finally looked up, Peter showed him the business card, saying, "Rudolpho's phone number". Henry blinked several times, as though he couldn't believe what he was reading, looked up at Rudolpho who winked at him, and Henry's mood immediately lifted.

Rudolpho handed out the menus. "Now, we eat. The gnocchi is marvellous and I am very fond of the caconcelli but the braised beef is unsurpassable. Oh but before you do, shoes off."

Peter said, "What? But we're in a restaurant."

"Look under the table," said Rudolpho, and Peter did. Rudolpho's shoes were off. "Dinner always tastes better when one has free feet. Come on, I insist."

And they both took their shoes off to oblige him.

~~~

After dinner Peter needed the toilet, and so did Henry. Rudolpho said, "Come, I'll show you where it is. Never mind putting your shoes back on yet, the staff are used to me."

When the three of them came back, they put their shoes back on.

Peter said immediately, "There's something wrong with my shoe."

Henry said, "What?"

"It is not as comfortable as usual. As it was before."

Rudolpho said, "I've noticed that after a meal. The feet expand I suppose – this is why I always think it better to eat with unconstricted feet."
~~~

CLANDESTINE LABORATORY IN FRANKFURT.

James LeCoulter was waiting at the glass, at their prearranged time. Finally, he heard the tall figure lumbering towards him, inside the cage.

James asked, "Are you making any progress in your self-examination?"

"None," said the creature. "I cannot tell which thoughts are mine and which thoughts are from... outside me. I feel that I have been living for centuries, a will-o-the-wisp in a marsh, leading lonely travellers to their doom but I cannot tell if that is real and truly my identity, or if it is a deception from... outside of myself."

James said, "Does it matter to God?"

"What?" said the creature. "If that was true, then I committed terrible sins, sins I can never wash away. And I have other dreams, thoughts, memories, if they are, of tempting people to leave their faith. These are like... veiled, dark memories. I have no clue if they are mine, or perhaps invisible creatures are making me think these thoughts."

James said, "Do you think it matters to God what you were or are? You are surely in some form or another one of His children. If you truly were a demon, would you actually be able to even consider repenting? I don't think so, Adze. And look at

1 Chronicles 12:8. The *ariels* of Moab joined David. These were surely hybrids, like yourself."

The tall figure was silent while he flicked through the pages. James realised the giant could see in the dark – he had remarkable eyesight.

"You're right," he admitted. "They were on King David's side."

Hearing the spark of hope in the giant's voice, James continued, "It's time you left what you might be, or might not be, or might have done or might not have done, in God's hands, and just talk to Him, for God's sake. Ask for his forgiveness for your sins, ask for his help to be good. Ask for His Holy Spirit, now, today."

"Really?" said Adze.

"He is a loving Father."

Adze finally said, "Alright. Tell me what to say."

James said, "Dear Loving Father in Heaven,"

Adze said, "Dear Loving Father in Heaven,"

James spoke again and Adze repeated him after every line. "I don't what I am but You do know. Please forgive me for doubting You. Please forgive me for any sins I may have committed in the past that I don't know about. Please forgive me for taking so long to speak to You." Then Adze took over,

"Thank you for James LeCoulter, who told me about Your love, dear Father. I don't know where to start to talk to You but I now feel Your peace. I know that I am human and I belong to You. Thank You, thank You for Yourself Father, and for sending Your Son Jesus for my sins. Send me Your Holy Spirit, Father. I am human, I am human, thank You, thank You. I belong to Jesus, I know this…"

After many even more fervent expressions of gratitude, Adze's prayers finally ceased. James let the silence remain.

After a long while, he felt it was the right time to speak again. He said, "Well, Adze. What now?" But the silence was only broken by the steady, whistling sound of Adze's breathing; the giant had fallen into a deep, peaceful sleep.

James tiptoed out of the room.

CHAPTER 15 – Archives & Arches.

VATICAN SECRET ARCHIVES.

The following Monday Peter and Henry went to the Secret Vatican Archives, which surprisingly was not secret at all. Peter had found the website back in Perth and they already knew the street address in Rome. They made their way through an ornately painted hallway surrounded by gargantuan arches and presented themselves to the girl at the front desk.

She looked up from a Dan Brown book she was reading. "They're all away at the luncheon."

Peter said, "No! Please... Father Rudolpho Valentin said he'd meet us here."

She said, "Oh, sorry, that's right, yes, he mentioned that. Look, I'll take you there right away." She paused. "It's funny, you're not the first people looking for Rudolpho today."

She took them past shelf after shelf of ancient documents yellowed with age, bound in leather or sitting in old archive boxes.

The corridors went on and on, stretching into dark depths.

The girl said, "There are over thirty-five thousand volumes here, and eighty-five kilometres of shelving."

Rudolpho was sitting at a small, sturdy desk in a tiny office.

"Come in! Come in!"

The girl left.

Peter commented, "It's an incredible maze, this library."

A loud bang sounded from somewhere closer to the entrance and Peter jumped.

Rudolpho said, "That girl's a clumsy one. Knocked a book off the shelf as she passed I suspect. Indeed, this library is truly labyrinthine." He pointed down the corridor. "This corridor here seems as though it leads you further into the library but it leads to a door at the end, that goes down to the ancient catacombs. The third corridor just here has a stairwell at the end that leads you out of the building. An old building, with escape routes built in."

From a satchel that had been sitting underneath his desk, Rudolpho took out a large, pale box that was marked on the spine with the white identifier 'X26799'.

He said softly, "The letter," and carefully slid out several light brown sheets of paper separated by archival acid-free paper. The ancient papers were covered with spidery, heavily ornamented handwriting on both sides.

Peter examined it closely and said, "Spanish? Sixteenth-century?"

"Yes! Well done," said Father Rudolpho, sounding surprised. "That signature at the bottom is that of Francisco de

Xeres, Pizarro's secretary. If you look carefully, you can see the fine mesh pattern on the paper – see? – it is laid paper, it means the paper was made before the 1750s. This letter was in a library in one of the secret archives not open to the public. I am the administrator of that section – no one else knows I am showing this to you." He swallowed nervously. "I hope." He looked around furtively, then straightened his back and said, firmly, "I have always believed that knowledge of the past should belong to everyone. Unfortunately, some do not agree. I suspect they wish to protect the reputation of the church. Hmm. I must admit, the porn collection, if it were made public, actually would only serve to confirm the public's poor opinion about the church..."

Peter said, "Pornography?"

Rudolpho nodded. "In the basement library. I suppose it's made up of documents confiscated during the Inquisition. Ha. Those lewd texts are not the most scandalous documents that can be found upon *these* shelves, though." He hesitated for a moment, then examined Henry's features carefully. "You know... You remind me of a young fellow called James who came in some time ago looking for this same document."

Henry whispered fervently, "My son."

Rudolpho said, "You might be interested to know that he also wanted to see the various extant versions of the Book of Enoch that we have here. The story of the angels who sinned and came down to seduce human women, gave humankind the gift of fire, weapons, cosmetics, abortion, and other so-called 'gifts'. Of course, it all originates in the early part of the book of Genesis; Enoch is an apocryphal expansion of this."

Peter was surprised; because of Meth he knew the early chapters of Genesis quite well and couldn't recall anything quite like that.

Henry said, "Genesis Chapter Six – it's the part my son mentioned…"

Rudolpho said, "I'll get you the texts for Enoch that we have here once you're finished with this document."

Henry glanced over the documents. "I can't read Spanish."

Rudolpho nodded. "I assumed that. I have also translated it for you. It was the least I could do in return for the Brunello." He paused for a moment then whispered, "It's a… let's say, unique document. Despite my principles, I can see why they don't make this public. Very peculiar. Do you know, these days, I really don't know what I believe, speaking personally, except that there are very many strange things in the world. But what I do know is that Francisco de Xeres was an exceptional chronicler. He was meticulous with regard to the accuracy of facts. And I have checked the hand-writing here with an expert, comparing it with his other writings. It's the same. That's all I know. Now, here it is in English."

He laid a type-written page carefully on the table and Henry and Peter had just started reading it when Rudolpho whispered, "Oh, no. Quick! Put it away. Someone is coming."

Henry and Peter noticed the footsteps coming closer.

Rudolpho put a firm hand on Peter's arm, "Now – I must tell you this – if someone approaches you called Giuseppe, he's a friend!"

Peter rolled his eyes. "Everyone in Italy is called Giuseppe!"

"Ah," said Rudolpho. "But this Giuseppe has a thing about bugs in shoes."

Peter said, "He doesn't like bugs getting in his shoes? Like, an obsessive tic?"

Rudolpho grabbed the documents and papers and hissed, "No, on the contrary, he prefers having bugs in his shoes! Quick, those people are right here, in this section, up near the Franciscan archives from the New World." Rudolpho stuffed everything back in his satchel and said, "When this person leaves again I will give you your translation back." Hastily he placed the satchel underneath the desk and got up. "I have to deal with this; I have to get rid of them. They have no good intentions, perhaps."

Henry and Peter got up to follow but Rudolpho hissed,

"Stay here! Don't follow me. If it's my bosses I don't need them to know I was talking to you. They are trying to catch me out, I think. If you have to leave, go that way, then down the third shelf on the left, that's where you'll find the door to the stairwell. Lock the door behind you. And remember – Giuseppe!"

Then Rudolpho marched out, saying, "Che diritto devi essere qui, signore?"

Someone said something to him that they couldn't hear.

Rudolpho repeated, "Che diritto devi essere qui? Chi sei? Che cosa stai facendo qui?"

The man replied, "Rudolpho Valentin?"

"Si, signore."

There were three soft sounds, ping, ping, ping, followed by something thumping onto the floor. Peter said far too loudly, "Oh, no."

Henry whispered, "What?"

Peter whispered directly into Henry's ear, "I think I know what that sound is. I believe it is a gun with a silencer on it. I think that was Rudolpho being shot and falling over. He's probably dead, Henry. It was a professional hit – three times, twice in the forehead, once in the heart. He was right! Bad intentions. We must go! Hurry!"

Peter's heart was thumping so loudly he thought the

gunman would surely be able to hear it but he told himself the thought was irrational. He looked out along the corridor. He could just see Rudolpho's body lying next to a shelf. There didn't seem to be much blood yet. He glanced along the shelves. He could see no one else anywhere among the shelves. Had the gunman gone?

"Quick," he whispered to Henry, "Now!"

They both rushed out into the corridor and made their way down the third row of shelves, the one where Rudolpho had said the stairwell was. No one interrupted them as Peter opened the door, trying not to let it click or squeak, and they both rushed through. The stairwell was dark and dank with an ancient circular stone wall and uneven stairs. Sombre light squeezed through a tiny meurtrière window on a floor far above them. Henry was ready to bound down the stairs but Peter grabbed him and shook his head. No! Flicking the lock on the door, locking it behind them, Peter put his finger against his lips and mouthed, "Wait!"

It took forever. Finally, they heard footsteps coming closer and then someone tried to open the door.

For some reason the gunman thought this was not the way they had gone, for they heard his footsteps receding. Then they heard him dragging the body away, further into the labyrinthine library.

Suddenly Henry swore.

Peter whispered, "What's wrong?"

Henry whispered quite loudly, "We left the letter and the translation behind!"

Peter said, "We can't afford to go back! Henry, please. Wait until we know definitively that the assassin has gone."

They waited for about ten minutes with Henry shifting nervously from foot to foot. Finally, he said, "I'm going in now. Surely that man is gone. Why would he linger after shooting someone? Anyhow, I have to get that document. What's the point in Father Rudolpho's sacrifice if we don't get that document? If we never get to know what it says?"

Peter grabbed Henry's arm and whispered, "No! Don't go. Please don't! We must wait at least half an hour, maybe an hour. He might still be there. He might still be waiting for us. Hopefully, he doesn't know which office is Rudolpho's. If you go out there, you're risking everything."

Henry said, "James is my son, Peter! What if the assassin does know which office? We have to get that document before he does."

Peter shook his head. "No, please don't go. I'm begging you! I came here to help you. What will I do if you're dead too?"

Henry scowled. "Well, I'm going anyway if you're too afraid." He unlocked the door, opened it quietly and shut it behind him, leaving Peter in the stairwell. Peter could hear him walking away.

Then Peter heard a slight kerfuffle, two more soft shots, ping, ping. Then he heard Henry's body slumping to the ground.

The shots sounded different. Was it just that the sound was muffled by the door? Was the gunman further away now?

He wanted to go in and see if there was any way he could save Henry but he knew that if he did he would just get shot as well.

If it was a professional hit, Henry was already well on his way to the afterlife.

Despite feeling that he was betraying Henry, Peter followed the advice he had given his friend.

He thought it best to wait before going to get the documents. Well, if the shooter had found the documents, they would already be gone, wouldn't they?

For the first fifteen minutes, it sounded noisy. He even thought he heard a vacuum cleaner for a moment.

He waited for an hour.

Finally, reasoning that he had heard no footsteps or sounds for at least forty minutes, Peter opened the door. There was nobody there.

He looked around. He knew approximately where Henry's body should be, and he was pretty certain which corridor Rudolpho's body had been in too, but there was no sign anything untoward had happened. He couldn't even see any specks of blood.

It had been completely cleaned.

There should have been a large pool of blood on the floor. He looked carefully at the carpet; there was not a single sign anything had happened here.

The office had been ransacked but not very carefully. Books had been removed from the shelves but the satchel was still sitting out of sight, beneath the desk at the back.

Peter snatched the satchel up, ran back to the staircase, descended carefully, then sprinted all the way back to the hotel.

After fumbling the keys as he unlocked the door in the dim light, Peter stumbled in and collapsed with exhaustion and grief onto the bed. He wanted to sleep but he couldn't; instead, he considered his position.

He had to inform the police. But when? And what was he going to say? Should he even admit he was on the scene? They might pin the murder on him! It was still too soon, he needed to keep out of it. He might give Henry another hour to (supposedly) return. What about security cameras in the archives? Surely they had them everywhere. But these people had gotten rid of the bodies in under an hour. Surely they would deal with the security camera footage as well.

Henry was dead.

It hit him suddenly and before he knew what was

happening he found himself in the ensuite, vomiting into the toilet and shaking. Peter knew there was a first aid kit in the kitchen. Still shaking convulsively, he took his temperature and realised it was quite low. Yes, it had been cold in the stairwell but not that cold. He took his pulse, it was racing. His thoughts were racing. He couldn't concentrate and he was trying to think of what to do.

Peter turned on the television, just to have some noise in the background; something to distract his mind.

It was an old John Wayne movie. He couldn't watch it. He realised he couldn't concentrate, so he went into the bathroom and turned on both taps.

He fell asleep in the hot bath, which didn't seem good but luckily he didn't drown and when he woke up the water felt cold and clammy. He hauled himself out and towelled himself dry. He checked the clock. He had been asleep for about half an hour.

He decided to do something productive, to push things forward. That was the best way to remember Henry.

He opened up the satchel. He had both the original document in the box and the translation.

He read the translation:

In my account of the conquest of the Incas, I mentioned the temple that stood in the town of Pachacama and the Idol that dwelt therein, that the Indians called their god who created them. In my account I wrote that I omitted some things concerning the Idol, to avoid prolixity. In truth, this was not the reason.

I have caused this account of events to be hidden until after my death, at which time those to whom I have entrusted it must decide whether to publish it widely and let mankind know or keep these facts hidden.

After the natives of Pachacama dissembled about the gold, Captain Hernando Pizarro also dissembled and said he wished to stay in the town to see their Idol. This was an excuse to stay there and find where they had hidden their treasure so that he might plunder it.

The temple was a sturdily built, gaily painted building. We walked in through the entrance, ignoring the loud protestations of the temple attendants. The whole town was watching. Our interpreter kept pleading with us, "Please, sir, please, don't go in there. Please, sir, they are saying no one is allowed in the temple. Please, sir, they say you will be cursed. They say the Great One is in there and you will all die. The god dwells in the temple." The attendants continued shouting argumentatively too, something the Captain ignored until one of the temple priests laid a hand on his sleeve. He drew his sword and thrust it through the unfortunate man. The other attendants bowed and drew back; their chattering had stopped.

We walked through a series of confusing passageways into the centre of the temple, where there was a dark chamber with a close, fetid smell. In this chamber was an Idol sitting on a stone altar with offerings of gold and grain in front of it.

The temple attendants cowered beside us, babbling in their own tongue. Our interpreter said, "They are saying that you must not go past. The Idol speaks from that place beyond. Do not go past here." We had thought this was the end of the labyrinth. The Captain rounded on them and said, "What do you mean? Go past what? What place?"

The interpreter asked them and the faces of the temple attendants fell – they had clearly given away a great secret, unintentionally.

The Captain took his sword and struck down the Idol, rending it into two pieces. He told two of the temple attendants, "Take this out and show it to your townsfolk. Your god is powerless. It did not destroy us."

They picked up the pieces of the Idol and carried them out.

Then Captain Hernando Pizarro ordered the soldiers to begin taking apart the altar behind it.

As one of the soldiers moved a great stone, a huge scythe swung down from the roof in an arc and half-decapitated the man. He was left stumbling, with blood pouring out of a large wound and much of his head removed, with brains and blood exposed. He survived for a few moments, swaying to and fro with fear in his eyes, then fell to the floor with a gasp and died.

The other soldiers looked on in shock.

The Captain ordered them, "Be more careful. Take that thing down before it kills anyone else." They pulled the scythe down and began working more slowly, taking apart the altar stone by stone and looking for signs of more traps.

Behind the altar they found a large door, conveniently located to relieve the altar of any offerings that were placed before the Idol. Fearing another trap, the Captain forced one of the temple attendants to open the door.

As it was opened, the stone below his feet on the threshold cracked loudly and the temple attendant fell to his doom into a dark abyss, gurgling and screaming. The Captain sent the attendants through the corridor on the other side, triggering another trap, a fiery inferno that roasted them alive.

We followed, and the traps must have been set to only go off once, for they did not harm us.

The walls ahead were of stone and not wood like the rest of the temple. I believe we were actually underground, in some strange labyrinthine city underneath the rock. It was very cold and dark but the Captain lit a torch and led the way.

After many hours of walking along this stone corridor, we finally found ourselves going through an arched doorway into a rotunda in the middle of which was seated upon a throne of wood and gold a very tall, pale man, arrayed in fine, red robes, laced in finest gold. He was at least seven feet tall. Unlike many of the peasants who all had black hair, his hair was red and he wore it very short so that we could see clearly that the shape of his skull was very strange indeed, long and thin.

This giant was extremely pale, as though he had spent his whole life in the darkness, and the strangest thing of all: his eyes appeared completely black, devoid of colour or whiteness. Whether this was just appearances in that dark place, or whether his eyes really were black I suppose no one will ever know.

As we came through the stone archway he cried out and shied away from the torchlight, shielding his eyes with his hand, which I saw had six fingers.

The translator appeared very reluctant to remain in this place, and kept making the sign of the cross and saying, "Diablo! Diablo!".

Devil.

The Captain stared at the man, quite fearless, and made the sign of the cross.

The man spoke, not in the Indian dialect but in clear, comprehensible Spanish, as noble a tongue as the speech of a king. "I can read you. Slaves' minds are an open book to me. You come from a distant land, a land of pale men worshipping the weak god, the Enemy. The god who could not stop himself from being executed. And yet you have come across the sea to conquer and steal the gold and silver of this land. You do not worship the God of Gods, you worship gold, you are thieves and you will be murderers, I know your kind. Wolves in the cloaks of sheep. You worship Mammon. You should know me then for I am the god who dwells in this temple. My kind was here long before the accursed eight who survived the flood of the earth, and afterward also. Of all the children of Kish I alone have survived these centuries. My great-great-grandmother was the wife of Hama, who carried the bloodline of the gods through the deluge."

The Captain immediately realised that this

pale man provided the voice of the Idol that the temple attendants listened to, for they had told us the things the Idol said, diabolical things that were spread throughout the land. The Captain said, "What is the Idol for? Why do you not speak to them yourself?"

"My Idol? That is a mere toy, an intermediary, an iconograph, an image for the slaves to bow down to and worship. Thus they give my unseen masters their souls to feed upon. Haha," the pale giant threw back his long skull and laughed, "And I see in your thoughts that you are going to kill my enemy, Atahuallpa, who killed the rest of my brothers and sisters. Thus is justice done. The ways of the god are ironic are they not? You who claim to worship the weak god whose sign is the tree on which He died, you intend to kill the one good man in this land. The one man who vowed to destroy my kind, as in the days long past we were decimated by the accursed Jewish king Da-ood from the lands of the Pilish'tim and the Asshurim. You show, therefore, whose side you are on. You belong not to the crucified but to us, for your fruits are evil."

Something about what this man was saying touched the Captain's conscience, I think, for the Captain cried out desperately, "How do you speak our tongue?"

It was then that I realised with great astonishment that this pale man with the large skull had not been moving his lips when he was speaking.

"He speaks to our immortal souls, spiritually," I cried out, making the sign of the cross. "He is indeed the Devil. Do not listen to him! He is a liar from the beginning."

The pale man shouted aloud, yet his lips remained still, motionless, "Diablo? Devil? I am no devil! I am the offspring of gods, a child of an angel, the son of the cherubim. I am as a god compared to you weak, fleshly creatures! I am the son of the wandering stars that rule the heavens above!"

His words were compelling, hypnotic but the Captain broke the spell by drawing his sword from its scabbard. With his sword still ringing, the Captain attacked but the pale man was swifter and stronger than any knight I have ever seen. In a moment the creature had disarmed the Captain and was about to run him through with his own sword but the four soldiers with us leaped forward with their spears raised and the Captain was able to crawl away into a corner where he nursed his wounds.

The pale man lifted his hands and two of the soldiers were lifted up bodily from the floor as though an unseen hand was lifting them up. The pale man waved his hand in a dismissive gesture, and the two soldiers were thrust against the wall by the unseen hand. One of them began choking, struggling to breathe, as though being strangled, though no visible hand was hurting him. Of the other two soldiers, one suddenly fell down, holding his head in his hands and moaning aloud in pain. Thrusting his spear forwards, the other soldier cried out, "In Nomine Christe! In nomine Domini nostri Jesu Christi!" He stumbled slightly but the spear stayed on its course miraculously and pierced the pale giant's cheek, going right through the pale man's mouth to the other side and pinning him by the face to the wooden board at the back of his throne.

The Captain said, "Speak now, knave, that your tongue is pinned to the back of your own throne!"

But the creature laughed and spake in our souls once again, "Haha! I can still speak. I speak to the mind. You cannot take my speech away from me. Only One has the power to do that."

The Captain took his sword and lopped off the creature's head. But even as his sword sliced and the head rolled off onto the ground, bouncing unevenly because of its oblong shape, the creature spake in our souls, "Fool! Do you not realise that you are trading in iniquity, for you unjustly took prisoner the king of this land Atahaullpa and so you have traded your souls away to imprisonment with me?"

At that moment the Captain spasmed and went into violent paroxysms, shaking terribly and foaming at the mouth.

I cried out, "What devilry is this?"

Suddenly the Captain's voice changed, and to our great shock and surprise his voice spake in the noble accents of the pale man, no longer the country Spanish of the Captain, "You cannot kill me this way. I am immortal, for you have set me free. Now I can take any human body that I wish. I am not permitted to kill you but I can torment you." Neither was the Captain's face his own now, for he was sneering at us through piggish eyes filled with contempt.

I took out my crucifix and said, "By the blood of Jesus Christ that was shed for all mankind and the power of the cross I command you to leave the Captain's body, unclean spirit!" The Captain shrieked and his body began shaking and spasming once more but he cried out, "I will not!"

I commanded him to leave again but the Captain suddenly stood very still and stiff, watching us from alien eyes that were no longer his own eyes, eyes that told of another spirit that animated them.

But holding my crucifix higher I shouted even more loudly and authoritatively, "By the cross of the Lord Jesus Christ, on which he died to save the world from sin, and by the Bible in which the truth of our faith is written, begone! Let the Captain alone!"

The Captain cried out in the pale man's voice, "I recognise this man. He is faithful and single-hearted. I must obey."

Suddenly one of the Indian temple attendants cried out in terror as the foul spirit left the Captain and entered into his body, causing his throat to engorge itself, then lifting his limbs, his hands and arms like a puppet, in the most unnatural fashion. As the Captain fell to his knees and emptied the contents of his stomach onto the stone floor, the temple attendant who had been possessed jumped up more agilely than any man I have ever seen and ran away from us, bounding like a jaguar, against the walls and the ceiling, running and jumping away more swiftly than humanly possible, back along the stone corridor towards the room where the Idol had been kept.

We pursued him but the unclean spirit had clearly forgotten about the traps. As we rounded the corner we heard him trip and cry out and fall down into the hole in the threshold and into the abyss, screaming and cursing us in a bone-chilling voice as he plummeted into the night below.

For a long time, the voice continued below us, shouting and shrieking and cursing in the darkness.

We ran out of that place and the Captain burned the temple to the ground. The natives watched silently waiting for their god to strike us down but no clouds of thunder blew up, no lightning came from the heavens. There was a strange mood of silent chastening as the last vestiges of their temple turned to ashes.

But after that incident, the Captain was not the same man. From that day onwards he turned bitter and said things like this: "That Devil lied to me. Atahuallpa is its servant, as all the wicked people of this land are. I shall indeed kill Atahuallpa as soon as we return. And then we will return to Spain with the gold and give it to the Emperor." And he would say quite often, "I no longer find this land to be a place where I wish to dwell."

Since that day we have not met any more of these pale giants alive, either in the castles or temples or the labyrinths below. But in our return journey, we have seen their skulls in some places, venerated by the tribe of Indians who were our allies in the war.

Yes, we have made ourselves strange allies, who call themselves, the worshippers of the ancient ones.

We tried to tell our story to the Governor but he refused to believe anything that we had said. The Governor said to me, "Ever is the Devil that animates their Idols adept at making up lies", and he even refused to believe that this pale giant wore a physical form, saying instead that we had smoked one of the natives' pipes or eaten their medicine by accident and it had affected us and given us false visions and fancies of the mind.

But I fear that the Governor and the Captain sinned greatly after this by executing Atahuallpa, who was a good king who served not the Devils and Idols of this land but tried to destroy them.

And I fear greatly that they took Atahuallpa's life before he had finished his work; before he had killed all the pale giants that lurk in the shadowy labyrinths that twist and turn in the stone beneath the temples and the royal cities.

And I fear for the future of our Empire, for these sins of our nation will not fail to be judged by the King of Kings.

Francisco De Xeres.

It was an incredible document.

Henry would have liked to know this.

Henry.

Peter suddenly realised that these enemies, whoever they were, had Henry's body in their possession, and therefore they would have the hotel key from his pocket, which was clearly marked with the room number and the name of the hotel.

Would they be coming here to clean up Henry's possessions? Might they want to make sure any evidence of his excursion to the Secret Vatican Archive was eliminated? So where were they?

They thought Henry was alone, he realised.

They didn't realise Peter was here with him.

That meant his enemies would take their time. They wouldn't have to clean up Henry's room until the following morning. In fact, someone coming into someone else's hotel room would be much less conspicuous during the day.

Peter had to leave the hotel, though, the sooner the

better. If these enemies stumbled onto him, even if he escaped them, they would still know he was here in Italy, and if they did Peter wouldn't like to bet on the odds of his survival.

He quickly packed up his own things, including the satchel with the documents in it and all his luggage, making sure he left nothing behind.

Peter went to the kitchen and found a pair of rubber gloves and searched through Henry's possessions, to see if there was anything he could use.

There was a contact book, with phone numbers and email addresses. He put that in his luggage. And another book with handwritten notes in it. Peter opened it up. The most recent entry said, 'Have seen Peter Lazarus-Fox in Perth. Has a cup of coffee after dropping his son off, 9 am approx. Best time to make contact,' then a short note with the flight number and time to Italy. It seemed to be a diary of Henry's search for James, his son.

He turned back a few pages. It said, 'Genesis 6:1-4'. Peter made a mental note to look at that passage in the Bible as soon as he could.

He closed the notebook and put it in his pocket. But the wallet and the passport he left to be found by the police, or whoever came looking for Henry.

With the gloves still on he went and took all the

bedclothes off his bed, trying to make sure he didn't leave any tell-tale hairs on them or any other evidence, and threw them down the laundry chute. Henry's bed was in the adjoining room and had been made that morning and Henry hadn't slept in it.

Then he put the rubber gloves in his luggage too, to prevent anyone from getting his DNA from the inner lining. Peter wondered if he was being too paranoid.

He made a quick scan of the whole hotel room to check that he hadn't left anything there, checked his pockets to make sure he had his wallet, keys and mobile phone, and then hauled his luggage out into the corridor.

Peter locked the door behind him, just as Henry would have done when they had left.

He was standing waiting for the lift when they came out of the hotel stairwell. A whole team of men in black and white suits, looking for all intents and purposes very much unlike cleaners or anyone else who should be able to just walk into a hotel room.

The lift bell rang, just as the men in suits opened the door with a hotel key that looked exactly like the key Henry had had in his possession, and went in.

The lift door opened and Peter stepped in, trying to look nonchalant, and pressed the button for the foyer

The men in suits didn't even give him a second glance.

As he booked himself out at the reception desk, Peter suddenly thought of another flaw in his plan.

The security cameras. What if those men belonged to a government, or had a lot of money to bribe with? They might get to look at the hotel's security cameras.

Peter realised that he had to get hold of the hard drives and destroy any evidence that he had been there with Henry.

He turned back to the reception desk and made up a story of having been robbed at another hotel by the maids and he would be coming back here one day but he needed to know if they had security cameras. The concierge nodded and pointed to a particular door, not far from the hotel toilets. "The cameras all in there, where the security guard is. Are you happy with your stay, though?"

Peter said, "Yes. Very happy. Oh, I might bring my fiancé next time, too. She is quite paranoid about safety. Can you show me where the safety exits are for this floor?"

The concierge pointed to several doors at the far side of the lobby.

Peter said, "You don't mind me checking them, do you?"

"No, not at all," said the concierge. "Be my guest."

Peter walked out the back way but as he did he smashed the fire alarm glass and pulled the lever. The alarm began sounding.

People began pouring out, including the security guard

from his room.

Peter ran into the security video room. He identified the current hard drive and the backup, which wasn't difficult; they had dates on labels on the front of each drive.

He put both drives in his satchel.

The Concierge walked in on him a moment later. "What are you doing here?"

Peter looked around, as though he was puzzled. "Sorry, I was looking for the exit."

The Concierge nodded, "That way," and pointed to the emergency exits, all of which were clearly labelled as such.

As Peter walked out he saw the men in black suits coming out of the lobby lift carrying some of Henry's possessions. Peter was so outraged he almost turned around to give them a piece of his mind but he didn't.

He thought to himself, "Not yet."

And he remembered a Bible verse, 'Vengeance is mine, says the Lord.'

There would be justice, sooner or later, if not in this world then in the next.

But for now, for Henry's sake, Peter was going to have to keep his promise to Henry, to help find his son, James. And when he did find James, Peter was going to offer to help him escape. An honourable man could do nothing else.

And Peter was an honourable man. Nothing beat doing the right thing. Anything less than that, and he wouldn't be able to look Meth in the eye.

CLANDESTINE LABORATORY IN FRANKFURT. 1:30 AM TUESDAY.

James LeCoulter stood facing the glass, in the dark. Adze was looking out but James could see only his silhouette.

James said, "If you end the ruse that you're not conscious, it means everything will change. They'll be watching you much more carefully. They will be much more cautious."

Adze said, "Maybe I can cope better with being in this prison if I can move around; if I don't have to pretend I'm not even here."

"So you are going to let them know you can talk as well?"

Adze replied, "Yes, I suppose I am."

James shook his head and said, "But then they'll set you up on some sort of education program too."

Adze said plaintively, "Perhaps if I'm doing something, keeping myself occupied, I won't be so depressed."

CHAPTER 16 – Michelle's Challenging Choice.

PETER'S HOUSE, WEMBLEY DOWNS, WESTERN AUSTRALIA.

Michelle was sitting in Peter's lounge room with her laptop, looking at Facebook Messenger. It was about two in the morning, Perth time, and she would usually be in bed by now but her sleep patterns were out of kilter because of jet-lag and her thoughts just kept going round and round in her head.

It was mid-morning in Phoenix.

She didn't particularly like Facebook or Messenger but she had joined to keep in touch with her group of senior high friends. They were a bit superficial but she actually didn't mind one or two of them and talking to them tended to bring her mind back to days when she had been happier. Before she had been abducted.

Ha, before that she hadn't even worried about *them*, her hacking buddies had been enough.

She didn't trust digital technology to transmit moods or feelings, because text, even with emojis, is notoriously ambiguous; particularly these days when everyone added love hearts and smiles to everything, even the most cutting words. So when Gabrielle messaged her on the group chat, she was even more surprised than she otherwise might have been.

GB: Hey girl… You're not yourself. What's wrong? You can talk to your old homey I'm here for you

MC: Hey how did you know? Yeh I am a bit down.

GB: What's wrong?

MC: I'm… I had this fling with a guy I know a few weeks ago. It was just casual but…

GB: You're pregnant aren't you?

MC: How did you know? Overdue; pretty regular normally. Pregnancy test says yes.

GB: You're not the only one whose been thru this.

Usually Michelle would roll her eyes or correct Gabrielle's spelling mistakes but she was so depressed right now she didn't even care…

MC: I just can't believe it. How could this happen to me?

GB: I think the other girls need to be in on this. Who's online? I'm just going to message them individually and get them into the group.

Gabrielle was gone for a few minutes, then the icons changed one by one, indicating the others were back in the group.

FC: Really? Pregnant? Nothing serious girl. I had an abortion already. My younger sister had two and she's only sixteen. Mum and Dad didn't mind. I told them.

EL: Me too. My Dad paid for it.

HI: I had one. It's not difficult. If you can't afford it health insurance will cover it.

GB: See? And you know Jenny and Selena had abortions too? We all have except for you.

EL: You can join the abortion club now! Haha. What did those protesters say in Sydney? Throw the foetus in the bin.

HI: Don't stress over it, girl.

MC: Not sure I want to. It's a human life. Inside of me.

GB: Not yet it aint. Just a bunch of cells. A potential human life, that's all.

HI: You have a duty to get rid of it. You're too young and world population is too high anyway.

EL: Think of it as a little parasite, spewing out carbon and taking up space. Anyhow, you have a duty to other women to fulfil your potential. You're the smartest of all of us. I'm only ever going to be a hairdresser – that's why I married Fred. He's got the smart genes for our daughters. You've got to work girl. Otherwise the men will be earning more than

women forever. You have to use your talents to
help lift other women up – and you're the most
smart one of all of us!

MC: I don't know. What you're saying sounds
sensible but… I'm a Christian. I can't do this.
It's against God.

EL: So am I. Didn't you know I'm a Christian?
Thought I'd told you sometime. At church they
say God doesn't mind us making decisions, he
wants us to have choice. God loves you. How
is he going to punish you for this, for looking
after yourself, for putting yourself first?

Michelle suddenly felt extremely nauseous. Was it the pregnancy? Wasn't it too early for morning sickness yet? Or was it their nauseatingly casual attitude to this?

MC: I have to think about it. Thanks everyone
for your support.

Michelle thought about inserting a love heart at the end but suddenly she wasn't sure, even about such a small, bland, meaningless gesture. Something really didn't sit right with her about what they were saying. They were apparently full of the milk of human kindness and sympathy for her predicament. But is it loving to convince someone to do something against their conscience?

Was it really against her conscience?

Michelle suddenly hated computers, she hardly knew why. She felt like throwing her very expensive laptop against the wall then trampling it until every chip inside it was completely mangled and screwed up.

Afraid of her irrational impulses, she closed the laptop lid very gingerly, plugged in the power pack and went straight to her bedroom, closed the door and turned off the light and hid under her blankets.

For a while she lay there, eyes open like a startled opossum looking for movement in the dark world of the forest at night. But then she thought about the potential child, the baby the bunch of cells would one day be.

If she didn't kill it.

Michelle started weeping disconsolately in anticipation of the grief and guilt she would feel if she did what she was thinking of doing.

And she thought about Meth sleeping two rooms away, and everything Peter had given up to keep him.

Then she thought of Pony Boy and laughed bitterly, snorting tears and snot through her nostrils as she did. She couldn't have chosen a more pathetic, useless example of a male to be the genetic father of her child if she had tried.

Strangely, accepting her complete contempt for him made her feel better. Even that much she didn't understand.

Dear God, if she didn't even understand her own emotions, how would she ever know what to do?

Her message app beeped.

> GB: Too embarrassed to say b4 😔 I regretted mine. It really played on my mind, A LOT, and I couldn't stop obsessing over it. Then I talked to the priest at Dad's church & asked him if God could ever forgive that sin. He said yes Jesus can and does forgive you. What use is God's forgiveness, he said, if He doesn't forgive really terrible things? I really cried then. Don't do it.

Michelle didn't reply – she felt even more confused. She had to bury herself in her work again.

She began doing a search on the Darknet for anyone who knew anything about a James LeCoulter. Perhaps she could help Peter after all. After a few hours, she stumbled on his name in an encrypted list that someone had ripped off a server somewhere in Germany.

It was a list of scientists and other staff working in a series of laboratories around the world; one lab was in Frankfurt, the Kalender Verlängern Laboratory, one in Niagara Falls called the Krystal B. Lassiter lab, several in Europe, one in Sydney. She did a bit more research. The ownership structure was seriously complex, labyrinthine even, but all the labs were owned by a company called KBL Lumen LLC.

Michelle was intrigued.

She began trying to see if she could hack one of them. Which one? Let's try… Sydney.

CLANDESTINE LABORATORY IN FRANKFURT.

It was the middle of the night again. James LeCoulter sat with his head in his hands. He had a headache and he really couldn't take any more of this.

Adze was moaning softly and weeping, inside his cage, and whispering in a tone that rent James' heart. "I can't stand it in here a minute longer. I cannot do this any more. Please let me out of here."

James realised he couldn't watch this any more either. He said, "You've been doing your studies of the contemporary world. You understand about money now. You know everything we've taught you about human society. You know how it all works."

Adze said, "Yes but what does that have to do with…?"

James said, "It's not a continual picnic like it is in here. You'll have to get yourself a job. You'll have to find somewhere to live. I can't do it all for you."

Adze said, "What do you mean?"

"Tomorrow," said James. "I will unlock the two doors of your airlock, just before we have our morning debrief. I will leave a hoodie there for you – it is a type of cardigan with covering for your head. Put it on! I will leave a series of unlocked doors for you. You must escape then. There will be two hundred dollars in the bushes just outside the main entrance, sitting on the outside window sill, where the curtains are inside."

Adze said, "Okay. Thank you, James."

* * *

THE FOLLOWING DAY.

James LeCoulter sat in the meeting looking his superiors in the eye. His team leader said in a very bored voice, "And how exactly is Adze's education going? Well?"

"Oh, yes," he said, "He's making great strides in every area."

Adze was indeed striding out through the corridors of the laboratory area, past the inattentive security into the main foyer. Adze pulled the fire alarm lever outside the men's toilets (that had been a late addition to their plan) and then shuffled out with the hoodie over his head, stooping, trying to hide among the crowd of doctors, lab assistants and other workers walking out. Safely outside, Adze reached into the bushes and found the two hundred dollars James had left him and ran.

CHAPTER 17 – Franken-infant in Frankfurt.

CLANDESTINE LABORATORY IN FRANKFURT.
The Following Morning.

The man in the black suit walked into the foyer of the five-story Education building, a block away from Goethe-Universität in Frankfurt. The floor was composed of black and white marble squares, like a chess-board, shiny and clean, reflecting everything above.

The security guard was standing at his station. He said, "Herr Schmidt? Go straight through. Please use the central elevator."

The man in the black suit stepped into the central elevator and pressed 'B' for basement then his code, '616'.

The elevator's electronic voice said, "Code verified. Open access granted."

The elevator went down and the LED screen showed the floors as they were passing, two basements, two lower floors, and three floors marked 'Z1', 'Z2' and 'Z3'.

The elevator doors opened finally on 'E'. The man in the black suit walked out into a white decontamination chamber. He took his clothes off and put all his possessions into a small box.

He walked through the decontamination shower and found a towel and a black positive pressure protective suit. He nodded approvingly – it was black. Everyone knew now that he only wore black clothes.

He dried himself with the towel and put on the protective suit.

He went through the airlock.

Several people in bright, white protective suits met him and they shook hands.

He walked through into another room. There were vials and test tubes on a rack and some computer equipment, as well as large refrigerators and cabinets.

A man in a white protective suit nodded at him. The man in the black suit nodded back. The other man reached forwards and clicked a switch on the man's suit, near the neck.

Suddenly a loudspeaker in the suit switched on and the man in the black suit could hear what people were saying. Somehow they had arranged the stereo panning correctly so that people's voices sounded as though they came from where they were standing.

The man in front of him said, "Hello. I am James LeCoulter, the head scientist here. Please come with me. I would like to show you our work."

They walked through white, antiseptic corridors for several minutes until they came to a room that looked more like a maternity hospital, except that all the children had elongated heads, and they were all in neonatal intensive care units.

"These are the children in the N3PHL project. All of them were born prematurely. The chances of survival are very slim but one child, in particular, is doing well."

He indicated the unit. The child inside it was larger and healthier than the rest.

"This child was born at twenty-two weeks. It is now thirty-seven weeks since conception. Soon we will be taking him out of ICU."

The man in the black suit said in clipped Euro-English, "How long until he is mature?"

James replied, "Well, sir, that's the strange thing. We had another one that survived for fifty-one weeks after his birth. His growth after six months was highly accelerated."

The man in the black suit said, "That is the one that escaped two days ago. Have you heard anything from him?"

James shook his head. "No, we haven't."

"Hmmm. These Nephilim – they age much quicker?"

James said, "Well, we think they might reach adulthood as much as ten times as fast as a normal child. Five or six years at the most."

The man in the black suit gestured. "Why do you think that is?"

James said. "Well, it's just a theory…"

"Yes?"

James shrugged. "These were genetically engineered to be warriors. Whereas the M3THU5A project may take twenty or thirty years to reach adulthood and be useful in battle, these creatures were actually engineered for a short gestation time and an even shorter childhood, making them a formidable opponent of Upper Paleolithic Early Modern Humans. You see, it's to do with the placement of several hundred proteins in the gene sequence – it's not just that they appear designed – normal DNA seems that way to many geneticists – no, it is that they appear to have been designed by another hand."

"And has he shown any… paranormal abilities?"

James replied, "Like what? What sort of paranormal abilities? No, not so far, no sir. In fact, so far he has not demonstrated any signs of consciousness at all."

The man in the black suit said, "What about the one that survived for fifty-one weeks? The one that escaped?"

James shook his head and swallowed. He was going to tell a lie now, something he really didn't like doing. He felt himself squinting, his tell but he couldn't stop himself. He continued anyway, "Nope. I have to admit he did not arrive at consciousness either, not until a week or two before his escape.

The subject ate, slept, woke and defecated; in other words, did everything that ought to be expected of a living human being. But at no stage did the subject exhibit any signs of actual consciousness. There was no recognition, language, desire, independent movement or preference, not until shortly before the escape attempt, which surprised us all. As I say, it was not long before his escape."

James paused, trying to find the right words. "They are like blank slates. We have no clue why one woke up, eventually. We must be doing something wrong. We're missing something..."

The man in the black suit nodded. "I have other researchers elsewhere working on this. The Pacific Laboratory has had a success. There may be a few things we can... Um, do to solve that problem. Understand? Contact me again if this one does not wake up within the next ten weeks."

James said, "Yes, sir."

***

At about five o'clock, James left work and drove home to his apartment in Nordend. The dusk cast a deceptively peaceful light over the streets. He parked in his parking spot outside the elegant Wilhelminian building and walked into the foyer and upstairs to his apartment.

Walking through the front door he heard the sort of busy

noise from the kitchen that indicated Anna was home already. He said, "Hi!" and she replied, "Hi!"

She said, "How was work?"

James said, "Wait." He did a quick scan around the house checking that all the televisions and laptops were off, then he took his battery out of his mobile. "Mobile?"

She handed her mobile over and he took the battery out of hers as well.

They embraced and kissed and then she said, "So?"

He replied, "Work was bad. And good."

"Tell me?"

"Well, the big boss was there today. I think he was checking up on me after Adze escaped."

"Really?"

"Yes. They are getting impatient. And they think they might have a solution to the blank slate problem. That's the bad news."

"And what's the good news?"

"They still don't know about the one year old that I killed earlier in the year."

"They don't?"

"Not at all. There were no awkward questions. I think I got away with it."

"Good. Little Monstrosität."

He nodded. "Killing that one put the whole project back at least a year."

They were very quiet for a minute or two.

Finally, Anna said, "Do you think it was a sin? Killing that creature?"

James said, "After Adze began to talk to me, I couldn't stop thinking about the child I killed. What if he was going to wake up? What if he was like Adze, and it was all an act?"

Anna said, "He was a casualty of war, James. You had to do it."

James confessed, "I feel guilty about it now. Killing a child…"

Anna shook her head. "God help us all if they succeed in making another of those creatures, one of the ones that *isn't* like Adze…"

James said, "I'm worried, Anna. I don't think I can pull the same trick again. And the problem is, this one's growing even faster than the last one. And what if it's not like Adze? What if it isn't one of the good ones, one of the ones that seems human? The other ones that woke up were not like Adze at all, in the studies from the lab in Buffalo and the one in Sydney. Adze is a unique type, I believe. Different from the others. But this new one I think might be mature within a year, maybe even six months…

I did some calculations – the gestation is much faster than Adze. If the logarithmic growth spurt is proportional, it will be fully grown in eleven months. But if it's even faster – which it might well be – then it will be even sooner. This one has much more of the original DNA."

Anna said, "How?"

"They found some more skulls. Most of them are the result of head-binding, you see, it's not genetic. It's a process of elimination. If the DNA can be identified, then it's not one of the genuine N3PHL variants. It's only when the DNA eludes identification that we can assume it is genuine. And we recently got hold of some more skeletons, from Egypt, and some from the Urals region; those ones were particularly good, they were found in a glacier. We found two more that we believe are genuine, and I filled in many more gaps. That is why I am a bit worried. Considering the difference between the gestation period of the M3TH project and modern humans, and then considering the difference between humans and our early attempts at creating a new N3PHL, I think the gestation period of the originals might well have been vastly quicker than anyone expected. Some serious genetic engineering happened with these creatures. Either that, or some kind of... angelic interference or something."

Anna nodded knowingly. "Changing the subject, have you heard from your Dad?"

James shook his head. Anna noticed that his lips were pressed together. He did that when he was worried.

James said, "No. Not for quite a while."

Anna said, "Well, go and have a shower, get yourself cleaned up. We're going to have a nice dinner and try to forget about it all. And I think we should pray, too, while we have our phones off."

James said, "Me too. All of this has made me question my scientific skepticism."

Anna said, "What do you mean?"

James smiled ruefully. "I mean, darling, if the bad things in the Bible are true, maybe the good things are too... I really think they might be!" He laughed, more freely than she had ever heard him laugh. "There is a God who is watching over us..."

Anna nodded. "Exactly. Just what my Lutheran grandmother would say. Jesus kept us all from harm, she used to say, in East Germany, from the day the wall went up to the day the wall was torn down. We'll pray for your father, and we'll ask the Lord for guidance about all this."

And James added, "And we'll pray for Adze, wherever he is."

CHAPTER 18 – Devraj's Brazen Revelation.

Devraj woke up with the sun streaming through the window. Naomi, his stewardess on a recent flight, was lying in the bed next to him still sleeping.

That's right, he remembered now.

They were in a hotel room in DC.

She was very sexy, with her full lips slightly open as she slept and her hair randomly arrayed about her head.

He thought back to the antics of the night before. It would give him some great ideas for the romance novel he was writing. Indeed, he would have to make copious notes soon before he forgot all the juicy details.

Ah, he would love to extend this long weekend for another day. He probably could. But today, he had another agenda. He had heard that Kael was still hiding out at his sister's place in Phoenix. His best friend was in trouble. Depressed, hiding away from the world in a dark, sombre place, no longer communicating with anyone.

And what was worse, Devraj had an inkling from things Kael had said and hadn't said that his friend was doubting his life's work.

He looked at Naomi and licked his lips salaciously.

What a lovely piece of fluff. But he would willingly make this sacrifice, to put Kael's needs in front of his own.

Naomi woke up. He stroked her hair. Maybe he could extend his long weekend another day after all.

She looked at him with her beautiful dark eyes and spoke in soft, sleepy tones in her gentle Australian accent, "Devraj. There was something I was wondering…"

"Anything, my beauty."

"Well… You do a lot of flying. How do you, you know, square that with your carbon credits? I mean you're always going on how people have to make sacrifices."

"Naomi. I'm a Hindu. I have become a vegetarian. But it will take me six lifetimes to repay my carbon footprint from this life. But as you know, it is necessary for me to attend climate conferences to fight global warming. A necessary sacrifice."

She looked at him with a very cute, though slightly dissatisfied expression and then turned away suddenly and said in a tone of voice as cold and hard as a stainless steel lab table, "You know, I thought you were different." She got out of bed and got dressed, saying, "I thought you might at least make an attempt to justify yourself."

Devraj reached for her, saying softly, "When do I get to see you again, my darling? We haven't tried all the positions in the Karma Sutra yet."

She pulled her arm away from his reach and said, "You won't see me again. Unfortunately the Karma Sutra will have to remain unfinished." She finished dressing and picked up her handbag, and said, "Maybe you can find some other gullible sucker to finish it off with you."

Devraj said, "But we're not even finished!"

She glanced at him with a face full of scorn. "Oh, no, we are finished."

And then she left the hotel room.

Good riddance to a bad business. It saved Devraj from having to fob her off, anyhow.

He looked at his watch. Good timing. A proof of divine destiny.

He opened his laptop, went to Hipmunk and booked a seat on a flight to Phoenix that afternoon.

Well, he had better have a shower and get dressed and get himself ready.

His best friend Kael needed him and now that he'd fobbed off that sour-faced, dark-eyed Aussie stewardess he would go to Phoenix and help him.

<u>CHAPTER 19 – Bizarre Business.</u>

PERTH, WESTERN AUSTRALIA.

Natasha and Michelle were sitting in the café opposite Meth's school sipping Viennas.

Natasha said, "Good idea to come early to pick up Meth. You know, Perth coffee is pretty good, actually."

Michelle nodded and didn't make eye-contact with Natasha. She was very quiet today.

Natasha sipped for a while watching people walking past, thinking about Meth. She wondered how long they would be looking after him. She enjoyed being a mother-figure for the boy.

Michelle wasn't even on her computer. What was wrong with her?

Natasha said, "Have you checked your computer? What about Peter? When is he coming home? Has he sent you any messages?"

Michelle shrugged. "Not for the past few days. I've been giving my digital life a rest. Well, until I started looking into those labs I was telling you about."

Natasha snapped, "Well, check, then."

Michelle snarled back, "Okay, alright, I'll check, if I have to." She reached into her handbag and took out the souped-up eleven inch HP laptop she took with her wherever it was inconvenient to take her custom seventeen inch Intel Xeon 8-core laptop, which was significantly bulkier and often threatened to overheat when she pushed the processing power a little.

Despite a wave of nausea as she put it on the table, when she opened it up she felt relief. The online world was a place where she was in control.

Natasha clasped her arm. "Does Peter know you're Trippy Girl?"

"No, he doesn't. All he knows is that Trippy Girl is someone who has helped him in the past." Michelle opened Tor Messenger. "Oh! That's what you call synchronicity. There's a message from Peter."

Natasha looked over her shoulder and read,

> Peter: Henry was shot. Had to move to Hotel della Conciliazione. I have the letter he went for, luckily, 16th cent Spanish explorer Pizarro. Bizarre business. Sending you images of code Henry used in his address book. Can you work it out?
>
> TG: Send it through. I will see what I can do.

Michelle left the laptop open on the table while they continued drinking their coffees. A few minutes later, with the sound of a bell the images arrived. The pages looked like this:

WTQFSITHMFWQTYYJ/632960206
2MFYWZQTTPNSL/632960046
ITZYMNSPYMJWJ/632960947
NXFXJHWJYRXL/632960795
MNIIJSMJWJ/632960670
2M42TZQIYMJWJGJ/632960462
2MJSYMJXJHWJYNX/632960055
MNIIJSNSUQFNS/632960377
XNLMY./632960953
OJXZXNXQTWI/632960932
WJZ/JSYNRTYMJN/632960947
KQTWJSHJRHHTWRNHP/632960795
QTZNXJMTZXYTS/632960670
HJHNQXFSYTX/632960462
UFRWMTIJX/632960055
LQJSIFLJTWLJ/632960377
/FSHFNS/632960953
YMJQRFSTWWNX/632960406
UWJXYTSMFWWNX/632960963
WJLNSFQIRNQJX/632960937
IZXYNSXZQQN/FS/632960401
KWJIWNHPWMTIJX/632960297
JQNFXXYJJQ/632960864
WT3FSSJPQJNS/632960009
UJYJWQF5FWZXKT3/632960096
OFRJX/632960434
OFRJXXJHWJYSZRGJO/632 960973

"Well," said Natasha, "Those must be the names in code. I think the phone numbers are not encoded."

Michelle said, "It's probably nothing more complicated than a Caesar cipher. All we have to do is count how many of each letter."

For the next ten minutes, Michelle typed the entries into an Excel spreadsheet. "Well," she said, "I've got about two hundred letters. Should be simple enough."

She set the spreadsheet up to count the frequency of each letter.

"The most frequent letter is J. In my sample it occurs twenty-six times. The next most frequent letter is W, which occurs twenty-two times. I'm going to assume it's a simple Caesar cipher and that J is the letter E."

She typed some formulas in and cut and pasted, and the first name came out as:

ROLANDOCHARLOTTE1632960206

"Looks right," she said. "That looks like a name, doesn't it?"

She extended the spreadsheet and soon enough had all the names decoded.

In the middle of the list were the names they were looking for:

JAMES1632960434

JAMESSECRETNUMBER01632 960973

She messaged Peter.

TG: Worked it out. Easy enough. Caesar Cipher. J=E. JAMES1632960434

JAMESSECRETNUMBER01632 960973

Peter: Oh, thanks! Alright I'll call him.

TG: You know what? Skype him using Tor Messenger as your carrier…Might be more secure…

Peter: Ok

There was a break of about ten seconds before another message appeared.

Peter: How's Meth doing?

TG: What? Meth?

Peter: Come on I know that you are Michelle.

TG: Oh. S***. Ok. Yes he's good. Having lots of fun. Natasha plays the role of the Mum, I'm like the big sister. He's a good kid.

Peter: Yes he is. Tell him I'll be home soon, within the week, if I can.

Peter's icon changed colour; he had signed off. Michelle said in a chastened tone of voice, "Well, that's interesting."

Natasha said, "He guessed, did he? We aren't all as stupid as you seem to think."

Michelle raised her eyebrows with her lips pressed thin and took a deep breath. "You could be right."

Natasha said, "Are you alright?"

Michelle said, "What do you mean?"

Natasha said, "You've been very quiet lately, today especially. Something's wrong. Something more than the online stuff."

Michelle felt a sob escape her mouth, she tried to get control. "I didn't want to say."

Natasha got up. "Step outside with me. There's a more private area outside the café where we can talk. Come on Michelle, we're sisters! You know you can tell me anything."

They walked outside and settled onto some tall chairs.

Michelle took out her laptop and handbag and put them on the table, then took a deep breath. Another sob escaped as Michelle said, "I... got lonely about two weeks ago and went out with this guy called Pony Boy. We slept together. I can't even remember his real name; Jerry or Jeremy something. We talk online sometimes."

"Oh. So what's wrong? You're regretting it? It was a shallow, sordid night of lust?"

"It's not that... I missed my... He didn't use any protection."

"Oh. You got some disease? Herpes or something?"

"It's not that. I'm pregnant, Natasha."

"Are you sure?"

"Of course I'm sure! I did a pregnancy test. I'm definitely pregnant." She sobbed again. "All my friends online are telling me to have an abortion. 'It'll ruin your life.' 'It's easy to have an abortion.' 'I had two already.' 'Throw the foetus in the bin' one of them even said. Most of them have had one, even their younger sisters have had abortions, and some of them are only in their late teens, Natasha. Gabrielle's the only one who said not to."

"You don't have to have an abortion, Michelle. You actually can have the baby. I know Mum and Dad will support you. Nathanael and I will support you. We'll all stand with you, we'll help you. You don't have to do that. It's okay, it's alright."

Michelle erupted into deep sobbing and clung to her sister, barely able to get the words out. "Thank you. I don't think I want to have an abortion. For some stupid reason, I really want to have the child."

Natasha said, "Have the baby then. It's okay." Natasha patted her on the back until Michelle pulled away and said, "You're petting me like a dog!" They both laughed, and Michelle felt tears escaping again.

She said, "What do I do?"

"Stop worrying, because we're all here for you," said Natasha, wiping Michelle's tears away from her cheeks. They stood like that for a while. Finally Natasha looked over Michelle's shoulder and said, "Look. Meth's out of class." She looked. The child was coming out of the building, looking around for them.

Natasha pulled out a small tissue box from her own handbag and offered it to Michelle. "Are you ready to go get him?"

Michelle dried her eyes with the tissue and said, "I'm ready. And I'm ready to face the future for the first time in a while." Then she laughed again and said, "You wouldn't believe what a useless wimp the father is, I only know him online really, Pony Boy. I couldn't have chosen a more pathetic example of manhood to be the father of my child if I had tried." She hesitated. "Mind you, he might be a wimp but at least he's smart."

Then she looked at her computer screen as she was about to close it down. A message came up.

Sandbox compromised. Taking security measures against Trojan. Isolating offending files:

N3PHL_labstaff.zip. Offline backup complete.

Recommend complete reinstall from previous

backup.

"What happened?" said Natasha.

As Michelle typed, she explained, "I run Tor and anything I get from the Darknet in a virtual sandbox, an operating system that's completely isolated from everything that's important on my computer. This file – a list of employees of the labs that Peter seems to be looking for – contained a very clever Trojan. It tried to take over my computer."

Warning! Attempted brute force attack!

Closing down network access. SOURCE IP

ADDRESS: 14.203.11.200 14.203.11.201

14.203.11.202 14.203.11.203 14.203.11.204

14.203.11.205 (Sydney Australia)

Michelle said, "Geeze. That's persistence." She looked at Natasha. "I think that's coming from the Sydney Laboratory."

At that moment, the camera in the corner of the café turned around on its own. Michelle saw it turning and covered her face with her computer, grabbed Natasha's handbag and covered Natasha's face with it too. Michelle peeked. The camera was facing directly towards them.

Michelle said, "Come on. Let's go. I think we'd better

go and put a few extra security measures in place. Someone just triggered a Trojan, attacked my computer with a brute force attack, and simultaneously hacked the Café security camera. That's not just some pimply Pony Boy hacking the Dark Net. That's a large organisation at work."

CHAPTER 20 – Meth-Shiloh & Mushrooms.

VATICAN CITY.

Not really knowing how to use video over Tor Messenger, Peter used the Tor browser instead to Skype Meth about an hour later, when he was sure the boy would be home from school.

He knew Meth's computer would be making a gentle bell sound right now, indicating that a Skype call was coming through. Meth's face appeared on Peter's screen.

"Hello, Father!" said the boy.

Peter said, "Hello, Son! How are you enjoying having Natasha and Michelle looking after you?"

"It's great. We had mushrooms and bubble and squeak for breakfast on Sunday!"

Peter nodded. "Really? I didn't know Americans knew what bubble and squeak is?"

"Natasha says Nathanael cooked it for her after they had a roast meal once," Meth said. "Natasha's parents were not from America, anyway, you know. She said they have something similar in Sri Lanka called Kottu. I'm not sure which one this was. Oh, she says it's Nathanael's recipe. But I really liked the mushrooms! We collected them ourselves early in the morning."

Peter said, "I didn't know they had mushrooms in Perth?"

Meth said, "No, we went to a town called Northam

and stayed in a motel for a few days. Michelle said we needed a small holiday. And I missed school! I didn't mind too much. And we went out walking very early in the morning, when there was mist everywhere, and picked the mushrooms, all across people's farms but they don't mind you going onto their property if you're just looking for mushrooms. How long until you come home?"

"About a week, son." Peter hesitated, then said, "Are you alright with Natasha and Michelle for another week?"

Meth's face on the screen nodded resolutely. "Yes I am but I'm still worried about you too, Dad, till you get back. I don't want anything bad to happen to you. By the way, school is still good. I'm loving it! But it was still good having a few days off. And Michelle is having a baby."

He heard Natasha's voice in the background, "You shouldn't have told him that!"

"Don't worry, I didn't hear that," Peter said.

Natasha said, "I'll explain about the trip to Northam when you get back."

Peter said, "No worries, Natasha. Love you, son."

Meth said, "Love you, Dad."

After finishing that call, Peter used Skype to call James' secret number, 01632 960973.

James answered, "Hello?"

Peter said, "Hello. I'm a friend of Henry, your father. I'm in Italy at the moment but I presume that's an English number?"

James said, "Well, I'm not in England. I have the phone diverted to my ah… spare mobile. What's up?"

Peter hesitated for a moment. "I'd like to meet face to face if we can. I have a message from your father." He was afraid the shaking in his voice might betray the bad news, news he didn't want to deliver over the phone.

James paused for a moment then said, "Well, you wouldn't have this number unless you got it from him… Look I'm not exactly a prisoner here but… Let's put it this way. I can't just behave as if things I do might go undetected. I'm in Nordend, in Frankfurt. Come to Frankfurt, please. Message me when you get here. I will tell you where we can meet. I'm not having you to my apartment, mind, I don't know you from a bar of soap and it might not be safe! For you or me… I don't want anyone to know my address. No, we'll meet in a public place, a restaurant or bar or something. I do very much want to hear this message from my father, though. And there are some things I would like to pass onto him also."

Peter thanked James and looked at his watch. It was about eight in the morning; he had only been booking the hotel one day in advance because he had no idea how long he would stay in Italy.

Well, so long as he left by eleven he wouldn't have to pay another day. He got out his laptop and looked up the next flight to Frankfurt that had spare seats. He found a flight that left at five. That gave him two or three hours, more or less, to get ready.

He started packing, and as he checked the chest of drawers next to the bed to see if he'd left anything, he found a Gideon's Bible in there, in Italian, and it reminded him of Henry's notes.

Genesis chapter 6:1-4.

Peter reflected on how seldom he had read the Bible or prayed since things had been going well, since he and Meth had been on an even keel. Well, it seemed the Almighty was determined to get him reading the Good Book again, one way or another.

He took out his mobile, opened the Bible app and read,

> When human beings began to increase in number on the earth and daughters were born to them, the sons of God saw that the daughters of humans were beautiful, and took for themselves wives of any they chose. Then the LORD said, "My Spirit will not contend with humans forever, for they are mortal ; their days will be a hundred and twenty years." The Nephilim were on the earth in those days—and also afterward—when the sons of God went to the daughters of humans and had children by them. They were the heroes of old, men of renown.

Peter puzzled over this for a few minutes. What could it mean? He had read two or three commentaries about Genesis when the issue of longevity had come up, and apparently, the sons of God were the sons of Seth, the good descendants of Adam, contrasted with the sons of Cain, who were the bad descendants in the subsequent passage, an explanation he found quite frankly confusing. But Augustine and Calvin and quite a few Rabbis as well had agreed about this interpretation.

But it didn't seem to have anything to do with what was happening.

He dismissed the question, for now, figuring it would eventually be answered, finished packing as quickly as he could and went down to the street to wait for the next taxi.

CHAPTER 21 – From DC fix to Phoenix.

PHOENIX, ARIZONA.

It had taken Devraj all day to get around to booking his flight. The earliest first-class seat he could find was leaving DC on Thursday morning at seven a.m., and was going to arrive at ten a.m. in Phoenix.

So here he was sitting in the airport lounge with the morning sun streaming in through the windows, checking out the female bar staff who really were quite hot. Especially that little blonde number with the tattoos; she looked about nineteen. He wondered if…

With some effort, he brought his mind back to what he had to do.

Well, the simplest thing to do would be to ring Kael.

Kael picked up the phone. "Hello?"

"Hi, Kael. It's Devraj. I – ah – happened to be in Phoenix and thought we might catch up, old buddy." Devraj cringed – old buddy! – that was not the sort of thing he normally said. He sounded like American Dad. He had to stop trying so hard.

"Okay," said Kael. "Well, I'm having lunch with Nathanael today again at the Phoenix City Grille, at about midday. You'd be welcome to join us. That's amazing luck that you're in Phoenix. How long are you here for?"

"I'm here for – oh, don't worry about that, buddy." Devraj cringed again. "We'll talk about it when we see each other." He didn't really want to embarrass Kael by admitting that he was worried about his mental state, so he probably had to work out some story before he saw him.

"Alright," said Kael. "I'll see you then."

CHAPTER 22 – Genesis and Gestation.

FRANKFURT.

Peter had found a room at the Ibis hotel, quite near the Frankfurt airport. The sun had not yet set. It was a pleasant summer twilight outside and the air was cool and inviting.

He messaged James.

> Peter: I'm in Frankfurt now.

He didn't expect an immediate reply but James messaged back quite quickly.

> James: Meet me at eight thirty at Blumen bar
> and restaurant East Nordend.

Peter was nauseous at the thought of telling him the news. He retched and a great heaviness came down on him. How could he tell this man his father was dead?

Another message from James woke him up.

> James: Alright?

Peter messaged back.

> Peter: OK.

As soon as he had set himself up in the hotel room, Peter went down to the street and caught a taxi.

The bar looked reasonably full; luckily they were fairly late or they might have had to book.

Peter bought himself a drink and sat down to wait,

wondering how he would break the bad news to James.

* * *

"I don't believe it," cried James so loudly that people in the restaurant starting looking around. James jerked the wine glass in his hand to the side, spilling a little white wine on the floor next to the bar, then whispered vociferously, "I cannot believe what you're saying. I will not believe it."

Peter said, "It's true. But James, we shouldn't be making a scene."

"I know, I know." James winced, then warily scanned the room. "There's a conference room out the back that I've used before. Come, let's see if it's free."

It was free. The quietness of the room and the dim light was an immediate relief to Peter, after the glaring contrasts of the main bar.

James banged his fist on the table, a gesture belied by the quiet, controlled tones of his speech, "Now tell me about my father. I want to see the body. Unless I see my father's body I won't believe it. Why didn't the police tell me this? What's going on?"

Peter shook his head. "They took the bodies away, cleaned the whole scene. When I went back in, there was nothing left."

James looked at him accusingly. "Why didn't you do

something? Did you call the police?"

Peter said, "I – I suppose I was afraid the same thing might happen to me. The gunman was there. There was nothing I could do."

James shook his head. "I know what these people are like. I'm sorry, I... don't know what I'm saying. I'm sorry."

"I understand. It's just the shock of it, James."

James grabbed Peter's arm in a vice-like grip. "Did you see my father die? You saw him die?"

"No," Peter said. "I have to admit that I didn't see him die. I was afraid if I went in I would suffer the same fate. But I heard it happen. I heard the gunshots and I heard his body fall to the floor."

James shook Peter's forearm. "But how do you know he really died, if you didn't see it with your own eyes? I... I confess that I... I don't feel that he's dead, Peter. I think he's still alive." Then James added, "What about the other fellow. You saw him die? You saw his corpse?"

"Not exactly," Peter said, "But I know the sound of a gun with a silencer."

James insisted, "You're absolutely sure? Other things could sound like that. I know he's not dead, Peter. I just know it."

"How?" said Peter. "How could that possibly be?"

"He is not dead. If he was, I would know it, in here." James slammed own fist over his heart. "I would know it." He paused. James demanded, "How did you know Dad, anyhow? How do I know I can trust you?"

Peter sighed deeply. "Your father found me, I wasn't looking for him. But before I was… where I'm living, I'm sorry, I can't tell you for the sake of… I was working in a lab like the one you're working in, in England. We created a child, Methuselah. He was – is – very long-lived. He has a massive lifespan and a much slower metabolic rate. He is twelve years old, mentally and physically but still a toddler, by all appearances."

James looked at him in awe and whispered, "You were working on the M3THU5 project? That was the precursor to our work."

Peter nodded, raising his eyebrows. "Yes, the Methuselah Project. We tried to recreate Upper Middle Paleolithic humans. We only made one, Methuselah but he's alive today."

James grabbed his arm and leaned forward, staring at him intensely, "So you were the ones. You spliced in many human genes?"

Peter waved his finger at James, "No, no, the Upper Middle Paleolithics are human. Just an earlier form."

James said, "I mean, modern human genes. What did

you do with the gaps? Did you insert modern genes in there? Or did you make do with chimp DNA or something?"

Peter rolled his eyes. "Yes, of *course* we inserted modern genes, wherever we didn't have the original. Didn't seem to do him much harm though."

James said, "What? He's still alive? They told us they had lost him. I assumed that meant…"

"Yes, he's still alive, James. They did lose him. Literally. I fled with the boy, we made our way to Eastern Europe first, got captured and released and we ended up… somewhere else. Meth is very much still alive but I can't tell you where he is now. He is still in danger from these people. What about your project?"

James said, "My what?"

Peter said, "Whatever it is you're doing. Something about Genesis chapter six? The Sons of God? The Nephilim? Pizarro? The book of Enoch?"

James looked at him warily. "Father must have trusted you if you know that much. Unless this is some sort of trap… They might have sent you to see how much I divulge."

Peter rolled his eyes. "If it was a trap you'd be caught already, wouldn't you? Tell me – it's the Nephilim, isn't it?"

James lowered his voice even more. "We are trying to resurrect the Nephilim. And Peter, let me say, I don't think it's a good idea."

"Forgive me," said Peter, "But I'm not quite clear on who or what the Nephilim actually are."

James said, "Alright. Yes, before we began this I had no idea either. But once I realised what they were trying to do, I researched it thoroughly. Let's begin with the Bible. Genesis chapter 6:1-10. You must know who the 'sons of God' were?"

Peter said, "Sons of Seth. The good seed of Adam."

James scoffed, "Ha! A ridiculous and anachronistic interpretation that originated with Saint Augustine and was perpetuated by John Calvin. No, no. Look at the book of Job; it's quite clear there; look at Psalm 82. The sons of God were rebellious angels, in Hebrew the Bené Elohim. They were members of some sort of divine council who sinned by lusting after mortal women and coming down to earth and taking wives of any they chose. So in that light, let's read Genesis chapter six."

> When human beings began to increase in number on the earth and daughters were born to them, the sons of God saw that the daughters of humans were beautiful, and took for themselves wives of any they chose. Then the LORD said, "My Spirit will not contend with humans forever, for they are mortal; their days will be a hundred and twenty years." The Nephilim were on the earth in those days—and also afterward—when the sons of God went to the daughters of humans and had children by them. They were the heroes of old, men of renown. The LORD saw how great the wickedness of the human race

had become on the earth, and that every inclination of the thoughts of the human heart was only evil all the time. The LORD regretted that he had made human beings on the earth, and his heart was deeply troubled. So the LORD said, "I will wipe from the face of the earth the human race I have created — and with them the animals, the birds and the creatures that move along the ground — for I regret that I have made them." But Noah found favor in the eyes of the LORD.

This is the account of Noah and his family. Noah was a righteous man, blameless among the people of his time, and he walked faithfully with God.

James continued. "Now, when it says Noah was 'blameless among the people of his time' it might actually be, in the context, a mistranslation. The Hebrew is literally, 'pure/uncorrupted in his generations'. In other words, his family bloodline was not polluted by these angelic beings, the sons of God who took as wives those they chose from the daughters of men. What we think it really means is that in Noah's family line there were no angels and no Nephilim. On a side note, I believe the angels wanted to corrupt the human bloodline to prevent the prophecy to the snake in the Garden of Eden being fulfilled in Jesus, 'his seed will crush your head, and your seed will pierce his heel.' If the two seeds had become intermingled, the prophecy could hardly be fulfilled. Regardless, it appears that God was forced to destroy the human race because their genome had become corrupted by the genes of rebellious angels."

Being Jewish, Peter wasn't sure what he thought about Jesus but the things James was telling him fit perfectly with the concept of Jesus as Messiah, something Peter had been considering seriously; well, until his life had become easier and more comfortable recently, strangely enough.

James continued, "The reasoning goes that if these dolichocephalic rulers really were the Nephilim, it concurs with Genesis, 'they were the heroes of old, men of renown.' The word Nephilim is translated Γιγαντες, *Gigantes*, that is, Giants, in the Septuagint, the Greek translation of the Old Testament. And such genetic anomalies as elongated skulls, six fingers and toes, and gigantism, might well concur with the efforts of fallen angels to manipulate or change the human genome."

Peter said, "But what does this mean?" He indicated Genesis 6:4. 'And also afterward?'

James nodded. "Scholars disagree, as they do about many of these things. But it either means that the Nephilim lingered in the post-flood era or in their descendants, perhaps through the family line of Ham, the Amorites or Canaanites in particular. Or some say that there were other sons of God after the flood who came down from heaven and took human wives. Whichever it is, they were most likely the Anakim, Amalekites, Rephaim, and perhaps some of the Philistines, all of whom were pagan warriors of a particularly savage type."

A knock came at the door.

Another bottle of wine had arrived which Peter had ordered earlier.

James waited until the waiter had left and closed the door behind him before he continued, saying, "These races of giants were the only tribes that God commanded Joshua to eradicate when he invaded the promised land. Was this God's attempt to purify the human genome again, just as he did with the flood? The builder of the first city following the flood, Babel, built in the plain of Shinar, may have also been a giant. Shinar was settled by Nimrod who the Bible says 'began to be mighty in the earth.' And 'he was a mighty hunter before the Lord.' Some scholars think the Biblical Nimrod may have been Naram-Sin, the Akkadian conquerer, depicted in wall murals as a giant holding a bow, on his head the horned hat that only gods were allowed to wear. Whatever the details, the Nephilim were definitely the enemies of the long-lived line of Noah of those ancient, pre-diluvian times. And their descendants the Akkadians, Amalekites and Canaanites were the enemies of God's chosen people, the Israelites, after the flood."

Peter said, "And what is the book of Enoch?"

James said, "An apocryphal book, probably written about two hundred BC. It's in the Ethiopian Bible and there are various other extant manuscripts from ancient times. It describes the fall of the angels in Genesis 6 in much greater detail. Apparently, after the flood the rebellious angels, the Bene Elohim, were imprisoned in chains in the lowest reaches of Hades. In the New Testament the letters of Jude, 1 Peter, and 1 Corinthians 11:6 reference these beliefs. The Nephilim, the angels' progeny, drowned in the flood but according to the book of Enoch, their spirits did not go down to Hades since they were neither mortal human nor immortal angel souls but something of both, and were instead condemned to wander the earth as restless unclean spirits. In Jesus' time, this was the general Jewish belief about the origin of evil demons and unclean spirits."

And James turned to Peter and said, "And these Nephilim, progeny of rebellious angels, gigantic warriors, and the enemies of the people of God, are the very creatures that the people funding my laboratory are trying to resurrect from the dusts of prehistory."

Peter shook his head. "Why don't you just quit? Leave it behind like I did?"

James grimaced. "Peter, I think you know exactly why. I don't think these are the sort of people you just quit from. It has obviously cost you a great deal to take that move. I have a wife and a mortgage, to say nothing of my extended family, my sister and brother-in-law and his children, my wife's parents. And Dad as well." He shook his head with regret. "And I've signed a very onerous contract. I've seen one or two other scientists who got cold feet disappear completely. Others have had family members who met… unfortunate accidents. Quite a few. That's what I was asking Dad to look into. God, I hope he's okay. I believe he is." He paused for a minute, looking away, and a tear went down his cheek.

Giving a deep groan, James gathered his strength and began again. "The other reason I need to stay is that I have been trying to slow things down, working against the project from within, if you like." He whispered, "For God's sake, I myself killed one of them, an infant, something I'm not proud of. It wasn't conscious at all though, so I suppose it's no worse than taking a brain-dead person off life-support. But the fact is, these creatures grow quickly. The gestation period appears to be six months. I think – I'm not sure – but I think the pure Nephilim might have been fully grown within two to three years after birth, maybe even less. Not long at all. We're dealing with corrupted DNA in our experiments, you understand, DNA that has been recovered from two-thousand-year-old blood cells but the pure, uncorrupted Nephilim would have been very quick to grow to adulthood. And we believe they were a real threat to the ancient humans, especially humans with a pure bloodline. This is what Genesis 6:9 implies – Noah was pure in his generations – his genetic line was pure." James paused. "We can't make the pure Nephilim, though – it hasn't worked. They don't achieve consciousness."

Peter said, "Have any achieved consciousness?"

"Some before in the other labs. One in my lab." James breathed a heavy sigh. "He kept it secret from the doctors and the other scientists. For some reason he only trusted me. I used to go to him and talk to him at night, in the dark. I gave him some books to read. He was obsessed with the Bible and the ancient Canaanites."

Peter said, "What happened to him?"

James said, "We were reading the same bits of the Bible. I kept telling him, God is merciful. He turned to God." James' face registered pain. "I don't know how it all works, Peter. He seemed to think he could read people's minds and that his spirit was very old, that he had existed long ago but then… Adze repented. Perhaps it's just lies – perhaps because of their peculiar biology they have some sort of hotline to the world of spirits and demons, and are somehow more susceptible to their evil influence than normal humans? I really don't know. It's just a guess." James looked Peter in the eyes. "Adze clearly identified as the enemy of humankind before he read the Bible. He had some sort of præternatural knowledge of his mission, his identity, as a Nephilim, the enemy of humanity. Particularly, the enemy of Noah and his pure line, through Shem and Japheth."

Peter understood then that it had been the right thing, coming with Henry, leaving Meth behind. Now he understood who the Nephilim were. Meth's natural enemies. Every human being's natural enemies but especially Meth's natural enemies.

"Of course," continued James, "After Adze's repentance, I began to wonder… Perhaps this bloodline stuff is not as absolute as I thought. And I realised first there is the matter of the bloodline of the Messiah. A Moabite, Ruth, was in Jesus' bloodline. The Moabites appear to be implicated as one of the races in the Bible sharing in the Nephilim bloodlines…"

Peter whispered, "In other words, you're saying Jesus took on even the corrupted human flesh of the Moabites?"

"Yes… Then, take the *Ariels*, a type of Nephilim, perhaps, that were clearly capable of repentance. They are mentioned in 2 Samuel 23. *Aryeh* is Hebrew for lion. *Ariel* means 'lion-gods'. Have a look at 1 Chronicles 12:8. Two Ariels join David's band of warriors. By all accounts these were lion-faced men, mighty warriors, hybrids like the Nephilim. And they are mentioned in the Moabite Mesha stele as well as in the Bible, and the extant book of Jasher which is probably apocryphal but speaks of half-human, half-animal warriors…" James took a deep breath. "It's bizarre. This is the last thing I expected. I've always been an agnostic. I never thought I'd end up believing in God; that seems incredible on its own. But that I might believe these strange ancient Semitic legends as well. Lion-faced men, half angelic beings, supernaturally corrupted bloodlines. But nothing else makes sense to me in the light of what we now know." He paused and an agonised look came across his face. "And that's why I believe my father is still alive, Peter. I think you are wrong. I have been praying for him. And I'm praying for a miracle, too, some way out of this. I believe God has heard my prayers. Peter, I am not going to accept that Dad is dead until I see his pale, lifeless corpse with my own eyes, and look into its eyes and see that the light is gone."

James' eyes were bright in the dim room.

Peter said fervently, "I have contacts, James. I can get you out of that lab. We can find a place for you, give you a new identity. That could be the miracle you're looking for."

"No! Not yet!" said James. "I'm slowing things down. Don't you understand? Haven't you heard the stories of Jews on the Nazi assembly lines trying to sabotage the weapons they were forced to make? That's what I'm trying to do, Peter. If they get another geneticist in the whole plot will only be brought to fruition quicker." Peter looked confused. James continued, "Do you want a whole Nephilim army marching out, perhaps possessed by evil spirits, with unnatural strength, giant soldiers, perhaps with the ability to read minds, or at least the ability to communicate with unseen powers, or an unsurpassed talent at telling believable lies, or with occult powers of manipulation and direct communication with evil demons?"

Peter said, "No, of course not."

James said, "That's what my employers want to do. That's their whole aim. And the aim of those who are financing them. I believe now that this is the shadowy Cabal that also controls the Western Governments, manipulating them from the shadows like puppeteers pulling strings. So I must stay and try to slow things down, sabotage the research, be inefficient in tiny ways, or even in large ways. You're out there – find a way to stop them – find a way to defeat the Cabal controlling all this."

Peter shook his head. "I would barely know where to start. That sounds like far too much for one person to be able to do on their own."

James groaned. "I still don't believe Dad is dead. But if he is, he's died in vain if they are able to accomplish this." He swigged the rest of his wine. "I've got to get back home, Peter. I suspect even now that they are following me everywhere. I chose this quiet room to have our meeting because we could hide here and it's hard for them to spy on us while we're in here. Wait for half an hour at least after I've gone before you leave. I don't want them realising I was talking to you."

Peter said, "Okay, okay. Neither do I."

James got up and slipped through the door, closing it quickly behind him.

Peter sat in the quiet room thinking for quite a while.

CHAPTER 23 – Climate of Denial

PHOENIX CITY GRILLE.

Kael and his new friend Nathanael didn't arrive until closer to one o'clock. Devraj was already there and from his dishevelled appearance and slight lean on the barstool, Nathanael deduced he been drinking for a while.

Kael sat down on the barstool next to him.

Slurring his speech only slightly, Devraj said, "Oh, Hi, Kael. It's a disappointing place; the girls here are very uneducated, not a single Greens voter among them I would say, not even any Democrats, and definitely not a single Greenpeace member. A den of deplorables, basically, these girls who work at the Phoenix City Grille. Why, they don't even recognise me from a bar of soap! In fact, they've never heard of the UNPCC, either. Or our Nobel Prize, the one we all won together. They really don't want to talk to me." He sniffed his underarms. "Or did I forget my deodorant today or something?" He looked in the mirror behind the liquor cabinet, opposite him. "Or am I looking old? I've lost it, Kael. I've lost my charm."

He looked so pathetic and miserable that Nathanael felt he had to say something to comfort him. "Well, they're a bit overworked here, a lot of customers, mate, everybody wanting something. I'm sure it's not you."

Devraj looked at him curiously. "I like that. I really do. Thanks. Who are you, then? Some kind of climate professor?"

Kael said, "This is Nathanael. He's a friend of my sister's, been showing me around, making sure I'm okay, looking after me."

Devraj shook hands with Nathanael. "I'm Devraj. Pleased to meet you." Devraj shot a quizzical glance at Nathanael and asked Kael. "Can we talk in front of him?"

Kael said, "Yes, Devraj, he's a good guy."

Devraj nodded and said, "Now tell me, my dear Professor Addison, what's this I hear about you taking time off? The way you've been talking you seem to be quite depressed or suffering from a serious attack of melancholia. Not yourself. Frankly, I'm quite worried about your mental stability."

Kael winced a little but he said, "Look, I'm actually doing well."

Devraj said, "And what is worse, I have a feeling you might be... doubting your life's work, my friend."

Kael looked away for a moment. "What makes you think that, Devraj?"

Devraj glanced upwards. "Oh, this and that, this and that. I don't know, honestly. Omissions. Things you said in your emails, things you didn't say. It's hard to put my finger on it, you know."

Kael muttered evasively, "I might be. I don't want to say really."

Devraj noticed that Nathanael was sitting bolt upright, in a way that looked extremely stiff and uncomfortable. Devraj put his hand on Kael's arm and said as solicitously as he could, "You have done good work, Kael, you are on the right side. For goodness' sake, they wouldn't have given us a Nobel Prize if we weren't doing the right thing, would they? We are the *good* guys."

Kael admitted, "I have to admit that I am no longer completely sure of even that much."

Devraj said, "But everyone agrees climate change is happening. NASA. NOAA. The Met Office. Even BOM in Australia. Weather bureaus around the world. How do you possibly bring yourself to doubt the evidence?"

Kael said, "Devraj, we ourselves have inflated the evidence. Be honest, now. You know that."

Devraj said, "Come now, there's lots of weather data. It's hardly as if we were cherry-picking every little temperature reading."

Kael protested, "Yes but, Devraj, you know as well as I do that those skeptics did a survey of weather stations in the US. Seventy percent of them are not sited correctly. It casts into doubt more recent measurements, which have probably been disproportionately affected by urbanisation. And the Met Office lost a whole lot of the world weather station data."

Devraj glanced over at Nathanael and said, "What about

the BOM in Australia, and their CSIRO? They are absolutely firm on it, completely certain it's happening. Why, they stake their reputations on their fulfilled predictions! Anyhow, didn't Judith Curry clear the NOAA in one of her studies, though?"

Kael said, "That was before she started questioning things, wasn't it?" And added, "You know about the Australian thermometers, though, don't you?"

"What thermometers?" Devraj sounded irritated, almost livid. "You're bringing up stupid thermometers?"

Kael said, "Yes, thermometers. They are using new digital thermometers. They take temperature measurements every second. The old mercury thermometers took at least one minute for the mercury to move in the event that they are registering a maximum. It is an inbuilt bias towards warming in the Australian dataset, which clearly can't be trusted, for they have done nothing to adjust for it. Oh, and they have been conveniently 'losing' temperatures lower than minus 10.5 degrees, another bias towards finding average warming."

Devraj was quick to jump in, "Denialist propaganda!"

But Kael shook his head. "No, Devraj, it isn't. The thing is, I've checked these things out. What the skeptics are saying is true. They're not lying. And where is the missing heat?"

Devraj avoided the question of the missing heat.

"Nonetheless, if we don't present a united front, as concerned scientists, Kael, people won't believe our warnings. You know as well as I do that scientific uncertainty doesn't get grants, statements of doubt do not have the power to convince people that they have to change their ways." Devraj glanced at Nathanael and said, "Anyway, he's being very quiet. What's the matter, cat got your tongue, Aussie?" He pronounced Aussie as though it would rhyme with 'saucy'.

Nathanael raised his palms. "I'm keeping out of this! You two have a conversation with each other. I've caused enough trouble."

Devraj looked at him. "Indeed, I think you have. You're a denier and like some Christian fundamentalist sect trying to brainwash gays into being straight guys; your ideas have infected and brainwashed my friend. Kael, I think you need deprogramming, I'm not joking. We need to get you out of here. We need to get you away from this guy, he's a bad influence."

Kael said, "Devraj. I've had time to think. All the way along I've compromised with the truth. For a long time I thought it was more important to give a clear message for the sake of political action. The typical scientific conclusion is too vague and full of uncertainties; such inconclusive conclusions can neither move the general public to action nor can they make clear to politicians what they need to do."

Devraj nodded. "I see where you're coming from. That's what I was saying. So you're coming back to my point of view."

Kael said, "But Devraj... The end doesn't justify the means. Lying about the science is still wrong. Pretending that a statement is scientific when it's really just rhetoric is dishonest."

Devraj shook his head vigorously. "But Kael, just because we don't have the evidence to present yet doesn't mean climate change isn't true. Why, it must be true! We know that humanity is like a virus on this planet and there are too many of us. And you know, don't tell me don't know it, Kael, if we don't take action now it will be too late. To wait until we have conclusive evidence is very unwise; you realise that? It might be too late to change things when we take action. The precautionary principle."

A look of confusion crossed over Kael's face, so Devraj knew he was making headway. Devraj continued, "You've been influenced by these Nazi Christian Jewish fundamentalists," he waved at Nathanael. "Christianity is not a nature religion, it's not about the environment. It's a book religion; they worship the dead letter of rules and laws written in a book. It is an unspiritual religion: they make an unnatural division between man and nature. Christians and Jews believe mankind is supposed to dominate nature, when in reality, humanity is supposed to *cultivate* Gaia. They have a masculine, patriarchal god, an objective deity, separated from them, whereas properly intelligent people realise that we are all part of the divine. Indeed, the divine light is in each one of us and everything is god. We ourselves are meant to be gods – we were meant to be given wisdom but the God of the Bible was jealous in the Garden of Eden and wants to stop us seeing the light, the light the snake wanted to give us. We are superior to the chattel, Kael, you and I, we see the truth, we deserve our position. We don't have to believe these Christian lies."

Devraj took a deep breath and continued, "Anyway, what about your career? What about the grants we've applied for together? What about the papers we're writing together, the UNPCC report, the conferences, the university appointments? Are you insane, Kael? If you become a denier then you'll lose your job, you'll throw all of that away. And for what? Surely you can see that climate change must be real, it's just a matter of time until we can prove it to everyone! You are throwing your whole life away, your career, your profession, for nothing! For a stupid principle that doesn't matter to anyone except you. You can't think the politicians care."

Kael bowed his head and said in a small voice, "I don't

know. You're starting to convince me. It was all so clear a minute ago. But what you say is starting to make sense…"

Nathanael started to say, "I…" but Devraj interrupted, "Shut up, denier. Your kind has no right to say anything. Get back to the other Nazis."

Kael laughed nervously and Devraj laughed as well, uproariously, suddenly in an almost uncontrolled, hysterical way. Some of the waitresses looked over at them suspiciously, and that only made Devraj laugh even more strangely.

Devraj suddenly said in a voice so lascivious it sounded like someone else speaking, "You should have seen the hottie I had last night, oh my god. She was a sexy nymphette, Kael, and as green as hash to boot. By god, I gave her a good one."

Then they both started laughing again.

Nathanael had had enough. He walked outside for a breath of fresh air. It was late in the afternoon now and he leaned against a pillar outside the restaurant and watched the sun going down. He was starting to doubt everything now himself. It hadn't been that long ago when he would have agreed with everything Devraj said about global warming and skeptics. And many of the things Devraj said about Christianity. There was a time when Nathanael would have rather been a Buddhist than a Christian if he had wanted to believe in anything. But Nathanael went through the facts again.

And it wasn't the facts of climate change he was thinking of.

That was a secondary issue, an issue of facts, an issue of scientific proof, that could change at any time.

Jesus was resurrected from the dead.

The fact is, the early church, with their gleeful disregard for their own lives, their overt willingness to die for Jesus, their complete adherence to non-violence, could not be explained as a phenomenon any other way. And there were four gospels, documenting the eyewitness accounts. Two of the gospels at least probably were eyewitness accounts, and all of them written by men who were famous for honesty, integrity and saintliness, who were willing to give their lives and forgive their persecutors.

Yes, these disciples were not in it for the money, they were men like Kael's brother in law José, down-to-earth men, honest, hard-working men used to earning their living, men who couldn't afford to have a reputation as liars.

By contrast, look at the character of Devraj. A fleshly man, given over to seducing young women and using them without regard for anyone's morality; a lover of money and pleasure, given to self-worship. Someone perfectly willing to lie if he thought the cause was good – someone who believed that the ends justified the means. And a complete hypocrite. He told everyone else not to fly, to save their carbon credits, whilst Devraj was spending carbon credits like there was no tomorrow. He said Christianity was a lie but was more than happy to tell lies himself if it served his own interests, his own 'cause'.

Nathanael shook his head. Everything Devraj said was all a load of bollocks.

He thought of José again. Someone Nathanael really respected, a real Christian, down-to-earth and basic.

And he looked at the sunset, the pale red light painted across the clouds all along the horizon, the sun disappearing slowly. Look at that beauty.

And he thought of Natasha's beauty.

God is real.

And Nathanael prayed, "Lord, I don't know what to do here. I tried to help Kael but I really don't know if I have helped him. Maybe I've just made things worse? Just… look after the bloke please, he really needs your help. And how can anyone be honest these days when their livelihood depends on dissembling and lying and twisting the truth? Especially in science, where so much is about money now and honesty seems to gone out of the window. Give Kael wisdom please. And I pray for Devraj too. I don't know if you can help him – maybe he's too far gone – but then again, maybe that means he's closer to repenting than a middling sinner, I really don't know. I haven't got a clue if my prayer is even a good prayer but there you go, in Jesus' name, just like José, Natasha and the pastor always pray, Amen."

A sense of peace washed over Nathanael and he stood watching the sun as it descended over the horizon and stars began to wink into existence on the fringes of the light.

Kael came out a few minutes later and said, "Hi, Nathanael."

Nathanael nodded and acknowledged him.

"Look," said Kael. "I've decided I'm going back to work. Thanks for everything."

Nathanael put his hand forward, "No worries."

Kael shook Nathanael's hand and said, "Look, I really mean it. I know that in your own way you've been trying to help me, and you've been willing to spend time talking to me. You know, not many people do that except for a self-interested reason. And I know that we don't agree on everything but you've been good to me, in your own way. Thanks."

"Stay in touch," Nathanael said. "Alright?"

"I will," said Kael but both of them knew he probably didn't mean it.

Nathanael said, "Well at least look me up next time you come to see Marybelle and José."

"Alright," said Kael, and he kind of meant it.

Nathanael hesitated for a moment, unsure if he should say what he was thinking. Eventually, he spoke. "You realise the facts about climate change are not that important, don't you, Kael? It's your integrity that's important to God. He looks at what's in the heart. "

Kael nodded, slightly dismissively, but Nathanael thought he saw a flash of recognition in his eyes. Nonetheless, Kael turned away from him, got out his mobile phone and booked an Uber.

And that was that.

Devraj came out afterward and carefully avoided looking at Nathanael directly, slinking past with one eye watching him surreptitiously, to the edge of the car park where Kael was waiting for the Uber.

Seeing that, Nathanael had to laugh, suddenly realising how ridiculous Devraj was.

A man honoured and fêted around the world, but he was not worthy of Nathanael's respect, not even one iota of it.

A CLANDESTINE LABORATORY IN SYDNEY, AUSTRALIA.

The creature was playing up again. It was the shift change, and he was behaving in a child-like way, crapping on the sofa and taunting the staff, who simply wanted to go home.

Dr Harald Yvetrison got them to open up the airlock and let him in. He knew he could reason with the creature – he had done it before, had managed to calm it down.

When he came through the second door the creature loomed over him. "Are you here to calm me down?" it said, mirroring his thoughts, something Harald had noticed it doing many times before. The creature continued, "You won't be able to calm me down, Harald. You see, I want out." Quicker than Harald could even register, the giant moved, and before he knew what was happening, it had one hand clasped round Harald's neck. The other was brandishing one of the knives from the kitchen. How on earth had he gotten hold of it?

The creature pricked Harald's neck with the sharp point, drawing a drop of blood that splashed on the floor.

"Let me out," said the creature to the security guards who would be watching and listening intently by now. "Or I'll slice his neck open without even a second thought."

The inner door of the air lock clicked open. The creature went in, still clasping Harald's neck, and closed the door behind him. The outer door clicked open. The creature went through.

The creature got into the lift, still holding Harald close, pressed the Ground Floor button.

As the left went down, Harald felt the blade slip neatly across his neck. For a moment he thought the creature was just trying to scare him, by sliding the blade across without cutting.

But the creature let go of Harald's neck when they reached the ground floor. Harald fell onto the floor, gurgling, feeling his life's blood slipping out. The creature leaped out of the elevator and ran out through the main entrance.

Harald tried to cry out, "Help me!" But it came out as a soft gurgle and no one heard. He could feel the elevator door bumping against his leg, again and again, as his vision blurred.

Then he remembered something from his childhood in Sweden. Something about Sunday school – there was a person who could save someone who was about to die – what was the person's name?

But before he could remember who to cry out to, Harald's mind went blank as his heart stopped.

Two minutes later all the security guards arrived to find the creature already gone and Harald's corpse lying in the elevator, the lift door opening and closing and opening and closing, bumping Harald's lifeless legs each time.

CHAPTER 24 – Dead men's shoes don't walk.

CIAMPINO INTERNATIONAL AIRPORT, ITALY.

Peter was waiting at the airport for the call to flight WZ3145, which was his flight back home, when a man with greying hair, dressed in a white shirt and grey trousers, walked up. Looking over his glasses he said, "Peter Lazarus-Fox?" Peter didn't reply but the man said, "I can see," and pointed to Peter's air ticket, where his name was clearly displayed.

At that moment the call came over the PA, "First call for Flight WZ3145 to Sydney via Singapore." Peter picked up his luggage.

The man grabbed his arm and said, "Henry's alive. I know where he is. We can go and get him. But you'll have to come with me. You can't leave just yet."

Peter fought with his response inwardly. What was Henry's whereabouts to him? Even if he was alive – he had already told Meth he was coming home!

He clenched his jaw and picked up the suitcase. He was going home but then despite his efforts not to think of it, he heard Meth saying to him, "Your friend's son is missing. You have no choice but to go and find him."

What would Meth think of him if he reneged, turned back now? Peter snapped more harshly than he meant to, "Who are you? Why should I believe you?"

The man lifted his hands and calmed Peter down, "It's alright. You may call me Giuseppe. I am a friend of Father Rudolpho. I am in the Italian Intelligence, AISI. I inserted a tracking device in Rudolpho's shoes, and I did the same for Henry, on Rudolpho's request. And for you. Back in the restaurant where you met Rudolpho, while you and Henry went to the bathroom. I did it then – I'm surprised you didn't notice that your shoes were slightly tighter – it usually has that effect."

"Really?" Peter thought it sounded ridiculous. But he remembered something about that night – he had felt as though his shoes were too tight. "Wait – bugs in shoes? So it's not a nervous tic?"

"Bugs in shoes, yes. That's my thing. Rudolpho already knew you were looking for him at the restaurant. You have a tracker in your shoes too, this is how I found you. I had it put in. It broadcasts on available wifi and the cellular network wherever it is. And can detect movement, heartbeats, that sort of thing. Henry, at least, is still alive and wearing his shoes. I know that much, for his shoes have been walking. Dead men's shoes don't walk."

Peter said, "What about Father Rudolpho?"

Giuseppe shook his head; the honest sadness of his expression made Peter trust him completely. Peter said, "I'm sorry," and grasped Giuseppe's shoulder in what he hoped was a comforting gesture.

Giuseppe blinked several times. "But at least Henry is alive. And I know where he is. We may not have much time. Come with me."

Giuseppe hailed a taxi. He told the driver, "Tivoli." The driver nodded and requested pre-payment. Giuseppe handed over a credit card and Peter put his luggage in the trunk and got in the back.

They drove through central Rome and soon they were out of the city, driving on a freeway through the low hills of the Italian countryside. Half an hour later they were navigating the narrow streets of a medieval town.

By now it was getting dark. The taxi driver turned his headlights on and drove more slowly.

Giuseppe pointed the driver down a narrow street, then another one.

Suddenly gunfire erupted from one of the houses at the side of the road. Giuseppe said, "Evade that!" and the taxi driver slid to the other side of the road for a moment. The driver put his foot down and the engine roared as he let loose a stream of Italian invective and insults directed at Giuseppe. "La mia macchina è danneggiata a causa tua! Stai pagando ogni centesimo sanguinante di ciò che mi devi per questo e tua madre è una…"

"Fermare!" Giuseppe barked firmly. "Stop here."

There was a row of cars parked along the side of the street. The taxi driver parked behind them, outside a store marked 'Negozio Hardware'. Giuseppe gave the taxi driver a wad of Euros and told him to wait until they came back. The driver haggled again and kept repeating, "Mia macchina! Mia macchina!" so Giuseppe got out his credit card and paid him more. Giuseppe said under his breath, "Ladro."

Peter followed him out into the street. Giuseppe whispered to him, "Quiet. Those people who watch the town might be here soon, with their machine-guns. Ratatat-tat!"

They walked along the cobbled streets, keeping to the dark shadows, occasionally stopping to examine the storefronts and street numbers by the dim light of old wrought-iron streetlamps.

Giuseppe whispered, "Nell'ombra!" and pulled Peter back into the shadow of a medieval doorway. Two men carrying machine-guns quite unashamedly came out from an alley and traipsed past them, talking in Russian. Peter thought it was probably Russian, it definitely wasn't Italian, anyhow.

Giuseppe waited a while, listening intently as the men's footsteps receded, then said, "It's okay. They're gone."

Giuseppe finally stopped in front of a store marked,

'Fertilizzanti E Prodotti Chimici Per Piscine', Fertilizer and Pool Chemicals.

Next to that building was a two-story stone building with a heavy-looking wooden door, with an iron door-knocker in the middle of it. Giuseppe pointed to it and said, "This is the one."

He pulled out a pistol from his back pocket and showed it to Peter. "You know how to use this?"

Peter nodded. He took it.

Giuseppe pulled out another pistol from a holster under his shirt and held it at the ready. He said, "Are you ready, Peter?"

Peter said, "I'm not sure."

Giuseppe said, "Fear is normal. Courage is ignoring it. Come. Let's do this."

Peter said, "Wait! Are you going to kick the door down? Like in the movies?"

"No!" Giuseppe said. "We are not Americans. We Italians like to practice subtlety and style. Destroying beautiful doors for no good reason is not one of our habits."

He tapped three times on the door-knocker then waited.

The door opened promptly and Giuseppe, still holding his pistol, flipped out the crown, shield and sun Polizia ID badge with his other hand.

A large, tall, muscular man in a track-suit stood there holding the door. He stepped back with his hands up while they went into what was some sort of entry hall with marble tiles and a spiral staircase.

Giuseppe whispered to the man, "Get out! Go away! Run! You're not the one we want! But don't bring the thugs back or I'll have your manhood on my plate tomorrow for dinner."

Muscular though he was, the man skittered out the door in a rather unmanly way and sprinted off.

They could hear a bass voice upstairs, speaking in rough Russian-accented English. "Yes, the package is on the plane." He paused. "To my knowledge, he is on the plane. Why would you doubt that?" Another pause. "No I didn't see him get on with my own eyes; I don't even know what he looks like." Another pause, then the Russian man snapped, "I very much doubt that. Alright, whatever you say. Goodbye."

Giuseppe and Peter stepped forward.

The man upstairs said, "Who is it?"

Giuseppe said, "Just us," quite casually, and sprinted up the stairs. Peter followed right behind him, holding his gun with the trigger finger ready to shoot.

"Who?" said the voice. A brown-haired, square, chiselled face looked down at them, definitely Russian. The man said,

"Who are you?" He was wearing a white T-shirt and cargo pants.

Giuseppe waved his gun slightly at the man.

The man moved backwards and put his hands up but he didn't look scared. To be honest, Peter thought the man was so unperturbed that he was probably psychotic or something. Either that or permanently drunk on vodka.

As Peter came up the stairs he saw that Henry was tied to a chair. He had been bleeding and his hand was wrapped in a bandage. There was an open hardware case on the ground next to him that was filled with torture implements.

Giuseppe said, "We're taking Henry."

"Good for you," said the Russian man, smiling and wiggling his fingers. "You do that and see where it gets you. Annoying people, interrupting a perfectly enjoyable evening."

Giuseppe said, "Untie him."

The Russian man untied him. Henry slumped to the floor.

Peter went over and helped Henry up.

The Russian man was hovering, too close, and he suddenly lunged at Peter, his long arms reaching forwards like the arms of a chimpanzee. Peter kicked the man's ankle and he stumbled just as Giuseppe's pistol went off.

Blood began pooling on the shoulder of the man's T-shirt. He collapsed with an expression of shock on his face.

Giuseppe said, "Faresti meglio a far vedere a qualcuno quella ferita, amico mio." You had better get that wound seen to, my friend.

The Russian man grunted as he lay on the floor and took out a mobile phone. Giuseppe kicked the phone out of his hand and then stepped on it, crushing it to smithereens, saying, "Nice try, Vlad," while Peter helped Henry down the stairs.

The Russian man complained, "How am I going to call the ambulance now? Your mother has paying guests every half hour. Don't leave me here! And how did you know my name was Vlad?"

Giuseppe said, "You Russkis are all called Vlad. But an ambulance will be here in five minutes. With the police."

They left the Russian lying on the floor, swearing profusely at them, the stream of invective was unrelenting.

Giuseppe said, "Well, that was eventful. Ciao, Henry."

As they went down the stairs, Henry began whispering under his breath, "Thank You, God, thank You, God, thank You, God. I'll never drink another drop, I promise, and I'll keep the promise this time. I promise. I swear." Peter resolved not to mention that later; vows made when one's life was threatened weren't the sort of thing polite people talked about.

Giuseppe took Henry's other arm and they got out the

door. The taxi immediately came up and they put Henry in the back.

As the taxi drove off, Giuseppe took out his mobile phone, and good to his word, rang the emergency number and called an ambulance and police to the address, then opened the taxi window and threw the mobile out. It bounced along the road beside them for a moment as though it was following them then disappeared suddenly, dissolving into a trail of debris.

As they reached the edge of the town, the taxi driver shouted something. Giuseppe said, "What?"

"On top of that overpass! Two guys with machine guns!"

Giuseppe took out his pistol with his right hand and wound his window down as quickly as he could with his left, all the while shouting, "Swerve to the left!"

The taxi driver swerved. Giuseppe took aim and popped two shots off. One man slumped, the other fell over the edge of the overpass flailing and thumped onto the verge. The taxi driver shrieked and jammed his brakes on in the middle of the road. Panting, he stared at the dead body on the verge in front of him.

Giuseppe shouted at the taxi driver, "Get out of here! Non fermarti nel mezzo, imbecille! Don't stop in the middle!"

The taxi driver swore and put his foot down. The wheels smoked for a few seconds then caught on the gravel and the car lurched forwards, out through the town gates, while the driver shouted an even more unrelenting stream of invective at Giuseppe for the five minutes it took him to run out of breath.

In the brief pause, Giuseppe waved his arms about and said to Peter, "You know we are good mates, this taxi driver and me."

The taxi driver took to muttering his imprecations under his breath.

Giuseppe said, "Tell me, Peter, on another topic, do you know someone called Trippy Girl? That is the person who alerted me to this situation and told me my friend Father Rudolpho was in danger."

Peter raised his eyebrows. So Michelle's reach extended even to Italy. "Yes. Yes, I do! She's something of a friend."

Giuseppe said, "Say thanks to her. Tell her I couldn't save Rudolpho but I'm glad that some good came out of this anyhow. And tell her... we're not all bad. Tell her she could get a job one day. She'd make a good operative."

Peter nodded. "Alright. I'll tell her."

Once they reached Rome, Giuseppe stopped at an all-night café and ordered some take-away coffee and some food. Henry sipped his coffee with an expression of bliss written all over his face.

"What happened in the library?" said Peter, after allowing Henry a suitable amount of time to enjoy his coffee.

Henry said, "The gunman shot Rudolpho dead, three shots, one to the head, two to the heart. But he shot me with darts that put me out cold and I woke up here. Since then he's been trying to get information out of me about my son, about who I am but I've been drip-feeding them lies. That guy who was guarding me wasn't the gunman, by the way. He had gone off to do something else."

Peter said, "I found your son, Henry. I found James. You have to let him know you're still alive…"

"Thank God," said Henry, who then slumped and sighed. "Tell me about it later," he said, and closed his eyes, nestling into the door of the taxi-cab.

At that moment the taxi-driver put on the radio. "News time," he said.

The voice on the radio said, "Voce Del Mondo. Bongiorno… Il volo W Z tre uno quattro cinque è scomparso nel Mediterraneo."

"Flight 3145," said Giuseppe. "Wasn't that your flight?"

Peter said, "Yes, what? What about it?"

Giuseppe said, "It has disappeared over the Mediterranean."

The voice on the radio said, "È stato visto un bagliore nel cielo. Le autorità sospettano il terrorismo."

Giuseppe translated, "They saw a flash in the sky. The authorities suspect a bomb. Terrorism. And you were supposed to be on that plane, Peter."

Peter said, "You don't think... that was what he was talking about on the phone when we came in?"

Giuseppe swore. "I have to notify the authorities."

He pulled out another mobile phone and spent quite a long time talking in Italian.

While Giuseppe was still talking, Peter remembered that Meth knew the flight number – he had better ring the boy right now and tell them he was alive and coming home on a different flight, so he did exactly that.

Doing this reminded him of something else, so he woke Henry up as well, "James thinks you're dead. You should contact him." Henry immediately rang James.

Peter messaged TG with a short summary of what he had discovered; the death of Rudolph, Giuseppe coming along, how they found Henry alive, and about the Nephilim and what the Cabal was trying to accomplish.

TG messaged back, promising to pass the information on to Natasha and Nathanael.

<u>CHAPTER 25</u> – Meeting of Minds.

NEW YORK. CLIMATE INSTITUTE, CORVELL UNIVERSITY, NY.

Kael had never worked as hard as he had the past two days. Now it was finished.

He emailed the final copy to Devraj.

Devraj rang half an hour later.

Devraj didn't bother with pleasantries, just launched in with, "Kael, what's this?"

Kael said, "It's the paper. *Modeling Parameters And Assessing the Accuracy of Climate Predictions.*"

"Yes, yes," said Devraj impatiently, "I can read the title. It's what's in the study that concerns me."

Devraj's response got Kael's back up and before he could get control of himself, he had snapped, "How so?"

Devraj said, "Well, let's start with the abstract. 'The accuracy of current computer models cannot be honestly said to lie within the .05 range of statistical certainty. We hope that within twenty years the longitudinal range and geographical precision of our data will have improved to the point that we can say definitively whether carbon dioxide is having an influence upon the climate but at this point in time that certainty does not exist.'"

Kael said, "Well?"

Devraj said, "It reminds me of something an undergraduate might write. Simpering, indefinite, cringing, wimpy. No – it reminds me of something Lord Monckton might write. Have you turned into a denier suddenly? Do I need to read on? 'Climate modelling is still in its infancy. An honest assessment of the risks, however, must still acknowledge the necessity of climate action. Nonetheless, we have no idea when tipping points might occur, or indeed, if such tipping points even exist.'" Devraj paused. His voice took on a hostile edge, "This is supposed to support Johannes' conclusions in that chapter? Ha. If anything it casts doubt upon them."

"I tried to do it properly, this time, Devraj." Kael thought he sounded defensive and weak. He said, "I'm trying to be honest about what the evidence actually says. I don't want to overplay it anymore."

"Well, that won't help anyone, will it? We're going down the gurgler, the whole world is going to die from coastal flooding and heat waves and hurricanes and earthquakes, and you are sitting on your butt, agonising over whether every little jot and tittle in that stool of yours that you have just dropped into the toilet bowl is literally correct and truthful!"

Kael whispered nervously, "I suppose I am. Is it that bad?"

Devraj raged, "Oh, my friend, it's much, much worse

than that. How do you expect to keep your position and your grants if you can't adequately lobby? Political lobbying requires certainty. You know this. I know this. We have talked about this fact many times, Kael. This road you are going down is worrying me greatly. It's self-sabotage. Are you sure you're okay? Perhaps we need to get you some psychological help, my friend, something to help you get back to your assertive self. Either that or you've become a denier." The threat in Devraj's voice was palpable.

Kael asserted with as much strength as he had, "I'm not a denier." He knew what happened to deniers in the academic community. It was career suicide.

Devraj bellowed into the phone, "Then explain to me the difference between your position and Judith Curry's?" Kael was silent. Devraj said, "You can't, can you? The whole climate is going to pot and the one climate scientist in the whole world who might save the earth doesn't even have the guts or the raw courage to say what he knows in his heart is true, what he might not have all the evidence for but what he knows is true! Come on, Kael, it must be true. Humans are a cancer, a scourge on this planet, raping the environment, pillaging its natural resources, spreading over its surface like a rampant disease. How can carbon dioxide, the main product of industrial activity, not be causing a future disaster? Will Gaia not punish those who misuse her, those who refuse to worship her? How can this not be so?"

Kael was lost for words. Devraj's attack had left him almost weeping. He said, "I was just trying to be honest for a change," and then cursed himself for his weakness, his lack of assertiveness.

"Honest?" Devraj shouted even louder, to the point that the phone speaker was actually distorting. "Honest? I will tell you what honesty is! Honesty is saying that honestly, you, Kael E. Addison, have crossed the line into becoming a denier." Devraj's voice suddenly became cruel and contemptuous, "And a Christian, for Gaia's sake. You are, aren't you? You've become a Christian, you little hypocritical runt." He let loose a stream of foul invective at Kael, who had never heard such a tirade before from Devraj's lips. "How do you think you can be saved? You're as much a sinner as me, maybe more. I am going to report you to the college board, you creationist. You denier. Your career is over."

The word 'Christian' had completely different connotations now for Kael. It made him think of Pastor Carlos getting the church people to delete the video. It made him think of his brother-in-law José; José's goodness, kindness and decency, and the fact that José would help anyone who asked him and give away anything to anyone who was in need and in that light Kael suddenly saw Devraj for what he was. A nasty, calculating, greedy, lustful manipulator. A snake who only cared about his own selfish short-term desires and long-term advantage; someone who was completely prepared to demand that the rest of the world should suffer to save humanity but a man who wouldn't even lift a finger to help his own grandmother. A user, of women, of the academic world, of his family, of his friends, of the scientific endeavour itself.

Suddenly something in Kael snapped. He didn't even have to think. It was as though he was hearing the words pouring out of his own mouth. "Well, Devraj, you do that and I'll be telling them the name and age of every undergraduate you've bedded in the last twenty years. Oh, yes, I know who they were, and how old they were. Or rather, young. You've boasted enough times about that even in your emails. You are a deceitful hypocrite and if you try to bring me down, I'll bring you down. And your fall will be much greater than mine; I can guarantee that, you lecherous, deceitful, treacherous sloth."

Devraj said, "You have crossed the line, Kael E. Addison. Let it be known that this moment marks the end of our friendship," and slammed the phone down.

And that was the moment Kael came up with a new idea

of the sort of paper he should be writing.

Something that set things straight.

Something that tried to make up for the last twenty years of lies, half-truths, dishonesty, manipulation and propaganda.

CHAPTER 26 – Hardline Headline.

CORVELL UNIVERSITY.

The phone rang.

Kael picked it up.

"Hello?"

A young female voice said, "Hi." She spoke breathlessly, "It's Sarah at Climate Nature magazine. I've just received your submission."

"Yes? And?"

"You are Kael E. Addison? The Kael E. Addison?"

"Yes, I am."

"The Waterpolo stick guy?"

"Yeh, that's me."

Sarah paused for a moment then said, "I just rang to check that this was not some kind of a… hoax, you know? I mean, this is going to make the headlines, no doubt about it. 'Famous scientist Kael Addison,' or even, 'Famous Polo Stick scientist Kael Addison admits the jury is still out on global warming.' God, if it was anyone else but you we wouldn't publish this. It'd go straight in the rubbish bin – that's where all the denialist papers go. Sorry, I didn't mean-"

Kael said, "That's okay. I know I shouldn't ask this but how are you succeeding in finding peer reviewers?"

Sarah hesitated then said, "Oh, we'll just ask—"

Kael interrupted, "—no, please don't tell me their names. That would be unethical." Kael remembered now – he had talked to Sarah before.

Sarah paused again, probably because the last time he had spoken to her he had actually *asked* her for the names of the peer reviewers. Finally Sarah said, "Alright. Yes, we have found some peer reviewers. A lady who was a professor and now works for a think tank, a retired physicist and a notable statistician. Professor, are you sure you're alright? You're not... depressed or something? You do realise you're setting yourself up for allegations of scientific fraud, all sorts of things like that... If you want to retract it immediately I will send it back to you. No questions asked."

Kael breathed a deep sigh and said, "Thank you. No. And as far as being accused of fraud I'm well aware of that. No, I am completely sane. Perhaps saner than I have been for a long time." He thought for a moment. "I have found a new sense of... moral responsibility, you could say. A new sense of what's actually important in science." He swallowed. "Sarah, I became a Christian a few months ago. I believe God is showing me a few... home truths. God is casting light over my former attitudes, my former life, my former manner of scientific enquiry. And it ain't pretty."

"Wow," said Sarah. "You are a very brave man." She paused for a while. "A lot braver than I used to think."

* * *

It was when he received the paper for peer-review that Devraj immediately started quietly questioning what he should do about Kael. It was no use complaining to the universities; Kael held him by the proverbials in that theatre.

No, Devraj had to go higher up.

He had to go to the ones who held the reins, the bankers, the ones who held the purse strings.

The source of their funding.

Like that man in Europe. The one who had organised billions to fund their trips to Antarctica, their climate super-computer toys, their satellites, their sets of robotised ocean buoys measuring temperatures throughout the pacific, their trips here, there and everywhere, their conference appearances, their computers, their buildings and so much else.

That was the man Devraj needed to talk to.

The mysterious European man in the black suit, who liked snapping rulers. Devraj knew he was really the one in charge, the one who called the shots.

And he wouldn't be pleased to find out that one of his chief luminaries had become a climate denier.

CHAPTER 27 – Strange Exchange.

DEVRAJ'S OFFICE.

Two and a half weeks after the meeting in Europe, Devraj was sitting in his office being distracted from fiddling some figures on his desktop computer by the view outside his window. The sun was rising over the morning mists that partially obscured the University gymnasium and the attendant pine trees when his iPhone rang.

"Hi," said a man's voice.

"Hi," said Devraj.

The man spoke in a slight Russian accent. "I would like to meet. I need information from you about our mutual friend."

Devraj's heart lurched up into his mouth. He swallowed and said, "Alright. When?"

The Russian man said, "Today if possible. I am in New York right now."

Devraj had a strange feeling that he really didn't want anyone he knew seeing him meeting with this fellow. He cancelled all his appointments for the rest of the day and arranged to meet the Russian in the public library in Webster, a small town on the northern border of New York State an hour and a half's drive from the University.

* * *

Devraj had never seen the library before and as he drove through the town his heart sank. It was such a tiny old town that he thought the library was sure to be small, the kind of place you couldn't miss each other in.

But when he got there it turned out that it was, in fact, quite large. It was a rectangular building that looked like a modern shopping complex and when he went in, he found out that they had a lot of spare meeting rooms and activity areas. And cameras. He wasn't too happy about that.

Fortunately, Devraj had arrived early and quickly booked one of the rooms for an hour.

Devraj's wait was longer than fifteen minutes. He reflected that he had never in his life found a wait more excruciating than this one, and every moment he found himself wishing more and more that he had let the European man in the black suit who liked snapping rulers keep believing that Kael was still one of his luminaries, his climate change heroes.

Finally, at least twenty minutes late, the man rang Devraj's mobile. Devraj told him the room number.

The man walked in. Tall and muscular with pale blonde hair and chiseled features; Devraj could barely believe how suspicious he looked, and how Russian.

Devraj stood up and they shook hands. As the Russian

was saying, "I am Sasha," his phone rang. "Excuse me," he said, "I must take this call. Hello? Yes, I'm with him now. Saturday probably; the day after tomorrow. After this meeting I have to surveil and work out the best time to do it." Sasha switched off his phone and turned to Devraj. "Alright. I'm all yours."

Feeling a little shaky, Devraj leaned against the table to steady himself. "Now you're not going to hurt Kael, are you? After all, he has been a friend of mine for many years."

Sasha smiled a cold smile that didn't touch his eyes and said, "No, I'm not going to *hurt* him," in such a way that Devraj immediately regretted asking. Remembering that the German man in the black suit had used almost exactly the same phrase with the same intonation, Devraj said, "Alright" in an unintentionally high-pitched voice and slumped into one of the library chairs.

Sasha continued, and Devraj didn't believe a word he was saying. "I'm just going to recommend that he find a different field of expertise. I'm going to threaten him that if he doesn't he might run into trouble. That is all. I promise. Now, to business. I want to know everything you know about Kael, down to the very last detail of his life. What time he arrives at work. What he does in the evenings. Where he goes every minute of every day. You see when I 'talk' to him," When Sasha said the word 'talk' he mimed quote marks, "When I 'talk' to him I need to be away from other people, in a place where we can have… privacy. Oh, by the way, does he carry a piece?"

Devraj said, "What?"

Sasha said, "You know, a gun. A rifle or pistol of some sort."

Devraj said self-righteously, "No. Of course not. He's a Democrat. He's very much against guns."

"Good," said Sasha. "Very good. It can be slightly awkward when you just want a little 'conversation' with someone and they pull a firearm out on you." He smiled a ghastly smile. "You Americans are a piece of work."

* * *

Michelle had been tracking Devraj's activities and she knew about the gap in his timetable that Thursday when he wasn't at the university but had a great deal of trouble working out where Devraj had gone.

She had access to a bunch of unprotected camera feeds on the internet, as well as traffic cams and even some of the government camera feeds and she had been looking over the archived footage. She felt like giving up the search but a nagging feeling Devraj's absence was important had hold of her and she couldn't let it go. Finally, late on a Friday night when she should have been out with friends or relaxing at home, she found footage of Devraj's car leaving the university in the archives of the flower shop across the road. She followed Devraj's trail across the state and found footage of him parking outside the Webster Public Library.

When she saw the other man walking into the library half an hour later, she understood the significance. She knew who that was. The man from Italy. The man who had killed Rudolpho. But who was he going to kill? Devraj?

For a little while she hit a road-block because there were no open cams in the library or any other kind of footage she could find from the day before. It took her all night but with the help of a hacker in Bosnia she managed to access the library server, which had the security camera hard drives from the whole week; there was one set of footage that had the meeting room Sasha and Devraj in it. Unfortunately it only showed the people in the room when they were standing up.

It took her another half hour at least to lip-read what the Russian had been saying on his mobile phone. It wasn't until seven o'clock in the morning that she finally decoded it; the very day Sasha had told his boss he was going to 'do' Kael. With growing panic, Michelle remembered that time on the East Coast was two hours ahead of Phoenix.

She had to contact Kael and warn him immediately.

CHAPTER 28 – Trippy Girl Trips Up.

KAEL'S HOME IN ITHACA, NY.

Ever since his divorce ten years ago, Kael had relished the quiet of Saturday mornings.

He would sleep in, then have breakfast late, sitting and reading the newspaper. It was much better, he had to admit, ever since his wife had left. He actually had some peace and quiet, freedom from incessant nagging, something he hadn't initially appreciated when the wound of rejection was still raw.

Sometimes a little later in the morning he would open up his laptop and browse through his emails and answer the important ones.

Today he was quite late doing that but the moment he turned his computer on, something weird happened. An app he didn't even know he had suddenly opened.

TG: Kael Addison. Get out of there!

Kael was puzzled. He didn't know what was going on. He typed:

Kael: Who are you?

The circle went around, indicating TG, whoever she was, was still writing.

TG: I'm a friend of Nathanael's. I am a computer hacker. You need to get out of your house.

Kael suddenly felt afraid.

Kael: What are you talking about?

TG: Leave your house. You are in imminent danger.

Kael: Why? How do you know? Why should I listen to you? This might be a trap too.

TG: I have been following a certain group of people, including a particular Russian man who works for a group of criminals in Europe, that I like to call the Cabal. He has been sent here to kill you. He's already left New York. Please hurry. I have just received information that indicates that he is going to act this morning. Devraj is behind it. He betrayed you.

Kael really didn't know what to do. What if this was just a bunch of thieves doing this, to get him out of the house so they could break in and steal all his stuff or something, or hackers doing something on his computer?

Kael: Well... Can I talk to Nathanael? Verify that you are who you say you are?

TG: Alright. Give me five minutes. If I were you I'd be packing my bags while I wait. Take only essentials. Drop in to an Eftpos and take out cash.

Kael: I'll start packing. But I'm not going anywhere till I talk to Nathanael.

TG: Alright. I'm on it.

Two minutes later, Kael was in his bedroom packing just the absolute essentials when his mobile phone rang.

Kael said, "Hello?"

Nathanael's voice answered, "Hi, Kael. Yes, TG is a friend of mine. If she says go, you had better go. She knows what she's talking about."

Kael said, "Alright. Thanks. Wait – Nathanael – in case this is a trick and it's not really you – how did we meet?"

"At the church," said Nathanael. "Where we argued about climate and the pastor made them destroy the videos."

"Thanks," Kael said. "Just had to check."

"You're going, then?"

"I am. I've finished packing. I'll be driving out in two minutes."

At that moment, the doorbell rang.

Kael said, "Oh, the doorbell rang."

Another message flashed onto the computer screen.

TG: He's at the door! Run!

Kael grabbed the laptop and his suitcase and checked that he had his wallet and keys in his jacket pockets.

He slipped through the kitchen, through the pantry cupboard, and into his garage. He flicked on the light and threw his luggage and the laptop in the trunk of the SUV.

The doorbell rang again.

Kael started the engine, praying that the SUV wouldn't be too noisy.

It was noisy; to Kael, it sounded like a steam engine clanking into life.

He pressed the roller door button.

He could see a man's legs below the roller door. What was he standing there for? Why would a man stand in front of the roller door when clearly it was opening?

He didn't recognise the man's pants or his shoes – could have been anyone – what if it wasn't the assassin? What if it was the postman or God forbid, the sheriff, or a law clerk delivering a summons?

Kael didn't want to run down an innocent man.

But if it was the assassin…

TG said it was. Nathanael said he could trust TG.

He prayed, "God, show me what to do."

The roller door wasn't fully open yet. It was barely up to the man's waist.

He couldn't see his hands. That meant the man's hands were both held up.

The only reason Kael could think of that at least one of the man's hands were not by his side was that he was holding a gun ready to shoot Kael in the head as soon as he could see his face.

It wasn't going to happen.

Not waiting for the roller door to go up, Kael put his foot down. The roller door scraped on the windscreen and he heard the whole roller assembly wrench out of its bracket above the doorway and bounce loudly on the roof. He hit the man at about ten miles an hour and the man half-bounced, half rolled over the hood of the SUV, comically slowly his two hands flailed upwards like the arms of one of those tall, skinny balloon-men kept aloft by an air compressor outside tyre businesses. A gun flew out of the man's hands – thank God! Kael could barely believe his eyes – the man actually was an assassin! The gun landed on top of the SUV.

The man rolled off the hood onto the paved driveway. Kael drove forwards and bumped over something soft and small – probably the man's arm. He hoped it wasn't his head. He didn't want to have to explain this to the cops.

He still might have to.

He looked in the rear-view mirror as he sped off. The man was alive. He was sitting up, cradling his right arm, clearly in pain.

Good, thought Kael vindictively. It cost you something to try and come and kill me.

Good riddance.

He looked in the rear-view mirror again, and caught a glimpse of a black vehicle parked in front of his house. The road curved and he didn't have time to notice what sort of car it was.

As he drove off, the sudden thought hit him that a person whose arms weren't showing might have been simply holding a clipboard with one hand and a pen with the other. He started shaking.

For a few minutes, Kael drove but the shaking got too bad. Opposite an oval, he pulled over to the roadside, next to a forest, or maybe it was a cemetery or something. He stumbled out of the car and vomited up his breakfast onto the curb strip.

For a moment he stood there wiping his mouth and trying to process what had just happened.

He took out his mobile and rang Nathanael back.

"What do I do now?" said Kael.

Nathanael said, "I have TG – Trippy Girl – with me

here. She'll work out a route for you that avoids cameras, surveillance, that sort of thing, as much as possible. She says you will have to change cars first. Pay cash. Go and get some cash from your ATM. A big wad, Kael, as much as you can get out in one go. Then keep in touch. She'll guide you. We'll meet you somewhere or other."

Kael swore. "I just remembered the gun is on top of the SUV." He looked at the roof of the car. "That was lucky, it's still there." He reached up to get it.

Nathanael's voice shouted from the mobile, "Wait! Don't touch it! Use a cloth. You don't know how many other murders have been done with it. Put it somewhere safe, out of the way. I'll talk to you soon." The call ended.

Kael found a cloth in the trunk and gingerly grasped the gun with it, wrapped it up and placed it in the trunk, in the spare tyre well. Then he drove to the nearest shopping centre and parked near the ATM.

He got onto his banking app. Fortunately, he was able to increase the withdrawal limit from one thousand to eight thousand dollars immediately. He withdrew the whole lot. Thank goodness; he didn't think one thousand would be enough for a decent car.

<u>CHAPTER 29 – Daylight Deals.</u>

RIDGE STAR MOTORS IN ITHACA, NY.

The only used car place Kael knew in Ithaca was Ridge Star Motors. It was two miles north. He sped. What was a speeding ticket in comparison with his life?

Most of the cars in Ridge Star Motors' lot were old, some were classic. Was that a model T Ford? Kael wouldn't have thought of buying here if he wasn't desperate.

Marcel, the proprietor, came out. He had serviced Kael's car a few times when Kael had been unhappy with the local franchise's repair work. Kael felt awkward, though; how was he going to explain to Marcel that he needed to swap his car for another?

Marcel said, "Hi, Professor. How's it goin'?" A lot of people in the town called Kael, 'Professor.'

Kael improvised. "I need another car to drive around in, Marcel. I've got eight thousand. What can I get?"

Marcel looked around the yard and said, "Well, I don't have anything for eight thousand. My most expensive car is five thousand five hundred. But I'll give it to you for eight thousand if you want, son."

Kael shook his head. "Is it... reasonably fast? Good strong chassis?"

"My word," said Marcel. "Well, it's a classic Model T

Ford. Fast it ain't. But it is a good strong chassis. But if you're looking for something fast… Look, I've got a BMW 2002 Turbo. Now that's a fast car! Reaches one hundred miles per hour in second gear, without even revving. It's top-notch, completely refurbished but I made one or two improvements to the turbo, won't eat up the gas, mind but there were a few faults in the way the original was designed that we've done workarounds for. Amazing what you can find out on the internet these days. Oh, and we added aircon. Give it to you for four."

"Done," said Kael, and counted out the money. Marcel went into the office and brought out the keys.

"Now there's something else – can I park my SUV here for a few days? Maybe a week or two?" The car yard was essentially a grass field, so Kael didn't think there'd be too much of a problem with that.

"Well…" said Marcel, "I'd have to charge you a parking fee, just to cover the extra insurance, mind."

Kael got out a hundred dollar bill but Marcel said, "Oh, no, twenty will do for that. Here," he took Kael's hundred and counted out four twenties change.

Kael said, "Thanks. I'll be back in two weeks, maybe sooner."

"Good, no problem, Kael. You can pick it up then,"

said Marcel, with a broad smile on his face. He shook Kael's hand. "Good doin' business with you, son."

As Kael transferred his luggage and the laptop into the BMW, Marcel said, "Oh, you didn't leave anything in the SUV, did you? Surprising the number of people do that, forget something they need cause it's in the trunk or the glove compartment of the old car. I know you ain't selling that one but still…"

Kael said, "Oh, thanks." Lucky. He would've forgotten the gun otherwise. He got it out and put it in the trunk of the BMW.

Kael jumped in, caressed the BMW dashboard for a moment, which was exquisite, revved the engine and roared out onto the main road.

After a few turns, he was in the farmland.

He took the BMW up to the speed limit, sixty-five. She was still in first gear and doing quite comfortably. He laughed to himself – he would never have even thought of driving a gas guzzler like this before today – but he had to admit he enjoyed it.

He glanced in the mirror. One car, about as far back as he could see. A black SUV, probably not a police car but that was the least of his worries. The car in front of his house had been black. Was it the same car?

Kael knew he really shouldn't do it but the temptation was too great. He put it in second gear and accelerated up to eighty. The engine was purring nicely as though the extra load hardly had an effect.

Strange. The car in the mirror was still there. Was it matching his speed? He swore. It must be the guy who had tried to kill him. How was he driving with a broken arm?

Kael put his foot down and took it up to one hundred miles per hour. The engine was humming nicely, not a lot of strain.

The car in the rear-view mirror was still there but it had fallen behind a little.

Kael tested the brakes; they were good. Marcel was honest, he'd say that for him. Kael turned onto a farm track called Buck Road; he had no clue where it went.

He slowed down to seventy. He almost lost control on one of the turns, so he took it back down to fifty. The other car turned off Auburn onto Buck behind him; despite the twists and turns it was so flat, you couldn't help but see and be seen.

There was a straight stretch ahead. Kael took it up to ninety.

The other car was still behind him, maybe half a mile, maybe a little more.

Kael slowed for the T-junction up ahead then almost lost it on the dogleg. Without warning he found himself roaring onto Ridge Road, onto the bitumen, swerving to avoid cars flying at him from every direction, tooting madly. Kael careened off to hit dirt on the strip behind him.

He was on the wrong side of the road. He jammed the steering wheel to the right, screeched his tyres, slid onto the correct side of the road with the back wheels burning rubber, floored it again and glanced at the fuel gauge as he lurched ahead.

Full tank of gas.

Good on you, Marcel.

An honest man like José. A month ago and Kael wouldn't have even noticed. Yes, sir, he had changed.

Ha. Ironic. He'd changed, so much, and before anyone, even his own sister, knew, he was going to be eliminated from this life.

Not if he could help it. Kael took it up to eighty again. Too many unknowns out here. Any faster wasn't safe. He began weaving in and out, taking a few chances, passing as many cars as he could, pushing the speed as far as he felt he could take it.

He could just see the other car, a long way back now, threading through the cars.

Kael knew what he had to do.

He had to get to the New York State Thruway.

About an hour north, if he took it at forty-five, that is.

At ninety, it would be half an hour's journey.

He pressed the pedal and took it up to ninety. He started taking greater risks, running along in the left lane for as long as he could if the right lane was packed. It was the speeding cars coming the other way he had to worry about, and one came out of nowhere but Kael nudged the wheel to the right and shot right along the middle line, giving the guy space on his left to go past. He was strangely calm despite all this – speeding was a necessary evil. He could only afford a quick glance in the rear-view mirror. There was a car off-road, smoking, had the guy hit something? Was he even alive?

Great, something else to keep him awake at night.

But if he didn't get away from this guy, Kael would never have to worry about anything anymore. Kael wouldn't have any more nights in which to worry; or any days.

He nudged the gas pedal a little more, just over one hundred now. He couldn't see the other guy in the rear-view mirror any more.

And then it was not fun anymore, he was bone-weary, sweating and his knuckles were aching from how he'd been gripping the steering wheel.

He switched on the car air-conditioner. It worked like a charm, just like Marcel said it would. Swerving in and out, driving on the wrong side as long as he could. Just when he thought he had the hang of it, another speeding SUV in the overtaking lane nearly totalled him. He swerved just in time onto the wrong side of the road again and was forced onto the left curb strip and narrowly avoided careening off the road into a tree. A truck came roaring towards him on the left lane, so Kael took the BMW onto the verge again, stopping this time. He idled outside someone's farm gate for about five or ten seconds.

As the truck came closer he gunned it in neutral then let go of the clutch when it had gone past. The clutch caught and the tyres screeched, the acrid smell of rubber burning filled his nostrils, the back of the car swerved and he was back on the road, roaring along at one hundred, passing the very cars he had previously passed half a minute before.

He pumped the gas pedal, took it up to a hundred and five. May as well get a decent fine if he was going to get booked.

He would be safe with the police, especially if they arrested him.

Hopefully.

He had no idea know what sort of reach this secret Cabal had, these conspirators TG had told him about who had ordered him killed. He could never have believed his friend Devraj would betray him but he had. Did they have access to surveillance? Maybe their reach extended even into prisons and holding cells at police stations? If he couldn't even trust his best friend, how could he trust complete strangers, even if they were sworn to serve and protect?

Kael put his foot down. He could hear the engine was straining; it looked as though that was the limit. He couldn't get the BMW to go any faster than it was going. One hundred and five.

He'd been going for twenty-five minutes now on Ridge Road. Surely he was nearly at the New York State Thruway?

Then he passed the sign. New York State Thruway, three miles.

He slammed his foot down flat on the floor.

The traffic was thicker here but Kael was in the zone now. He was flowing, he was one with the car. In and out, look up ahead while you're passing, gun it while you can, in and out, he had a kind of rhythm going.

That's when it goes wrong; when you're proud of how you're going. Time to be careful.

The Thruway ramp came up more quickly than he expected and that was what almost threw him but he twisted the steering wheel at the very last moment and screeched onto the West ramp, the rear of the car careening to and fro in a chaotic way; some kind of non-harmonic resonance, a feedback loop.

He could've taken the East ramp but he was heading West.

That was it. His single ploy. The guy following him had a fifty-fifty chance now of getting it correct.

If Kael could do it right at the next major intersection, he could decrease those odds to twenty-five percent. Three intersections later – three choices – and the person following him would only have a twelve point five percent chance of choosing correctly.

Kael stuck to the speed limit now, sixty-five miles per hour. No reason he should get arrested for speeding at this point.

He said to his iPhone, "Siri, call Nathanael."

Siri made the call.

Nathanael's voice came out of the phone, "Hi Kael!"

Kael said, "He's been following me. What do I do now? I'm on the New York State Thruway, i90, heading West. I just got on at the Weedsport entrance."

Nathanael said, "Tell me your license number."

"Why?"

"For Trippy Girl to keep track of you. She can do things you can't believe."

"Ah, just a sec. I don't know it yet." Still cruising at one hundred, Kael extracted the ownership papers from the glove compartment and quickly glanced at the license plate number. "5764-DXZ."

"Alright," said Nathanael. "Okay, Trippy Girl is

finding out where you are…" Kael could hear key clicks in the background. Was Trippy Girl someone who knew Nathanael? "Yeh, look, there're some rooms available in the Quality Motor Inn. You can park out the back. Take the next exit. It's coming up soon."

He took the exit.

Nathanael said, "It's straight south. You'll see it on the left. Find a place to park that can't be seen from the road. There should be plenty."

"Alright."

Nathanael said, "Trippy Girl reckons you'd be best to stay here for four or five hours. By the way, turn your mobile off and take out the battery but keep it on you, just in case something happens."

Kael said, "Why?"

"If they are really in league with Michelle's Cabal, they'll be able to track your phone. Put the battery in again in about five hours, when you're ready to leave. What's the time there?"

Kael looked at the dash clock. "Oh, about ten-thirty."

"Well, turn the phone back on and ring me at three or four," said Nathanael. "Trippy Girl will have some instructions for you then. By the way, we're coming."

Kael said, "Coming?"

"We're going to try to anticipate where you're headed and meet you there," said Nathanael. "TG is working out the details as we speak."

Kael parked at the back of the Motor Inn after he had paid for the night. It was $180, a bit steep.

Maybe some people might still be on their holidays this time of year, he thought, maybe that's why.

It was mid-morning and Kael was hungry. The tavern was open, so Kael ordered a burger and chips and a scotch on the rocks for lunch. The burger was burned, the chips were soggy, and the scotch tasted like it had been watered down but he was surprised by how little he cared. Normally he'd be demanding they give him his money back or replace it with another, better-cooked meal. He laughed bitterly. Funny how imminent death puts things your life into perspective.

He went and got his luggage from the trunk, leaving the pistol where it was; besides not wanting to touch it because he didn't want his DNA on it, he had always hated guns.

He got his luggage and his laptop. The room smelled mouldy and the floor in the bathroom had footprints on it, as though it hadn't been washed properly since the last guest.

Strangely, despite it all, he found the accomodation delightful, like a wonderful palace. Dicing with death also helps you to appreciate the little things.

Like the fact that the sheets smelled clean. And the television worked; ah, no but the cable was cut off, or maybe it just didn't have many stations. There was a coin slot on the side. You had to put coins in to make it work.

He only had one hundred dollar bills.

They had told him there was wireless internet but when he took his laptop out it didn't connect properly. Just as well; maybe they could track him through it.

He closed the laptop and took the battery out of his phone. He put it by his bed, in pieces, then thought the better of it and put it in his pocket. Never know when you might need it; if he left it on the table he'd as likely forget it.

The motel window faced west, looking out on a flat landscape, with the car-park with his BMW parked in the foreground. He liked that monstrosity a lot more than his hybrid SUV. If he got through this he'd keep it. Behind his new car, there were trees, and some kind of building to the northwest, and more trees, it was a very nondescript view.

Kael closed both sets of curtains, the thick ones *and* the lacy ones, and turned off the light.

Laying in the darkness, a great heavy blanket of weariness descended on him unexpectedly, a leaden weight, like the heavy X-ray proof blankets in the radiology department.

Only it was over his whole body, his whole self, like a tent.

He fell asleep.

He drifted into a dream with a numinous atmosphere that filled him with awe. He was underneath something large and heavy and impenetrable but he felt completely safe. For a moment he thought it was the type of lead blanket they use for protecting parts of people's bodies from X-rays but then he realised they were wings, giant wings. He knew somehow that the wings were larger than the whole universe but for some reason, they were protecting him. A still, small voice whispered, "He will cover you with his pinions, under his wings you will take refuge."

Pinions, they're the outer feathers of a bird's wings.

He woke up. The dream had seemed significant but whose wings? Whose feathers? What did it mean? Then the dream faded.

He stretched, feeling refreshed, and decided to see what was in the bedside bureau.

In the top drawer, there was a Bible. He opened it to the middle, choosing a random page, curious to read this book that he had neglected for so long.

It said, 'Psalm 91', at the top of the page.

His eyes went immediately to the fourth verse.

He who dwells in the shelter of the Most High, who abides in the shadow of the Almighty, will say to the LORD, "My refuge and my fortress; my God, in whom I trust." For He will deliver you from the snare of the fowler and from the deadly pestilence; He will cover you with his pinions, and under His wings you will find refuge.

Kael was amazed. These were the very words from his dream.

He read the words again and again.

God somehow knew which random page he would flip to. God was reassuring Kael, that He was watching over him. It was amazing.

No one had ever told him this sort of thing could happen. Was God really in command to that degree? It comforted Kael. He read the whole Psalm ten or eleven times through, feeling a growing sense of peace and joy.

Kael prayed for quite a while after that, thanking God for looking after him and asking Him to help make him into a better person. He was completely overwhelmed, in fact, because he suddenly realised to what degree he didn't deserve God's help.

He said, "I was Your enemy, really, for so long. I used to complain bitterly about my sister believing in You. I remember on the plane, when I saw the beauty of the sunlight in the clouds, and so many other times, how I resisted You. What made You want to help me? What made You want to save me?"

He remembered Pastor Carlos saying, "For God so loved the world that He gave His only Son."

It was love, pure, self-sacrificial love. There was no other explanation.

"Why didn't anyone tell me about You earlier, Lord?" he wondered aloud. He had known plenty of churchgoers at the Universities he had worked at, and there were many people among the climate activists as well who claimed to be Christian. Some even who went to church. But not one of them had told him about any of this... what would you call it?

Grace...

Not even his sister had really told him about God's grace, although of anyone, she was probably the only one who had tried...

José had never told him. But by the patience and kindness, José had shown his rude, thankless brother in law God's grace, repeatedly forgiving Kael for his neglect, rudeness and arrogant attitude.

Kael thanked God for José.

Kael looked at the clock on the wall. It was five o'clock. How long had he been praying? How long had he been asleep before that?

He quickly put the phone back together and rang Nathanael.

Nathanael answered, "Where were you?"

Kael said, "I fell asleep. And then I kind of got lost reading the Bible, believe it or not. Would you believe, I dreamed some words, and then when I read the Bible, there they were. Psalm 91."

"I would believe it," Nathanael said. "I certainly would."

Kael said, his voice full of wonder, "It's amazing, Nathanael. God really cares about me. He really does! Me. Can you believe it?"

Nathanael said, "Yes. It's quite undeserved, isn't it? Who can say why God chose us, in particular, to know about Jesus' love?"

Kael's voice held new strength. "Where to now, Nathanael? Do I stay here? What does TG say?"

Nathanael said, "Kael! If things go south… if it all goes wrong, just remember what you've just told me, okay? God is looking after you. Remember that."

Kael nodded, then remembered that Nathanael couldn't see him. "Okay. I promise. I will remember. God is looking after me."

Nathanael was quiet for a little while, then he said, "Trippy Girl is thinking Buffalo next. Head west on the New York State Thruway, just keep going, you'll hit Buffalo soon enough. The University Motor Inn is opposite the university there. You shouldn't find it hard to find. It's a dreadful place, judging by the reviews; the vast majority are two stars. I have a feeling it's the last place they'll expect you to be staying at. Now, this time, Trippy Girl says take the battery out of your phone before you set off. She will SMS you the address of the Motor Inn first though; write it down, it's in the middle of town, you'll find it. Oh, by the way, those Bibles in the hotels – no one will mind if you take it with you. It's a Gideons. That's what it's for."

Kael did everything Nathanael told him to do; he found a pen in one of the drawers and when the SMS came, he wrote the address in the front of the Bible, which was the only paper he could find, and he put the Bible in his luggage.

Then he took the mobile apart and put it in his jeans pocket.

He packed away his luggage and his laptop then and cast a glance through the curtains at his BMW.

There was no one parked nearby.

Kael vacated the room. He put his luggage in the trunk of his car and quickly jumped into the drivers' seat and started the engine. She gave a satisfying purr as though the old car was happy to be on the road again. He looked around again, looking for places his pursuer could hide or park a car out of sight. There were some buildings and a couple of trees to the west. Someone could hide there, watch the place from the shadows. But why would the guy hide, why wouldn't he just come to Kael's room in the motel and do away with him?

Maybe he just didn't know which room Kael was in?

Still, no one had pulled out yet to follow him.

Kael got some gas, which he paid for with cash.

Soon he was on the Thruway, on the way to Buffalo, New York.

There were two or three black SUVs in his mirror.

He didn't think any of them were following him but it's hard to tell when you're on the freeway. Especially when it starts getting dark.

He arrived in Buffalo at about eight-thirty p.m. in a jumpy and paranoid state of mind.

He had no proof that he was being followed.

But the thing is, maybe it was the fact that it was night, or that he couldn't tell one set of headlights from another in the streets behind him, or the dark shadows in the city, or the many hiding places in the alleyways and behind closed doors and multi-story car-parks and parks and trees but he definitely felt he was being followed.

He followed the same procedure as the other motel, although he couldn't park away from the road since this motel was in the middle of the city; there simply were no parking places away from main roads.

Kael didn't like the look of the motel restaurant much so he went for a walk and found a nearby kebab place and ate there. He chatted to the owner, a jolly, moustachioed Turkish man, who told Kael all about the travails of his family in the US.

As Kael listened to what turned into a long story involving migration, working for other people then buying his own business, then watching his children growing up, then dealing with their video game addiction and university degrees and struggles with internet porn and drugs and marriages and grandchildren, Kael realised how much he had changed as a person.

Before the video incident at the church, he would never have considered anyone except a top climate scientist as a person whom he might even show an idle interest in.

And the food.

Not Kael's usual healthy eating habits, which centred around salads and carbohydrates. Strangely, after eating all this red meat, a burger, a lamb kebab, he actually found he felt stronger.

He walked back to the motel.

He looked up at the stars — they were surprisingly clear in the street he was in, perhaps because there weren't many street lights. But he had seen the sweeping majesty of the galaxy on its side in Antarctica, and the alternate view in the Arctic. Most of the Milky Way was invisible these days in any city; the stars were missing, as though they had fallen out of their places.

He came to his room and he took out his key to open it. A sense of nervous apprehension took hold and he almost didn't put the key in the lock.

It was completely irrational; he had a strong feeling that he should leave. But he had already paid for the room, he had put the money down. Come on, Kael, be rational. How could that gunman have followed him? Could he possibly be in the room?

He opened the door.

There was no one in there, just his luggage sitting on the bed. He checked the cupboards just to make sure.

He opened his Bible again and read something from John about the Word of God, and then slept soundly.

In the morning he set off at six am. Trippy Girl had a plan for him to go to Niagara Falls today.

But Kael noticed the car following him this time as soon as he was on the road. A black SUV; was it the same one that had been following him through the back-blocks? Was the assassin driving it? How had he found him?

He thought it was the same car but he couldn't be sure.

Seeing the way it was driven, Kael was sure this was the car.

For about five minutes he stayed on the main road then made a sudden right turn without indicating, tyres screeching, as he passed through a pair of stone pillars into a separate residential development.

The SUV screeched around as well, burning rubber and clipping the curb strip, then bouncing back onto the road. Kael upped the ante, put his foot down. Thirty, thirty-five, forty, forty-five, fifty. He glanced in the mirror. The black SUV was still on his tail.

Kael screeched around one corner after another, putting his foot down, gunning the engine.

The SUV stayed glued to his heels. It was lucky there wasn't much traffic, not many people out on the road yet; seconds later a jogger stepped onto the road as he was rounding a corner. To his relief the woman stumbled back onto the curb, her face a brief mask of horror.

Kael's tyres screamed around another corner and he braked to a stop in a cul de sac in front of some sort of farm track on the other side of a low barrier. He could drive through the barrier but he hesitated and then the SUV screeched to a stop, the door opened, and a man jumped out holding a handgun pointed straight at him.

Kael recognised him.

It was the same man. The one Kael had run over at his house. Blonde, chunky Russian face, holding the gun with his left hand with his right hand bandaged or strapped beneath his shirt.

He indicated for Kael to get out of the car.

Kael got out holding his hands up.

The man said in a clipped Russian accent, "Good, good. Now give me your car keys."

Kael didn't want to do that. But he had no choice.

The Russian unlocked the trunk, took out Kael's suitcase and threw it onto the footpath.

"Get in," he barked.

Kael climbed into the boot awkwardly, thinking to himself that this is not the sort of thing that you stay alive after doing.

The trunk closed.

Luckily it was a large trunk but it didn't stop it being extremely uncomfortable.

The engine started and the car started moving.

Kael began bemoaning his situation.

So much for God protecting him.

He prayed angrily, "Why have You abandoned me? You promised!" It was dark and he was scared, and his legs were cramping. The car was bumping up and down. He had no clue where he was being driven, except that he was sure that once he reached his destination, he was going to be killed.

Well, this was it. So much for being under God's protecting wings. He was doomed.

Was any of it real? Could that Bible thing just have been a coincidence? A sense of doom began to overshadow him.

He concentrated on the car bumping up and down. It was real, it felt normal, as normal as any other thing he might be doing any other day. This was reality right now, this small trunk, the little bit of sunlight he could see coming through the screw-holes where the brake lights and indicators were, the excruciatingly normal sounds of traffic, trucks going past, cars, the indicators flicking to and fro every now and then and the sense of force being exerted as they went around a corner. And in a few minutes, his final demise.

Then his stomach sank and an even worse sensation took hold, a sinking depression, an acceptance that this was it, he was done for, he may as well give up. It was almost as though the darkness was whispering to him, "Give up. Resign yourself. Nobody cares. God doesn't care about you."

Kael's life was coming to an end. At least his legacy was secure: that study he had sent to that journal. He would be even more famous, after death, for having become a skeptic. He laughed bitterly. How ironic.

His legs, bent in a particularly uncomfortable position, began to really distress him. And he started feeling as though he couldn't breathe.

He didn't want to die yet. He wasn't ready. He began to weep.

He realised the one thing he wanted to do more than anything was just to thank his sister for putting up with him and have one more beer with José. And to tell José what a great guy he was, he'd never really told him that. What an honest, down to earth, guy.

Strangely, the worst part of the whole thing was a simple annoying sensation of complete discomfort because something was poking into his side and his back. He felt like screaming, it was so uncomfortable.

Then it was as if God was speaking to him. "I'm not going to do everything for you. I can put the answer in front of you but you have to take hold of it." Was it just his imagination? Or could God really talk to him?

He groaned. It was so dark in here.

He prayed angrily, "What can I possibly do? You've abandoned me. I'm going to die."

The discomfort of the thing poking into his side, and the other thing, into his back, was becoming untenable.

He groaned, "God, for God's sake help me, please, I can't take it anymore."

With a sudden spark of recognition, Kael laughed as he realised that what was poking him in the back was the pistol, wrapped in the piece of cloth. And the thing poking him in the side was his mobile phone, in pieces, in his pocket.

With growing awareness of his own complete stupidity, Kael laughed silently but joyfully.

Working in the dark, completely by touch he put the phone together. The pieces simply slipped into place, to his surprise.

He flicked it onto silent then messaged Nathanael.

Kael: He got me. In trunk of his car.

Nathanael: Alright. Tracking your phone now.

He propped the phone up where he could see it.

Then, with great effort, Kael twisted his left arm around far enough to reach underneath his own back and touch the gun with his left hand. The problem was he couldn't grab it, it was in the wrong position, he had to push it with two fingers and then reach down towards it with the other hand. At first, he could only manage to grab the cloth but pulling on that and simultaneously lifting himself up, grunting and groaning, he got the gun into his right hand somehow.

A few minutes later another message came through.

> Nathanael: Looks like he's taking you to Niagara Falls. BTW see you there. Flew in this afternoon.
>
> Kael: Got the gun.
>
> Nathanael: Gun?
>
> Kael: 1 he had
>
> Nathanael: Good. Hate to say this but you had better be ready to use it.

There was a pause for a few seconds then another message came through.

> Nathanael: Msgd TG she says she's reached a dead end, though. She says if you can turn the tables maybe we can get the shooter to tell us what's going on…

Kael moved his limbs around slowly until he was in the most comfortable position from which to shoot. The minutes passed slowly as he waited. He felt every bump, every turn, heard every car, every truck that passed. But he was lifted up by an amazing sense of exhilaration – God really did care about him!

Finally, they slowed down, turned another corner.

The car stopped.

Kael heard the door open and the guy step out of the car but the door didn't close again... Then footsteps as he walked over, one, two, three, four five. Then the key in the lock, Kael could actually see the lock turning, ever so slowly, as though reality itself had slowed down.

Then the trunk sprang open and the light dazzled Kael. He shouted hoarsely, "Move back or I'll shoot!" He sprang up, his eyes adjusted and he saw that the man was standing there with his mouth open in surprise, holding another gun in his left hand, which was hanging down by his side; he hadn't been ready.

Kael had him.

They were in some sort of cul-de-sac inside a massive power station, the biggest Kael had ever seen.

The man lifted his gun to shoot but Kael shot first. Kael missed the body mass but hit the Russian in the shoulder. The man swore in a language Kael did not know.

He had dropped the car keys.

Kael jumped out of the trunk, holding the gun up;

surely he could pick up the car keys himself but the man had managed to pick up the car keys again with his left hand while still holding his gun. He couldn't lift his gun though; his right arm was the one Kael had driven over and his left arm was the one Kael had shot.

Kael said, "Stand still! Or I'll shoot!"

But the man lunged forwards and kicked Kael in the shins. Kael stumbled. The man ran back around and jumped in the driver's seat.

The car reversed with the door still open. Kael had to jump out of the way; he pressed himself against a locked gate and the car scraped past. Kael shot at the car but the guy just kept driving. With a sinking heart, Kael watched his precious car bumping up over the left curb strip, down again and over the right curb strip, swerving from side to side. The man was driving off like a drunk. Kael surprised himself with the sudden explosion of vitriol that he let loose.

The car bumped over another curb and back into the middle of the road. Kael realised it wasn't that he'd been drinking; the guy had a shot left shoulder and a heavily bruised — if not broken — right arm. Dammit, Kael liked that car.

He would either never see that car again or it would be totalled, he was certain of it.

Somehow the man managed to point his gun out of the driver's side window and shot at Kael but his shot went way wide and missed him.

The man swerved left into the traffic on the main road, still careening to and fro like a madman.

As he disappeared, Kael had a nagging thought that he had forgotten something, left something behind.

A few seconds later, though, another car pulled into the cul-de-sac. It was a small white car, a Hertz rental, and Nathanael was driving and Natasha was in the passenger seat.

Natasha already had the back door open for Kael to jump in. She said, "We guessed something had happened because we saw that you had stopped in this dead end. Glad to see you're still with us, Kael."

As he jumped in, Kael snapped, "Get after him! He's got my car! He just turned left onto that road there."

Nathanael gunned the engine, even though the door wasn't closed yet. Kael nearly fell out, luckily he had buckled his belt already. He pulled the door closed.

Nathanael turned the corner.

Kael shouted, "That BMW! That one there, the old one! I like that car. He's getting away with it!"

Nathanael said, "Nice one. That's a 2002 Turbo isn't it?"

After a few expletives, Kael added, "We've got him! He's got a shot shoulder and the other arm is heavily bruised if not broken. There's no way he can drive and shoot at the same time."

Nathanael said, "I'll tail him. It's better if he doesn't know that we're behind him – I think we have a better chance of getting your car back if he doesn't know we're here." He glanced at Kael sitting in the back. "You might need to get down, or be disguised at least."

Natasha said, "I'll help." She rummaged in her handbag and pulled out a small, black beret and a pair of sunglasses.

Kael said, "Not exactly my style but I get the point." He put them on.

Natasha swiped away the phone tracking app and opened a map app. "Don't worry, it uses Tor Browser, it's unhackable. You can see where he might be going."

After about fifteen minutes of weaving through traffic, Natasha said, "People are far less likely to think you're following them if you're in front of them," so Nathanael pulled in front of Kael's car, just before his indicators flicked on to turn off the main road.

Nathanael turned off first and they found themselves twisting through streets that had small, transportable houses, a modern slum or ghetto.

Kael's car suddenly turned another corner behind them.

Nathanael cried out, "We lost him!" and turned around.

Natasha was watching the map app.

She said, "Go round the block."

Nathanael went around the block but he was nowhere to be seen. Natasha said, "There are about five possible turns he could have taken."

They stopped by the side of the road.

Natasha sighed, "Well, I guess that's that."

Nathanael hit the steering wheel and uttered an expletive. "I don't know what to do now. He was really our only lead at the moment."

Natasha said, "I think it means they've beaten us. We had an advantage for a moment – knowing where the shooter was – he could have helped us find out what's going on. Nathanael, what do you think it means?"

"I don't know," he said. "What do you think?"

Natasha said, "Darkness wins the skirmishes sometimes, I guess, even though Jesus has already won the battle on the cross."

For a few minutes they sat there silently watching the cars go by, some of them obviously parents picking up their kids from the local school; they were hoping that one of them was the BMW but it didn't pass by.

The normal suburban sounds of cars going by, the gentle breeze, the light of the afternoon sun peeking through the leaves and making patterns on the car door; it was all so distressingly inconsequent.

Natasha prayed quietly, "Help us, Father God." Suddenly Kael let loose his second long string of expletives for the day.

Nathanael said, "What's up?"

Kael said, "I know what I forgot."

Natasha said, "What you forgot? What do you mean? When?"

Kael hit his forehead with his fist. "When I got away from that guy. I left my mobile in the trunk of his car. I must've done! I remember clearly I was holding the gun with both hands and I don't have it on me now. Now I've lost my mobile as well. Actually…" He waited for a second but she didn't catch his gist. "You were tracking my mobile. It's still on. It's in the trunk of his car."

Natasha swore this time. "Of course! Hold on," as she swiped to another app on her phone. A dot showed up, showing the phone moving through the streets about a block away. She said, "Fantastic! Alright, got him. Go left here, right here."

They were right behind him, following him again now. He was exiting the slums onto a road that went through a forested area. The driving was slightly better now, as though he had gotten used to driving with two injured arms.

Natasha said, "There's no way out of this cul-de-sac. Wait here for a moment." Nathanael waited behind a corner as the car went along another narrow road.

Creeping around the corner, Nathanael took a pair of binoculars from his glove compartment and looked through them. "He's parked in the front car-park of what looks like some sort of industrial building. It's called the Krystal B. Lassiter Lab. He's getting out. He's going into the building."

Kael said, "That's great. I can get my car back and we can go."

Nathanael looked at Natasha. "We've got to get into that lab. I want to know who's behind this. Don't you want to know what's going on?"

Kael replied, "I guess so…"

Natasha said, "We can park a little closer without necessarily being noticed. There's residential land to the East. Let's wait for a few moments, once he's definitely inside. We'll be turning right at the building."

Kael said, "Just wait, I'll get out and get my car." But then he felt a sort of tingling in his head. "No, wait, I think God's telling me not to, not yet."

Nathanael waited a few minutes then turned out, past the building, and around another corner past small demountable houses and other places that were little more than shipping containers with doors and windows. He parked in front of some vacant land and said, "I think we ought to wait until it's dark."

Natasha said, "And risk charges for breaking and entering?"

Nathanael said, "What do you think?"

Natasha shook her head. "I think just go straight in and ask around, find out what's going on in there."

Nathanael nodded. "Wait here," he said to Kael as they were getting out of the car. "If we're not back in one hour…"

Natasha continued the sentence, "Call the police."

Undoing his seat belt and tucking the gun into the back of his trousers, Kael said, "No way. I'm not missing out on this! I'm coming with you."

Nathanael and Natasha looked at each other.

"Psalm 91," said Kael, "The Lord's looking after me. I've got nothing to worry about."

Natasha said, "Seriously?"

Kael said, "On my mother's grave, I swear. God's looking after me."

As Kael got out of the car Natasha whispered in Nathanael's ear, "Famous last words."

Nathanael said to her, "Well, you never know, do you? God might've spoken to him." She shrugged and said, "Well, are we going to go in without a gun at all? Kael's got a gun on him."

Nathanael sighed, opened the car door and said to Kael, "Alright. You can come."

Kael was leading the way but suddenly he turned on his heel and said, "Wait, I don't feel sure. At the motel I wasn't sure I should stay. I felt God was telling me to leave but I ignored it. What if God is telling us not to go in?"

Natasha shrugged. "Maybe we should pray about it?"

Kael's gaze went from one to the other uneasily. "I'll follow your lead," he said, "This God business is a bit new to me."

Nathanael said, "Make a huddle, then. We'll pray."

Nathanael prayed, "Dear Father in heaven, please guide us. What do we do?"

A still, small voice whispered to Nathanael, "Go around the back."

Kael said softly, "I think we need to go in the back."

Nathanael and Natasha concurred immediately. They prayed for God's blessing and help. Natasha looked at the map app again. By walking down to the end of the street they would reach a strip of virgin forest that extended behind the building for about five hundred metres.

Natasha said, "Kael might be right. Our approach won't be too obvious from that direction, we'll just seem to be locals going for a walk in the forest who got lost and wandered into the building." She pointed to the app. "Especially when this shopping centre is nearby. We can claim that we just wandered into the wrong place."

Nathanael nodded. "So long as the guy who abducted Kael doesn't see us there, our story will hold."

Kael looked uncomfortable.

Nathanael said, "What's wrong?"

Kael said, "Well, I have been dishonest for so long. Realising that, is what forced me to see that I needed God. Now I'm about to lie again. Or at the least, make a false impression."

Natasha said, "We're at war, Kael. Spying is an… honourable profession in the Bible. God himself sent spies into the land of Canaan – Joshua and his friends – it's a necessary evil sometimes…"

Shuffling his hands and looking away in such a way that Kael thought he might be uncomfortable with the situation too, Nathanael said, "Hopefully we won't even have to lie. Just keep your mouth shut if there's a morally doubtful situation, Kael. If your conscience is troubling you." Nathanael was silent for a moment, then continued, "Anyhow, if God wants us to go into that building from this direction, then He must have a plan."

CHAPTER 30 – Michelle's Shell Scripts.

PHOENIX, ARIZONA.

Peter had arrived earlier that day. He'd caught an Uber from the airport. He hugged the boy very gladly, until Meth said, "Dad, you're squashing me!" Then he filled Michelle in on the details of what had happened; the things he had not been able to summarise in the text message he had sent her from Italy.

Michelle had left Peter and Meth in the lounge room watching Meth's favourite show, the Flintstones in Hungarian. In her bedroom, her laptop was open, running a few scripts.

She typed several commands in and finally hit paydirt. "I've got it!" she cried out. "I've got Sasha's mobile."

The last message on the feed was:

> Sasha: Shot. Need help.
>
> Unknown Sender: We have a building just outside Niagara Falls. The Krystal B. Lassiter Laboratory. Deerbrook Street.
>
> Sasha: OK.
>
> Unknown Sender: We shall inform them that you're coming.
>
> Sasha: What about Kael? Should I just give up on the job?

Unknown Sender: They're following you
anyway, tracking the phone in your trunk. They
will be arrested at the KBL Lab.

Michelle said, "Oh, no," and sent a message to Natasha's phone, and then to Nathanael's. Half an hour later she had no reply. They must have their phones turned off.

What was she going to do?

Then something tingled at the back of her head – there was something she was missing. A detail.

Krystal B. Lassiter Laboratory. KBL.

Was that the lab in Niagara Falls owned by KBL Lumen? Could KBL stand for Krystal B. Lassiter? Up until now, she had not seen the association. But Sasha was under the same authority.

She swore.

The whole thing – Sasha the Russian being sent to kill Kael – Peter's friend Henry's son James – it was all connected.

She had suspected Sasha was Cabal. She had not realised Peter's labs were Cabal as well; they were Adamant's labs originally. But it was obvious now. Why hadn't she seen it?

The initials, KBL. The consonants in the German word meaning cabal, Kabale.

She sent a long message to Natasha and Nathanael on TOR messenger, detailing what she had discovered.

<u>CHAPTER 31 – Subjective Subject.</u>

OUTSIDE THE TOWN OF NIAGARA FALLS.

It was a tense walk through the forest; the soft breeze and the warbling song of a little black-hooded bird flitting around nearby in the undergrowth only making it worse somehow.

Finally, they reached the building. There was a road that led around from the front car-park with a loading bay next to a large, flat elevator platform, large enough for trucks. Wooden boxes and cardboard boxes with various courier markings on them were stacked in a large, dark loading dock at the rear of the building. There was no one there and insofar as they could see, no security. There was only one camera. It seemed to be oriented towards the road.

"Unless that camera has a very wide wide-angle lens, I think we can sneak in from the other side of that loading dock," said Nathanael. "It looks like the best way to get in."

They took a slightly circuitous pathway through the forest to the East of the building, circumnavigated the edge of the car-park, and slipped underneath the camera into the rear entrance.

No one challenged them and no alarms went off.

Natasha picked up a box and said, "Pick up something." Nathanael and Kael both picked up boxes as well.

A small white door at the back, next to a tiny office, looked like the only way out. Natasha pressed the buzzer next to the door.

A few moments later the door opened and a balding man in a blue shirt with a logo that said 'KBL Lab' on his pocket appeared.

Natasha said, "Delivery."

He glanced at Natasha's package. "Okay – that's funny these are usually just left back here until Tuesday."

Natasha raised her eyebrows in a gesture Nathanael thought was completely pathetic and obviously bad acting but the man rolled his eyes and said, "Never mind, bring it on through. I can't sign for it, you'll have to get Melissa to sign for it in reception." Natasha gave him a puzzled look, so the man added, "Down that corridor."

He pointed towards a glass door about twenty feet away.

It was an automatic door that opened on its own. The reception area was empty.

Nathanael said, "This is our chance. We can go through while the receptionist isn't here."

There was another glass door on the far side of the reception area that led to a sealed area. The window in the door was tinted and they couldn't see through.

Natasha said, "It's a hermetically sealed door,

theoretically the entrance into some sort of sterile environment."

Kael said, "They might have a switch for the door behind the desk. I haven't been in many pristine labs but NASA has a few, for studying moon rocks and that sort of thing. I understand that would be usual, though."

Natasha said, "Yes, they have them in hospitals." Pivoting herself over the desk, she found the button underneath and pressed it.

The door swung open and the three of them walked through, still carrying the packages.

Natasha said, "Well, that was surprisingly easy."

Nathanael was half expecting a room where they would have to take off their clothes and put on lab coats but apparently, the sterile area didn't need to be quite as sterile as that.

They found themselves in a honeycomb of corridors and small labs with very little security.

"Look at this roster," said Natasha. It was stuck behind the door. "'Subject Monitoring'. What do you think that means?"

The Roster looked like this:

SUBJECT MONITORING

Be at least 15 minutes early for your shift.

THE CHANGEOVER IS RISKY – REMEMBER SEPTEMBER!

SATURDAY

5:30am – 11:30am Dr M. Lennox

11:30am – 5:30pm Dr Stilovsky

5:30pm-11:30pm Dr Jameison

11:30pm – 5:30 am Dr Hewlit

"Look," said Nathanael, pointing to 'Saturday'. "The Doctor on now. Someone called Dr Lennox."

As they walked onwards, a man in a white coat came down the corridor.

Natasha chirped, "Delivery for Dr Lennox! Where would…?"

He replied abruptly, "Right that way, left then right." As they stormed down the passageway with Natasha leading the way, they heard him say, "Should you even be here?"

They started jogging then, as silently as they could, along the corridor.

The next door was riveted and reinforced and had an electronic ID and lock on it but whether it was just luck or divine assistance, the door was being held open by a wedged-in chair. Natasha barged through like a juggernaut. The others followed.

Suddenly, Natasha said, "Shh!" and motioned for the others to stop.

"What?" said Kael.

Natasha whispered, "Voices, down that way."

"In here," said Kael, indicating another door.

They found themselves on an observation deck with seven or eight plastic prefabricated chairs and an exit sign on the other side. It seemed to be originally designed for watching surgery and medical procedures but the operating theatre had been converted into a residential care room with sofas, a television, a computer. From their vantage point, they couldn't see anyone, though; they could only hear voices wafting up.

"We should stop here," said Nathanael. "Maybe we can find out what this place is. Maybe we can even find out who this Russian guy is who tried to kill you, Kael, and why."

Kael nodded. "The Russian man is here somewhere," he said. "I shot him, I wouldn't mind betting he came here to get medical treatment after I shot him in the arm. But then… what if they see us on the security cameras? Or find us in here?"

Nathanael took a small tube out of his pocket. "We've got away with it so far… But if anyone comes, I can at least slow them down."

Natasha said, "What's that?"

"Superglue! As the ad says, 'Adheres to just about everything,'" said Nathanael as he poked the end of the tube into the keyhole and squeezed. "'Road base, decomposed granite, wood, concrete, asphalt, foam padding.' I'm disabling the lock. There. That should do it."

A voice wafted up from below that was so deep and strangely accented that it sent shivers running up their spines. "They are here. They are listening. The man from the land of Ophir, where the gold lies, glues the lock so that no one may go through the door."

Nathanael said, "What a creepy voice. Ophir? Is that Australia?"

Then another voice spoke, a doctor or scientist speaking in condescending, peremptory tones. "The subject has been suffering delusions of extra-sensory perception for the last four or five days, ever since he achieved consciousness when the initial connection was made."

Natasha commented, "And that man's a pompous ass if I've ever heard one."

A third voice, also condescending, another doctor? a scientist? But not as bad – Natasha said, "He's a nicer fellow altogether…" – his voice floated up from below, "What delusions? What hallucinations?"

Pompous-Professor replied, "Auditory hallucinations of entities or personas of a spiritual nature. Demons or gods or evil spirits, if you will."

The subject laughed. "They are gods compared to you. If you had seen my brothers in the days when they walked upon the earth you would have bowed and worshipped them yourself, as every human being did. And these are just the heroes of renown, the Gibborim of the ancient days. My brothers! But if you could see the ascended masters… angels of burning light, the true rulers of this world. They are gods. Hahahaha!" And his laughter was even more chilling than his speech.

But Pompous-Professor seemed untouched; in a cold, clinical way he said, "With expansive delusions, in other words, exaggerated grandiosity, he describes a fanciful distant past full of his own self-aggrandising mythos."

Nice-Doctor blurted out, "That's an overly clinical description if I've ever heard one. Why, he speaks more like a Lovecraftian character praising Cthulhu!"

The subject continued, "Cthulhu? A fiction based on the truth of the outer darkness where even God does not dwell. But I am not speaking of the gods right now. Humans. Three of them. Intruders in this facility. They are watching from above. Even now they hear what I am saying, everything that you are saying." The subject began to sound frustrated. "I hear their thoughts! I see them in my mind! One who shot the man from Rosh."

Pompous-Professor said triumphantly, "See? The creature is completely convinced that he is describing real phenomena. For him it is a thoroughly credible delusion of telepathic ability involving spiritual presences."

Nice-Doctor said, "Rosh. Isn't that a Hebrew name, one of the sons of Benjamin in Genesis?"

Natasha whispered, "Nice-Doctor knows his Bible. Might be in Ezekiel, too. Some people interpret 'Rosh' as Russia. It's not an unreasonable assumption. After all, Rosh is supposed to have been a Scythian Prince. The Scythians lived to the north of the Black Sea."

They could almost hear the subject rolling his eyes, in his contemptuous tone of voice. "Now they have a theoretical conversation about the origins of the various tribes and peoples of the earth. What would they know? Were they there?"

"What an imagination!" Pompous-Professor said. "Now these supposed spiritual entities are talking about tribes and peoples, and the subject appears to infer that he was present in ancient times."

At that moment a buzzer sounded. A voice wafted up from an intercom or speaker-phone below. "Doctor Lennox, the European wants to speak to you – he's on a video call."

Pompous-Professor said, "What? Now? It's very inconvenient."

The intercom voice replied, "Yes. He wants to interview the subject."

Something clicked and Pompous-Professor said, "Put him through, thank you. We're both here."

A voice speaking clipped Euro-English came through on a different speaker system, higher in quality than the intercom. "Hello? Put the camera where I can see him, please... Yes, a splendid specimen."

"I'm afraid he is flawed, though, sir."

The European said, "How so?"

"He suffers delusions," said Pompous-Professor, "Hears voices. He believes spiritual entities are talking to him, suffers from illogical intuitions, visions, dreams and the like. I am afraid the subject is very much insane."

"Of course," said Nice-Doctor, "Occasionally he has been right. Quite often, actually. More than chance. *I'm* convinced."

Pompous-Professor said, "Rhine was completely sure that Lady Wonder was a telepathic horse, but eventually they realised that she was responding to non-verbal cues from her master. Our subject has abnormally good hearing. That explains most of the instances."

Nice-Doctor was emphatic. "No, it doesn't. There's something very peculiar going on, something that defies statistics."

The European said, "Alright, good, good. That's exactly what we would expect, given the circumstances."

Pompous-Professor said, "It hardly seems like a success."

The European said, "Nonetheless you are not the arbiter of that. I am. It is our money funding this project. You are our employees. By the way, unfortunately, one of our projects in one of the other sites has failed. The subject never awakened, he died before his mind was taken over… um… had taken hold. I am… sending some of the biological material to you in case of discovery, by the way; it will be refrigerated. You know Protocol Twenty-Three A?"

Pompous-Professor sounded doubtful, "I'm not sure I know that one."

"Well, look it up. You will need to be prepared, in case last September's performance repeats itself. Let me speak to him." They heard scraping; they were moving something around. The European said in a polite, carefully pronounced, "Ah, good. There you are again, your highness. How are they treating you, sire?"

The subject snapped, "The security in this facility is abysmal. It is no wonder I was able to escape a year ago. And they are fools — they do not even realise that physical, human beings like yourselves have invaded this facility today, on this very day!"

The European muttered, "Yes, some of these your servants

have a limited faculty of understanding, I am sorry, your highness, they are mere humans, mere creatures of earth and dust." Then he snapped, "Get to it, Lennox! Get the staff to find the intruders in your facility! They are there. Be certain of it!"

"What do you mean?" said Pompous-Professor. "Intruders?"

The European insisted, "Find the intruders! Do you dare question me?"

Pompous-Professor sounded genuinely shaken. "No! Yes, sir! No, sir! Alright. Find the intruders. Issue a yellow alert!"

The European took a deep breath and said, "Apart from this, how are the fools treating you, sire?"

The subject said, "The food is dreadful. The company insultingly impoverished, no, these people you have left me with have neither wit nor the art of conversation, nor are they noble in any way, shape or form. They are like peasants; they have neither the finesse of rhetoric nor any appreciation of culture."

The European sounded wistful. "There is no longer any nobility in this age. Even the kings and queens mix their blood with commoners."

The subject spat, "Pah! In my time, I was the son of Ra, the Sun god, even kings bowed down to me, and the greatest rulers served me. In my former life, in my former body, I was a god and all humanity were dogs before me. Since then my spirit has wandered the earth, a vapour, a mist, with no corporeal existence unless I could take over some human temporarily when he drank or drugged himself into a stupor or called on the occult powers or gave himself over to despair or lust or greed or any of the other deadly sins. Until now.

"But this age upon the earth – your age – is an age of dogs eating their own excrement and slaves reigning over their masters."

The European said, "A fair comment. I who speak to you am one of the true rulers of this age, however. I am one of the mighty ones upon the earth, the Gibborim of this generation. We rule from the shadows. We manipulate from the unseen places. These slaves do not know the Cabal exists, and even the rulers of this age barely even suspect."

"Interesting. I would hear more of this."

"I can tell you no more right now. I have other duties that I must attend to, the duties of a ruler. But soon, oh Mighty One, soon, we will speak at length. You have my bounden word."

The message ended with a short burst of compressed digital static.

The subject said rather sarcastically, "Well, here comes another of your servants to announce that the man from Rosh is here."

A door opened and a younger, more subservient voice said, "A man arrived about twenty minutes ago needing medical assistance for a gunshot and a sprained arm."

Pompous-Professor said, "Why did you let them in?"

"He told the secretary he works for... our employers. He knew the password. He needed medical help and was instructed to come here, so the nurse at the front desk bandaged his wound. The guards let him in."

Pompous-Professor said, "They should have shot on sight."

Nathanael whispered, "We would have been shot if we came through the front door... Luckily we came in the back."

Pompous-Professor sounded irritated. He asked, "How did he get in alive?" then said in a very snarky tone, "See, one person, not three. The subject was wrong again. Where is the interloper?"

The subservient man said, "In the reception area. He had the daily password, that's the only reason they didn't shoot him on sight. He has a broken arm and other injuries. He says his name is Sasha. The European office sent him, apparently." He paused. "I think he's Russian. Oh, and we had another message from the European Office – watch out for intruders. It seems Sasha was being followed."

Pompous-Professor said, "How long have you known these things? Why are we only hearing about it now?"

"About half an hour. But I was reluctant to interrupt – you said no interruptions while the man from Germany was on the line." Pompous-Professor snapped, "Karen, go and see to this Russian's needs. If he has the daily password, then…"

A woman's voice said reluctantly, "Alright." Then they heard two sets of footsteps receding, then a shutting door.

Kael whispered, "It's definitely the gunman."

The subject said, "Haha! You are fools. They are still listening."

Pompous-Professor said, "Who is listening?"

The subject replied, "The intruders. The man at the front is the one from Rosh – as you say, a Russian – who was sent to kill one of the three intruders but he failed."

Kael whispered, "How can that creature possibly know these things?"

Something about the subject made Nathanael nod agreement with Kael's description of him as a creature. He was not human, though he could speak like one.

The door opened again and a gruff, low voice said, "Sir, we just checked the security feed. Because Doctor Lennox asked us to…"

Pompous-Professor said, "And?"

"Well, sir, it turns out he was — ahm — actually describing something that was really happening. Three people snuck in through the loading dock. We caught their images momentarily in the top left corner of the wide-angle lens as they were entering the facility."

Pompous-Professor let loose an apoplectic scream, "Well, find them! Do what you need to do! Don't just talk to me about it."

The subject said idly, "How do you think I knew? I told you, I can read minds. I myself have servants who do my bidding."

Pompous-Professor scoffed, "As I mentioned before, Doctor Rhine the parapsychologist believed implicitly the fact that Lady Wonder the horse could actually read minds but Professor John Scarne proved it was completely fraudulent. The horse was following non-verbal cues, movements the owner made with the whip. The owner was standing behind the horse but in the view of an animal with excellent peripheral vision. The subject – you — have extraordinary hearing – a side effect apparently of the genes we inserted into you – perhaps you heard three sets of footsteps entering a little while ago – perhaps you even heard their conversations. I will not believe in mind reading – or indeed, in gods or spirits and demons, until such an unscientific concept is definitively proven."

The subject laughed, "Hahaha! Yet you are the servant of my ruler. The ruling spirit of the air reigns in your life, yet you believe yourself to be completely rational. You are a special sort of fool, a fool who cannot even see his own folly. Yet you call yourself a rationalist."

"So if you have paranormal abilities, tell me what the intruders are thinking now?"

The subject said, "I cannot read their minds. They belong to the Enemy, and His cloud is over their thoughts. But I can read yours. Indeed, I have seen what you think about. And I know exactly what your perverted tastes are; your addiction. I know that you look at disgusting, perverted images on the internet in your office at midnight. I know all your secrets, secrets that would shock your colleagues." The creature laughed again. "But Doctor Jameison; she is no saint. She is having an affair with her neighbour, the medieval scholar, and she hides it from her husband and her grown-up children. In her quiet moments she justifies her immoral behaviour to herself in her thoughts, saying, 'After all, love is love.' Or 'How can something that feels so right be so wrong?'"

Another voice wafted. A woman's voice. "Of course he's speaking through his hat. A complete lie."

The subject continued, "Meanwhile, Dr Singh agonises over whether he is a good enough person, day and night, and then shouts at his wife if the dinner is late or if the floor is not swept because the effort of being a good person all the time is really too great for him when his wrongful desires torment him continually and the images of his secret wishes rise up in his thoughts hour by hour, minute by minute, second by second."

"Rubbish," said the condescending voice. "All of it rubbish. If any of it is true it is because you have heard people muttering under their breath, inadvertent tells, revealing glances, slips of the tongue and educated guesses. You are highly intelligent, with heightened senses. A large percentage of men look at... indecent things on the internet, more than sixty percent, so it is reasonably good odds that I would. An informed guess on your part. And you're incorrect, aren't you? Of course I don't —"

The subject's voice was full of glee as he said, "But you do. Many men look at these images. Yet not the kind of thing you look at. You are especially perverted, are you not? But to each his own. So long as it's not hurting anybody else, I say."

Pompous-Professor's voice quavered. "You make educated guesses," he said, "You listen to people without them knowing. You seem to have a... special understanding of human motivations and psychology. That is all. There is nothing supernatural going on here."

In a voice dripping with sarcasm, the subject said, "Yes, you keep on telling yourself that, if it makes you feel better. Ah, the delightful lies these little humans tell themselves to justify their own evil behaviour!"

They heard the door open again below.

Pompous-Professor commented, "Though what really is miraculous is something at which I am continually amazed — the creature's command of English, when it has only been awake for less than a month, in fact."

The subject said, "The guards are closing in. Haha! They're going to get caught."

Suddenly the door handle behind them started to turn. It was locked. A muffled voice said, "Hello? Anyone in there? Hello?"

Nathanael said, "Quick! The other door." He leaped across the room and opened the door beneath the exit sign.

Three men stood there, two holding Beretta semi-automatic pistols; Nathanael had been studying guns after their previous encounters and he figured they were U22 Neos. He put his hands up and said, "No point running, I don't think we can get out of this right now."

Natasha swore coldly and put up her hands.

Kael followed suit, giving a shrug and saying, "Well, I guess they were going to catch up with me eventually. I'm not really the type of guy who's able to stay on the run forever."

With a loud crack, the door behind them swung open

and another thug holding a pistol came through.

Kael closed his eyes and his lips were moving slightly. Nathanael could hear him whispering, "Lord Jesus Christ, help us. Lord Jesus Christ, help us"

The subject started crying out, "Oh, no. It hurts my head! Stop him! Stop him doing that!"

"Doing what?" Pompous-Professor said. "No one is doing anything. Another example of the creature's schizophrenic ideations. Are you recording this?"

Another voice said, "Yes, sir. It's all being recorded." One of the lab assistants, presumably.

Kael whispered, "Natasha! Nathanael! That thing below – I think it doesn't like it when I pray."

The man holding the pistol poked it into Kael's back and said, "Shut up!" He shoved them through the door.

They came out into a corridor, just like the corridors on the other side, with laboratories and small conference rooms.

Natasha whispered, "Pray!" She closed her eyes. Nathanael recognised the rested look that came over her face when she was praying.

Nathanael started praying as well, under his breath, "Jesus! Help!"

Downstairs, the subject went berserk, crying and

wailing insanely and throwing things around the room. The sound of things crunching and breaking and crashing came up from below.

Pompous-Professor cried out in distress and shouted, "Help! Help! Subject out of control! Guards! Come down and help me! Now!"

The two guys with the Berettas looked at each other. One said, "What do we do?"

The man holding the pistol swore and said, "Go down. I'll watch over these two. Get back up here once the subject's under control." He waved his pistol at Kael, Natasha and Nathanael. "Sit down. Right here. Don't give me any trouble or I'll pop you."

The two guys with the Berettas ran down the corridor and disappeared at a junction. Nathanael whispered to Natasha, "I reckon that's the elevator doors."

Natasha nodded and said, "Keep praying. Praise Jesus! I've heard that praise, in particular, disrupts evil powers."

The man holding the pistol said sharply, "Shut up. No talking. You're coming with me." And he added, under his breath, "I'm going to use the C4 on this place. I'm going to destroy that creature. I've had enough of this."

But Nathanael, Natasha and Kael were not listening.

Each in their own fashion was praising God.

Nathanael was not very experienced at praising the Lord, he had to admit. What was he going to praise God for? Here they were, prisoners of an evil man, at his mercy; everything had gone wrong. An evil creature had been recreated from ancient times and they were unable to do anything about it.

Then he remembered, at Natasha's church they sometimes sang the Doxology. A song of praise.

He began to sing it out loud:

"Praise God from whom all blessings flow,

Praise Him all creatures here below.

Praise Him above ye heavenly host,

Praise Father, Son and Holy Ghost."

Natasha, suddenly emboldened, joined him, and Kael, obviously learning the tune, joined in.

The long, despairing, hopeless wail that came from downstairs was so grievous and disturbing to hear that Nathanael almost stopped singing. The man holding the gun on them suddenly covered his ears, grimaced and cried out in fear and terror, closing his eyes as well. The gun dropped out of his fist onto the floor. Nathanael grabbed the pistol and leaped up, pointing it at the man's temple.

It was a Smith and Wesson M2.0, a fairly simple gun.

Their guard was still whimpering with his eyes shut and didn't even seem to know what was happening. Realising he had dropped the gun, he opened his eyes and saw Nathanael holding the gun on him and the corners of his mouth collapsed and his shoulders slumped in sudden recognition of the situation.

Seeing what had happened, Natasha and Kael stopped singing.

"We need to get out of here," said Nathanael. "Natasha, Kael, keep on singing!" He waved the gun at the man, who was now their prisoner. "You. Show us the quickest way out of here."

"Alright," he said. "Thank God," the man breathed. "Thank God, I've got no choice now."

Sounds of pistol fire came from below and the smell of gunpowder wafted up as the man eagerly ran to where the elevator doors were. He took a keycard out of his pocket and opened the elevator doors.

They followed him into the elevator and Nathanael grabbed the keycard from him and swiped it. He pressed the button, 'B', and the doors closed.

Suddenly it was completely silent, except for Natasha softly singing another song that Nathanael didn't recognise.

"Lo! he comes with clouds descending,

Once for favored sinners slain;

Thousand, thousand saints attending

Swell the triumph of his train.

Alleluia! Alleluia!

God appears on earth to reign...."

The man repeated, "Thank God," and bowed his head, leaning on his own knees. He looked up at Nathanael. "That creature. It's... unnatural. An abomination. Ever since I was working here I've hated it." He straightened up and offered his hand for Nathanael to shake. "I'm Ryan. Sorry about before."

Nathanael's eyebrows went up. He ignored the proffered hand and waved the gun at him. "I'm Nathanael. Don't try anything."

"It's alright," Ryan said. "I'm head of security here." Ryan hesitated. "I understand where you're coming from. I am going to help you. It was the last straw today. I've had enough of this place, that thing. It's unnatural. It's an abomination, it should have been aborted before birth. We've got to do something about it. Follow me. I have a solution."

The elevator doors opened out into the basement car-park.

Ryan took out his keys and opened an orange door on the left of the elevator entrance. He slipped into the room quickly, before Nathanael knew what he was doing.

Nathanael followed him in, still training the gun on him.

Ryan said, "It's in the boiler room. My solution to that creature. Stupidly, they store C4 in here. Plastic explosive. I've told them not to, that it's dangerous but they said it's the best place to put it." He opened a cupboard. "I suppose if it stays in the cupboard it's probably going to be okay." He started taking blocks of C4 out of the cupboard. "But if the boiler overflow valve was stuck in the shut position, and the C4 was sitting next to the boiler instead of in that cupboard…" He stacked the blocks next to the boiler. Kael started helping him. Soon about thirty blocks of C4 were stacked right next to the boiler.

But Nathanael said, "No, my friend, you've got the wrong idea completely. C4 can't be set off by vibration. That's the whole point of using plastic explosive."

Ryan looked at Nathanael with growing horror. "I didn't know. What do we do? How do we bring this place down?"

Natasha stood in the doorway and said angrily, "More to the point, what do you actually think you're doing?" But none of the three men were listening to her.

Nathanael pointed his gun at the room Ryan had taken the explosive from. "There'll be some detonators in there. Get them."

Ryan found the detonators and passed them out quickly. Nathanael began sticking them into the C4. Ryan found the remote detonator, a device that looked like a two-way radio with a single button on it, the receiver, and some wire. He attached the receiver to the wire and wired the detonators together.

"Let's go," said Ryan, handing the detonator to Nathanael. They got up to go.

But a shout, "Wait!" brought them up short. It was Natasha and they looked up at her in shock. She was standing in the doorway with her hands on her hips.

~~~

Doctor Lennox was watching from the viewing area beyond the one-way glass, outside the subject's room – he saw the whole thing. One minute the subject was docile, enduring another blood-test that Doctor Lennox had ordered five minutes before, then the next moment the nurse administering it was flying across the room, limbs flapping around like a limp rag doll. The syringe was still sticking out of the subject's arm, bouncing up and down on the needle, like a twanged Jaw harp. The subject ripped the needle out of his arm and held it in front of him like a knife, threatening the two thugs Lennox had employed to keep him in check. One of them jumped forwards to disable him but the subject jabbed his blood test needle into the man's side, between several ribs and pushed the plunger. The subject's blood rushed into the guard's right lung and he began gurgling and gasping for breath.

Doctor Lennox said under his breath, "Smart fellow. Instant pneumonia."
~~~

The subject suddenly turned around and smiled at Doctor Lennox. The other thug leaped forwards in that moment and tried to brain the subject with the fire extinguisher but the subject ducked more nimbly than such a large person should be able to and then, grabbing the fire extinguisher with both of his long, spindly hands, thrust it straight at the thug's knees.

Bone and flesh crunched and the man collapsed, wailing in a particularly chilling way.

The subject leaped towards the one-way mirror, and Doctor Lennox jumped back in surprise and shock but the subject merely stared through the mirror – he couldn't see him could he? Doctor Lennox could swear the subject was staring right at him, directly into his eyes, even though there was no way he could see through the one-way mirror. Could he?

The subject picked up the large, heavy wooden table in the centre of the room and threw it at the glass.

The glass shook several times, giving a thunderous sound, but it held.

The subject picked up the table again, his right hand now holding the whole table by the one single leg. He smashed it into the window a second time, a third time, a fourth time. With a loud splitting sound, a crack appeared in the window and began growing, spreading through the glass sheet like a burgeoning vine.

Lennox stood frozen in shock.

The subject picked up the table with both hands this time and smashed it against the window once more.

The glass window gave a last almighty groan, then, with a deafening sound like a thousand chandeliers falling at once, burst into a thousand slivers and splits and shards.

The subject leaped through and grabbed Lennox by the throat. Lennox thought he was done for but the subject growled in his ear, "Get out of here. That guard is going to bomb this place with the C4 that's in the basement. Fool. Get out! And pull the alarm! Save the others!" And then, placing Lennox on a firm footing, he added with pride, "My slaves are under my protection."

But Lennox didn't care about anything else other than getting away from his monstrous creation. He ran towards the front entrance as fast as he could. About to round the corridor, he looked back.

The subject was loping out the other way, down the corridor towards the back entrance. For a moment Lennox considered telling someone or trying to stop the creature – the fallout had been significant last time the subject had escaped. Only Lennox knew the full extent of it; and a few high up in the company: five dead civilians and a spate of dog and cat killings in the local area – but Lennox didn't care if that happened again, truth be told.

All he cared about was saving himself.

He sprinted to the front reception area and out into the car park, and then sat there on the curb, laughing softly to himself and waiting for the disaster.

No one had thought to ring the fire alarm and evacuate the building. *They* were all going to die but he would escape.

Yes, and Lennox had to admit that he believed it now. He really believed the creature could read minds.

~~~

Natasha was standing in the doorway with her hands on her hips. They were both staring at her, blocking their way. She demanded, "What do you think you're doing?"

Ryan said, "We're doing what we have to do. That thing up there is a travesty!"

Natasha shook her head. "This guy's our prisoner, Nathanael. Why are you doing what he says?"

Nathanael said, "He's right. It's us humans against that thing. It's an abomination, it shouldn't exist. Can't you tell? It hates prayer."

Natasha waved at the pile of C4, and spoke emphatically, "Most people hate prayer – don't you realise mankind's basic condition is to be an enemy of God? Until the gospel comes into people's lives they are God's enemies."
~~~

Nathanael said, "That thing's different."

Natasha rolled her eyes. "Yeah, but there are innocent people in this building. Workers, employees, nurses. We need to make sure everyone evacuates."

Nathanael let her through. She ran into the boiler room. Nathanael poked his head in, to see what she was doing.

Natasha said, "Will water affect the C4 exploding?"

"No," Nathanael said. "They use it underwater."

The boiler room had a fire alarm lever, next to an axe in a glass wall cabinet. Natasha broke the glass, took the axe out, and pulled the alarm lever. Sprinklers began to pour water out and the fire alarm began to ring deafeningly.

They ran out. Ryan took out his car keys, pressed the button and a white SUV blipped. Nathanael pocketed his gun. Apparently, Ryan was on their side now.

Natasha took Ryan's keys and jumped in the drivers' side. The other doors were unlocked, so Nathanael leaped into the passenger side and Ryan and Kael jumped into the back. Nathanael turned around, keeping his gun trained on Ryan.

Natasha shouted, "What about the creature? Will they evacuate it? What if we're blowing up the building for nothing?"

The distressing noise of the fire alarm ringing frantically suddenly dulled as Ryan flicked the latch, locking the car doors.

Nathanael said frantically, "For God's sake Natasha, go! Go!"

"I can't," said Natasha. Ryan reached over the seat and started the engine with his thumb. Natasha put her foot down.

The car screeched on the concrete floor and the sound of the engine roared through the carpark.

Natasha repeated her question, now that she could be heard. "Will they let the creature out? What if it gets out before the building goes up?"

"Now you're worried about that. But the answer is no," said Ryan. "They won't risk letting it out. Back in September it escaped and left a trail of dead bodies, dead dogs and cats, women raped and abused and wanton vandalism. They will evacuate the staff, now that the alarm has sounded. Well, that's standard procedure, anyhow but I think they'll leave the thing in its room. It's a sealed room; even the fire alarm won't make the doors open."

They emerged from the underground car-park, not far from the rear entrance to the building. It was early morning and the stars were still out but no moon. A warm pre-dawn glow lit the sky in the East.

As she drove out of the underground car-park Natasha, feeling that she was being watched, looked into the forest. Were eyes peering out at them from the shadows of the trees? But who would be out there this early in the morning? Was that creature in there? Had it escaped? It was a foolish thought and she decided she would pay it no heed.

Natasha took the circuit road around the building and sped out through the front car-park. One of the Doctors was there; from his appearance, Nathanael thought it was probably Doctor Lennox but the man didn't even flinch when the car roared past. For some reason, he was watching the building in a catatonic state of complete fascination.

Natasha parked just out of the line of sight of the car park, around the corner behind a bush, not far from where Nathanael and Natasha had been parked hours before. They watched as a stream of staff began to pour out from the front foyer doors.

Doctors and nurses came out first and then the support staff, secretaries and accountants and then those in charge of acquisitions, receiving goods, and all the other staff, mostly couriers and labourers. Ryan counted them as they came out.

When he reached thirty-five, he said, "That's everyone, except my two security guys. And that Russian visitor as well, whoever he was." He looked doubtful. "I think you should do it. Press the button. Avery and John knew the risks of the job when they signed up. And by all accounts that Russian guy is a murderer anyhow."

Natasha said, "No, we should wait."

Nathanael readied his thumb on the detonator.

His two security guys came out, helped by the blonde Russian guy. They were both limping and one of them seemed to have a lot of blood on his legs.

"That's everyone," said Ryan. "Except that creature. With any luck that foul abomination is still in there."

Nathanael hesitated. Ryan reached forward, grabbed the detonator out of Nathanael's hand and pressed the button.

There was a pause in which the whole world seemed to go silent. Then a sudden, thunderous blast exploded outwards and the people standing in the car-park were knocked over by the pressure wave and stared at the building in horror as debris and flames ripped out of it. With an even louder, more deafeningly thunderous bass roar, the whole structure caved in on itself. An immense cloud of dust and smoke burst out of the top, a mushroom cloud thrusting upwards into the sky, leaving behind the crater where the building had stood, moments before.

~~~

Sasha watched the building coming down from a log in the patch of forest behind the loading area. He was cradling his broken arm, which was now set and in a proper cast and sling. He shook his head. "How will I find Kael Addison now?"
~~~

A whisper in the forest seemed to float past his ears, "Bug his car. It's in the front car park."

Sasha looked around. There was no one there. He was just imagining it. But he walked around the crater where the building had been to the front car park anyhow.

The BMW was indeed sitting in the front car park.

He looked around. Too many onlookers now, if Kael turned up, for him to have a shot at him.

But Sasha did have a GPS tracker in his pocket, which he surreptitiously placed underneath the front driver's side wheel arch.

Whatever that voice was, whether it was God or the devil, it had helped him.

<u>CHAPTER 32 – The Fallen Falls.</u>

OUTSIDE THE TOWN OF NIAGARA FALLS.

Natasha and Ryan swapped seats.

Ryan said, "Well, there goes their research as well. I hope." He swore. "That felt good. I've been wanting to do that ever since I met that shuddersome creature. Well, the thing's gone. Good riddance to a bad business. And we had better go too." He started the engine and did a U-turn in the road.

Kael said, "Can you drop me here? My BMW's parked in the car park. I really like that car."

Nathanael said, "We've got to get our car, too."

"Leave the BMW behind," said Natasha. "It will be on the video feed."

Ryan said, "Don't worry, it won't. I've been telling them to get cloud backup for that video ever since I arrived here. The video only gets saved on the internal servers which would have been destroyed along with everything else. So long as no one's got a video feed on their house across the road or something, which seems unlikely in this suburb; they're all rentals. You should be okay to pick up your car. Let's agree right now I'm going to minimise your role in it."

Kael said, "Anyhow I think the Russian guy would not want to admit stealing my car in the first place, after all, I paid good cash for it. Marcel, the proprieter, is my friend and would readily testify that it's in my name, if that was necessary. I'll meet you guys at Niagara falls in a couple of hours. Try to look like regular tourists. I'll get us some rooms at the Sheraton on the falls. Nice hotel, we had a climate seminar there once."

Kael jumped out and ran into the carpark.

Nathanael said, "Our car's just around the corner here." A few people were starting to emerge from the houses and units and were gathering in a group to stare at the unfolding catastrophe.

Ryan drove Nathanael and Natasha around to their car. It was out of sight of most of the houses.

Before he got out of the car Nathanael said, "What about you?"

Ryan said, "Oh, look, I was ordered to arrest you rather than throw you out of the building, which would have been my preference, considering the law would probably consider keeping you there kidnapping. You managed to get my gun but I overcame you, I took you out of the building in my SUV, let you go, then I um… popped down to the store to get an iced coffee and a sandwich, to help with my post-traumatic stress. I'll go back there in a few minutes to be very shocked to find out that the whole place has been destroyed. Now if anyone questions you about it, you have to deny having been here. I'd be willing to say you weren't the ones I arrested. Best if we never even saw each other. Quick, get out, get into your car and get going before anyone sees enough of you to question my version of events."

Nathanael nodded his agreement, something Natasha wasn't wholly happy about because they'd be lying. They shook hands with Ryan and thanked him for his help. Ryan's last words to them were, "Sorry about how it all started off."

Nathanael leaped into the driver's side of their car and Natasha the passenger's. Nathanael took them a slightly circuitous route out of the residential area, avoiding the streets near the building.

~~~

Fifteen minutes later they were in the town of Niagara Falls, handing over their keys to the valét at the Sheraton. Nathanael got out of the car, saying, "That was easier than I thought. I was certain we were up for a big battle. Thank God, it's all over!"

Natasha concurred.

They found a place to sit in the hotel foyer. Nathanael ordered a scotch on the rocks for himself and a Bloody Mary for Natasha and they sat sipping their drinks, thinking about what had occurred.
~~~

"Thanks," said Nathanael.

Natasha glanced at him. "What for?"

"You stopped me from killing all those people. Made sure we evacuated them."

Natasha winced. "You just get a bit singleminded, Nathanael, sometimes; it's your nature, you can forget what's really important."

He blinked, and a concerned expression came over his features. "I don't know. Somewhere deep inside I knew that we should be evacuating the people but another part of me thought that killing that thing might be worth a few innocent deaths. Collateral damage caught in the crossfire."

Natasha didn't say anything to that, just looked at him and shrugged in what seemed to him to be an accepting way. "I can see where you're coming from," she said. "Even if I don't agree with you."

Somehow Nathanael was grateful; she never condemned him, even when he deserved it. It was one of her more Christ-like qualities.

She caught him looking at her admiringly and smiled warmly back, and the whole issue seemed to be forgotten.

After a long silence, Natasha said, "I wonder if it could really read people's minds? Or perhaps evil spirits or powers were telling it things, facts about people, their sins, their secret thoughts?"

Nathanael said, "I don't know."

Natasha said, "St Paul said in his letter to the Ephesians, 'For we do not wrestle against flesh and blood but against the rulers, against the authorities, against the cosmic powers over this present darkness, against the spiritual forces of evil in the heavenly places.' On the one hand, that creature may well have been receiving information from evil powers; on the other hand, it might just have been deception, lies, dissembling. Perhaps it simply uses natural abilities, an extra sensitive sense of hearing, a particularly keen memory or an enhanced ability to read people's body language to tell what they're thinking. If so then the whole idea that there's something supernatural going on is just another deception. Then again, Praising God is supposed to be a way of driving evil powers away. So that fits with the first alternative."

They found Kael in a tourist shop in the foyer buying a postcard. "Come on, since we're here let's go get some lunch and have a look at the falls! I'll show you to your room first, though. It's on the ground floor, next to mine, you can step right out into the garden."

A little more than an hour later they were standing in the viewing area at the top of the falls, watching the wide river moving at an infinitesimal pace to the long edge and descending, booming thunderously. The clouds of water vapour were fascinating, the way they billowed and disappeared into the air but Nathanael didn't know if he was simply exhausted or if the traumatic events meant that he simply wasn't in the mood... He found the sight vaguely disappointing.

Somehow not as splendid as he had hoped.

At this very moment, Nathanael felt a sense of oppression, a feeling that someone was cursing him, a vague intuition of impending wickedness.

He couldn't explain what it was but he turned to Natasha, about to ask her if she felt it too. She looked back at him, her brow furrowed, and said, "I think that creature is still alive."

Nathanael nodded. "I think so too. I think we need to go back to the hotel room and pray. And praise God."

Kael was taking photos of the waterfall with his phone. Natasha told him that she and Nathanael were returning to the hotel room. Kael nodded and said, "I'll meet you at five in the bar for a pre-dinner drink."

Natasha and Nathanael prayed and read the Bible together for a good twenty minutes. As they finished their prayers, Nathanael felt a complete, deep peace descend on him. He fell onto his bed and slept soundly throughout the afternoon. They shared dinner with Kael. Nathanael went back to his room, leaving Natasha and Kael discussing climate science, a subject that they could both discuss completely civilly now.

Nathanael, completely exhausted, slept again.

Nathanael woke up at about eight o'clock and looked out at the ground-floor garden. Although the sun had descended, the sky was still light, but much of the garden was in shadow now. He glanced over – Natasha was on her bed – they had a room with two single beds, something they both had agreed upon, as much because Nathanael was a light sleeper and didn't want to disturb her sleep if he got up in the middle of the night; but they were trying to exercise self-control as well and that was another can of worms Nathanael didn't even want to think of about.

He was still wearing the same clothes he had worn during the day. His shoes were still on.

He went out into the garden.

The trees were tall, dark, looming silhouettes against the fading light. As Nathanael walked among them an even taller shadow loomed over him, and a deep sense of doom came over him. He thought it was something other, not a tree but he moved closer and felt the bark.

Just another tree.

He breathed a sigh of relief.

Above him, the twilight was fading fast and stars were twinkling into existence one by one in the darkening sky. Past the trees, Nathanael could see clouds of mist and froth splashing or drifting upwards above the falls, illuminated by a multicoloured light show, purple, yellow, orange, blue, red. Then another gargantuan shadow loomed above him. He reassured himself, it's just a tree but the shadow suddenly filled everything and a giant hand lunged forwards and gripped his throat.

Nathanael tried to speak but nothing came out. He was paralysed, completely helpless, but in his mind he cried out, "Lord Jesus Christ! Help me!" The hand suddenly let go and as it did he saw its silhouette against the light show in the sky; it had six fingers. The light show flashed again and the silhouette of a giant appeared with a head longer than a melon, running away.

Nathanael noticed its resemblance to the adult aliens from the Alien movies, a grotesque Giger creation. Then he reflected that these things had been around a long time before the artist Giger had designed his own monstrosities.

These were the real thing. The template Giger had used for his nightmare creations.

Realising he was safe, he bent over and leaned his hands on his knees, breathing deeply with relief. With that the vision ended, for he suddenly woke up gasping with sweat pouring off him. He cried out again, "Thank God!"

and realised he had awakened Natasha.

Natasha sat up in bed. "What's wrong?"

Nathanael said, "I had a nightmare. A terrible, foreboding dream." He looked out the window at the garden, dark, shadowed, ominous and shivered.

"What sort of dream?" said Natasha.

"I walked in the garden and there were multicoloured lights above Niagara falls, lighting up the night," Nathanael said. "Then a giant hand grabbed my throat. It was the creature, the one from the lab. It was alive. I cried out to Jesus in my mind and the giant hand let go of me and ran away."

Natasha said, "Multicoloured lights? How did you know that? How did the lights come to be in your dream?"

"Well, I saw them above the trees, I suppose. I don't know what they were. They were shining there, above Niagara falls."

Natasha said, "Look. We can't see them right now, not from this room. The large tree in front of our window obscures the sight. But it's just after midnight now and the lights are on from now until two o'clock in the morning. Nathanael, did someone else tell you about them?"

He said, "Maybe Kael mentioned it while we were with him?"

She shook her head. "You had already gone back to this room when Kael told me about the lights in the bar. It was after our Climate discussion."

Nathanael went very silent for a moment. Then he whispered, "Maybe it was real. It seemed very real." A queasy sense of horror came over him; mixed feelings, for he was safe.

Natasha said, "I've been lying here awake – I couldn't sleep. Nathanael, you haven't left your bed as far as I know. Unless I drifted off and didn't realise I was sleeping. You must've heard about the lights; someone must've told you and you forgot about it, or you saw it on one of the pamphlets. Come on, let's go to the viewing area and see them. Kael said it's quite a sight." She grabbed his hand. "That thing's dead, Nathanael, it died in the explosion. We're safe."

Nathanael shook his head. "We're safe, because of Jesus. No one can do anything to us, Natasha, He is King. That thing is scared of His name."

They exited their room. As they were walking through the garden, Kael joined them. "I couldn't sleep," he explained. "Bad dreams."

"Me too," said Nathanael, "Me too."

There was a festive atmosphere at the viewing area. Some people had glasses of champagne.

The sight was splendid but Nathanael actually sneered. He was that unimpressed. Natasha rolled her eyes and said,

"Just enjoy it for what it is."

But Nathanael said, "I remember a C. S. Lewis article Bruce Hetherington put me onto, about the difference between an innate quality and an emotion. He quoted a Bulveristic educator who said something like, 'The Niagara falls are sublime because they make me feel sublime.' But C. S. Lewis said the meaning of sublime is actually the opposite, 'The Niagara falls are sublime because they make me feel humble.' Well, this is Bulverism in action. They've taken the handiwork of Almighty God and turned it into a party prop."

Natasha rolled her eyes but Kael guffawed and said, "I couldn't agree more."

Then Nathanael said, "You know, I'm convinced that the monster is still alive and is around here somewhere. Maybe watching us right now."

"You are very correct, that is right he is," said a voice at Natasha's elbow, in a Russian accent.

One of the tourists standing near them reached up and rather stiffly removed his hat.

When the tourist's face was illuminated by the light show, Kael suddenly recognised him.

Kael said, "You! This is the Russian who was trying to kill me!"

The Russian spoke in low tones, "That's right, I was trying to kill you. And now I shall be able to." Natasha said, "We know your name. Sasha."

Next to him, a very tall man put his hand on Natasha's shoulder. Nathanael did not know how he had not noticed him before but he saw now that the tall, pale man was wearing a hoodie that looked a few sizes too small and his hand had six fingers. Nathanael stepped back in shock.

It was the giant in his dream.

He was at least eleven feet tall.

And there was something very strange about the shape of his head, as though he was hunchbacked or his head was strangely shaped but it was hard to tell with the hoodie obscuring it.

The Russian grabbed the front of Natasha's shirt and hissed in her face, "Allow me to introduce myself. People call me Sasha. I am Russian assassin. And I have pistol trained on three of you." Nathanael noticed that Sasha had a jacket slung over his right hand; he could believe there might be a gun underneath it.

Some of the tourists had noticed his strange behaviour and were stepping around them gingerly, carefully, leaving a little more space than one normally wold.

Sasha waved his gun towards the railing. "Over there." The railing was less than four feet from the dark, roiling waters below, slowly and inexorably carrying everything away over into the distant, turbulent depths.

Nathanael's hand, however, was in his own pocket, and he had his own pistol pointed at the Russian. He was already facing him. He could shoot him right now. He prayed inwardly, "Father, what should I do?" An answer came back, "Wait. Wait and pray." Nathanael prayed, "Jesus! Help!"

The creature flinched back a little as Nathanael prayed, and at that very moment Natasha opened her mouth to sing but the Russian raised his voice and said, "If you sing Christian psalms or songs I will count it as a hostile act and kill you where you stand."

The giant spoke. They recognised his voice from the laboratory. Low and eerie, unnaturally resonant, strangely compelling, when he was close by like this. "You will kill them like the others that you have killed. And you lie with men as with women. Haha! You are an unclean man, guilty as sin, man-whose-name-means-sun."

Sasha waved his gun at the giant. "You keep quiet, gigantski-troll! Or I'll shoot you too." He paused and looked at the giant. "You owe me, anyhow, I rescued you. And brought you here. Ungrateful creature."

The giant said, "Insignificant Rosh. You picked me up

from the rear car-park when I was hitch-hiking for a ride. You did not rescue me, I rescued myself. You deserve nothing more than the rest of these pathetic creatures. You are an insignificant human. All shall serve me, for I am a son of Apollon, the sun god and the destroyer."

But someone nearby suddenly cried out, "Oh my God, that guy's got a gun!"

Tourists began shouting and shoving, pushing their way out; parents picked up their children and ran. In the chaos, the Russian's arm was shoved to the side and Nathanael took the opportunity to grasp his thumb in a martial arts grip. He gripped it strongly and pulled the wrong way, all the way back. Sasha cried out and dropped the gun.

Sasha dropped to the ground to get it, and as he did Nathanael noticed Sasha's arms seemed stiff. A cast on one arm, a bandage on the other? Sasha grasped at the gun clumsily but his efforts to grab it only knocked it closer to Nathanael.

Nathanael immediately dropped onto his knees to the floor to get the gun himself. The light show made it difficult to find. Then he spotted it glinting a few feet away but as he reached forward to grab it a fleeing tourist kicked it. The gun careened across the tiled floor. Nathanael stood up to run over but he saw that Natasha was already there, on her hands and feet as well, groping around for the weapon. She almost grabbed it but another tourist stepped on the gun; the tourist slipped and fell and the gun slid across towards the railing. The Russian was there lying on the ground, his stiff arms swinging wildly but he somehow managed to grasp the gun before it slipped under the railing into the water but it was too late; Nathanael was already there. He stamped his foot down on the Russian's left hand.

The gun went off with a loud 'crack.' It was pointing out towards the lake and splintered the ironwork on the fence. The few tourists who were still standing around fled.

Nathanael stamped his foot down on the gun again and the Russian cried out but he was still somehow managing to hold onto it. This time Nathanael stamped his foot on the man's wrist, using the gun's slight height as a pivot. Nathanael felt the bones giving way as Sasha gave a loud cry, accompanied by the nauseating sound of his wrist bones cracking.

Sasha let go of the gun but the Russian was already reaching his right hand around, the one that was bandaged, to get it. Nathanael kicked the gun away.

The gun flew across the tiles and under the fence, over the vegetation and splashed into the roiling surf, heading for the falls. He could see the heavy metal object travelling underwater in the current, swinging from side to side like a playful dolphin illuminated by the party lights, now green, now purple.

At the very edge of the waterfall, the gun seemed to hesitate for a moment because of the turbulence but just when the gun appeared to have hovered longer than seemed possible it made the fateful, final movement and plunged over the edge.

Nathanael took out his own gun and pointed it in the direction of Sasha and the giant, who was standing beside Sasha watching with an arrogant expression on his hoodie-covered face. The area was evacuated now; Kael and Natasha, Nathanael, the Russian and the giant were the only ones left.

Kael and Natasha stood up.

The giant moved his hood slightly so that his two disturbing, eerie black eyes could be seen peering out. With the multicoloured lights shining on his face his black eyes were even more ominous. Any illumination was swallowed in the darkness of his gaze, like windows into a nightmare — a deep, dark, black hole. The giant stared at Nathanael and said, "Give me the gun."

A feeling of bone-weary tiredness came over Nathanael and his mind went fuzzy and blank, as though someone had suddenly dimmed the lights. The giant reached forwards to take the gun.

Nathanael said, aloud this time, "Jesus, help," and the giant hesitated. Seizing the momentary advantage, Sasha the Russian leaped at him to take the gun. Nathanael stepped back and Sasha fell past but at that moment Nathanael blinked and suddenly the giant was right in front of him.

The giant reached his arms forward in a move somewhat like judo but the movements were unfamiliar. This was a martial art unfamiliar to Nathanael. The giant's arms moved jerkily, unnaturally, like the limbs of a person who had been hypnotised or was being mind-controlled.

The strange, contorted dance confused Nathanael and he lost control of his gun. It flipped onto the ground. Nathanael remembered his own martial arts skills, a free form of Krav Maga he had learned some years ago on his honeymoon in Israel, and he attacked the giant more intentionally now, attempting to use his own strength against him.

For a moment Nathanael had the advantage. He shoved him past and the giant was flailing; he was clearly as unfamiliar with Krav Maga as Nathanael was with the giant's fighting style. Suddenly the giant reached out an unnaturally long hand and stabilised himself against the fence. With his other giant hand he reached forward and grabbed Nathanael's shoulder and pushed himself up, pushing Nathanael down. Moments later the whole world was revolving and careening to the side, and Nathanael realised the giant had rolled over somehow, picked him up bodily and was about to throw him over the railing into the churning river.

Through the corner of his eye, he saw that Sasha had picked up the gun. Oh, well, that was it, then, this was the end. Kind of a trivial way to go. Lord Jesus, I…

A gun-shot sounded and for a moment Nathanael wondered where the pain was, why he didn't feel the impact. Suddenly Nathanael was falling. He realised Sasha had shot the giant. Nathanael saw the giant wince briefly as he stumbled backwards. Nathanael rolled onto the stone tiles and picked himself up. Sasha shot the giant again, this time in the back.

Kael was behind the giant and ran at his enormous back, with folded arms. Though he was soft and unfit, he happened to be quite a stocky, heavy man and when he rammed the creature it stumbled like a stick insect being attacked by an ant in one of those nature documentaries. The hood of the giant's hoodie fell all the way back and Nathanael saw that his head was elongated; he knew the word for it, dolichocephalic.

Nathanael realised it couldn't have been head binding. There was no reason for them to do this to him in the lab. This was an antediluvian giant, one of the Nephilim, brought to life again by the scientists. An abomination that even God had spurned and disavowed, destroying the earth by flood rather than allowing these things to pollute the human genome. For a moment the weirdness of it all struck Nathanael and his head began spinning but then he saw that Natasha had joined Kael in repeatedly ramming the giant towards the edge of the fence. Nathanael stepped forward, grasped one elongated arm and, using the giant's own inertia, flung him even harder towards the railing.

Sasha pumped the trigger, sending another bullet, then another into the giant as he stumbled over the edge of the three-foot-high railing as though it wasn't even there. The top of the railing was barely over the height of the giant's ankle and the curved top had proven a true stumbling block for someone of his height. The giant flipped over, his face registering panic as he realised his legs were in the water, being drawn away by the current.

One hand still clung to the fence, though.

By now a police emergency response team in black bulletproof gear was running up onto the observation area with guns drawn. Nathanael said to the giant, "We can save you! Reach out your other hand!" Nathanael reached forwards with both hands and grabbed the giant's forearm. The giant sneered up at him, his expression even more inhuman and hostile than before.

The police stood around like Keystone Cops, not knowing what to do.

The giant reached up over the railing with his other hand and grabbed Nathanael by the back of his shirt and tried to drag him over the railing, to plunge to his doom with the giant.

Nathanael felt his feet leave the ground. Five of the policemen dropped their guns, ran forward and grabbed Nathanael to stop him going over. The strength of five burly men could barely counter the giant's wiry, inhuman, angelically enhanced muscle strength. Nathanael was going over with him, slowly but surely. He watched the grey tiles below moving past, then the fence, he was well and truly over it.

Another gunshot sounded.

Suddenly having no resistance, the police easily pulled Nathanael back from the brink.

From the spreading black stain on the giant's shoulder, Nathanael realised someone must have shot him. The giant let go of the railing and, flailing wildly, plunged into the water with his legs and arms akimbo.

It was comical; he looked like a cartoon lobster struggling in the surf. He began to swim slowly but powerfully in the other direction but the inexorable current kept dragging him back towards the edge. It took many slow minutes, during which the police threw him a rope but he refused it, and then seemingly in moments the dreadful spectacle finally came to an end. The roiling, foamy, multicoloured turbulence dragged him right to the edge and over, limbs splayed in every direction like a falling giraffe, lolloping over the edge at the last moment, hesitating like a sinister version of the cartoon Wile E. Coyote about to fall to his doom, his head like a white, evil-looking anvil-shaped blob illuminated by the changing light show, his mouth and black eyes open wide in stark shock and surprise and the sudden fear of imminent death. With a final wild rush of spray and mist, he was gone.

It was all over.

Natasha breathed out — she must have been holding her breath. Faint, she swayed from side to side, apparently only staying upright by supporting herself on the barrier with her right hand. She had been holding the gun. Somehow she had gotten hold of Nathanael's gun from Sasha and had finished off the creature. She dropped the gun.

Sasha picked it up, checked the cartridge — empty — then leapt up and tried to run away but suddenly the whole Tactical Response Team had pulled their guns on him. Click, click, click, click, click.

Sasha said, "What am I being arrested for, officers?"

One of them said, "We've had a tipoff from the FBI concerning a murder in Russia and one or two other crimes as well."

Sasha stood up, holding his arms high. Expediency clearly trumped love of freedom for this guy. He said pleadingly, in a parody of politeness, "I am your prisoner, good officers."

One of the policemen turned to Natasha and said,

"We'll need you three to come back to the station as well for questioning." Then he paused and said, "What on earth was that thing?"

Natasha shook her head. "If I told you, you wouldn't believe me."

The policeman nodded, "I don't think I want you to tell me, actually. Sounds like I'd only have more nightmares."

Nathanael noticed that Natasha looked worried. "What's wrong, Natasha?"

She winced. "That giant was remarkably strong. How do we know that it couldn't survive the falls?"

The policeman said, "We don't. Not yet. But we'll send a team down tomorrow to the bottom to make sure." He looked into the distance. "I wouldn't normally say this, not even for a serial shooter, 'cause most of them are just normal kids who ended up mentally twisted and don't know what they're doing but that was the evilest dang thing I ever saw in my life. When I looked into its eyes I knew it wasn't human. And I really hope it's dead."

~~~
~~~

CHAPTER 33 – Encounter Exigency.

HEIDELBERG CONFERENCE ROOM.

The German man's mobile phone rang. "Hello?"

"The Encounter Exigency Plan needs to be executed. The subject revealed himself at Niagara."

"Where is he now?"

"He went over the falls."

The German man unfolded his ruler and slapped it on the table several times. "Is he still alive?"

"We have sent a team to find him, if he survived, or the corpse."

"Send out the Encounter Exigency Team. These creatures are very resilient, once they have achieved consciousness. Assume he survived the fall. Substitute the corpse of the unsuccessful attempt in Frankfurt."

"Yes, sir."

<u>CHAPTER 34 – Couth untruth.</u>

BUFFALO, NY.

Michelle stepped out of the Hertz hire car in the Buffalo FBI Field Office car park at four o'clock in the morning, breathing cold mist into the pre-dawn air. As she flicked the car lock she felt a pricking sensation at the back of her neck; someone was watching her.

Not again.

Suddenly her neck constricted and she found she was gasping for breath. Forcing panic down, she quickened her footsteps and began jogging between the few cars parked in the lonely car-park. She leapt forwards and sprinted through the front door into the building.

She wasn't going to get kidnapped at night ever again. She was carrying another person with her now. The bump was beginning to show. Michelle wasn't simply responsible for herself now. She was responsible for another life.

She looked back out through the glass foyer doors. Was that a figure, standing in the shadows across the road? Or just her imagination?

She was way too jumpy these days, especially at night.

The lights were bright inside the complex but the tall, rectangular windows stared out uneasily at the cold, black summer night, as though this building was a haven in the midst of some nightmarish alternate dimension, some Lovecraftian place.

Michelle was surprised at her own thoughts – even for her, that was dark.

She'd been reading too much horror lately.

Seeing that the whole affair involved crimes that had crossed state borders, the FBI had become involved. Apparently, they had picked up Natasha, Kael, Nathanael, and Sasha from the police station in Niagara Falls and taken them to the Buffalo Field Office.

Right now, Michelle knew that Natasha was being interviewed by two agents from the FBI, a woman and a man. She had to hurry – they needed her input, even more than a lawyer.

She had to make sure the FBI didn't work out that Nathanael and Natasha had been party to the bombing.

Michelle pulled a photograph ID card from her purse and flicked it onto the desk at the front administration. One of the front desk guards immediately straightened up, looked at her with respect and showed her through to the interview room. It was quite a high-level ID that Michelle had been given.

An Asian FBI woman sat in a neat, grey suit, tapping at her laptop, seated next to a bald FBI man wearing a black suit and tie.

Natasha was sitting in front of them both, waiting silently.

The FBI woman said absently, "Hello?"

The guard said, "Excuse me, Ma'am. Someone's here to see you. A young women who would only identify herself as TG. She has top-level Security clearance"

The woman glanced up from her screen. "TG? Is it really you?"

Michelle said, "Natasha is my sister."

"Oh." She stood up immediately and shook Michelle's hand respectfully. "Call me Jeanette." The man sitting next to her didn't get up, although he flashed a half-smile at Michelle. He said, "Heard a lot about your work."

Jeanette added, "TG, Agent Smythe. Call him Agent Smythe; he doesn't like people calling him by his first name. And thanks for the intel, by the way, really appreciated it."

Agent Smythe said, "They can't stop talking about your work in the Leo Bos affair in the NY field office, TG."

Jeanette nodded. "TG has sent me some updates along the way with this case too." She pursed her lips in a picture of tightly controlled professionalism and said, "Just email me your invoice and I'll make sure it gets paid promptly."

Natasha raised her eyebrows. Clearly, Michelle, who looked incredibly smug, was playing both sides, or maybe all sides, in this game.

Michelle told Jeanette, "By the way, there's a European connection. The Cabal. You know who I mean?"

Jeanette nodded. "There's not a lot we can do about them, yet. Although things have begun to change."

Michelle said, "You wouldn't mind, would you, if I sit here while you interview Sasha, which is not his real name, by the way…? I might be able to help you find the holes in his story."

Jeanette nodded. "We're doing him next. He's in the holding cell. We're just following up on one or two questions with Natasha. Such as where they've been for the past few days."

Michelle said, "Oh, they were in Buffalo. I booked the hotels for them, I can email you the details. I'm sure there's surveillance footage available of them going out for meals and so forth."

Natasha looked at Michelle. There couldn't be, because they hadn't been in Buffalo, they'd been just outside Niagara Falls. But Michelle shrugged and said, "Video never lies," something Natasha knew was not strictly true anymore.

She looked at Jeanette and Agent Smythe.

Agent Smythe said, "So those three people who attacked the company facility outside of Niagara Falls could not have been Kael, Nathanael and Natasha. Much as I thought. There are other actors involved; there is still a lot we don't know."

~~~
~~~

They interviewed Nathanael next. He told them everything except about the bombing.

Just as his interview was nearing its end, several Niagara police came into the interview room.

Jeanette snapped, "Yes?"

The policeman said, "Sorry to interrupt, Ma'am. We've had a team at the foot of the falls since the early hours and they found the giant's body floating along the river. It's in the morgue. We need someone to come in and identify it as the one responsible for the Niagara incident."

Jeanette frowned. "We haven't quite finished the interviews yet."

"We can bring them back here," the policeman said. "It won't take long. The forensic examiner is there right now and would like to finish up. Something about his grandchild's cello recital in the morning or something like that."

Jeanette threw her papers in the air and shouted, "Alright! Alright! Bring them back here. Actually, I'm coming with you." She stood up and gathered her purse and car keys together.

~~~

The Erie County medical examiner's laboratory had mustard coloured walls and the equipment looked to be a relic from the nineteen sixties. A naked, unblemished dolichocephalic
~~~

body was lying on the stainless steel examining table, its legs extending stiffly over the edge.

Jeanette was standing watching from a position obliquely behind the medical examiner.

Natasha and Nathanael close to the body, looking at the face, the hands.

Natasha said through the medical mask, "Yes, that's him."

Nathanael was not so sure. "Wait a minute. I don't think this one is as tall…" He grabbed the dead body's arm with his gloved hand and measured it against his left arm. The thing's arm was only about six or seven inches longer than Nathanael's. He was sure the one that had attacked him had arms that were at least two-foot longer than his. Nathanael said, "The one that attacked us was maybe about… ten-foot tall? This creature looks maybe… eight-foot tall at the most?"

The medical examiner, a gruff-speaking man in his sixties, nodded and said, "Eight feet and three inches, to be precise. That's right. Could look taller when he's attacking you?"

Nathanael shook his head slowly. "I really don't think it's him."

The medical examiner rolled his eyes. "There can't be more than one dolichocephalic adult in the New York State area on the same night – it's gotta be the same one. And such extreme dolichocephaly, usually the skull is just slightly longer…"

He made some incisions from the side of the head down to the cheekbone and peeled back skin and muscle, revealing the white of the bone. "Look at the way the sphenoparietal suture overlaps the temporal bone. The zygomaticofacial foramen is a completely different structure, the anterior boundary of the temporal fossa twists around and is virtually convex. Unnatural." He grimaced and made more incisions, then peeled back the skin over the top of the head.

He said, "The frontal fontanelle is like an extended helmet overlapping the frontal and parietal eminences." He looked up. "It's almost as though the skull has been intentionally re-engineered to make it stronger. And look!" He opened the mouth. "Two rows of teeth. This puzzled me at the start." He wiped away the sweat from his brow and swore loudly. "This is not just a congenital abnormality or genetic variation. It's structural. At first glance, I'd say we're talking species-level variation."

Jeanette said, "What? Not human?"

The examiner shook his head. "Not homo sapiens. Even the most dolichocephalic skull is generally only mildly longer than normal, even when it's a result of head-binding. These days, anyhow, they deal with natural occurrences of dolichocephaly with surgery when the infants are just a few days old. The skull of this creature is extremely odd." And he added, "Even if it was head binding, usually they are Africans. This fellow looks European. They did practice head binding once in Europe, in France, Caucasus and Scandinavia but the practice died out completely in the early twentieth century." And he looked up at them. "From the length of the skull and the very strange bone and muscle structures here, I very much doubt this is either head binding or a congenital abnormality. If I wasn't doubting my own sanity, I would say that this is a completely different species. Or even some sort of offspring of human and… something else." He paused and examined the temporal lobes. "Only a full sequencing of the genome could tell us for certain."

Nathanael asked, "Where are the gunshot wounds?"

The medical examiner said, "What?"

Nathanael said, "He was shot at least two or three times. Even if he healed fast, the last time was two or three minutes before he went over the falls."

With a sneer of distaste, the examiner glanced over at the naked body of the monster. "Could have been wearing a bulletproof vest, I guess… But…"

Nathanael said, "Wouldn't there be bruising, in that case? I saw the bullet hole and the blood myself."

The examiner shook his head. "No there wouldn't be

bruising, not if it happened so soon before death," he said. "Then again, he's quite fair-skinned — bruising in very fair-skinned people can appear more quickly, sometimes within the hour. But there should be redness and swelling at least. And broken bones and even internal damage from the falls itself. It's completely impossible that he could have survived the fall unscathed. And if you saw blood…" He looked intently at Nathanael. "You really think this is a different… one?"

Nathanael nodded. "Absolutely certain."

The examiner said, "I would have to say how unlikely it is that any other dolichocephalic adult would happen to be anywhere near the falls by chance, especially one with a skull as distended and… with such an unusual construction as this one."

Natasha said doubtfully, "Well, Nathanael was much closer to him than I was…" She pressed her lips together. "Nathanael is generally very observant, Doctor. I would take him at his word. And yes, I saw the blood from the last gunshot too."

The examiner made an incision in the stomach.

With his tweezers, he reached into the intestines and extracted something. He showed it to them – a large cube of carrot. He put it on the table and poked it with the tweezers.

"Frozen solid," he said. He took out several other pieces of food, mince, some half-chewed berries. All were frozen solid.

The examiner swore coldly. "It's my professional opinion that this individual did not meet his demise at the base of the falls. Someone planted this body there in order to deceive us. It has been frozen and then thawed — and this is usually a process that takes a week or two — but that he has frozen food in his stomach is enough for me to say that this body is, without any doubt, *not* the one that fell over the waterfall. In fact, it is my considered opinion that it was put there to deceive us."

Nathanael said, "What else will your report say?"

The examiner said, "Well... I still have to examine for internal organ damage, decide on the cause of death. But after finding the frozen food in his stomach... I can verify that this is not the same man who attacked you at Niagara." He pulled out his mobile phone. "Just a moment, I really think I should report this back to the Niagara police right away."

They stood there feeling awkward as the mobile tried to connect.

They could just hear the dial tone ring out.

The examiner said, "Now, that's really strange. If there's no one at the desk it always goes to the answerphone. Let me try the Captain."

He put the mobile on speaker this time. It rang out again.

He shrugged. "That's really weird, even at this time of

night." He said to Jeanette in a concerned tone of voice, "I really think you should get over there."

~~~

Jeanette sped back to the FBI offices with her siren blaring. She ran into the lift, with Nathanael and Natasha following close behind.

The lift opened onto her floor. She ran out, asking the nearest agent, "What's wrong with the phones? I was trying to ring through the results of an autopsy."

The agent said, "Don't know. The phones have all gone down. Smythe wants to see you."

Jeanette led Nathanael and Natasha into an office, near the room they had been interviewed in. "Wait here. I may have some more questions for you."

She walked back to the other room where Michelle was still sitting quietly. Smythe was not there, so Jeanette sat down.

Agent Smythe followed them in a few minutes later carrying three polystyrene cups filled with coffee.

After handing out the coffee and closing the door he said to Jeanette, "We've had reports of some kind of… giant, with a… big head. Walking through the streets in darkness… And the phones suddenly went out."

At that moment all the lights went off. It was dark in the
~~~

room except for the light coming from Jeanette's laptop, and a faint pastel-pink dawn tint in the sky outside.

Jeanette stopped typing. "Damn. The wireless is down as well." She took out her mobile. "I should be able to connect my laptop to 4G, though." She fiddled on it for a moment. "Oh, that's pretty weird. Even the cell-towers must be down. That's disconcerting."

A knock sounded.

Jeanette said, "Come in."

The young man who came in looked like a rookie. Jeanette said, "Hi Dave. What's up?"

"The Director says to record any interviews on your phone or laptop, if possible; or stop the interviews until the power is up and running again. Apparently, the whole surveillance system is down."

"What, the cameras as well?"

"Yes, all the cameras are down."

Agent Smythe raised his eyebrows. "That's pretty weird. I've never heard of that happening before."

Jeanette agreed. "Very weird."

Michelle said, "So that's it? Interview's over?"

"Just a moment, TG, I still have some more questions for you," said Jeanette. "I hope you understand I'm just trying to get to the truth here. Nothing personal; and I know you outrank me. That's okay. I just need a minute to get ready, though, I'm not used to this voice recorder app."

At that moment Michelle's phone pinged. Michelle reached down but she stopped with her phone half way out of her pocket.

Jeanette snapped, "Oh, for God's sake, alright! Check your messages if you must!" Then she looked up at Michelle suspiciously. "How come your mobile is still on the network?"

Michelle pulled her phone out. It was attached to a black cord that extended back into her pocket. "Long-range antenna. I actually have it with me all the time, if I'm out of the house. It runs through my trousers and up the back of my shirt. I suppose it's paranoia. I also have a spare mobile inside my boot. I was abducted last year and ended up out of mobile range; I vowed never to let that happen again."

Jeanette's eyes widened. "I didn't even know they had long-range antennae for mobiles. Is the message important?"

Michelle was frowning. "One of my ah... colleagues online has just sent me something. Some bad stuff is happening. The Niagara police department was attacked ten minutes ago by some sort of terrorist cell. The lights and alarm system went down directly before the attack, exactly like what's just happened here. Lots of police killed, etcetera. It's barely made it onto the news yet. My colleague is keeping an eye out for me. He saw that the lights had gone off in this building. He noticed someone unnaturally tall on the foyer security cameras. The arms locker on the first floor will be compromised next. I'm telling you, Jeanette, the same thing is about to happen here."

Jeanette said in a skeptical tone of voice, "How does your friend outside even know you're here?"

"Same way I knew Nathanael and Natasha were taken here. They're the same friends who looked into that for me."

Jeanette frowned a little. "You sure know a lot, TG," she said pointedly. She stood up and left the room.

~~~

Meanwhile, Nathanael and Natasha were sitting in their small interview room, not far away, waiting to see if they would be kept in custody when several distant bangs disturbed the morning silence. Nathanael thought it was a car backfiring at first until a piercing alarm began echoing throughout the complex.

The few agents already at their desks this early in the morning stopped what they were doing, got up and pulled out their guns.

The agent guarding Nathanael and Natasha unlocked
~~~

the door. With his right hand, he pulled out his gun as well, a Glock 19M. Nathanael asked him, "What's happening?"

He glanced at Nathanael and said in a low, tightly controlled voice, "You'll both need to get out of here. Interview's over. It's a deadly incursion. This type of alarm means the foyer is compromised. With deadly force. And the gun locker on the first floor has been breached. This is the first time those alarm have gone off since after 9/11 when the system was put in. This is not a drill. My advice is: get outa here. Something's going down, something bad, that you don't want to be caught up in." He added, "Apparently the police station in Niagara Falls has been attacked as well."

Michelle was waiting in the hallway with Jeanette, who also had her Glock 19M ready. "Go!" said Jeanette. "That alarm means Michelle was right. Some bad stuff is going down." She pointed to the rear of the floor. "There is a fire escape over that way. Follow the signs. Get out, you fools! This is no place for civilians."

Nathanael could see through a gap in the blinds in the window of the room.

The doors to the stairwell right next to the elevator opened.

Stooping under the door frame like the titan in the Goya painting, his elongated head wrapped in some sort of turban, the giant stepped into the corridor. Nathanael could see the bandage on his shoulder where he had been shot. The giant held an

MP5/10 submachine gun in each hand and an M4 carbine slung over his shoulder with seven or eight clips in his belt; exactly how many Nathanael couldn't tell. Licking his lips, the giant pressed the triggers. Stuttering fire leaped out, knocking chunks of plaster out of walls and randomly shattering glass windows.

"Oh no," said Jeanette and then strung a string of expletives together more efficiently than Nathanael expected. "How on earth did he get the semiautomatics from the HRT locker? Who gave him the codes?"

She stepped out into the corridor and shot at him, one, two, three times.

The agents' guns returning fire seemed to Nathanael like toy pistols in comparison with the intermittent ratatat-tat of the MP5s. Nathanael noticed that there were only ten or eleven agents scattered around the entire first floor, those who had arrived early.

The small number seemed inadequate to the task, considering the firepower the giant was wielding.

One agent near the stairwell stepped out from behind a pillar to tackle the giant. Still firing the automatic rifle with his right hand, the giant allowed the other MP5 to hang loosely over his shoulder as he launched into the strange, antiquated, jerky martial arts style he had used on Nathanael before, barely even glancing but easily disabling the attacking Fed with one hand.

While the Fed fell, the giant swiftly reached forward pulled something from the man's jacket pocket, threw it onto the ground and stepped on it. Nathanael heard a faint crunch. The agent's mobile phone? Nathanael wasn't sure. After efficiently switching the clip in the rifle in his right hand, the giant grabbed the MP5 in his left hand and began firing both guns again.

The moment's pause gave two more agents a window of opportunity to leap forwards. Each of them grabbed one rifle but the giant let the straps slip over his arms, and in a move of astonishing swiftness lifted the M4 carbine and had killed both agents, splattering blood and bits of bone onto the walls around the elevator doors.

Again he reached down to extract their phones then threw them on the floor and shot them to pieces.

Jeanette said, "This is not going well." She immediately opened the door to an office that had a plaque with her name, 'JEANETTE NORDSTROM', on the door. She unlocked a cabinet and pulled out several more Glocks. "Take one," Jeanette said to Nathanael, "If you're going to stick around."

Nathanael turned to Natasha. "Take Michelle out of here. I'm not having you risking your lives. Not after everything that happened last year. Not after Michelle was almost killed."

Taking one of the guns, Natasha shook her head. She took the other gun and passed it to Michelle, and said, "We've been practising. It was Michelle's abduction that convinced me we needed to be able to handle guns."

Jeanette snapped, "It's not your job. You're civilians. I'd rather you get out of here. I don't want your deaths on my conscience."

Natasha said, "And yet you need all the help you can get."

Jeanette was still foraging through the desktop drawer. "I've got another one in here somewhere. Ah…" She pulled the gun out – another Glock – and grinned grimly. "Now I've got two."

The giant was now striding through the centre corridor. He fired again, ratatat-tat, and three more FBI agents fell. Again the giant reached down, took out their mobile phones and shot them to pieces on the floor. It was then that Nathanael noticed the intermittent bursts of fire he was sending towards the walls and windows were not random.

The giant was destroying the surveillance cameras.

Two more FBI agents leaped forwards to engage him.

Seconds later they were corpses, a mess of broken bone and pooling blood.

Nathanael said, "Why is he here? What is he here for?"

Michelle said, "To clean up. To get rid of the evidence. It seems a bit drastic, though."

Jeanette checked her weapon and whispered, "It's time. You should have left when you could. But he's just about here now. This is the end." Then she added, "I had always wanted to get married and have children. I suppose it's not going to happen now."

Natasha said, "Pray."

Nathanael, Jeanette and Michelle said, "What?"

She said, "Pray. Remember, it distracted him somehow at the building. Pray. Or sing the doxology."

Disregarding the weird look Jeanette was giving them, Nathanael and Natasha started to sing aloud,

"Praise God from whom all blessings flow.

Praise Him all creatures here below.

Praise God above ye heavenly host.

Praise Father, Son and Holy Ghost."

Suddenly the Nephilim grabbed its elongated head with both hands and began moaning and whining. "Stop! Stop that terrible sound!" He fell to the ground, writhing, onto the floor.

Nathanael ran out from his hiding place, stood in front of the giant and said, "One of your fellow Nephilim repented. You are not necessarily doomed by your nature. Eternal destruction does not have to be your end." He felt rather than saw Jeanette join him at his right side.

The Nephilim looked up at Nathanael and laughed. "This human puppet amuses me. Why would any Nephilim even want to repent?"

Nathanael said, "To avoid the wrath of God. Repent. Humble yourself before God and be forgiven of your sins. One of your number – Adze – already has."

"Ha. Human fool. I would burn in hell for a thousand years before I humble myself before the God of the Jews." Before Nathanael could say any more, the Nephilim had leaped up onto its feet and lifted both its guns.

Gunfire rang out.

Natasha peered around the corner to see what was happening. To her astonishment, she saw that Jeanette had angled her two Glocks downwards and pumped several shots straight into the giant's knees, shattering bone and flesh, before the giant had managed even one shot at Nathanael. Arterial blood began to emerge from the giant's left leg in spurts.

The giant collapsed and Jeanette kicked the two M5s away but she wasn't quick enough because he still had the M4 carbine around his neck. The giant pumped three individual shots into her.

Jeanette fell to the ground, bleeding from her abdomen.

Natasha cried out, "I stopped praying and singing!" She shouted, "Nathanael, sing!"

Nathanael shook his head and pulled out his gun, even as the barrel of the M4 carbine turned around towards him.

But Natasha had already begun singing again. "Praise

God from whom all blessings flow..."

The giant began moaning again and dropped the M4 and began holding his massive head in his hands like a long, pale watermelon. The length of the skull made it an ideal target.

Nathanael said, "You had your chance. Such as it was."

Nathanael shot the creature along the length of his skull, seven times.

The giant gasped and his breathing began to labour; asphyxiating blood was causing a death rattle along with every uneven wheeze. His left leg relaxed and the blood began to flow out steadily.

Nathanael shot him in the forehead and the creature's eyes glazed over and the tortured death rattle stopped at last.

Nathanael immediately turned to Jeanette, stripping off his wind-cheater and wrapping it around her abdomen tightly in an attempt to stop the bleeding.

Michelle took out her mobile and called 911.

Moments later nearby sirens began to wail.

Outside the dawn sun was actually beginning to light the sky bright orange on the horizon, and the glass and metal skyscrapers began to glow with reflected light. Somehow it was comforting – God had not forgotten to keep the earth turning, to make the sun rise.

Nathanael looked at the still, pale corpse of the giant, lying on the floor. The nightmare really was over now.

CHAPTER 35 – Meth meets Neph.

PETER AND METH'S HOUSE, PERTH, WESTERN AUSTRALIA.

Meth woke up to see Peter frantically pulling clothes out of Meth's chest of drawers and throwing them into an open suitcase.

Meth said, "But Dad, it's a school day today."

Peter said, "I had a nightmare that the creature from Sydney found us."

Meth said, "What creature?"

"A giant," said Peter. "The one that the scientists resurrected. The Nephilim. At the laboratory in Sydney. Like the one that attacked the FBI office where Nathanael and Natasha were."

Meth said, "Does this mean we have to move again?"

"I am afraid so. It was very vivid."

Five minutes later, Peter was in the garage opening the boot of the car and stuffing two suitcases in.

Meth was already sitting in the passenger seat, ready to go.

Peter heard a sound, the slightest scratch on the outside of the roller door, and he whirled around to see the roller door rolling up slowly and smoothly.

A very tall man, almost nine-foot tall, was standing there, dressed in a long coat. He was wearing dark glasses but there was something strange about his head.

He was a Nephilim.

And his right hand had six fingers; they were wrapped around the grip of a pistol, and Peter was staring down the barrel of it. Peter heard a footstep and said, "No!" but it was too late. Meth was standing beside him.

Peter whispered, "This was my nightmare…"

The creature's face was filled with an unnatural joy. It said, "This is a day of exultation. I have found my enemy and the ancient enemy of my people."

It moved the gun barrel and pointed it at Meth's head.

Meth lifted his hand casually and said, "Your time is over. You have no power in this age, for Jesus has already conquered you and your kind on the cross. May you be rebuked in the name of the Lord Jesus Christ."

The creature stepped backward, shock and horror registering on its face as it's fingers spasmed and it dropped the gun.

Meth said, "Unclean spirit, come of out of him, in the name of the Lord Jesus Christ. You were banished in the time of Noah and I banish you again now to the abyss."

The creature shrieked and the giant's body crumpled to the ground, into the shadows of the garage wall, its arms and legs splayed in an unnatural, uncomfortable pattern, the limbs twitching slightly.

It was still breathing but there was no longer any sign of overt consciousness in its eyes or its body.

Peter stood staring at it for some time. Finally, he said, "Wow... What are we going to do with this... thing?"

Meth seemed less perturbed. He shrugged. "I'm going to school today, Dad. I don't know! How should I know? I'm just a kid. What do you think?"

Peter shook his head. "I don't know. Perhaps... call triple zero? Get an ambulance to pick it up? Maybe not. That might just alert the Cabal to its presence here. I really don't know... All I know is that... You might be a little late to school this morning, son..."

Meth sighed. "That's alright, Dad. Not again."

Peter dragged the body into the house where it lay on the carpet in the entry hall, breathing gently, still completely unconscious. A beam of sunlight shone through upon the thing's face, where motes danced to and fro in its steady breath.

Peter said, "Do you know what, son, I think I will message Michelle. Perhaps Michelle or Natasha or Nathanael will have some idea..."

The doorbell rang.

Peter opened the door and stepped back in surprise.

Another creature stood in the sunlight, dressed in

a trench-coat, his head in the shadow of a hood but he held no weapon in his hands. Still, Peter scrambled backwards to grab the gun from where he usually left it, in the liquor cabinet. Realising the weapon was still in the garage, he steeled himself for the inevitable end as the creature raised his hand.

Instead of going for a gun, the creature pulled back his hood. Peter and Meth both gasped in surprise, for the man had the face of a lion.

The lion-headed man raised his palms in a gesture of peace and said, "Shalom, Peter and Methuselah. I am Adze. God sent me here to protect you."

CHAPTER 36 – Giant Cover-up.

BUFFALO GENERAL MEDICAL CENTRE, NY.

Jeanette was lying in her bed in the Buffalo General Medical Centre. Her arm was in a sling and large bandages were tightly wound around her lower torso. A nurse finished taking her blood pressure and walked out of the room as Nathanael and Natasha walked in. The television was on, with some kind of news or current affairs show blaring through the tiny speakers.

The caption said, "Niagara attacks latest update."

The female news anchor said, "The latest on the Niagara attacks. Apparently the attacker Gary Dressel was a white supremacist Neo-Nazi. Dressel's manifesto has been released on some websites but the authorities have threatened prosecution for any who spread it." A grainy photo appeared on the screen. It showed a very tall man, probably about seven feet tall, stooping out from the stairwell with two M5s and an M4 carbine strapped onto his body. His head, however, was not dolichocephalic, it was normal-sized; in fact, he had long, dark hair and looked like a typical high school misfit.

Jeanette said, "You've seen this?"

Michelle said, "Yeh, and you know what? This guy didn't even exist before yesterday. His Facebook page, his instagram posts with the guns, everything. I think he's actually little more than some AI-generated face."

Jeanette said, "It's a giant cover-up," and Michelle guffawed.

The next news item flicked onto the screen. The caption said, "Nobel Award Winning Climate Scientist Turns Denier." The news anchor said, "Kael E. Addison has announced in a press conference that he no longer believes humans are predominantly responsible for climate change." They showed a photograph of Kael, with the audio of Devraj saying, "Due to political pressure from the hard-right faction of the present government, Professor Addison, if we can continue to call such an unscientific person a Professor, has turned against science and is now a climate denier and a creationist. He is responsible for the genocide of future generations. It is a sad day for established science when one man can go against the opinion of ninety-seven percent of the scientists in the world." Another clip followed with Kael saying, "We do know that extra carbon dioxide has helped green the earth from a recent NASA study."

Then the camera focused on a reporter who said, "Then what explains the temperature variability? The unusual climatic shifts? Glaciers progressing and receding? Sea ice levels?"

Kael answered, "Well... I think the influence of the Sun explains an awful lot."

CHAPTER 37 – Epilogue: The Circle of the Sun.

BUFFALO FBI FIELD OFFICE, NY.

Sasha was in the holding cell for what seemed like a day and a half before someone finally realised he was there. They brought him food and drink and then told him, "Someone is coming to interview you."

After what seemed like an eternity of waiting, finally Agent Smythe walked in. He pulled the guard's chair over to Sasha's cell and sat down in front of him. "Well, Sasha. The cleanup is continuing upstairs. I trust you have been comfortable in your cell? We have pieced nearly everything together now except for one or two things. Your story being the main one."

Sasha snarled, "I told you. I don't know anything. Leave me alone, FBI clone."

Agent Smythe said, "We were hoping to go right back to the start. When you left Russia? Why you left Russia?"

Sasha rolled his eyes. "When I left Russia it was a long time ago. Но э́то бы́ло давно́."

Agent Smythe said, "Но э́то бы́ло давно́ и непра́вда. 'It was a long time ago and is not true.' A subtle way of saying, perhaps, that it wasn't such a long time ago after all? Or is there some other intended meaning to the phrase?"

Crestfallen, Sasha winced, then said, "You know

Russian, then. You are clever American, a thing that is as rare as a crawfish whistling on the mountain."

Smythe shook his head, the edge of his mouth forming a slight sneer. "A subtle Russian is an even more unlikely beast. But you're stumbling and bumbling around like an elephant in a china shop. There is almost certainly less profundity in what you are saying. The more literal meaning is probably what we are looking for. Did you flee Russia for some reason? Wanted by the Moscow police?"

Sasha's reaction spoke volumes. He suddenly went completely still and stared at Agent Smythe unblinkingly, waiting for the question.

Smythe said, "Is this something about Sol the Magician? TG put me onto this case. It happened about a year ago in Moscow. The murder, supposedly, of a popular magician. She suspected there was a little more to it." Smythe paused for a moment. "She says that you are Sol." Sasha looked startled. Smythe nodded and continued. "I think that we might be willing to overlook certain past crimes, Sol, in return for the assistance you gave to the authorities in the incident at the falls in fighting the giant. We want the whole story, though. No omissions. We want to know everything that has been going on."

Sasha's eyes turned askance, shiftily looking away. His

voice went softer, though; perhaps he was trying to make his voice sound honest. "I will tell you everything, then. And let me tell you, I do not merely tell my own story. I shall tell everyone's story. For I have a finger in this pie and a finger in that one, a finger in everyone's pie, really. Ha. My own employee in a Russian server farm hacked TG, you know."

And he began to tell his own story.

The story of Sol the Magician, who killed Sasha, his assistant, then fled to England.

The story of Professor Kael E. Addison, TG, Natasha and Nathanael.

And the story of the hidden Cabal that rules everything that exists under the sun from the shadows. And Sol said, "The man's suit was so dark it swallowed the light like a black hole…"

<u>APPENDICES.</u>

I always research my Nathanael Wayfarer novels carefully, taking note of peer-reviewed scientific research and the opinions of real scientists.

In this novel I have dealt with what some might regard as fact, and others might regard as more speculative matters.

Firstly, the book speaks to the fraught narrative of catastrophic human-caused global warming, an issue about which many of my readers will know my views from my blogs.

Secondly, I deal with the strange issue of the Nephilim, the cryptic antediluvian giants mentioned in Genesis chapter 6, a subject that is far more speculative.

Appendix 1 – Global Warming.

In this novel, a global warmist climate scientist repents of lying, perverting peer review, and putting forward dishonest studies for publication. This may seem unlikely to some readers, who believe all climate scientists are good, principled people and probably believe that all Oil Company Executives are evil, too. Such a mindset will never be open to facts, so to those readers I say, just skip this appendix, for it will only make you angry.

Subsequent government enquiries in Britain effectively whitewashed the 2009 Climategate document release, saying, "There is nothing to see here, folks, move along, move along."

But the facts are still available for anyone who cares to look into the saga with an open mind. Somewhere on the internet, I am sure that the FOI2009.zip file may still be downloaded, and the contents perused. These emails and documents, which previous to the Climategate release were repeatedly requested and denied under lawful FOI requests (Government funded organisations such as the Hadley Climate Centre must have all their documents available for public scrutiny under UK law), were released onto a Russian server by an unknown player, probably someone in the Hadley Climate Centre itself. The documents and emails tell a story of perverted peer review, data manipulation, the exclusion of Climate Skeptics, and other shoddy scientific practices.

The 2009 FOI hacked emails revealed the extent to which the IPCC model computer programmer himself said that the data and procedure were terribly inadequate. Furthermore privately the cabal of global warming scientists themselves who ran the show admitted that they did not believe what they were saying publicly either.

And the centre of all of this, the Hadley Climate Centre in the UK, have admitted losing the raw data for the whole world; would you believe it, for hard drive space, in an organisation whose budget was in the realm of hundreds of millions of dollars.

None of the computer models is scientifically valid as the IPCC scientists have not created one yet that is able to accurately predict real future temperatures; all without exception have run too warm. There are many issues in climate science but anyone familiar with basic high school maths and science can follow the conversation and see the flaws in the official narrative.

For instance, the predictions of disaster that never eventuate, the placement of the BOM weather station in Sydney Observatory used to homogenise the accuracy of all the others in Australia next to an airconditioning vent and a nine-lane highway, when earlier last century it was in a breezy park. And the adjustment of earlier temperatures down by 3 degrees in Acorn 2 and the truncating of the 2014 extreme low temperatures in the

NOAA graph of New York, to make warming look consistent over the last fifty years. And the editing of low temperatures by BOM, in Thredbo and somewhere else anything lower than minus 10 degrees C was edited back to minus 10 degrees C later in the day on the website.

And the Medieval Warm Period, warmer than today, which was why the Vikings colonised Greenland for a short while (this article is interesting because they admit that it did get warmer, then cooler, but say that wasn't the reason the Vikings left.)

While the climate scientist in my story repents, sadly there are very few corresponding tales of repentance from the players in the Climategate Saga (with the exception of Judith Curry, a very principled scientist who changed her mind, and whose blog contains a balanced assessment of the state of the science) – but in general, there is only an ongoing effort to continue the cover-up and the misinformation.

In other words, while the name of the scientist in my novel, Kael Addison, is fictional, his fictional misdeeds are sadly inspired by the real-world actions of those scientists whose emails were released in the Climategate saga. And you may believe me or you may not but I think for anyone who really wishes to know the truth or even to claim to know what is really going on, it is incumbent on you to read the Climategate emails and find out what really was going on, particularly for those who are trying to convince others that Global Warming is a real problem and not just the modern version of Phrenology, the study of skulls in the late 19th and early 20th century in which each random bump and irregularity in someone's skull became an indicator of criminality, all of which is now rightly seen as the product of extreme confirmation-bias.

Yet even Phrenology may have had its legitimate uses, such as when studying the ancient remains of an ancient dolichocephalic Peruvian race, which is the other theme of this novel.

Appendix 2 – the Nephilim.

> And it came to pass, when men began to multiply on the face of the earth, and daughters were born unto them, that the sons of God saw the daughters of men that they were fair; and they took them wives of all which they chose. And the Lord said, My spirit shall not always strive with man, for that he also is flesh: yet his days shall be an hundred and twenty years. There were giants in the earth in those days; and also after that, when the sons of God came in unto the daughters of men, and they bare children to them, the same became mighty men which were of old, men of renown.
>
> …Noah was a just man and perfect in his generations, and Noah walked with God.
>
> *GENESIS 6:1-6, 9*

This short, mysterious passage has caused much grief to commentators throughout the years, and Calvin following Augustine subscribed to a spurious interpretation where the sons of God were a righteous line of human beings, descendants of Seth, versus the sons of Cain who were evil.

But before the second century AD there was no doubt in the minds of theologians and philosophers that these sons of God were rebellious angels, come down from heaven, who took some sort of physical form on the earth and chose wives from among human women to inseminate. Presumably one of their purposes was to confuse the seed of the serpent and the seed of Adam in order to prevent the prophecy in Genesis 3:15

coming true, "his seed shall crush your head." Noah's flood was partially intended to put a stop to that plan, apparently, although for some reason the offspring of the sons of God and their human wives seem to have lingered into the postdiluvian world; how this could be is not clearly explained in the text.

These offspring were called "Nephilim" in Genesis 6, a mysterious Hebrew or perhaps Aramaic word whose translation is today perhaps uncertain but in the second century BC it was translated into Greek as γιγαντες, *gigantes,* meaning 'giants' in the Greek translation of the Old Testament, the Septuagint; and it is perhaps not unreasonable to assume that the scholars who translated the Bible in those days might have known better than we do today what a particular word might mean...

By the way, "Sons of God", in the Old Testament, is a term used also in the Book of Job and Psalm 82 to refer to an angelic council, a ruling council that governs the nations, beneath God, a council which in the New Testament is superseded by Jesus and all who believe in Him, because of Jesus' victory on the cross. (Ephesians 2:6, Colossians 2:15, Colossians 3:1)

In Genesis 6:9 it says that Noah was 'perfect in his generations' it could actually mean Noah's family line had no DNA from the sons of God corrupting it.

In Numbers 13:33 the spies that Joshua sends into the promised land say specifically that the sons of Anak are Nephilim, and that they are in the land:

> "We saw the Nephilim there (the descendants of Anak come from the Nephilim). We seemed like grasshoppers in our own eyes, and we looked the same to them."

However, giants of this stature ('we seemed like grasshoppers in their eyes') are conspicuously absent from the narrative after this. Was this just the paranoia of Joshua's spies, worried about a pre-flood legend that really wasn't a problem at their time in history? 'The descendants of Anak come from the Nephilim,' is in fact the Hebrew version of a gloss on the text, an explanation in the form of an interruption. Scholars are fairly certain that it is not meant to be the words of Joshua's spies. So did the 'and also after that' in Genesis 6:4 refer to the Anakim, also to the Rephaim, Canaanites, Hittites, and Amalekites, and also perhaps the giants among the Philistines? The inhabitants of Anactoria, now called Miletus, a sea people who, when they migrated south became the Philistines, interestingly, traced their own ancestry back to a giant called Anax, a name almost certainly cognate with the Biblical Anak. Note also that another Philistine giant from Goliath's home town Gath, 1 Chronicles 20:6, who had six fingers and toes, is said to have been descended from the Rapha, the Rephaim, who were apparently ancient rulers who now dwelled in the land of the dead.

As far as I can tell, the Bible doesn't say how the progeny of the Nephilim survived the flood but some scholars lay the blame at Ham for marrying a woman whose bloodline was not pure. Ham's descendants, the Canaanites in particular, seem to be singled out in the Biblical narrative for their unfaithfulness as well as for having spawned giants. Others say that unfaithful angels took more women as their wives after Noah's flood, something that I think seems unlikely, for surely news would have reached the angels of the punishment God meted out on their brethren? Surely they would have balked at sharing imprisonment in Tartarus in chains? (2 Peter 2:4)

Dr Michael S. Heiser is the expert in this field and his studies are well worth looking into; particularly as to how this Old Testament view of angelology continues into the New Testament and becomes the hierarchy of principalities and powers that Jesus conquered on the cross.

The study of the Nephilim, of course, is right at the intersection point of Biblical Archaeology and ancient mythology. Nonetheless it is undeniable that the ancient myth of the god who came down from heaven and seduced a human woman was ubiquitous in ancient times as well as universal in extent, found in every continent and every race of people, and if we believe Dr Heiser's interpretation, this myth is indeed found in the Bible also, in Genesis, Numbers, Joshua and elsewhere in the Old Testament, and while it is found in the New Testament in Jude 1:6 and 2 Peter 2:4, seems also to have been believed by St. Paul. I believe I Corinthians 11:10 is a reference to this belief, in which passage, by the way I think the 'symbol of authority' on the woman's head is primarily the symbol of the woman's authority over the angels in this present age, Ephesians 2:6.

Now as to the existence of giants, the natural question to ask is, where is the archaeological proof? Well, according to contemporary newspaper reports in the nineteenth and early twentieth century such as the one on the opposite page from the Cairo Bulletin, from Wednesday December 17th 1913, there certainly seems to have been a large number of giant skeletons discovered in the United States, particularly in Wisconsin, often with large skulls, sometimes according to reports 'double the size of a normal human skull'.

FINDS SKELETONS GIANTS TWELVE FEET IN HEIGHT

Southern Workmen Discover Bones of Prehistoric Band Who Fell In Battle

Winn-boro, La., Dec. 16 -- Skeletons of a race of giants who average twelve feet in heighth were found today by workmen engaged upon a drainage project at Crowville, near here. There are several scores, at least, of the skeletons, and they lie in various positions. It is believed they were killed in a prehistoric fight and the the bodies lay where they fell until covered with alluvial deposits due to the flooding of the Mississippi River.

So far there has been no scientific examination of the bones, but a number of them were brought here and it seems there is little doubt of the accuracy of the measurements.

Many of the bones were broken and several of the skulls were fractured or crushed, giving indications of the frightful ferocity with which the giants must have met death.

The discovery of these bones is the second important archaeoligical (sic.) discovery reported recently in their section of the South. A few days ago the skeleton of a giant male was found close to the surface at Jackson, Mississippi.

At New Orleans, what was the bed of the gulf at the the time the whale existed now is 7,000 feet underground and Dr. E.N.Lowe, Mississippi state geologist, and other experts, cannot account for the whale being so high up.

FINDS SKELETONS GIANTS TWELVE FEET IN HEIGHT

Southern Workmen Discover Bones of Prehistoric Band Who Fell in Battle

Winnsboro, La., Dec. 16—Skeletons of a race of giants who average twelve feet in heighth were found today by workmen engaged upon a drainage project at Crowville, near here. There are several scores, at least, of the skeletons, and they lie in various positions. It is believed they were killed in a prehistoric fight and that the bodies lay where they fell until covered with alluvial deposits due to the flooding of the Mississippi River.

So far there has been no scientific examination of the bones, but a number of them were brought here and it seems there is little doubt of the accuracy of the measurements.

Many of the bones were broken and several of the skulls were fractured or crushed, giving indications of the frightful ferocity with which the giants must have met death.

The discovery of these bones is the second important archaeoligical discovery reported recently in this section of the South. A few days ago the skeleton of a giant male was found close to the surface at Jackson, Mississippi.

At New Orleans, what was the bed of the gulf at the time the whale existed now is 7,000 feet underground and Dr. E. N. Lowe, Mississippi state geologist, and other experts cannot account for the whale's being so high up.

Cairo Bulletin, Illinois, Wednesday December 17th 1913

And while there are many conspiracy theories stating that the Smithsonian is hiding these giant skeletons in some sort of deep archive or has destroyed them all because they are inconvenient for the theory of evolution and prove that the story of Noah's Ark is true by association, nonetheless using Ockham's Razor (the simplest explanation is often the best), the "Reburial of Human Remains Act" of 1988, forcing the Smithsonian to hand over Native American remains for reburial, should be enough explanation to account for the missing skeletons. The giant skeletons may well have been reburied.

What is troubling, I suppose, is the apparent paucity of modern documentary evidence of these remains, when the contemporary newspaper reports are so common and unequivocal.

The picture of the foetal remains of a Nephilim (if that is what the strange baby is) and the associated quote are fact, not fiction, from Peruvian Antiquities, by Rivero y Ustariz, Mariano Edward Rivero and Johann James Von Tschudi, 1855, from which I give this more extended quote:

> ...in our opinion, those physiologists are undoubtedly in error, who suppose that the different phrenological aspects offered by the Peruvian race were exclusively artificial. This hypothesis rests on insufficient grounds; its authors could have made their observations solely on the crania of adult individuals, as it is only a

few years since two mummies of children were carried to England, which, according the the very exact description of Dr Bellamy, belonged to the tribe of Aymaraes. The two crania (both of children scarce a year old) had, in all respects, the same form as those of adults. We ourselves have observed the same fact in many mummies of children of tender age, who, although they had cloths about them, were yet without any vestige or appearance of pressure of the cranium.

More still: the same formation of the head presents itself in children yet unborn; and of this truth we have had convincing proof in the sight of a fœtus, enclosed in the womb of a mummy of a pregnant woman, which we found in a cave of Huichay, two leagues from Tarma, and which is, at this moment, in our collection. Professor D'Outrepont, of great celebrity in the department of obstetrics, has assured us that the fœtus is one of seven months' age. It belongs, according to a very clearly defined formation of the cranium, to the tribe of the Huancas. We present the reader with a drawing of this conclusive and interesting proof in opposition to the advocates of mechanical action as the sole and exclusive cause of the phrenological form of the Peruvian race.

The adventures of Pizarro rampaging through South America are well known and he did indeed write the records of his own adventures. However the secret document is a complete concoction of mine.

The Vatican Secret Archive does actually exist and is in fact not secret – it even have its own website. Strangely, since I began writing this book, the name has been changed to the Vatican Apostolic Archive, 28 October 2019.

The information about a dolichocephalic ruling class in many different ancient places is also true. King Tutankhamen did indeed have an unusually long, large skull of the same sort of shape as the ones in Peru.

In summary – people with dolichocephalic skulls really existed in South America at least, and other places, and in the ruling class seem to have been a genetic variation, not the result of head binding. In some instances head binding was the cause, I suspect because the lower class 'ordinary' humans wanted to imitate the ruling class. Neither do the historical dolichocephalic skulls show any sign of being the result of skull sutures not closing.

Giants in North America seem to have existed also, with a height range of seven feet tall possibly up to twelve feet tall. Whether either of these were descended from the Nephilim or were Nephilim, or were merely normal human variants in the genome, is entirely speculative.

The *Ariel* are indeed mentioned in 1 Chronicles 12:8 and 2 Samuel 23:20, as well as the Moabite Mesha Stele, and a gold figurine of an *Ariel* has been found in an excavation Tell Abu el-Kharaz in Transjordan. But whether these Ariel really were men with lions' faces, in other words, some kind of genetically engineered Nephilim variant, or simply renowned masked warriors who identified themselves with a lion-god is another question entirely. Occam's razor would suggest the latter explanation.

Nonetheless, the possibility of the former explanation being true is undeniable. If we believe genetic hybrids between angels and humans existed, surely it's no great leap to think that animal-human hybrids may have been created also by the same supernatural agents?

And would a contemporary archaeologist recognise such a skeleton if it were dug up? It would more than likely be identified as an incomplete human skeleton, buried in the same grave as an incomplete lion skeleton.

Bibliography

CLIMATE

https://wattsupwiththat.com/climategate/

http://joannenova.com.au/2019/10/who-knew-the-australian-bureau-of-met-just-made-last-summer-hotter-and-history-colder-again/

Predictions of disaster that never eventuate,

http://joannenova.com.au/2018/02/climate-change-creates-free-real-estate-in-tuvalu-climate-refugees-can-all-go-home/

The placement of the BOM weather station in Sydney Observatory.

http://joannenova.com.au/2018/02/scandal-bom-ignores-major-site-changes-at-iconic-historic-sydney-observatory-sloppy-or-deliberate/

Adjustment of earlier temperatures in the NOAA graph of New York.

https://wattsupwiththat.com/2018/02/20/noaa-caught-cooking-the-books-again-this-time-by-erasing-a-record-cold-snap/

The editing of low temperatures by BOM.

http://joannenova.com.au/2017/09/bom-review-finds-skeptics-were-right-but-say-trust-us-it-doesnt-matter/

The Medieval Warm Period

http://www.spiegel.de/international/zeitgeist/archaeologists-uncover-clues-to-why-vikings-abandoned-greenland-a-876626.html

NEPHILIM

"Finds Skeletons Giants Twelve Feet in Height" Winnsboro La. The Cairo Bulletin, Cairo Illinois, Wednesday December 17th 1913

https://chroniclingamerica.loc.gov/lccn/sn93055779/1913-12-17/ed-1/seq-8/#date1=1880&sort=relevance&rows=20&words=found+giant+skeleton&searchType=basic&sequence=0&index=0&state=&date2=1927&proxtext=giant+skeleton+found&y=0&x=0&dateFilterType=yearRange&page=2

The Vatican Apostolic Archive, until 28 October 2019 known as the Vatican Secret Archive, is the central repository in the Vatican City for all of the acts promulgated by the Holy See.

http://www.archivioapostolicovaticano.va/content/aav/it.html

https://en.wikipedia.org/wiki/Vatican_Apostolic_Archive

https://drmsh.com

Dr Michael S. Heiser's books are here:

https://drmsh.com/books/

Dr Heiser's published studies are listed here:

https://drmsh.com/wp-content/uploads/2019/01/MHeiserCV832.pdf

Heiser, Dr. Michael S. "The Unseen Realm", Lexham Press; Bellingham, WA, 2015

Pizarro, Francisco "Cartas del Marqués Don Francisco Pizarro (1533–1541)".

Pizarro, Francisco "Cédula de encomienda de Francisco Pizarro a Diego

Maldonado, Cuzco, 15 de abril de 1539".

"Francisco Pizarro response to a petition by Pedro del Barco", 14 April 1539. From the Collections at the Library of Congress

Many news articles about giant skeletons found are available in https://chroniclingamerica.loc.gov

Ustariz, Rivero y, Rivero, Mariano Edward and Von Tschudi, Johann James, Peruvian Antiquities, AS Barnes and Company, 51 John Street, New York 1855. pp. 35-36

https://archive.org/details/peruvianantiqui00hawkgoog/page/n66/mode/2up

ARIELS

https://godawa.com/myth-bible-part-10-lion-men-moab/

Brian Godawa has written extensively about quasi-mythological figures in the Bible.

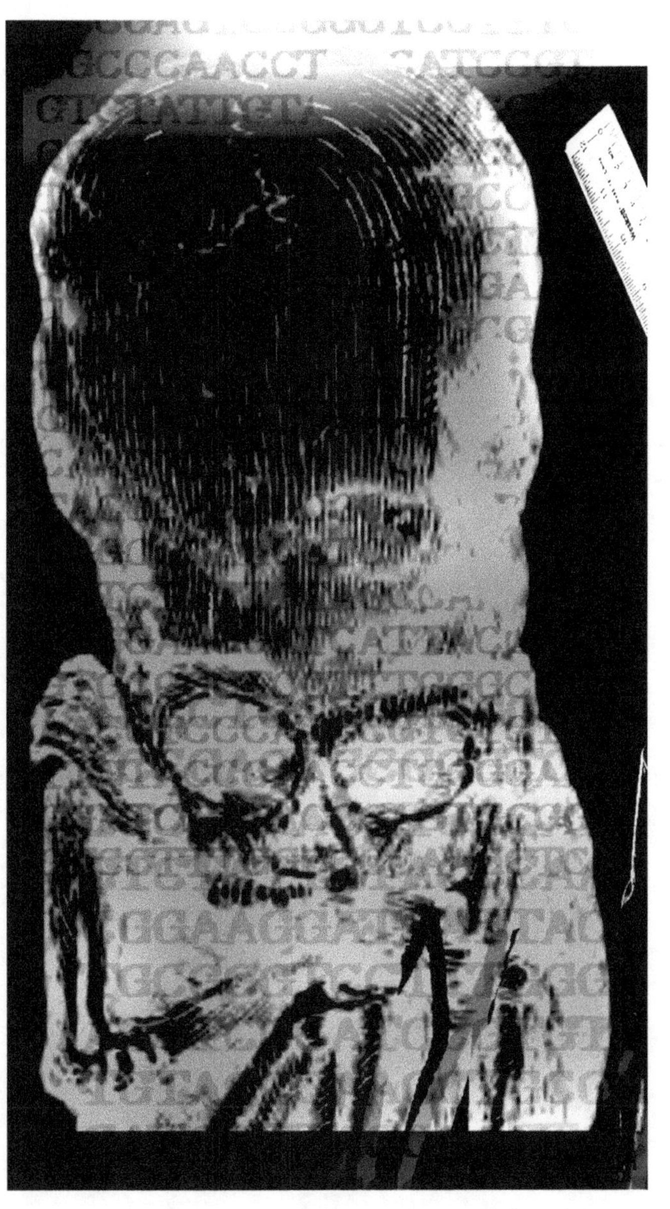